I0593279

Golden Valley

Marjorie Gadd is a teacher, musician and writer.

She is co-founder of the Tasmanian Heritage Fiddle Ensemble and the Huon Heritage Ensemble, two groups dedicated to the propagation and revival of traditional Tasmanian country dance music.

She was principal writer in the multi-media productions *Jane Franklin – an Examined Life* and FIRE, a history of the 1967 Tasmanian bushfires.

She is the author of *Eureka One: a creative approach to beginning violin* and co-author of *On the Fiddle* and *The Tasmanian Heritage: Apple Shed Dance Tunes Book.*

As a sixth-generation Tasmanian, and long-time resident of Southern Tasmania, she has a vital interest in Tasmania's unique and evolving culture.

Golden Valley is her first novel.

Golden Valley

Marjorie Gadd

ASHWOOD
PUBLISHING

Copyright ©Marjorie Gadd 2022

All rights reserved. Apart from any use permitted under Australian copyright law, no part may be reproduced by any process without the written permission of the author.
Enquiries should be directed to the publisher.

This is a work of fiction. The characters, events and places mentioned are fictitious or, if real, are used fictitiously. Any resemblance to any persons living or dead is purely coincidental.

ISBN: 978-0-6452045-4-4 (paperback)
ISBN: 978-0-6452045-5-1 (ePub)

ASHWOOD
PUBLISHING
Cradoc, Tasmania
www.ashwoodpublishing.com.au

Cover art based on 'Sleeping Beauty from Grove 2, Tasmania', original oil painting by Richard Stanley, www.theartofrichardstanley.com.au
Used by kind permission of the artist.

'The Fairy Glade', lyrics by E. Dougas Taylor, *The Dominion Songbook*, Auckland, Whitcomb & Tombs, 1930, public domain.
'My Mammy', lyrics by Sam Lewis & Joe Young, 1918, public domain.

A catalogue record for this work is available from the National Library of Australia

Acknowledgements

For their steadfast love, support and encouragement I'd like to thank my husband, Steve Gadd, and my mother-in-law, Jane Gadd. This book would not have been completed without you. A big thankyou to dear friends Erin Collins, Susan McGowan, Dorothy Bruck, and Paddy Riley for reading the original manuscript and offering helpful suggestions. For those who have helped me with specific details I'd like to thank Janet Fenton, Dave McNamara, Ruth Young and Paul Gibson. And for being kind, thoughtful and wise, I'd like to thank my editor, Susan Young.

Chapter 1

1971

'PUSH!' THE NURSE GRABBED LOUISE'S hand. 'Push like you're going to the toilet. When the next contraction comes, give a really good push. There's a good girl. It won't take long now. You're off to a good start.' With an iron grip, the nurse lifted Louise's left leg and placed her ankle in the stirrup. She rushed to the other side of the bed and did the same on the right. 'It's much easier like this,' she said. 'It'll all be over soon.'

Louise couldn't focus through the pain. She could barely understand what was being said. Was the nurse talking to her? It seemed that no-one in authority had spoken *to* her for months and months. Was it her they were talking to? Or was it simply about her? She would wait for another person to intercede. Perhaps one of her friends from the Home would come. If only one of them were here. She had known the baby would come out between her legs. She hadn't known she would be tied up like a side of beef. She hadn't known the pain would rip through her body like an angry demon squeezing every nerve and sinew and muscle till she moved in great involuntary shudders, rolling from one side of the bed to the other.

'Now breathe in with me, dear. Breathe in, ahaaaaaaaa. Now

out. Whooooooo. That's it, dear. Again. Ahhhhhhhh. Now out. Whoooooo. You're doing well, ah' – she took a quick look at the patient chart – 'Louise. Louise you're doing well. Next time the pain comes take a really deep breath and then push as hard as you can. You're doing fine, Louise.' She repeated the name as if to make sure she remembered it. 'It'll all be over soon, Louise.'

Two more nurses rushed into the theatre, and positioned themselves on either side of Louise, each taking a hand. One of them smiled at Louise. 'You'll be fine.' They gripped Louise's hands like arm wrestlers as she heaved and writhed through the next contraction.

———

The doors of the theatre swung open. 'Shop! Shop!' Dr Michael Althorp strode into the centre of the room, holding his hands high. 'Come on Nurse Chapman, what do you think you're doing? What do I have to do to get some attention around here? Have the baby myself?' He pirouetted on his toes, and then held out his arms for Nurse Chapman to dress him in a surgical gown. As she fitted his arms into the garment he moved closer towards her, sidling forward till he could feel her breasts against his paunch. 'Oh, that's better,' he said. 'Now tie it nice and tight, there's a good old duck!'

Without raising his eyes to look at her, Althorp pointed to one of the nurses. 'What's she doing here? This is an illegitimate isn't it?'

'Yes, Doctor. But we're short staffed. And Nurse Stevens has to start sometime.'

'Oh! Nurse Stevens has to start some time, does she?' he said in a mocking falsetto. 'And why doesn't she start with a proper birth?' Nurse Chapman knew it was a rhetorical question. 'Tell her to hang the sheet out to dry.'

———

Louise felt the hold on her left hand disappear and grabbed hold of the mattress, her head rocking backwards and forwards to the rhythm of the pain. A trembling arm stretched a pillowcase in front of Louise's face. 'It's to stop you seeing the baby,' a voice whispered. 'It's better that way.'

It caused her to panic. Louise could see nothing but the shaking pillowcase. Were they going to suffocate her? She started hyperventilating, panting and screaming. She heard the impatient voice of Dr Althorp. 'Keep her steady, Nurse Chapman.' She heard a rattle of instruments.

'Come on, come on, come on!' The doctor again, from over near the window. 'Tell her to get ready, Nurse Chapman.'

'Big effort, Louise. We're nearly there.' Louise felt Nurse Chapman's hand on her leg. 'Come on, Louise. Push really hard now.'

In silence Louise felt her body flex and convulse. Crying and screaming were beyond her now. In shock, her mind lifted from her body. She saw her legs high in the stirrups, the nurses bending over her as if bowing to some ancient god, and felt the wet head of the baby pushing through her body in a welter of sweat and blood and pain.

Nurse Chapman caught the baby, her deft hands ensuring that the umbilical cord was free.

Althorp spun round. 'Well. There we are,' his voice almost kind. 'Now just hold on for the afterbirth.'

Louise hadn't heard of afterbirth. Was it a ceremony? A ritual cleansing? She felt a long way away. Remote, in a silent world. She felt her throat make a high-pitched keening sound and then went silent, listening with her entire being as she heard a thin wail from the baby.

When the afterbirth spread itself out on the stained sheets, the veil of the pillowcase was lifted. She instinctively looked around, but the baby had gone. Back in her body, aching and shaking, she was released from the stirrups and covered with a fresh sheet.

Althorp lifted his head from the patient chart and for the first time looked directly at Louise. As if he were a bit player in a melodrama, he dropped the chart onto the foot of the bed, strode to the head and began stroking Louise's hair. 'There, there,' he chanted with his head on one side. 'It's all over now. You'll be back at school in no time, and no-one will know what happened.'

He turned to Nurse Chapman. 'Another one for the Pope is it?' She didn't reply at first.

'No, it's one of your mob,' she said as she wheeled the stirrups out of the way.

———

Nurse Stevens laid the baby down on the preparation table. She washed her carefully. Every little crease and fold, she straightened and wiped. Every little wrinkle, she traced with absorbed attention. The baby's pink skin glowed as her blood rose to the surface at her touch. The toes and fingers were miniature perfections. A small red mark on her ankle, the only fault.

Althorp spun round on the balls of his feet and flicked his theatre coat into bin. 'Well done everyone.' Pushing the doors aside with both hands and taking one last look at

Nurse Chapman's fulsome breasts, he headed to the doctors' staffroom. He enjoyed the sound of his leather soled shoes clacking on the polished linoleum floor. His mind strayed to Louise. Good lymphatic system. Not too much swelling in the legs. Probably well-defined ankles when the body returned to normal. Small bones and fine skin. Quite a beauty really. Couldn't tell about the face. One never could under those circumstances. Gorgeous hair! Every now and then the working class threw up a beauty... the lottery of genes. She could be one of those. She could be the daughter of his wife's bridge partner for all he knew.

———

The smell of lamb's fry and boiled cabbage hung in the air behind the hospital. Evening was setting in as a group of nurses sat on the fire escape waiting for the change in shift. Nurse Chapman sucked hard on a Craven A.

'Can get a lot harder than that,' she said. Nurse Stevens didn't doubt it.

'Althorp,' said Nurse Chapman, to change the mood. 'Despicable bastard! You can't do anything about him.' She drew hard on her cigarette. All the nurses had at least one story about Althorp's abhorrent behaviour: making you bend over to retrieve an instrument he had accidentally thrown on the floor; rubbing up against you in a crowded corridor; catching you in a cupboard, his hands flying all over you; pretending to flick dust off your uniform as an excuse to brush your nipples; tripping you up and throwing you backwards onto a bed.

'Just ignore him and get on with it,' she said. 'There's nothing you can do, so just forget about it and move on.'

'If he tried anything on me I'd kick him in the balls!' said one of the more brazen nurses.

Nurse Stevens didn't know what she would do. Probably cry.

The back door of the hospital kitchen swung open. A Sister from the Home for Unmarried Mothers held the door open. Louise came out in a thin paisley shift, with rubber thongs on her feet. Her hair was wet. Shivering in the cool air, she wrapped her arms around her abdomen. The Sister took her by the elbow and propelled her along the dirt path. Louise kept her head bowed, focusing on the tiny white flowers of sweet Alice growing beside a paling fence. She tried to avoid a greasy puddle and nearly slipped.

Nurse Stevens, sitting on the fire escape, looked up to the indifferent shapes of the roofscape silhouetted against the fading pink sky. The bland cross of St George's Church a mute condemnation of the shivering girl in the thin dress.

'Louise!' she cried. 'It was a girl, Louise. She's beautiful! She's got a birth mark on her right ankle.'

Louise turned around, tears in her eyes. 'Thank you,' she said and turned back, fixing her gaze on the path ahead.

'You watch yourself, Nurse Stevens!' said Nurse Chapman.

Chapter 2

1965

'It seems an awfully long way,' said Marion. She rolled down the window of the EH Holden.

A Hillman had been her preference: slim lines, subtle colours and fine chrome work. Overall, a more English look, understated and elegant. When she'd put the case for a Hillman, Malcolm had laughed. 'That's because you're English,' he'd said. 'There's no way I'm going to be seen driving a beige Hillman!' She smiled at the thought of it. The Holden suited him. She could feel the pride he felt when he took the wheel. Still, one day she'd have her licence, and she wondered how it would feel, driving a great black beast.

'It's not long now,' said Malcolm, resting his elbow on the open window. His shirt sleeves were rolled up, his arm catching the sun and the breeze. 'How are you going in the back there?'

Robert and Louise stretched and leant forward. The red leather upholstery stuck to their legs.

'Can we stop soon?' asked Robert.

'When we get to the top of this hill. There's a picnic ground with swings.'

'Good!' said Robert and slumped back on the seat. Louise rested her head on her forearms and held her face in the slipstream from her father's window.

The road to the lookout led them past wooden farmhouses exuding an air of untidy busyness. Verandahs with wrought iron balustrades were decorated with washing. Corrugated iron roofs reflected the dazzling sun. Marion eyed off the front gardens, heavy squat hedges and flower beds of perennials. Veggie gardens proliferated. Chooks were everywhere. Dogs, mostly tied up, barked and barked.

The view from the top of the hill took their breath away. The valley below was a patchwork of industry. Apple orchards marched up the slopes in neat rows. Dark forests overlapped the tops of hills. In the far distance, mountains embraced the foothills. Every now and then a cliff-face emerged among the folds of green. In some places the bare earth was exposed, shaved of all vegetation.

———

The picnic ground provided tables and benches. They seemed to be made for giants. Robert climbed the bench and stood on the table. 'I'm the king of the castle and you're the dirty rascal!' he yelled to the valley below.

Marion flicked the tablecloth at him. 'Off there this minute!' He scampered down and ran to the swings.

Louise, already occupying one of the swings, shifted her weight to ease it into motion. Lifting her feet high then down to the ground, holding her arms taut on the heavy chains. The seat was a slab of well-worn wood, broad and comfortable. Marion watched as she swept forward. At the end of the arc, she seemed more part of the sky than a creature of the land, her body suspended over the valley in the spiralling blue air. In the moment of weightlessness she straightened up to see the valley below. Marion thought she was like an eagle, part of the sky. Below, quaint details of domestic life, but up here nothing but the warm, clear air.

Robert threw his body over the second swing, facing downwards with his stomach on the seat. 'I'm the king of the castle and you're the dirty rascal!' he chanted again. His feet caught the muddy slurry at the base of the swing. Speckles of brown water appeared on the backs of his legs.

'Come on, you two. Lunch is ready,' said Marion. 'Robert! Why is it that you can never keep clean from one moment to the next! You only have to look at mud and there it is all over you. So who's the dirty rascal?' She ruffled his hair. A grand day like this could not be dragged down by pettiness.

'What have you got for us, dear?' said Malcolm.

'Ham and tomato sandwiches, curried egg and parsley sandwiches, raspberry jam sandwiches, apricots, prunes, a thermos of tea and some Madeira cake... my dear!' Marion chanted in a sing-song voice. Malcolm smiled his *dear* smile and butted out his cigarette. He took a couple of sandwiches and remained standing, stretching his muscles after the long drive. Marion, Louise and Robert sat at the picnic table. Seeing his father take two, Robert did the same.

'Robert! One at a time.' Marion slapped him gently on the hand.

'But Dad took two!'

'I've got a bigger mouth,' said Malcolm, popping a whole sandwich into his mouth and chewing it as if he were a wild beast.

Robert looked in envy at his father. 'I don't think we should have table manners on picnics,' he said.

'Neither do I,' said Louise. She leant over the table and picked two sandwiches out of the Tupperware box.

'Louise! Stop that this minute!' her mother said.

'Watch out!' Malcolm cried in mock seriousness. 'I can see the Queen coming round the corner.' Marion's face tightened. Robert snuck a quick look down the road as if to make sure a sovereign was not patrolling the outer regions of her crumbling empire.

'Look!' he cried. Everyone turned.

———

Approaching them at a slow clip-clop was a large draught horse harnessed to a dray. The reins were held by an old woman. She was thin, small and wizened, the size of a child. Marion had seen horses and carts as a child in England. Malcolm remembered his Scottish grandfather, a silent, brutal man who would use his whip indiscriminately on cantankerous horses or rowdy boys. Louise saw the tiny woman as a queen in disguise, travelling through her realm to check on her subjects. Robert looked in awe at the enormous horse clomping in slow motion as if it had emerged from the last century, resolutely plodding through the next century and on to eternity, looking neither left nor right but steadfastly holding the line for Time itself.

In her younger days Iris would have stopped to chat with the strangers. They were city types and might have interesting tales to tell. She would have let the children pat the horse and give him an apple or two. But nowadays there were so many new folks coming to the valley, either to settle or just to have a look around. Her bones were fixed in the seat and she knew that if she got down now, she'd have trouble getting back up. Alfred, the horse, was equally averse to any change in their gait. Now that the last big hill was behind them it would be a quick and easy trot home.

'G'day to youse,' she said.

'Good afternoon,' replied Marion.

'Hello,' said Malcolm.

'Nice day for a picnic,' said Iris.

'You've got a big horse,' said Robert.

'Yes, he is a big horse,' Iris replied. 'Youse are lucky. You've picked the right day. Usually a lot of wind up here on the hill.' Iris was now past the point of conversation. Alfred maintained his steady plod. They were too far down the road for any words to be heard.

'Goodbye,' said Louise. Iris raised a hand in a farewell gesture, but didn't turn around.

———

The Johnstones continued their journey. Robert and Louise played 'I-spy'. Marion looked back over her shoulder at them. They were gentle with each other and didn't disagree or fight. She knew the idea of moving to the country, away from all their friends, had filled them with a sense of loneliness and vulnerability. They would have to rely on each other.

As the journey continued, Marion's anxiety was slowly growing. The view from the picnic ground, while being grand and beautiful, had overawed her. She felt adrift. It was as if her soul slid off the road and flew over the green hills looking for an anchor, some point where she could gather herself together and stop the feeling of being swept away: a picket fence she could hold onto.

As Malcolm steered the car around yet another bend,

she noticed the houses getting smaller. Front fences no longer appeared. The paintwork on the wooden cottages was becoming flaky. Some houses had rusty roofs. Gardens became sparse and lawns had patches of moss showing through. One front yard was filled with car wrecks and old farm machinery. Not Marion's choice of neighbour. The afternoon clouded over.

'Not long now,' said Malcolm. 'There's a shop and a post office, and a school.' Marion offered no response. 'There's a bus service too,' he added.

'How often do the buses run?'

'I don't know,' Malcolm replied. Marion looked at him. So many details he had not taken into account. Getting the job with the Huon Council had been the big thing. They'd been over the moon. It was a move upwards.

The dead part of the afternoon had arrived. The children became listless and bored.

'Not long now,' said Malcolm.

'You just said that, Dad!' said Louise.

'Did I?' he said. 'Well I tell you what... It's not long now!'

'Daaaaad!' came the chorus in the back seat.

Marion gazed out the window. The road had straightened. Tall poplars lined the right-hand side of the road. Malcolm slowed and took a turning to the left. Marion looked up to see the road sign painted in white on a short piece of weatherboard nailed to a large old gum tree. 'Happy's Road!' she exclaimed. 'Malcolm, do you expect us to live in a place called *Happy's Road*? Who ever heard of such a thing!' It made her feel strange and light-headed just saying it. Louise laughed and Robert broke into song.

'Happy! Happy! Happy!' he sang as he stretched out every muscle in his body.

'So you think we're going to live in Happy's Road, Golden Valley, do you?' she teased Malcolm. The liberation of being ridiculous hit them all.

Over to the right was a solid brick house. It looked as if it had been transplanted from the wealthier suburbs of Hobart. A pear tree, tall and dishevelled, grew close to the outside of the garden wall. It leant slightly forward as if bowing to the newcomers. Malcolm slowed down and stretched his arm out the window, indicating a turn to the right. There were no cars behind him. It was simply for effect.

'Oh!' cried Marion. 'This is it?'

'This is it,' replied Malcolm with a broad smile, pleased that he'd kept the address from them.

Chapter 3

'It's brick! I'm so glad its brick. I was thinking I might have to spend every waking moment with a paintbrush in hand. Oh, Malcolm! It's lovely!'

'I knew you'd like it.' Enormous relief flooded through him. 'Wait till you see inside. It hasn't been done up. Everything is original, but in very good condition.'

The dirt driveway led up the side of the house. Malcolm parked and the children leapt out. The real estate agent, Mick O'Connell, had given Malcolm the keys, along with some personal particulars about the nearest neighbours – some invective regarding the local council – his opinion as to whether the Valiant was a superior car to the Holden (he was a Valiant man but did recognise the improvements in the Holden EH, although only time would tell whether it would be dodgy in the gearbox department) – cows were much less trouble than sheep (he'd let the neighbours know they could no longer run their chooks or graze their cows in the garden) – and women needed a good night out every now and then. He had a son at the Matriculation College in Hobart. He was doing alright too! His daughter wouldn't need to go to college. They (women) can always find a bit of work before they get married. Malcolm had let him rattle on. Best to say nothing till he learnt the lie of the land.

Malcolm saw the tension lift from Marion's face. All doubt had vanished as he turned the key. Two hallways led off a small alcove. To the right were three bedrooms, the last one being the master bedroom with a spacious bay window.

Malcolm pointed to the range of mountains to the north. 'Look. See the highest peak? That's Sleeping Beauty's nose. See the way it's shaped like a woman's face? There's her nose, and there's her lips.' He leant forward and kissed her. Marion smiled and reached for his hand.

All the rooms had dark stained dado boarding. The plaster walls were spotless. Simple rosettes in scalloped tiers decorated the ceilings. The light shades were classic Art Deco with lined patterns in thick glass, the colours soft and muted. The master bedroom was painted a pale yellow. 'I might need to change the colour,' said Marion.

Malcolm sighed. 'Just live with it for a bit.'

The children's rooms were painted sky blue.

'Blue's boring,' said Robert.

'We can always paint it, dear. If you don't like it,' said Marion.

'That's a fine bit of paintwork and it's staying where it is,' replied Malcolm crossly. *How can a colour be boring? Why does the boy have to say things like that?*

'Which room do you like, Louise?' asked Marion.

'I don't mind.' Louise gazed at the hills rising gently beyond the pear tree outside the window. 'This room is really nice.'

'That's settled then,' said Malcolm.

At the other end of the house the hall led into the living room. 'Oh! Whoa!' cried Robert. He stood in front of a double door of frosted glass panelling. 'Look at this!' His hands glided over the billowing sailing ships etched into the glass.

'Oh! Isn't it lovely!' said Marion. She looked at the fine details of shading and texture, the clear sweeping lines of the composition. 'Malcolm! I can see you on that sailing ship!'

'That's a clipper in full sail,' he said, his eyes wide and dreamy. 'That's not the reason I want the house, Marion. It's got other features.'

After examining the living room, the children ran to the other end of the house. Malcolm and Marion followed. An old Kelvinator with a wringer sat in the corner of the laundry.

'That will have to go,' said Marion.

'The bloke at the agency said it still works.'

'They're very dangerous, Malcolm. You can catch your fingers in the rollers if you aren't careful.' Robert poked his finger in the wringer. Malcolm swiped at his hand.

'Well then, you just have to be careful.'

Marion switched her attention to the floor. 'Look at the linoleum. Isn't it in good condition?'

'Yes,' said Malcolm, quick to find common ground. The four of them stood in the laundry looking at the linoleum.

'Let's see the kitchen,' said Marion. They filed out, Robert trailing his fingers along the dado boards.

Malcolm felt the tension return.

'Malcolm. I don't want to live in the Stone Age.' The Aga slow-combustion stove seemed to scowl at Malcolm.

'Yes, they're a lot of work,' he said.

The kitchen cupboards were spacious and there were plenty of them, rising from the floor to the ceiling. The children opened every one of them, the hollow popping sound of the catches echoing round the room. Nothing was found except a packet of rat poison solidified with age, an old breadboard with tea stains on it, and a small tin of Ajax cleaning powder. There was a faint smell of mutton lingering around the stove. A dark wooden kitchen dresser stuck out, obscuring the view from the window. Its feet sat stolidly on the floor with no tapering. Although it seemed out of place, as far as proportion was concerned, it appeared to have been there a long time. Malcolm lifted one end to test its weight.

'I think I can fit it over on the other side, next to the stove. It looks like there's room.' Marion moved to the other end of the dresser to help move it into place. They shuffled to and fro as if performing an awkward dance, zigzagging across the room. Where the feet of the dresser had been, the linoleum was a fresh bright green.

'Look!' said Robert. Lying on the dusty floor where the dresser had stood was a single row of dentures. He picked them up. 'They're mine! They're mine!' he cried. Robert had a special box of prize possessions – a rabbit's foot, a three-penny bit, a bullet, the skeletal head of a rat, a pocketknife, four square-cut nails, a ribbon (that he stole from his sister) and an army badge. A row of upper dentures was definitely a collectable item.

'Robert! Don't be disgusting!' said Marion. 'They're filthy. Leave them in the sink and we'll throw them out later when we do a proper clean-up.' Robert did not look dismayed. He would grab them later. 'Fancy them being there all this time,' said Marion. 'You'd think it would be hard to eat without your teeth.'

Once the dresser was in its new place, it became obvious why it had been put against the window: the glass was cracked from top to bottom, with a large hole in the right-hand corner.

'Will you look at that!' exclaimed Marion. 'You'd think the estate agent would have had that fixed!' Indignation brought her hands to her hips. 'Malcolm, you'll have to have a word with him. He shouldn't be allowed to sell a house with a broken window. I can't believe they wouldn't have known about it. You must be able to see it from the back yard. The cheek of him!'

Malcolm smiled. He knew now it was a done deal. Marion was taking ownership. She liked the place. Everything would be good. He could contact Mick O'Connell in the morning and see the bank manager in the afternoon. He had three more days off before his new job started.

Louise looked into the sink at the row of dusty teeth and then at the broken window. Someone had been without their teeth in a house with broken windows for a very long time.

'It seems sad in here,' she said.

Chapter 4

THE LIGHT STREAMED IN THROUGH the dining room, giving a warm glow to the frosted glass doors. Marion sat at the dining table among half-unpacked cardboard boxes. A small space between the crockery and pots and pans gave her room to write.

Dear Mum and Bo-Bo,

We've made the big move! It's so lovely here, you can't imagine. As soon as I find the camera I'll take some photos so you can see it. The house is solid brick and all on one level, so no stairs to put up with. The children have a room each and Malcolm and I have a bay window in our bedroom. The kitchen needs a lot of work. A new cooker and a fridge will make a big difference. There was a dreadful old wood stove that we had to get rid of. It took four men to move it! Malcolm says we can sell it at the salvage store in Huonville but I don't think we'll get much for it. Also, the lino needs replacing and there is a broken window that needs fixing. They sold the house with a broken window! Can you believe it?! Malcolm said it wasn't worth arguing the point, so we let it go but it just shows you how careful you have to be.

There's lots of space to run around in. In fact we're

surrounded by fields, but the neighbours are not very far way. It's surprising how many people live here, but you don't see them very often. There are some fruit trees in the backyard. Our own orchard! A pear, an almond, a mulberry and a Kentish cherry. At the moment it's quite warm, but they say the weather will turn at the end of April. Malcolm wants to put in a veggie garden, which I think is a good idea. There is so much land that we feel we should make the most of it. He also wants to build a garage. First he'll lay a concrete slab and then go from there. He's never done anything like that but he seems very confident. We've enrolled the children at the local school. It's quite small but I think that's good, in a way.

Malcolm's job is very similar to the position he had in Hobart, but he has more responsibility and the salary is higher. He says he'll enjoy having a bit of land to muck around with when he gets home from work. It's only ten minutes into Huonville. There's a bus service once a day from here, but apparently the locals all give each other lifts into town to do their shopping, which is nice. It is a little isolated compared to what we've been used to, but there are lots of organisations you can join, like the Country Women's Association and the school Parents and Friends Association. Malcolm says the Lions club is very big in Huonville and there is also the Freemasons' Association. I think the Lions Club sounds more modern than the Freemasons, but it all sounds a bit posh to me. Malcolm's Dad is fairly high up in the Masons. He's a chief Sitting Bull or something

*like that. They seem a bit too serious to be taken
seriously if you get what I mean. Anyway, it's another
opportunity to get to know people.*

*I hope Bo-Bo's sciatica is better. I'll send you some
eucalyptus ointment when I next go into town. It's
very good for all the aches and pains. They say it
can get below freezing here, but not very often.
When everything is unpacked I'll get started on that
jumper I promised Lucy, and I haven't forgotten it's
Jeremy's birthday next month.*

*I'm off for a walk now to the shop, which is also
the post office, as you'd expect in a country village.
It's such a beautiful day!*

Love to everyone,
Marion

She read the letter back. It sounded boastful. 'We've got this
and we've got that.' But Marion was excited about the new
start and wanted to share it with her family. They were having a hard winter with three children still at home. Jeremy
was seventeen and had a job. By now he should be thinking
of moving into his own flat. It would be less pressure on
Mum and Bo-Bo, but he didn't seem to get the hint. Sophie
had already left home and married. She was nineteen and
was working as a stenographer until she started a family.
Phillip was fifteen and in his final year of school. And then
Lucy – she was eleven now. Eleven years and eight months.
She had been two years old when Marion married Malcolm
and left for Australia.

Marion remembered the cold wrenching feeling as she
and Malcolm stood high above the wharf, looking down.

Everyone was excited. The passengers around her yelling and waving. Coloured streamers whizzing all around her. She held tight to the twisted red streamer that looped and crossed others before being traced to Lucy's tight little hand. Bo-Bo held Lucy in his arms, her little mouth turned down.

Marion was silently crying. When Malcolm felt her nearly double over with a huge sob, he held her tight, cupping her face, kissing her forehead, wrapping her in his warm arms.

———

Marion folded the thin airline paper and slipped it into an envelope. In her best copperplate writing she wrote the address. With each line she felt herself further and further away from its destination.

This was her first trip to the shop. The afternoon was warm, but she decided against wearing a hat. She didn't care for all that nonsense about 'English complexions' and didn't mind the feeling of the warm sun on her face. She thought gloves would be a smart touch. She had two pairs to choose from: a satin pair, cream with a pearl button at the wrist, demure and formal. A good choice for church. And a pair of pink polished cotton with white embroidered lily of the valley around the cuff. They were very pretty and a little too ornate for day-wear. Marion hesitated. Then thrust her hands into the pink ones. Flat black court shoes were all she possessed, apart from a pair of sneakers. Pleased with her decision to forgo the hat, she ventured forth with wicker basket in hand.

The unsealed road was dusty in the heat, and it was not long before her shoes were coated with a fine film. *Not to worry,* she told herself, *dust soon brushes off.* The verges were overgrown with fireweed. Gorse bush was in full flower. The occasional pop of a seed pod startled her at first. Then it became part of the auditory background: the gentle rustle of the tall eucalypts, the distant susurration of the river and the high-above *thaaaark* of ravens. Wrens and fantails danced and frolicked at the side of the road, their voices bursting with chatter. It was a golden day. Perfect for this first outing. As she approached the shop, a quick sudden rustling came from the side of the road. She looked around but saw nothing. Marion had never seen a snake. But this was a built-up area so it was unlikely to be a snake, she reasoned; probably a lizard of some sort, or a cat.

The shop was an old weatherboard building with a small verandah. A curtain of beads slid over Marion's cooling skin as she entered the shop. The old floorboards gave a startling creak. She looked around and saw no-one. The air was thick and stale. Bags of chicken grain lined the front wall. Above them was shelving up to the ceiling, containing all manner of household goods.

Marion explored the shop with interest. On the side wall, thick rubber gumboots and lined check jackets, a pile of raffia sun hats, spools of ribbon and hat elastic, handkerchiefs in cellophane packets, a set of mixing bowls, several sieves, a glory box of Chinese design, some pipes, one compact with mirror, a jar of nail scissors, a dustpan and brush, and a linen tablecloth in a rectangular cardboard box. Marion picked up a pale blue bri-nylon nightie – size 22. On the floor below the shelving sat a huge laundry copper holding a vast collection of children's plastic sandals. The colours ranged through pink, orange, red, light blue and the new fashionable pearl. All the boys' sizes came in a dull brown. A zither was leaning against the copper with a beginner's manual threaded through its strings.

The opposite side of the room held grocery items. Sugar, flour, curry powder, tomato sauce. There was a whole row of Spam, and the top shelf was devoted entirely to rolled oats in bulging two-pound bags. The middle shelf, at eye level, was crammed full of packets of biscuits. Arnott's Mixed Creams in family packs, Iced VoVos, Milk Arrowroot, Ginger Snaps, Scotch Fingers, Monte Carlos, Fruit Slice, Chocolate Royals, Chocolate Creams and the new variety, Tim Tams. The lower shelf displayed a collection of once-fresh fruit and vegetables. Potatoes in large sacks slumped on the floor, emitting a mouldy smell.

Still no sign of the shop's owner. Marion held her basket tight against her waist and picked up the bell on the counter, hoping it would give a polite and refreshing tinkle.

Klank! Klank! Klank! She quickly put it down. The door behind the counter opened and the drone of a radio tuned to the races flooded the shop. The chromatic rise and fall of it, along with the buzz of flies, had a slightly mesmeric effect. An elderly woman of matronly proportions shuffled through the doorway. She wore a full-bodice apron over a faded floral dress, and her grey hair was set in planes of crinkles emanating from her brow to the crown of her head where it stood up like a surprised halo.

'Hello, duck,' she said as she peered at Marion through thick glasses.

'Hello,' said Marion.

'Can I help you?' The woman cocked her head to one side.

'Yes. I was wondering if I could post a letter,' Marion said.

And then a little slower, 'A letter to England.'

'Oh yes, duck. We can do all sorts of letters, not just the local. England you said, was it?'

'Yes, England. I only need the stamp. It's airmail paper and envelope. I have the letter here.' Marion took the letter out of her basket.

'Looks like a standard one to me. How many pages inside, dear?'

'It's only two pages. It usually costs one and six.'

'Yes, that'll be right. One shilling and sixpence for that one.'

She bent down to a drawer below the counter and took out a manila folder. Slowly she filed through until she came to the appropriate stamps. The purple head of the Queen in profile, resolutely looking to the right, cloned a dozen times. She detached a stamp from the top right-hand corner, carefully holding the edges of the perforation so that it didn't tear. Marion noted that her fingernails were long and dirty. Her hands were a fatty yellow colour.

'Are you new round here?' the woman asked.

'Yes. We've just moved in. We're ten minutes down the road. The brick house.' Marion tried to keep the pride out of her voice.

'Oh! Oh! You're in old Mrs Cunningham's place.' A delighted smile. 'Oh, that's lovely. I'm glad that someone's there at last.' She raised her voice to full throttle, turned around and hurled it through to the room behind the counter. 'Merv! Merv! Can you hear me? There's people in Mrs Cunningham's place at long last!' There was a grunt the length of three syllables. The woman turned back to face Marion. 'My name's Vonnie, dear. Yvonne's the long of it but Vonnie's what everyone calls me. The kiddies call me Mrs Vonnie and that's alright by me.'

'My name's Marion. Marion Johnstone. My husband has just started a job with the council here in the valley.' Marion thought this might be too much too soon.

'Well I never! Last I heard they were cutting jobs to try and save money. Save our rates from going through the roof! And your fella's got a job just recent, has he?'

'Yes, but I think he is replacing someone. I don't think it's a new position.'

'Oh, well that different then isn't it. It's not like they're getting in another bean-counter just to make things easy for themselves.'

Vonnie settled into chat position, leaning one arm on the counter and the other on her hip and letting her ample bosom slump forward over her forearm. She looked up at Marion. The thick layer of grease on her glasses made her eyes look large and vague. 'Got some kiddies yet have you?'

'Oh, yes,' replied Marion. 'Louise is nearly nine and Robert is seven.'

'Well! You look too young to have any at all!' Vonnie quipped. 'Mine have all grown up now. There's just me and Merv. It gets lonely sometimes. It's just as well I've got the shop.'

Marion thought it was time to move the conversation towards a conclusion and looked down to the stamp that Vonnie held on the flat of her thumb. As she opened her purse to find the money, Vonnie continued. 'They done alright, my kids. Only one of them went bad and it wasn't his fault. Led astray. Easily influenced he was... six out of seven's not bad. Three of them's married, you know... I'm a grandmother three times over, but do you think I ever see them? Hardly ever. Only Christmas and birthdays. Breaks my heart... They left the valley, ya see. No jobs, they said. No jobs be buggered! There's plenty of jobs for those that want to work. There's apples that need to be picked and pruned, but no. They wouldn't have it. Sick of the sight of apples, they said.'

Vonnie's enlarged eyes roamed the room, looking at the pressed tin ceiling. Marion placed the shilling and sixpence on the counter.

'You'll love old Mrs. Cunningham's place,' Vonnie continued. 'She was a great cook. The sponge was her speciality. She could make a sponge cake that melted in your mouth. Oh, she won a lot of competitions with her sponges. Some say she cheated by adding cornflour like the Americans do, but I don't think so. Cornflour gives a pasty taste and hers weren't like that. No. They were rich and yellowy. Ya know what I think it was?' Marion raised her eyebrows. Vonnie lifted her weight off one elbow and placed it on the other. Her bosoms wobbled to find their equilibrium.

'It's that stove!' she said emphatically. 'That stove up there in that house is a marvel! It can cook anything, but it's especially good at sponges.'

Marion snapped her purse shut. 'I must be getting along.'

The close, stale air seemed to coat her skin, making her feel dirty and clammy. The flies buzzed and the radio barked out the results of the races in long flat vowels that seemed to scrape her ears. She wanted to be in the fresh breeze outside. Her hands felt awkward and clumsy in the gloves. They seemed so inappropriate now.

'Nice gloves,' said Vonnie.

'Thank you,' said Marion.

A silence followed as Vonnie examined the ceiling once

again, the stamp still stuck to her thumb. Marion was horrified at the thought of having to lick the stamp in order to attach it to the letter. The thought of placing it on her tongue, with all the germs and dirt from Vonnie's hands, filled her with revulsion. The Queen's imperious glare remained resolute.

As the two women contemplated each other, the stale air in the shop was invaded by another powerful smell. 'That'll be the onions,' Vonnie volunteered. 'I always put a pan of onions on the stove this time in the afternoon. Just on low with a good dollop of dripping. I make my own dripping, you know, from the Sunday roast. A couple of spoonfuls of dripping and three or four onions and just let them simmer. That's all I have to do to keep my Merv happy. Loves the smell of onions. I keep them cooking very slow till I'm ready to put the veggies and the meat on. I can go away and leave them and get on with whatever I'm doing. They can cook there for an hour and I'll only need to stir them once or twice. And he's happy. As long as he can smell the onions he knows that tea's on the way.'

The radio halted its meandering rhythm for the news bulletin. It was delivered in a deep, testosterone-laden voice, punctuated with what could only have been a burst of flatulence from the unseen Merv.

'God bless him,' said Vonnie and stood up, her bosoms reorganising themselves across her rib cage. She licked the stamp. An excessive amount of spittle clagged onto the back of the Queen's head and she thumped it down onto the envelope. Little bubbles of dribble squeezed out around the edges. The stamp was skew-whiff and smudged with grease.

Marion looked at the envelope, the greasy stamp carelessly

placed above its neat copperplate writing. By the time it got to England it would be worn and tattered anyway, she reasoned. She was enormously relieved and a little grateful at not having to lick the stamp.

'Thank you,' she said. 'It's been nice to meet you.'

'And you too, dearie. Margaret was it?'

'No, Marion.'

'That's right. I'll remember now. Marion. Like Maid Marian in Robin Hood. Oh! I love that show!'

'Thank you . . . Vonnie,' Marion said, relieved that the encounter was at an end. She walked with measured steps towards the door.

'Good luck with that stove,' said Vonnie as a final farewell. 'She's a beauty!'

Outside, the air was warmer and the breeze had picked up. Marion took a deep breath, wondering whether she'd made a friend or an enemy. The basket remained empty. There was nothing in the shop that she wished to buy. Perhaps she could purchase some plastic sandals for the children at a later date. Yes, that would be wise: to return with the intention of buying something. Vonnie had obviously been there since the year dot, so it would be expedient to maintain good relations. Having made up her mind, Marion strode back along the dusty road.

As she turned a corner a gang of boys whizzed past her on bicycles. School must be out. Like a storm of locusts they parted their ranks to make way for her without seeming to see her, their eyes fixed on some future destination, maintaining their speed and direction. They were a silent posse, the itch of their wheels on the gravel the only sound. Marion stopped still in the cloud of dust they left behind. It had flown high in the air and whirled back towards the earth in spirals that clung to her skin and hair. For a moment she felt like crying. But Robert and Louise would be home from school by now, and it was important that she be a strong and happy presence for them. She could laugh it off. What a day! Wait till she told Malcolm about it. They'd have such a laugh, especially if she was as dusty-looking as she felt. She walked on, head held high, lengthening her neck and straightening her shoulders.

She was nearly home when she became aware of a strange smell. Not the sweet, sickly smell of Vonnie's slow-cooking onions, or the natural freshness of the bush. This was a strange, metallic, sour smell that caught in the back of her throat. The small birds had disappeared. An ominous quiet prevailed. Looking ahead she saw a long black object hanging from a telegraph pole. Maybe a belt that someone had lost – perhaps another person had found it and hung it on a nail on the telegraph pole. She moved closer. No, it wasn't a belt. A four-foot-long tiger snake was nailed by its tail to the pole. Its head was smashed in, and blood dripped out of where its mouth would have been. The large ventral scales around its stomach were swollen where its last meal lay undigested. Parts of its body were crushed flat where the boys had taken pot-shots at it.

Marion looked at the deep blue-black gloss of the snake's back. The intensity of the colour fascinated her. Nowhere in the surroundings was there a colour so bold and deliberate. A night-time colour. A colour for dreams. The underbelly of the snake, the sleek black armour giving way to stripes of insipid grass colours. She was surprised by its scaliness. She wouldn't have expected such a strong resemblance to a fish. Each shiny scale pristine in its shape and texture, over-lapping the next in geometric precision. The sticky blood that dripped to the ground had been discovered by a nest of ants. It was another detail to add to the narrative of the day. What stories she would have to tell! The children, of course, would want to come and see it. She hurried back home. The gate was within sight when she heard the children calling. 'Mum!... Mum!' Such a cheery sound.

Chapter 5

BASHER BARWICK HAD SHIT ON the liver. A night at the Aberfeldy Hotel had left him with a vicious hangover. In his student days, when he was young and fit, he'd been able to drink all night and play footy all the next day. But that was ten years ago. These days he tired easily. But the drinking habit had stayed with him.

In all his years of teaching, he'd only once had the opportunity to teach at an inner-city school. He'd been there six months when a parent had started a campaign against him.

All he'd done was teach her son a lesson. The smarmy little bastard had set him up: always making comments just under his breath when his back was turned; taking too long to do a set task; full of excuses when he hadn't finished his work – and answering back one too many times. The insolent look on the boy's face drove him wild with fury. Barwick caned him hard. Three cuts on both hands. The snivelling little creature had yelled and cried without restraint. It only made him want to give him more.

Basher had been banished to the country, where parents were still in awe of any man with an education. If a boy was caned at school it was in his best interests to keep it to himself. A word about it at home and he'd be likely to get another hiding from his father.

The cane came down across Scott Donohue's desk. Grade 6 and the boy still couldn't read!

'Read it out loud, Donohue! Stand up and let's hear it from the beginning!' Basher shouted at the boy. Scott stood up with the reader in his hand. He thought he might as well hold his hand out and get the caning over and done with. He held the reader up close to his face and looked at the page. The white of the paper, with its black squiggles, confused his vision. He tried to focus.

'The . . .' He hesitated and looked at the picture. 'The Eskimo . . . lyves . . . in an—'

'Lives! You stupid boy! Lives! The Eskimo lives!' Barwick came closer. Scott could smell his stale breath.

'The Eskimo lives in an igloo.' Scott managed to get the sentence out in one breath. He looked up and took another breath and then put his head down to tackle the next sentence.

Making Scott read aloud from a Grade 3 reader, when he was in Grade 6, was just one of Basher's amusements. Scott focused on the next sentence. With effort he could lift the squiggly black lines out of the glaring white and decipher the words. But now they seemed to lift themselves right off the white paper and hang above the page. The letters were moving slightly backwards and forwards and curving round towards the end of the line. He blinked several times to try to clear his vision. 'Come on, darky, we haven't got all day!' Basher was losing patience.

'He . . . wears . . . an . . . i . . . mal . . . he wears animal skins and lyves on—'

'Lives! You cretin! Lives!' Basher shouted in his face. 'You stupid little mongrel! This should help you to read!' He lifted the cane. 'Hold out your hand.'

Scott stood with his shoulders hunched. He bent slightly forward. From top to bottom he looked a picture of misery: like a character from a Dickens novel, all tight and bony, trying to maintain a toughness on the outside, as all within was turning to water. His kneecaps were braced with tension. Already his mouth was tightening. *I won't cry*, he said to himself. *I won't let him make me cry.* He held the book to his chest with his left hand and held out the right.

Thirty-four pairs of eyes watched Basher Barwick raise the cane. Three of the bully boys sitting in the back row sniggered.

'It's not his fault, sir.'

Barwick's bloodshot eyes looked around in disbelief. His florid face turned white. A new level of fury overtook him.

'Stand up, the person who said that,' he said in a deathly whisper.

There was a scrape of wooden desk against wooden floor. All eyes turned towards the sound. A small girl in the third row slowly swung her legs into the aisle. She swivelled her body around, positioning herself on the edge of the chair. Looking down, she checked to make sure the calipers on her legs wouldn't catch on the lower rung. Hands under her thighs, she shifted forward. With one hand on the back of the chair and the other flat on the desk she slowly hoisted herself into a standing position. The heavy shoes that held the vertical rods in place around her lower legs had no give in them, so she shuffled to separate her feet a little more and spread her weight evenly. The cage of iron that supported her lower legs rose up from the bulky shoes and ended below the knee. Although the band around the knees was lined with leather it still rubbed the skin, and several Band-Aids were positioned carefully every morning by her mother to minimise the rubbing. The back of her dress was ruffled up and creased. All the girls in Grade 6 managed to smooth their dresses over their bottoms and thighs before sitting. This required a degree of muscular strength that she did not have. She lived with the crinkled look.

Her face was blazing red. *In for a penny, in for a pound.* 'It's not his fault, sir. His eyes don't work the same as everyone else's,' she said in a clear high-pitched voice.

'What!' cried the incredulous Barwick. 'What are you saying . . . GIRL!' This was an unbelievable affront. Before he had time to think, the GIRL continued.

'Scotty can't see properly when it's black writing on a white page. He's alright when it's on the board and he's alright if it's scratched in the dirt. Mrs Smith in Grade 3 uses blue cellophane over the page and that helps. I know 'cause my little brother's the same.' Her face was still scarlet. She'd said what she had to say and now she stood waiting for the consequences. The class held its collective breath. She stood as straight as she possibly could, just her fingertips touching the desk for balance.

That was the moment Ronny Cracknel fell in love with her.

No-one in the class had witnessed such as act of bravery before. Even the bullies in the back row fell silent. Was Basher going to canc a crippled girl? Would he stoop so low? You never knew when he would use the cane, and he did seem to like it. He seemed to think it would make children more intelligent. The chances were that he would hit the girl, even if she was a cripple.

'You can cane me if you want to, but it's still true,' she said with unbelievable audacity! By hook or by crook she was going to hold her position. Nothing like this had ever happened before. This was beyond everybody's experience. Julie Butler was making history right there in front of everyone. Basher's jaw dropped and his face, which was white with fury, changed to a sickening grey. He was lost for words. Scotty surreptitiously lowered his hand.

'So you're an expert are you, carrot top!' was all Basher could manage. In the long silence that followed, nobody breathed. The sound of the clanging bell for recess was the loudest it had ever been. It was the sound of salvation. 'Get out of here the lot of you!' he roared. With that he turned to the door, nearly wrenching it off its hinges.

———

Julie was usually the last child out of the classroom at recess and lunchtime. Because she moved awkwardly and slowly, she would wait until the coast was clear. Laboriously she made her way outside.

Long benches ran the full length of the verandah. Underneath each bench was storage space for bags. To retrieve her bag, Julie had to sit on the bench then double over and reach with her hand for the strap of the bag. If other bags had been pushed in after hers, she couldn't always reach it and would have to ask someone to get it for her. She'd thought of asking if she could keep her bag on top of the bench but hadn't got around to it yet. Maybe she would ask. Yes. She'd go straight to the headmaster and ask his permission, rather than try to reason with Basher Barwick.

Poliomyelitis had struck Julie when she was six years old. For five years she'd worn the calipers. The doctor had said that with exercise and determination she could eventually walk freely. Her mother had set her an exercise program to do at school, but somehow she lost heart when she saw everyone else running around. She was supposed to walk twice around the basketball court at recess, then at lunchtime do ten sit-and-stands on the bench without using her hands and then walk down to the front gate of the school and right up to the back where the rubbish bins were kept. It was uphill all the way and the only reward at the top was the stinking smell of rotting garbage. At least going down to the front gate gave her a chance to smell the roses that grew along the path.

Often she was so dispirited she just sat on the bench with Melanie. Sometimes she sat alone. But today everything was different. Still standing with a burning hot face and eyes wide and watery, she was surrounded by classmates. Cries of 'Well done, Julie!' and 'Julie, you're a hero!' and 'You've got real guts, Jules!' resounded around her. Melanie Squires, who was Julie's best friend, was pushed aside by Shirleena Robertson and Angela Metcalf. Shirleena and Angela, self-appointed social secretaries of the class, saw that there were gains to be had by being with Julie. In the past they had ignored her. Not even a sense of pity had moved them to acknowledge Julie's existence. But now things were different. Julie needed a new set of friends to go with her new status as slayer of monsters.

Angela grabbed her by the hand. 'I'm alright!' said Julie. 'Just let go of me!'

Melanie was waiting on the bench with Julie's bag. 'Thanks

Mel,' she said and sat down next to her.

Shirleena and Angela stood close by. Shirleena unpacked her playlunch and to her delight found two Chocolate Royal biscuits. She quickly gobbled one of them, and then thought to offer the second one to Julie. She held it out to her, but Julie was busy unwrapping a paper bag. Shirleena took a large bite out of the second biscuit. The remaining half she proffered again in Julie's direction.

'Here,' said Shirleena. 'This is for you.' A Chocolate Royal was something special even if it did have fingerprints all over it and a bite missing.

'Gee! Thanks, Shirleena!' said Julie, genuinely delighted. Shirleena felt noble. Angela thought of what she could give to bond with the new sought-after friend but could only offer Vegemite sandwiches. She decided to hate Shirleena for a little while.

Scotty shuffled over to the girls' area. 'Thanks Julie. You're a real sport.' It was all Scotty could think to say. 'I won't forget this.' He flashed a wonderful smile. Julie looked up and blushed. It was not that she was keen on him or any-thing like that. She just wanted to address an injustice.

'Basher's a real bully. It's not your fault about the read-ing. You ask Mrs Smith. She understands. He shouldn't be allowed to get away with it!' And with that she stuffed the Chocolate Royal into her mouth.

'Thanks, anyway. That was very brave! Braver than me. I couldn't have done that.' He gave her another smile and moved off to join the boys. He'd be accused of turning into a sissy if he hung round the girls any longer. He ran off to the gravel patch at the back of the garden shed, where the boys played football. His heart felt light.

Angela, still smarting from Shirleena's victory with the Chocolate Royal, had a brilliant idea. 'Stay still, Julie. I'll do your hair!' Angela was good with hair. She produced a small comb out of her dress pocket. Julie had fine, frizzy red hair. Not the type of hair that took kindly to combs. She had a freckly complexion and big sparkling blue eyes. In eighteen months' time people would begin to notice how pretty she was. Until then people would see only a small skinny crippled girl with a mass of unruly red curls. Carrot Top.

Angela pulled the comb through the top of Julie's hair. Julie felt her scalp lifting.

'Ouch!' she cried. 'Leave me alone!' She got to her feet in the usual shuffling increments and headed out into the yard. 'Mum says I have to go round the basketball court two times. Do you want to come with me, Mel?'

'Yep!' said Mel. 'Let's go.'

Halfway through the second circuit, Scotty came running up to her.

'This is from Ronny,' he said and passed her a note. Julie had never received a note from anyone, let alone a boy. Ronny Cracknel was the class captain. He was bright, alert and intelligent. His school reports used the word 'mature' a lot. 'What's it say?' asked Scotty. Julie unfolded the bit of paper.

'It says, *Do you want to come to the school social with me? I like you. Yours in admiration, Ronald P. Cracknel.*' Julie stood looking at the note. The Grade 6 social was the event of the year. A whole world of possibilities was opening up to her. Never in her wildest dreams could she imagine going to the school social. Even less, partnered with a boy. 'I won't be able to dance,' she said. 'Tell him

I can't dance. He'd be better off taking someone else. Tell him thanks for asking, but I'd feel guilty with him being normal and that.'

It was the sensible thing to do. People were just getting carried away by what happened in the classroom. She was still the same old Julie with the crumpled dress, red hair and calipers. Nevertheless, a spark had entered her heart. 'Come on Mel, I think I can do three rounds today.'

Scotty ran off and was soon back with another message. 'Ronny says he doesn't like dancing. Especially the Pride of Erin and all that muck. He says he just wants to sit with you.' Julie couldn't believe the feelings she was having. Excitement, terror and a wicked gleefulness. Was it possible that girls like her could have a boyfriend? She knew instinctively that Shirleena and Angela would not approve. Relations with boys was their territory. Her role in life would be, at best, handmaiden to the likes of Shirleena and Angela. But the feelings inside her were saying something different. Her heart was thumping at the possibility. Her breath was light and fast in the top of her chest. She looked down at her two little breasts lifting and falling in rhythm. Ronny was nice. He was kind and had a steady look in his eyes. She'd work on her legs every day as hard as she could. Maybe she could get the calipers off by the time the school social came round.

'Tell him only if he's real sure.' Scotty ran off, dodging basketballs, tripping over marble games and skirting groups of Grade 4 girls playing swap cards.

It was a done deal. By the end of recess Julie and Ronny were an item. Shirleena and Angela were shocked, disgusted and affronted. It was even more necessary to stay close to

Julie. If Ronny came to his senses and dropped her, either one of them could be next in line.

———

Louise was looking through her swap card collection when Scotty rushed past. Thumbing through the last of her cards Louise hesitated. She was looking for a swap for Sally's card of a Maine-Coon cat, an animal ridiculously big and fluffy. Not having a cat of her own, Louise thought to make do with a picture of one. The card she thought to swap was one of the national dress series. A Greek boy in full costume. His white tunic looked like a girl's skirt. The blue ribbon around the hem made it even more feminine. His shoes were covered by large white pom-poms and on his head he wore a high tapered fez. It was an odd card. All the national costumes seemed to be colourful and idiosyncratic. They spoke of exotic places, far away in time as well as geographically. A fantasy land of bright colours and eccentric adornments far removed from the dull conformity of the grey school yard. It was not a beautiful card. It didn't have the high gloss of some of the newer series. The stance of the boy reminded her of Robert. It was bold but slightly silly. But it still fascinated her. She hadn't reached the point of aesthetic exhaustion, that moment of disappointment when looking at the picture revealed nothing new. She held onto it and flipped through until she found a stylised tiger leaping out of its frame. She held it out to Sally. 'A tiger for a cat?' Sally nodded and the swap was made.

All around them the school yard was alive with gossip. The story of Julie's brave stance had filtered through the ranks. The Grade 4 girls looked up to the Grade 6 girls, admiring their toughness and resilience. There was no way any of them would be able to live through a year with Basher Barwick. Louise, only in Grade 4, felt certain she was going to die before getting to Grade 6.

On the Bus

Shirleena is proof that the world is round. She's a galaxy of spheres. From the tiny puffballs of flesh around her knuckles to the great mounds of her buttocks, she exudes a moving roundness. Even when she's stationary, some small parts of her remain revolving and rippling, reluctant to settle around her hidden bones. Long, dark, lustrous hair frames her pretty face. Sometimes she parts it low on the left side and lets it hang over her right eye. One of her enemies refers to this as a *sexy boy-trap*.

Shirleena likes to sit at the very back of the bus. Preferably in the left corner. From there she can survey the goings-on of other girls. She's the first to know if *sexy boy-traps* are being laid, and for whom. Shirleena likes to be the first to know of such events and to judge the suitability or otherwise of such flirtations. She knows instinctively that knowledge is power.

She sees Louise and sneers in a mocking way. Louise sits up the front. She doesn't look to the back of the bus and tries to pull an air of self-absorption around her. She's aware of Shirleena and is afraid of her. She's younger than Shirleena and can feel the power that she might wield. She sits just behind Clancy the driver and gazes out the window.

———

Shirleena likes helping her cousin in the fish and chip shop in Huonville. This gives her opportunities to be the first with snippets of gossip and scandal. A fledgling coven of teenage girls hangs around the shop. Friends of her cousin who know about makeup, boys and periods.

Saturday afternoon, Shirleena's cousin has slipped out the back for a ciggie. One of those smart-arse city types comes into the shop. He's tall and skinny with quick, businesslike movements. He wants a takeaway. Shirleena points to the board. He takes his skinny hand out of the pocket of his leather jacket and points slowly down the menu. Every now and then he flips his hair back out of his face. A real ponce.

Suddenly he starts laughing. 'I'll have two salmon patties. With no *ells* thank you.' Shirleena feels her eyes glaze over. Her mouth tightens. She smooths out the apron against her stretch slacks. She hopes her cousin comes back soon. He's making fun of her. She's not sure how, but she knows she's the butt of some sort of smarty-pants joke. It takes a while to heat up the patties. In the meantime he wanders round the shop as if he owns the place. Most people just hang around the counter. Make conversation. This bloke, with his straight back and leather jacket and nose in the air, goes around picking things up and then putting them back again. Sometimes on the wrong shelf! He's getting on her nerves.

'Two salmon patties,' says Shirleena. 'Didyawantanythingelse?' She gives him a sullen look.

'No. That's all thanks. Did you take out the *ells?* he asks with a smirk. She steps back from the counter as if expecting a physical assault. Her mind's on full alert. 'Salmon's got an *ell* in it, lovey.' He winks at her and strides out of the shop.

Shirleena doesn't like to look a fool. She wasn't the person who wrote up the board. And she's not even supposed to be here. When he's far enough away on the other side of the street, she turns to look at the board. *Samon patties* is written as clear as day and has been there for at least six months. If there was an *ell* in it, as the smart-arse ponce seems to think, it is clearly not needed. She moves around the board as if skating round a wild animal, not taking her eyes off the offending word. The chalk's in a tin underneath the counter. Slowly she picks up a piece and considers where to place the elusive *ell*. In her mind Shirleena hears Basher Barwick's loud abrasive voice. *SOUND IT OUT IN YOUR HEAD. SAY IT SLOWLY OUT LOUD AND THEN WRITE IT DOWN.* Shirleena says it out loud, just to be sure. 'Samon' she says with her teeth tightly clenched, still angry at the poncy customer. She dusts out the *a* and replaces it with an *e*. That makes sense. 'Semon'. She says it again. Louder this time. It doesn't seem quite right. Out comes the *o* and in goes an *i*. 'Semin' she says. That must be it. Well even the smart-arse in his leather jacket might be wrong. It sounds right, but looks odd. Maybe there is an *ell* in there somewhere. She pulls the chalk heavily down the board. 'Selmin'. No. She has a dim memory of silent letters and their odd placement. Suddenly, she knows what to do and thus, raising the humble salmon pattie beyond its station in life, she withdraws the *ell* from the middle of the word and places it at the end. 'Seminl!'

———

And now here he is on the bus. He's wearing check pants, his fancy leather jacket, and a cravat round his scrawny neck! Only poofters wear gear like that. He doesn't see me. How could he with his nose so far up in the air? What a weirdo! He doesn't see no-one else on the bus. Just opens his big newspaper and drags on his fag. Doesn't stand up for a lady or nothing. Just sits there. Right up himself.

Shirleena rests her arms on her wicker basket and gives her sullen face to the window. The window gives back a generous reflection. Her hair is bouncy with curls, and her eyes have a simmering glare. She half closes them to judge the effect. The buzzer buzzes for the next stop. *There he is, stretching himself up and folding the newspaper. Mr Weirdo.*

Chapter 6

'WHERE HAVE YOU BEEN?' ASKED Sally.
'To Sunday school,' said Louise.

'What do you do there?'

'Sing. Play games.'

'We have biscuits and cordial and we make up plays,' said Robert. 'Miss Crisp makes up stories and she draws on the board. She's a really good drawer. And she's got these big cards. She did this one of a big apple and a little apple and she said which one would you choose and I said the big one and Louise said the little one, 'cause it might be a trick. And then she changed the card to show what was in the apple and the little apple was nice and juicy inside and the big apple had a worm in it! But I said to Miss Crisp that all the apples have worms in them, even if they are small. Dad says that all the good apples go to England and all we get are the bad ones that aren't good enough to send away. And I told her, but she didn't take any notice.'

'It wasn't supposed to be a real apple, Robert,' said Louise.

Louise and Sally smiled at each other. The conspiratorial smile that older children share when they realise that they inhabit a universe far more complex than their younger siblings. Having reached the age of ten, they were in possession of a sophisticated world view that gave them some insight into the tricks adults could play on gullible children.

———

They were in the same class at school. Sally sat in front of Louise and often borrowed her pencil sharpener or rubber or sometimes her coloured pencils. Sally was on what was called the 'free list'. Her parents were unable to afford, or refused to pay, school levies which covered the cost of stationery and books. The teacher kept a supply of pencils for these poorer children. When Sally needed a pencil she would slowly raise her hand and ask, 'Please, Miss Rudolph, may I have a new pencil?' Miss Rudolph would ask for evidence that the present pencil was entirely used up, worn right down to the stub and no longer capable of being sharpened. Then Sally would begin the solitary journey to the front of the classroom. All eyes would follow her as she stood by the teacher's desk and waited. Eventually, Miss Rudolph would finish the task she was doing – marking maths or correcting spelling. Then she would give her attention to Sally.

She would put down her pen and slowly open a drawer full of paper and pencils. Once she had extracted the appropriate pencil she would hold it in both hands and snap it in half. A crisp *takk* and the pencil's integrity was lost forever. The mutilated end would be rammed into the pencil sharpener and ground into a perfect point. Half a pencil was considered enough for the children on the poor list.

It was a lucky day for Sally if she was given the top half of the pencil rather than the lower part. At least the top part looked as if it had once been full length.

To turn around and ask Louise for a loan of a pencil was infinitely more appealing than taking the long journey up to the front of the class and asking Miss Rudolph for the item and then waiting silently for the snap of the breaking pencil, and a dry comment: 'Try and make it last this time, Sally.'

Sally's revenge was neither spiteful nor hateful. Her sanguine nature smiled at the world and laughed at misfortune. 'Silly old bag,' she'd say under her breath when she was comfortably back in her seat.

Louise's desk was tidy and orderly, whereas Sally's was chaotic. They were complementary personalities and welcomed the difference of the other. Louise found Sally's presence exciting. She seemed to be always on the move, always had something to do or to ask or to tell. She was a child who seemed to be facing into the wind with joy and abandon. Louise loved being with her. With Sally the world was filled with adventure and danger and delight. She loved company and Louise was a good companion. She was steady and timid, which made being adventurous even more of a challenge. Always, Louise needed to be drawn out of herself, but once she was there, she was as foolhardy as Sally.

———

'Do you want to come to my house?' asked Sally.

'Yeah!' said Robert.

'We had better go home,' said Louise. 'We're supposed to always go straight home after Sunday school.'

'It's only just down there,' said Sally, pointing to a shack overlooking the river. The rusty corrugated iron roof was all that was visible.

'Yeah! Come on Lou. Let's go! Just for a little while. Mum won't mind,' said Robert.

Louise hesitated. 'Miss Crisp did let us out a little early.'

'Yeah! Yeah! Come on. Let's go! I want to see Carl!' Robert was already bounding down the crooked path. Caught by

Robert's exuberance, Louise ran down leaping from one uneven step to the next. Sally, knowing every step, followed as if sleepwalking, her arms outstretched as if she were hovering in the air above the visitors.

The front door was open. Sally led them through a dark passage into the back of the house and the kitchen. She opened the door and the warmth and light from an open fire lit up the room. The fire was roaring. A pile of logs sat next to the chimney and bits of bark lay around the hearth. A line of thick string adorned with several pairs of men's socks ran from one end of the mantelpiece to the other. A pair of men's overalls hung over the back of a chair in front of the fire, steaming in its heat. The owner of the overalls was leaning against the mantel, drawing hard on a hand-rolled cigarette.

'Well g'day,' he said in a friendly tone. 'And who would you two be?'

'This is Louise and Robert from up Happy's Road,' explained Sally.

'Well I'm very pleased to meet you, Louise and Robert,' said Sally's dad. His soft voice sounded tired, and his eyes were red-rimmed. He smiled at the children with gentle weariness. Salt streaked his wild and matted hair, and his skin was leathery and dark. He took one last draw on the cigarette and threw it into the fire. 'Sally's friends are always welcome here in this home,' he said. 'You can call me Salty.'

'And I'm a friend of Carl's,' said Robert.

'Well, are you now!' Salty brightened up. 'He should be around somewhere. You go find him, Max, and tell him a friend is here.' A small boy slid from the kitchen table down onto a chair and from there jumped onto the floor.

'Don't let anyone eat my chips!' he said and ran out the back door yelling 'Carl! Carl!'

Twin boys sat in identical highchairs at the end of the table. In the centre of the table was a plate of crayfish broken into bite-sized chunks, and beside it another plate heaped with chips.

'Youse have come just in time for a bit of tucker and you're very welcome to join us,' said Salty, his voice once again slow and steady. 'Everything's shared in this house. Everyone gets as much as they need. Isn't that right Alice?' By the sink stood a tall woman wearing a black silk dressing gown wrapped tightly around her body and tied with a red sash. Long white hair framed her face. She smiled at Salty. Her face reflected his soft gaze. It was a smile that was alive and questioning, a smile that took no notice of others present in their company.

Louise had never seen adults being their adult selves when children were around. She felt the deep currents between them, unmodified by concern for children's understanding. *So this is what real love is like,* she thought.

Alice turned around, displaying the fiery dragon on the back of the dressing gown. She took half a dozen plates from the rack above the sink and handed them to Sally. Sally put them on the table. 'Don't be shy,' said Salty. 'There's plenty there. Good fresh crays. I picked them off the ocean floor meself. If you eat them all I'll go back and get some more.' He laughed a kindly laugh and smile lines creased his face from chin to forehead. 'Have you ever eaten crayfish, Louise?'

Louise looked up at him. 'No,' she said. The look in Salty's eyes made her feel that she couldn't possibly tell him less than the full story. 'Mum says it's too rich for children to eat. Sometimes we have scallops,' she said apologetically. Salty's soft gaze released her anxiety.

'That's true, Louise,' he said in his slow, deliberate way. 'You have to be brought up with it. Some people can't take it. They puff up and become sick.'

'I've had crayfish,' said Robert. 'Me and Carl had some down by the river. He said it was leftovers.' Both Salty and Alice laughed.

'So youse two are already friends,' said Salty.

'Yes,' said Robert. 'We've been friends since last year when we moved here.'

'And where did you come from?' asked Salty.

'We lived in Hobart. Lou and I were born there but Mum comes from England.' Sally handed Robert a plate of chips and crayfish. 'Oh! Whoa! Thanks so much!'

'Your mum's English is she? Well! We've got something in common. My grandfather was English. That's where I got me eyes. Green eyes like me grandfather. Same as Sally,' he said, pointing to Sally's sparkling green eyes.

Salty picked up a crayfish leg. 'You try just a little, Louise. If it's not to your liking you can spit it out in the fire. Or if you blow up like a balloon we'll take you to hospital,' he joked.

He took the red-speckled leg and bent it at the weakest point, flattened the crusty shell and carefully pulled the claw away from the leg. The pale juicy flesh hung loose.

'Just take a little bite from here and see what you think.'

The children looked up to see Louise's reaction. She looked him full in the face and opened her mouth. Salty placed the morsel on her pink tongue as if giving her communion. She tasted the fresh tang of it and smelt the sharp bitter smell of tobacco from his fingers. She bit down on the white flesh, chewed and swallowed. It was sweet and succulent, subtle in its richness, creamy and moist.

'Thank you, Mr Salty,' she said.

'Mr Salty! Mr Salty!' The children cried. 'Mister Salty! *Mister Salty!*' They laughed and laughed. Even the little ones caught the mood of hilarity and banged their hands on their trays.

Max came running into the room with Carl. 'Hi Robert,' said Carl. 'What's everyone laughing about?' Robert shrugged his shoulders and munched on a chip. Louise blushed.

'It's not that funny,' said Sally. 'Lou called Dad 'Mr. Salty' and everyone thinks it's a big joke.' Carl, still full of momentum from running around outside, rushed up to his father and threw his arms around him.

'He's our Mr Salty!' he said triumphantly, squeezing Salty round the middle. Salty picked him up and hefted him over his shoulder where he crawled down his back and onto the floor. Salty picked him up again and gave him a kiss, twirled him round to face the table.

'You better tuck in before it's all gone,' he said.

Robert looked at the happy face of Carl and wondered what it was like to be hugged and kissed by your father. Louise stood red-faced, looking down at her tartan skirt.

'It's alright, Louise. You can call me whatever you like,' said Salty. 'As long as it's in friendship, I'll answer to any name. We're all together on this earth and it don't matter who you are or what you're called. As long as there's love in your heart for your fellow human being. That's all that matters. What's in your heart. You call me mister and that's a great sign of respect. More than I get from this mob!' He smiled at his children. 'And respect is a wonderful thing. Without respect for each other where would we be? Got to have respect. Young for old, and old for young. Neighbour for neighbour. All people as equals. Everyone to love one another. Youse two have lovely manners and kind hearts. That'll see you through life. Good manners and a full heart and you'll be right. What do ya say, Alice?'

Alice crossed her arms and leant her head on one side. 'I think they're fine words,' she replied and then added, with her eyes twinkling, 'Mr Salty!'

The children once again took to laughing with exaggerated hysteria. Max staggered around the room holding his belly like a comedian from a silent movie. Sally rolled her eyes and looked to Louise. But Louise was entranced by Salty. She had never been talked to by an adult in this fashion: as if she were just as important as an adult. Even in Sunday school the words were not as real as the ones Salty had uttered. He spoke of his feelings and ideas. She felt the deep sincerity within him and this, in some way, ennobled her: as if he had shown her some power in the world that she was not aware of. It felt giddy and strange.

Sally grabbed a handful of chips and a big chunk of crayfish and plonked them on a plate. 'We can share these on the couch,' she said and led Louise away from the fire to the back of the room. They sat on the couch, heads bent over the plate.

———

A very different household, this, from the Johnstones'. The room was drafty. Cobwebs hung from the ceiling, waving slowly in the heat from the fire. The linoleum was worn through, showing the floorboards beneath. A single light bulb, layered with sticky dust, hung from the ceiling. The sink against one wall was the size of a laundry trough and made out of solid Huon Pine. A clothes-horse off to one side of the fire held a drab collection of off-white clothing. The mantelpiece above the fire held a profusion of small items: boxes of matches, a tobacco pouch, scissors, a mouth organ, a postcard from Sydney, a candle in an enamel mug, a ball of grey wool skewered with two knitting needles, a packet of Aspro, a roll of digestive tablets, a hammer, a ball of string and a row of jars. The jars were clearly labelled: RENT, GROCERIES, BUS FARES, BIRTHDAYS AND CHRISTMAS and MUM'S TEETH.

A bookcase next to the couch was crammed full of books and magazines. Charles Dickens sat comfortably next to the complete works of Karl Marx. *Paton's Patterns for Winter Socks, Scarves and Hats* was wedged between *W.H. Auden: Selected Works* and *Poems* by Emily Dickinson. A well-thumbed copy of *Monsters from the Deep* lay across eight volumes of *Cassel's Book of Knowledge*. Two volumes of *Lands and Peoples* were equally well-thumbed. Sally, Max and Carl would spend many rainy afternoons gazing at the forlorn faces of native peoples from around the world. In fading sepia the native peoples looked back at them in bewilderment, their astonished defiant stares a silent echo. The *Webster's Dictionary* sat on the floor like an immobile pet.

The fire formed the centrepiece of the room, not only adding a great blast of radiant heat but a focus for the eyes and ears. Every visitor to the house gravitated to it, paying homage to the elemental. The fire gave of its spirit: its lively crackle and pop and the joyous curve and leap of its flames. A galaxy of sparks flew up the chimney every time Salty trimmed the logs.

The children too reflected the fire's wildness. As if they fed off its energy, they leapt and spun around in a dance of floppy limbs, testing the hardness of the world, throwing themselves against couches and chairs. Or outside: rolling down the grassy hill to the gurgling river below. Their voices loud and high, filled with exuberance.

———

When they had finished the crays and chips, Louise surreptitiously wiped her hands on the couch. 'I think we ought to go home now. Mum might be worrying.' She thought Mrs Saltmarsh would be thinking it was time for Louise and Robert to return home. Louise waited for a signal from Mrs Saltmarsh. But Alice seemed unconcerned. She made no move to urge Louise and Robert on their way.

'Come and see my room first,' said Sally. She led Louise down the hall through a panelled door with a missing handle. 'This is my room.' She pushed the door open and flopped onto the bed. The cover was a crocheted blanket in bright reds and yellows. 'Isn't this lovely?' Sally lifted the edge of the bedspread and wrapped it around her shoulders.

'These are my pictures.' She pointed to the walls. Nearest the bed was a brightly coloured tea towel printed with a picture of a large tulip, with 'Holland' written above it in arched lettering. On the far wall was another tea towel displaying the Eiffel Tower, 'Paris' on a flag waving from the top.

'I like your bedspread,' said Louise. 'Yellow's my favourite colour. I'd better find Robert and go home, now.'

They moved down the hall. 'I know where they'll be,' said Sally. 'In the bathroom!' This seemed rather odd to Louise. 'Wait till you see our bathroom. You won't believe it!' Sally laughed and skipped through the kitchen and out the back to a room on the right-hand side of the shack. Louise gasped as she came through the doorway.

Before her lay Golden Valley, spread out in all its glory. The river was churning and sparkling, racing over boulders and into whirlpools. The massive gum trees that stood on the banks seemed like giants holding hands, gazing down at the endless whirl of the water.

The room had lost its southern and eastern walls. The floor was intact and the foundations solid. Half the roof was missing. There was only cover for one small dresser and a hand basin. In the centre of the room was a large bath half full of steaming water.

'The bath is for Alice and Salty,' explained Sally. 'They always have a bath together when he gets home from fishing. The walls fell off when we had that big storm last spring. The landlord is supposed to fix it but he hasn't yet. So we get to bathe out in the open. The boys think it's great but I don't. Mum hangs a curtain around the bath when it's my turn. It's so annoying having brothers, don't you think?'

'Yes,' said Louise, not knowing what else to say. 'We had better go, or I'll get into trouble. Thanks for asking us in.'

'You can come any time. I've got lots of secret places that the boys don't know about. See if you can come down tomorrow.'

'Thanks, Sally. I'd better find Robert.'

They eventually found Robert and Carl down by the river. The boys had lost track of time, absorbed in making a fish trap out of rocks. With a sudden feeling of panic Robert scrambled up the riverbank, and together he and Louise ran up the path.

'We'll get into trouble,' said Robert.

'Not if we explain things properly. We didn't mean to stay so long, and it would have been rude to leave earlier. Mum will understand. She's always going on about politeness and doing the right thing. We couldn't have left any earlier. Sally would have been disappointed.'

'What did you think of the bath?'

'I wouldn't want to bathe in it. I'll ask Mum if Sally can use our bath so she doesn't have to be outdoors. Just until their house is fixed up. Isn't her father strange? He was like a prophet from the Old Testament. And their mum, did you see her dressing gown? It was very beautiful. And fancy having a bath in the middle of the day! And together! Robert, we had better not say too much about the house, I don't think Mum would like it.'

'Yes, you're right. We'll just say we had to go there because it would have been not polite to say no. I've been there before anyway but don't tell Mum or Dad.'

'No, I won't.'

The children ran the half-mile home as quickly as they could. Louise was still excited by the visit, and all the little details of it played back in her head. She would like to tell her mother everything. Yes, she decided. She'd tell her every detail and then she would be sympathetic to their predicament. If she knew how awkward it was to get away, she could not possibly be angry. The rules of good manners demanded that they stay for as long as they had. She wouldn't mention the food. That was probably not a good idea. Her mother had fixed ideas about food.

Salty talked about friendship and respect and love, all qualities that Miss Crisp at Sunday school would approve of. Maybe Salty could become friends with her father, and then her father would become a little like Salty – brave in his ideas about the world and good, like in the Bible... Her mother couldn't possibly be mad at them for wanting to hear these things... Yes! It was like what they learnt at Sunday school... Love for everyone. Salty must be a saint of some sort, only those in the Bible talked like that. Her father had never said the word love. Nor had he ever talked about grand things like equality and respect... They could use the story of Jesus in the temple to explain why they were late! Yes, that was a great idea – they were listening to the wise words of Salty and lost track of time. Just like Jesus had! They raced up the road and through the back door.

———

'Your father wants to see you in the living room.' Marion's eyes blazed. Her apron was pulled tightly round her waist and the sinews on her neck stood out. 'Get in there immediately!' She pushed them out of the kitchen.

'Mum, it wasn't our fault,' Robert began, but Marion wasn't listening.

'We didn't want to be rude.' Louise started her rehearsed explanation.

'Tell that to your father! Not to me!' Marion turned her back and plunged her hands into the kitchen sink.

The children moved down the hall. The frosted glass doors were shut but they could see the shadow of their father sitting hunched in the big armchair. Robert's eyes began to water. Louise had not given up on her prepared explanation and thought now, that her father would be more reasonable.

After all, it was Mother who was always adamant about being on time for meals – that was probably what had upset her the most. The fact that they were late for lunch. But her father was often late for lunch… He'd always have an excuse of some sort: he had to finish this or that, or he had met someone who needed his help in some way, or he'd simply got caught up with friends – just like they had today! Once he understood the situation, he would see reason. And, in fact, see that it was just the same situation that he himself had been in lots of times! All was not lost.

'Louise! Come in here! Robert! You too!' Malcolm's voice sounded angrier than they had ever heard it. They opened the door and stood by the big chair. Louise's prepared explanation seemed to disappear, as if her voice box froze. There was a violent storm in the room that stripped them both of their wits. They became dumb and mute, filled with terror at the strength of the rage that overtook Malcolm. He stood up from the chair.

'Louise,' he said, not looking at her. 'Lie on the couch. Face down.'

She made one last attempt to think clearly. Something else might have upset him. It might not have been simply that they were late for lunch. But her insides were trembling. The power of his rage was overwhelming. Any explanation she had would have to wait until he calmed down. She stood there not moving, paralysed with fear. Never before had she seen her father like this. He must be having an attack of some sort.

'Did you hear me?' he yelled into her face. Still she couldn't move. Robert started whimpering and held his penis tight. Malcolm grabbed her by the hair and pushed her down onto the couch, his foot in the small of her back so that she couldn't move. He undid his leather belt and, holding the buckle in the palm of his hand, he wrapped the leather round a couple of times. He pulled up her skirt and let the leather come down hard on the backs of her legs. Louise gasped with the pain. Then he did it again, this time right across her bottom. She bent her knees to try to protect herself but the belt came down hard again and the foot in her back was pinning her to the couch. 'And here's one more to make sure you remember!' He let the last stroke be the hardest.

Robert's whimper had become full-on sobs. His father turned around and grabbed him by the ear and gave him six quick lashings across the back of his legs. Robert yelled in terror and urine ran down his legs. Louise made to get up but Malcolm pushed her back down.

'You're not going anywhere! Do you hear! Let this be a lesson to you. You don't go down to that house! Never go down to that house again. Do you hear me?'

'Yes,' she stuttered. 'Yes.' She knew now that her father had gone completely mad. Her only hope lay in her mother. Her mother would give her time to explain. All she could do now was submit and wait for it to end. Her legs and bottom were throbbing and stinging with pain. She wondered if she would be able to stand.

'Go to your rooms and don't come out until I say. Is that clear? Now get out of my sight!' Malcolm put his belt back on and pointed at the door.

Robert ran out bawling loudly and headed for the bathroom. Louise lifted herself off the couch. She felt dizzy and stumbled a little but grabbed the door handle and moved out of the room as quickly as she could.

But she wasn't going to her room. Not yet. Even though the pain was excruciating, she wanted to see her mother. Surely she would understand. She found her in the kitchen, her arms still in the sink. 'It's not fair,' she said. 'We didn't do anything—' but before she could finish, Marion swung round and slapped her hard across the face.

'Don't you ever question your father or you'll get more of what you've just had!'

In disbelief Louise turned and went to her bedroom. In the long stretch of the afternoon she lay on the bed, not crying with sobs, but just allowing the tears to course down her face. She wondered what it would be like to lie on Sally's bed, on her pretty bedspread, and whether her father ever belted her. Somehow she couldn't imagine it. It simply didn't make sense. Salty didn't seem like the kind of man that would hit his children. Being a little late for lunch was not a crime worthy of such a beating.

As the sun was setting Marion came into Louise's room with Robert. 'Sit up, Louise, and listen to me,' she said. 'Robert, you sit on the end of the bed. I am very disappointed in both of you but especially you, Louise.' It sounded like a prepared speech. 'You are always to come straight home after Sunday school. You are not to talk to anyone and certainly not to go into *that* house. Is that understood?'

'But we were invited,' Robert began.

'You say *no*, and keep walking,' replied Marion.

'But can't we go down there at all?' Robert asked.

Marion's voice rose. 'No! Not at all! Those children are half-castes and that woman is a communist!'

Robert began again, 'But... what's a half-caste?'

Marion scowled. 'Your father should be explaining all this.

They're half aboriginal. Their father is an aborigine. It's a wonder those children haven't been taken into care. Do you know what I'm saying?'

'But Salty isn't an aboriginal, he's not even black. His grandfather was English! He said so himself. He said he has English eyes. You tell her Lou.' But Louise's eyes had closed down. A hard veil of pain and disbelief had filled her mind. Hearing Robert say his name had brought the episode vividly back to her. Nothing she could say was going to change her mother's mind.

'He is an aboriginal. He's a fisherman who can barely read or write. He's from the savage races and they are doomed to die out. That's the best thing that could happen to them. This country's ours now, and there's no room for them.' Marion stood up as if to end the discussion, but then she thought of one more thing. 'If you marry an aboriginal, the government can take your children from you and put them in homes and you can never see them again.'

All this information settled around Louise like fallen ash. *Saint Peter was a fisherman*, she felt like saying. 'What's a communist?' she said instead.

'Your father's the one who knows about politics!' Marion said. Then added in a rush, 'A communist doesn't believe in God.'

'What do they believe in?' asked Louise in a flat voice, not looking away from the pattern in the carpet.

Marion's voice rose again. 'You will not talk back to me like that! You will both stay in your rooms until you go to school tomorrow morning and I want nothing more said about any of this! You are never to talk to those children again and never, ever go into that house! Is that clear?'

'Yes,' said Louise, still staring at the carpet.

'Yes,' Robert mumbled.

On the Bus

The school bus pulls over at the bottom of Happy's Road. Robert and Louise slowly board.

Sally's holding a seat for Louise. 'Here, Lou,' she says and removes her bag. Sally threads her arm through Louise's and takes her hand. 'Ya know what Salty says?' She smiles at Louise.

'No,' Louise says, sullen and listless.

'Salty says you're my new posh friend!'

Louise feels overwhelmed by a new betrayal.

'I'm not posh,' she says and tears run down her face. 'I'm not posh,' she repeats.

'What happened?'

'Dad belted us.'

'What for?'

'Just because we were late getting home.'

Robert's standing in the aisle holding onto the back of the seat. 'That's right. It's so unfair!' says Robert. 'He got me with his belt right across here!' He turns around and shows the backs of his legs. A small crowd of children gather around.

Sally feels a cloud envelop her. She was looking forward to a close friendship and now it seems it won't happen. She puts her arm around Louise. 'I'm sorry, Lou. It's probably all my fault.' She had pushed for them to come down to her house.

A heavily set boy leaves his seat and comes up to Robert. 'Look at this,' he says, lifting up his shirt to show red welts across his back. 'That's a belting! My dad did that. I don't even know why he did it! He was drunk and he just felt like hitting me.' He pulls his shirt down. 'When I grow up I'm going to kill my father,' he says. Robert looks in awe at the big boy.

The rest of the journey is taken up with stories of beatings and bashings that take place behind the closed doors: tales of mothers being hit with saucepans; children being strung up and whipped as if they were convicts; mothers holding their children under water in the bath tub; fathers being tripped and kicked when returning from a night at the pub; children being lined up and belted on a Sunday night – a precautionary beating, just in case they might have done something wrong during the week.

'Has anything like that ever happened to you?' Louise asks Sally.

'No,' says Sally. 'Salty and Alice don't believe in corporal punishment. Every now and then they have a bit of a yell, but it's mostly at each other, not at us. Salty say violence is not the way. Max and Carl fight a bit but it's never serious.'

'My parents say the same thing.' A small girl with clear skin and a high forehead joins the conversation.

Sally doesn't borrow anything from Louise that day. At recess she helps in the sports cupboard, although she isn't rostered on. At lunch time she asks the teacher if she can tidy up the small bookcase. Louise asks if she can help her. 'Oh, if you really want to,' Sally replies, without looking at her.

Chapter 7

'THEY HAVE TO LEARN,' SAID Malcolm, drawing heavily on his cigarette, jaw clenched. Smoke curled out through his nostrils above his downturned mouth.

'They have to learn!' Marion agreed. She sprinkled Ajax over the sink and rubbed it in with the dish cloth. When she'd finished she pulled her apron over her head, and hung it on the back of the door. 'Even if it's the hard way,' she added.

'Hard? Cripes! It can get a lot harder than that! Believe me.' Malcolm stubbed his cigarette in the ash tray. 'Never mind, it's over now. Honestly, Marion, I hardly touched them. Nothing like what happened in my day. My grandfather with his bloody whip! By jeez he used to go to town on us. And for no reason. A little bit of grog and off he'd go. Anyone who got in the way was in for it. One time he went to clout me and I ducked, and my cousin Elsie collected it instead. Right on the nose. Blood everywhere! But do you think he regretted it? For a moment he looked a bit sheepish then he threw her a tea towel and chased me out of the house.'

Marion gave him a sympathetic look. Her upbringing, by comparison, had been haphazard but gentle. She could never imagine Clown Bo-Bo hitting anyone. He would be more likely to cry if he thought any of his children had done anything wrong. He was a softy: un-masculine and sensitive. He was a witty man in an age when men needed to be uniformed and strong. That was one reason she found

Malcolm so attractive. At times she found him unimaginative, dour, literal-minded, and lacking in wit or humour, but he was strong, solid, uncomplicated and forthright. Reliable and dependable.

———

This crisis with the children gave Malcolm and Marion a chance to repair their relationship after 'the incident' at Flo and Barry's party. Families, like some nations, maintain their unity by looking outward to the world beyond their borders to re-establish their difference, and be united in a common purpose. And so, when things became a little fractious after 'the incident', the crisis with the children came as a blessing. Like a nation having problems with domestic policy and seeking to deflect attention away from it by starting an untidy little war in some unfortunate country, so Malcolm and Marion sought to cement their marriage by focusing on the few areas where they shared common ground.

The issue of mixing with Aboriginal people was one such case. They both agreed that Australia was a white country and it was important that it remained so: Aboriginal people were to be pitied but not befriended; they would be allowed to die out and their blood lines eventually reduced to nothingness by the white population. Malcolm and Marion saw this as a natural part of evolution.

———

'The incident' was the most fun Marion had had in a long time.

Flo and Barry Highcroft were holding a house-warming party. All the neighbours were invited. A lot of their friends from the city had come as well. The city crowd were loud and raucous. They'd come laden with crockpot casseroles, meat loaf, wholemeal bread, curries, homemade sausages, and lasagne (which neither Marion nor Malcolm had ever heard of. Marion tried it and thought it was quite nice but a little too rich. Malcolm refused it outright). There were cakes, flans and cheesecakes, home-brewed beer and cider.

Malcolm was horrified when he entered the kitchen. A young man with extremely long bleached hair, wearing a girl's school uniform, was waving a spoon of toffee syrup over a pile of cream puffs. Without looking up, the apparition spoke to Malcolm. 'What do you reckon? Does it look like the Queen Mother's hat?' Malcolm had no idea what he was talking about. He hadn't expected the apparition to speak and was taken aback to be addressed in such a familiar tone. He left the kitchen without responding.

Alice Saltmarsh was sitting next to the fire sipping a glass of claret. Two young women were by her side, talking quietly. Salty was on the back verandah drinking beer with Barry. In the living room Malcolm found a couple of neighbours and joined their conversation: weather, cows, sheep, cricket. They were joined by Flo and Barry, who introduced them to a middle-aged couple.

'This is Ray and the Professor,' said Flo, with a twinkle in her eye.

Malcolm extended his hand to the man. 'How do you do, Professor?'

'Ha! Works every time! Malcolm, you've been had!' Flo laughed and pirouetted with her empty glass on her head.

'She's extremely wicked,' the woman said, in a crisp English accent. 'Her mission is to embarrass every man in the room.'

'She's the professor, old boy,' said her partner. 'I could never hope to achieve a fraction of her elevated status. For one thing I'm far too political and far too lazy. I'll be lucky if I ever get tenure. They don't like radicals like me, but Alison had made a name for herself in literary circles and the university is quite amenable to heads of departments having a national profile. As long as it's in literature and not politics.' Ray shoved both his hands into the pockets of his cuffed jumbo corduroy pants and swung back on his heels. He continued in a rounded, fruity voice to complain about the administration of the university.

Malcolm felt like more than just a fool. He had indeed been set up. How could a woman possibly be a professor? Perhaps in England or somewhere else, but here? ... And what was she doing at a party in the country? No – there was something fishy about it. She didn't look like a professor... More like some kind of communist – those unattractive brown slacks straining at the zip over her stomach, and some kind of lumpy knitted cardigan buttoned up to her neck. No effort made with her hair at all. Marion wouldn't be seen dead looking like that! ... These were not people to be trusted.

He grabbed one of the homemade sausages and took a bite. 'Oh, gawd!' he cried and rushed outside. The sausage was full of garlic. Spitting it out under a hydrangea bush attracted the attention of Spangles, Flo and Barry's Labrador. With his head cocked to one side, Spangles waited. 'Here, mate,' said Malcolm. 'It's all yours,' and he handed Spangles the sausage. The dog followed Malcolm back inside. Malcolm found an empty chair and Spangles rested his muzzle on his knees, every now and then lifting his eyebrows in an attempt to gain another treat. Malcolm obliged with another sausage.

Marion was in the kitchen with Flo, Professor Alison and several other women. Flo took the top off a flagon of hock and splashed it into ceramic goblets. 'It's a very mediaeval touch,' she said handing them around. Taking a large slurp she cried, 'Let's move the table back! Let's dance!'

Chubby Checker was hollering out the Twist. The music went straight to their hips and the women ground and pumped with abandon, throwing their hips forward and backward, arms and hair flying in the air. Flo leapt onto the table and kicked off her shoes.

Bobby Darin was next on the turntable. Malcolm heard 'Beyond the Sea' from the living room. It was a song that moved him more than he could say. This was their tune. His two great loves: Marion and the ocean. His heart swelled as Bobby Darin's mellifluous voice penetrated every cell in his body. His fingers started clicking and his toes were tapping. He wanted to hold Marion tight and shuffle around in a slow two step, feeling her tiny hand in his and burying his face in her hair.

Marion put the specialness of the tune out of her mind. She didn't want to think of Malcolm and the sea. This was a time for silliness and revelry: a time for being with the girls. Of course the music demanded that they all form a chorus line to perform a slow-motion version of the Swim, improvising moves as they became mermaids of the deep. It was so ridiculous they all ended in breathless laughter.

'I can't quite grasp the concept of the modern dancing,' moaned Professor Alison. 'There are not enough moves in it. I can't see the form, or is it that one has to invent the form oneself? Does the form just come out of nowhere? The subconscious perhaps?' Marion looked at her blankly. Flo quickly went to change the music. Perhaps the professor would relate to something from an earlier era. Soon they heard the hiss and crackle of a 78 record. Barney Google issued forth on his trusty pony, Sparkplug.

Marion was quick to catch on. 'Try the Charleston,' she said. 'It's quite stylish. Look. Left foot back, eyes to the right, circle in the hands, round and round. Right foot back, eyes to the left, circle in the hands, round and round. Crossing the knees, over and back, heel, toe, heel, toe, oth-er way.'

'Oh, what a lovely metre it has when you say it!' said Professor Alison. Marion had started going through the routine again with Flo and a few others in tow. 'Can I try it?' asked the professor, looking on with delight. 'You have to slow down a little. I'm too old to go at that speed. You have marvellous footwork, my dear. Where did you learn to dance?'

'Oh, I learnt this one from Clown Bo-Bo the First,' said Marion.

'Clown Bo-Bo the First! How extraordinary!' exclaimed Professor Alison.

'Oh, I'm sorry. I haven't explained that very well. Clown Bo-Bo the First was my grandfather. My father is Clown Bo-Bo the Second. My parents run a dance and drama school. It's very small but they make a living. Clown Bo-Bo the First – oh, sorry, my grandfather – was in vaudeville for many years.' Marion stopped to get her breath. Her cheeks were flushed and her eyes were sparkling with joy. She hadn't danced for years. There seemed to be no room in her life for dancing these days. She had been brought up in the chorus line, but somehow she'd let it slip. It was so much fun! Flo filled her glass again. They were both laughing and panting.

To Professor Alison, anyone with a grandfather called Clown Bo-Bo the First qualified as an 'interesting person'. The story of Marion's upbringing was obviously unique and quirky, both qualities she found enriching in the otherwise desolate culture beyond the ivory tower of the university. To her, the descendants of convicts held to an absence of culture that seemed to be bone-headed obstinacy: as if resistance to culture was a virtue. Professor Alison did her best to enrich the bland lives of the lumpen daughters of burghers and farmers with Shakespeare and Wordsworth. She sought to encourage the especially talented to leave their homeland as quickly as possible and travel back to England to immerse themselves in the transformative experience of a living, continuous culture.

She flung off her shoes. 'Let's go again! From the top!' she cried.

A glass or two later they were still hoofing away in the kitchen when Flo suggested they change dance. Barney Google had ridden his pony into the scratchy sunset and there was a moment of silence.

'What about the Can-Can! Marion, you can have the table.'

Marion flounced and twirled her full skirt, then sat on the table crossing her legs and cupping her face in her hands: a Doris Day pose. Then she leapt to her feet and up onto the table. Immediately they all started singing and shuffling, twisting and pouting in a coquettish fashion. The laughter was irresistible and others gathered to watch the display. Marion was in full flight, her dark curly hair tumbling around her glistening face, toes pointing, and fingers held just so, skirt flouncing, revealing knees and thighs. Ray popped his head around the door.

'I have it on good authority that the Can-Can was originally danced without knickers. Girls! You're not being authentic!'

'Out of here! You rogue!' cried Professor Alison. Whistles and hoots followed as the women continued to twirl, kick and gyrate. 'I can't do the splits! I'm going to rip my trousers! Oh!' The professor landed on the floor with a thump. 'I'll pay for this tomorrow,' she said, hauling herself into an upright position.

The rest of the women were looking at Marion's perfect posture on the kitchen table.

'Are you doing the full splits?' asked Flo. She looked at Marion and saw her front leg extended and toes pointing. Then she inspected the back leg. 'Yes! She can do it!' she cried. 'The full splits! Ladies and gentlemen, we have a true dancer in our midst!' Marion posed with her chest thrust forward and her head high, eyes to the ceiling, arms outstretched.

A round of cheers and applause followed.

'Extraordinary!' exclaimed the professor. 'Quite extraordinary!'

Malcolm stood in the doorway. 'Marion, we're going home!'

———

'How could you make such a spectacle of yourself?' Malcolm was shaking with rage. 'All those people looking at you, laughing their heads off. Where's your dignity? What are people going to say about you? About us! It's not how you should be behaving, Marion! What are they going to say at the office? How am I going to live this down! Do you realise what you've done?' Marion flinched as Malcolm flung the Highcrofts' gate back against the fence. 'You're just too stupid to think aren't you! There are people on the council who respect me and respect my judgement. What if this gets back to them? What'll they do when they find out my wife drinks like a fish and behaves like a tart? I'll probably lose my job over this.' He spat the words at her as they walked down the hill towards their home.

'I'm sorry, Malcolm. Let's just forget it shall we?' Marion pulled her cardigan around her shoulders. 'It was just a bit of fun.'

'Bit of fun? You call that a bit of fun! I call it shameless exhibitionism. I'm not going to put up with other men looking at you in that way, and believe me, Marion, if you behave like that they will and where does that leave me? I don't want to be known as a man with a trollop for a wife! No wife of mine is going to make a fool out of me! Is that clear? Do you understand? You're not a child, Marion.' Malcolm thrust his hands into his pockets and strode off into the dark.

The shadows of the gums swallowed him. Marion was left alone. The noise from the party came in waves riding on the night wind. She heard swells of laughter and music rushing towards her. Overhead the sky was filled with stars. Twinkling, laughing stars. A gibbous moon bobbed through the trees. She saw it rocking like a pendulum. Suddenly the earth shot round and hit her on the head. She rolled over trying to find which way was up. But the earth kept turning. Each time she thought she knew which direction to move, everything swivelled and shot away. The stars rushed towards her, spears of light needling into her as the ground slipped and rolled. She found herself against a tree at the side of the road. Her stomach knotted. She threw up a mixture of hock and roasted peanuts. The relief was almost immediate and gave room for a few quiet sobs of remorse followed by an attack of giggling. Marion found her shoes, which had dissociated themselves in the tumble, and fitted them to the appropriate feet. This took some time. Eventually she achieved an upright position, dusted off her dress and rearranged the cardigan. *There!* she thought. *Let's try again.* And she stumbled down the road.

The music from the party had changed as the ephemeral shimmer of close harmonies from the fifties gave way to a brutal toughness. One hard note after another pierced the restless night. Bob Dylan had hit the turntable and the Times They Were a-Changin'. The surroundings seemed to grow sinister as the raw voice chanted its clarion call. Marion felt forlorn, abandoned and desperately disappointed in herself. She'd make it up to Malcolm somehow. What if the children saw her like this? She had no idea she had become so drunk. But it had been fun! Exhilarating, unadulterated fun! She started laughing again.

Marion and Flo planned to see each other regularly. There was a macramé class starting up in Huonville in a couple of weeks and they were both keen to enrol. She wouldn't tell Malcolm that Flo was doing the class with her. Not unless he specifically asked. He didn't need to know little details like that.

The moon was leaping from cloud to cloud as she rounded the last bend before home. A dark figure with his hands in his pockets was walking through the shadows towards her. His head was down. He looked so lost, so lonely. She started running. He opened his arms and scooped her up.

Chapter 8

'So I didn't seem an embarrassment?'

'No! If anything, it was the most delightful thing that happened last night.' Flo took a sip of coffee.

Marion put her cup down and relaxed. 'The way Malcolm went on, you'd think I stripped naked in the men's bar in Huonville.'

Flo laughed. 'You made a lovely impression. People appreciate someone who's a bit different.'

'Different! I don't want to be different! I'd rather just blend in.'

Flo smiled and cupped her hands around the mug. 'You are who you are,' she said.

'Last night I felt like my old self. I feel different in Australia. I was such a *child* in England. Here, I'm an adult. So terribly grown up! Last night I slipped backwards.'

'To your old self. Impish and cheeky!'

'Well ... yes. But I can't afford to let that part of me out very often. Two children make you feel like a very responsible person.'

Flo took another sip and abruptly changed the conversation. 'Did you have any difficulty getting pregnant?'

Marion sat up and crossed her legs. 'No! Never any difficulty. Are you trying for a baby?'

'Yes. We've been at it for some time. I don't seem to have the knack.'

Marion was a little taken aback. She sensed Flo's need to talk, but felt reluctant. 'Keep at it!' she said. 'All in good time.'

'Anyway, while I've got time on my hands, I'm going to help Alice with her twins. They're still in nappies! Barry says it will put me off completely!' Flo laughed.

'Well,' said Marion. 'Good luck with that. You're quite comfortable going there?' Flo made no response. 'Well . . . you know Malcolm says where there's black blood there's always trouble.'

Flo snorted. 'You don't believe all that rubbish do you?'

'Well,' Marion started, 'when I was a child my aunt used to talk about a black man in Ireland. I don't know how he got there, but she said he went completely mad. Right in the main street of Ballyrowen. She said he wasn't made for the cold weather.'

'Yes,' said Flo. 'I grew up with those stories too. "Smooth the dying pillow", my grandmother used to say. Or "put them back in the jungle". It's all nonsense, Marion. It's all about colonialism and capitalism.'

'I suppose you're right,' said Marion. She felt out of her depth. Flo seemed so confident. She had no idea about colonialism or capitalism. Far too many isms for her.

'Alice needs time for her personal development,' Flo went on. 'If there's no time in your day-to-day life for conscious-ness-raising, your life can get very tedious. I'm thinking of starting a group.'

Marion made no response. She'd heard of the radical women's libbers, but she never thought she'd meet one. A bunch of hairy lesbians, Malcolm had called them.

'There are meetings at Uni, of course, but there's nothing down here in the valley. What do you think?'

Marion was startled by the question. Perhaps she'd talk it over with Malcolm first. 'Oh, I don't know,' she said. 'I've really got my hands full with the children and the house. There's always so much to do.'

Flo put down her empty mug and stood up. 'Anyway, Marion, it was a lovely night and thank you for coming.'

———

Flo had felt utterly foolish when she entered the Saltmarsh household. They would see her as some type of 'do-gooder' trying to change them somehow. Like the women from the church in ridiculous hats and gloves, pursed lips and a sanctimonious expression on their faces, carrying the burden of imperial colonialism into the twentieth century, clothed in the martyrdom of righteousness, looking for heathen victims.

She tried to make her proposal to Alice and Salty. 'I won't do them any harm... smack them or anything.' They were silent. Looking at her. 'And I think it's terrible that you're not recognised...' a heartfelt plea to Salty. Then looking at Alice, 'I'm trying to have a baby,' she said, and she burst into tears.

Alice and Salty felt a rush of compassion and their defences melted away. 'Oh, lovey,' said Salty in his soft liquid voice, patting her shoulders as they rose and fell with uncontrollable sobs. Alice made a big pot of extra strong tea and they sat together at the kitchen table. Flo felt for the first time the complete burden of her problem. In this dusty, dirty house with its plain wooden table, the love of strangers settled round her like a warm blanket. They knew nothing about her except her most intimate life. The problem sat with her without any distractions. She felt its weight, its thickened obstinacy clouding her life. They had no solution or advice. They were simply kind and gentle. Alice touched her hand and squeezed it gently, her face open and soft. Salty stayed, when many men would have run to the nearest shed. 'It'll happen, dearie. All in good time,' he said.

After the tea, the warmth, the sadness and the expression of hope, Flo left feeling empty but somehow renewed. Any reticence Salty may have had was washed away by the baring of the poor woman's soul. But he made it into a bargain. If there weren't any crays to be had, he'd fix them up with some flathead for their trouble. That way it wasn't charity.

Alice had thought it best if they got together with the children first of all, to get to know Flo. Flo and Barry would be like family. It would be good for the children to learn of the kindness of other people. It was settled. The first few times were filled with joy and strangeness for both women. Soon it became routine. Alice had felt a mighty wrench the first time she took the bus without the twins. But once she alighted in Hobart she headed for the library without a moment's thought.

———

Marion was returning from Vonnie's shop. She'd run out of eggs. Fortunately, Vonnie kept chooks in her backyard so it was never a problem to buy them by the half-dozen or singly if necessary. As she came to the corner of the road, she heard voices far below on the track by the river. It was some distance away but she recognised Louise's voice. She guessed the other voice to be Sally's. Moving to the verge overlooking the bank of gorse, she could see the two girls skylarking about. They were dawdling along, their school bags on their backs. One would start singing, then the other would join in, and then they'd break off in fits of laughter. They must be making up their own words, she thought. Marion was too far away to hear what they were saying, but when singing, their laughing voices were high and loud, echoing through the trees, as bright as the sparkling river. What a freedom, she thought. A rush of envy filled her and she stood still, watching them.

Never in her wildest dreams could she have imagined having a childhood like this. The grey brick streets of her youth stood tight in her chest. Suddenly she wanted Louise's girlhood. She wanted to roam along the riverbank and through the paddocks, up into the mountains and by the waterfalls. She wanted the lazy freedoms that abound in the countryside.

Louise belonged here. She was part of the river, part of the hills and mountains: part of a pre-word world. Louise's inner world drew its strength from beyond language. She could be as silent as a tree. A strange creature who knew the world without the filter of language, who could stretch with the dawn and fold with dusk.

When it came to experiencing nature, Marion couldn't quite give over. She'd grown up with people: always there were people. Not for her the strange silences of nature. Narrative – stories, conversation, dancing, singing, acting – was her way of making sense of the world.

Her envy was a momentary thing. Louise was not like her. She loved the dreamy creature that was her daughter. She loved her easiness with the natural world. But she was happy to take the role of the practical wife and mother. And she felt strength in that.

She'd allow this friendship with Sally. They seemed so right together. Malcolm didn't need to know everything.

———

'I saw you down by the river with Sally,' Marion said. She handed Louise a cup of tea.

'Please don't tell Dad! Please! Mum. Don't tell him!'

'It's alright, dear. I won't tell him. You can be friends with Sally. Just don't bring her here. Alright?'

'Yes, I promise.'

'I'm good at keeping secrets. It's just between us.'

On The Bus

Alice slowly pushes her lips forward then draws them back, exposing her new teeth. In her mind's eye she sees the reflection of the smile she's been practising in the open-air bathroom. She tried not to get carried away with what she saw in the mirror: the reflection of her younger self. The new teeth feel like a mouth full of bones crammed into her face. They rub on her gums and dig in when they hit the lower molars. She's having to learn to speak again. There's a slight whistle as her lips work overtime forming words against the hard white bones. Nevertheless, her soul feels light, her spirits high.

Her back is straighter. She's styled her hair the way she used to thirteen years ago before it turned from flaxen blonde to dull white. Taking the bangs from either side of her widow's peak, she's braided it in the French style from the temples to the crown, loosely coiling the remainder and fastening it with a tortoiseshell clip.

'Hello Clancy,' she says to the driver. She's aware of every syllable and enunciates perfectly. Clancy draws himself up and pushes his cap to the back of his head.

'Alice!' he says her name as if giving colour to a black and white world. 'You look grand, lass!' He looks her over, meaning nothing but admiration. She sees him look at the sleeveless blouse. It's turquoise silk, cut on the bias, the folds hanging below her collarbones. She made it from the lining of her silk dressing gown. But nobody knows that.

The black linen skirt, she's had for years. It never seems to age. Gently gathered at the waist, it falls in random folds to her shins. No-one can see the varicose veins clustered behind her knees. Her fawn-coloured shoes are new. A crepe sole. She feels she's treading on air, they're so light.

There are passengers waiting behind her. Keeping her smile, she pulls her lips over the teeth and takes the proffered ticket. Her string bag knocks clumsily into the seat railing. It's an awkward shape. Full of angles. Full of books. There's also a pound of mince: a paean to domesticity. Taking a seat by the window she places the string bag on her lap. *I'll wait,* she says to herself. *I'll wait until we're well underway.* She hopes no-one sits next to her. She tries to emit an air of aloofness, a mood of not wanting to talk. Of preoccupation. Aloneness is what she's seeking. The richness of solitude settles round her like a charm. Marion Johnstone walks quickly past her with her nose in the air.

Once the bus is chugging its way up the hill, Alice relaxes and searches the bag for a small book. When she finds it she feels a rush of adrenaline. The nerves in her hands prickle with excitement. She opens the book but the words lie flat against the page. She's so full of wanting. The words won't speak to her. Her thirst is so intense that she can't drink. Her mind's like an electrical storm. It's frozen with desire.

Breathe. Letting the air out of her feathering lungs she looks through the window. Stone. Tree. Sky. Cloud. Falling back into the mundane world, she lets her hand rest on the chrome bar on the back of the seat in front of her. Earthed by the metal. Breathe. Wait. Breathe again.

She looks at the page. Now she's ready. The words begin unfolding their story. Like rain on dry land she soaks them up.

Island

Such freshness! All the day seemed morning.
The sun as happy as a cherub, bouncing on the waves.
The salt air, strong medicine. The wind, a friend.
Clicking and klokking, the oars straight in the rowlocks.
Your wide broad hands.

I saw a bird. You saw a sea eagle
And knew its drifting flight.
I saw a shadow beneath. You saw
The kelp forest and felt its mystery.
With surprise, I pointed to the full moon.
You touched my belly.
Special. You said.
The rasp of wood on sand on the
Far side of the island.
You left me tending the fire
And dove for crays.
Gulls cried in the late afternoon.
We washed and laughed.

Then I wept. 'Am I a beginner at life?'
Settled in your way of being
You frowned. Confused.
Then you came to me as a small boy.
'Just hold me,' you said.

Alice's eyes sparkle. Mary-Ellen Smith's poem epitomises her life and reminds her of the early days with Salty.

———

Like a nautilus shell, she'd cast herself on the waves. Tossed away from a comfortable existence. She'd turned her back on a pretentious family set on bolstering their emptiness with private schools, big houses, big cars, big parties and gossiping acquaintances. And like the nautilus, she'd moved with the tide and felt the peaks and troughs of each wave, driven by some inner certainty locked in the chambers of her soul. Salty found her, scooped her up and made her his own.

'She's made her bed. Let her lie in it!' Alice's mother spat out the words in the harsh flat vowels of her childhood. 'The little bitch!' she added for good measure as the rows of pearls hissed round her neck, her throat all blood and sinews. Not only was the man a fisherman, for God's sake, he professed to being an aborigine. If this was not beyond the pale, he was also full of ideals. Socialist ideals. Communism! A smack in the face for the likes of decent people like herself!

Alice's father had gaped wordlessly. His love too deep for gesture. His cataracts seemed to grow overnight, and the world became distant and clouded. The everyday betrayal of daughters.

Alice became emboldened in her lover's arms. The world was much greater without her family. There were thinkers, philosophers, trade unionists, feminists, musicians and artists. There was the whole rambling, boisterous family of Saltmarshes: brothers, sisters, aunts and uncles, innumerable cousins. Salty's mother, gentle and frail, lived with the wind on Flinders Island. His father, long since dead. And then there were their children, adding their own cacophony and charm to her life. There was barely a chance to think about the past and her own family. Her favourite sister, Trish, stayed in touch with occasional letters and sent gifts from journeys overseas and presents on birthdays.

Chapter 9

Two words. Two words that made Robert shimmer with mirth or congeal with apprehension. 'Yes, Dad.' 'YES, DAD!' was his constant reply to any summons, be it a simple chore like carting wood, or lighting the incinerator or cleaning the car. If it was an initiation into the mysteries of car maintenance, or an invitation to kick a football, 'Yes, Dad!' was his instant reply. Even if the request came from Marion, it was 'YES, DAD!' in the exact same tone of voice every time.

Marion felt like throttling him.

Malcolm's constant worry was that Robert might have 'artistic tendencies' inherited from his mother's side of the family. To alleviate any of these tendencies, Malcolm initiated a constant stream of physical, male activities. Splitting and stacking wood was one of Malcolm's favourites. He taught Robert how to position the log on the chopping block and how to align the grain of the wood with the arc of the axe. 'All it needs is brute strength after that, son.'

'Yes, Dad!'

Robert was particularly good at splitting kindling. With the tomahawk he could split the wood to the dimensions of a twig.

'That's thin enough, son.'

'Yes, Dad. I just want to see how thin I can make it.'

'I know what you're doing! I'm just telling you that you've

gone far enough! Do I make myself clear?'

'Yes, Dad.'

In stacking the wood, Robert was equally conscientious.

'You don't have to make every bit of wood flush with the next one. This isn't bricklaying, son.'

'Yes, Dad,' he'd reply. 'But it looks nice.'

'Nice isn't what we want, son. This is a pile of wood.'

———

'It's a beautiful morning,' said Malcolm. 'Perfect for fishing.' Robert knew he was in for long moments of nothing happening. They sat silently in the fresh morning air. Robert hunched over his line, willing the flathead to take the bait. He felt a nibble and gave the line a tug.

'Pull her in, Rob! Pull her in, you've got one!' Robert reeled it in as fast as he could.

When they had half a bucket full, Malcolm started the gutting and cleaning. Crouching on the grey, worn planks, he held the flathead by the lower jaw and scraped the scales off. 'You hold his tail still. Here. Use this fork.' Malcolm handed Robert an old fork. The scales flaked off like jewels in the clear light. When sides and back were done, he rolled the fish over.

'That's his vent, Robert. His bum,' he said, pointing the tip of the knife at the small hole. Robert sat up on the backs of his heels and felt his sphincter tighten. 'Now watch. You'll be doing the next one.' Malcolm pressured the knife into the vent and slowly drew it up the midline. Robert blanched as he saw the flesh fold open and the purple, green and grey guts slide out. 'Now the easiest way of getting rid of the guts, is to do it by hand. There's a little bit of pulling and then just cut the last little bit off. Have you got that?' Malcolm performed the action in one quick movement.

'Yes, Dad,' came the reply.

'Now you have a go.' Malcolm handed over the knife and positioned a fish on the bloodied plank. 'I'll hold the tail.'

An audience of seagulls gathered around to watch the outcome. In his fastidious way Robert scraped the scales off. He could feel the strength of them as the knife pulled and flicked. Glutinous secretions caked the knife. He wiped it clean on his shorts, proud of this manly gesture, unprompted by his father. He smiled up at Malcolm, and Malcolm gave him a nod of approval: allies in the hunt, beyond the petty concerns for cleanliness and appearance. Malcolm seemed reassured.

'Roll her over, son.'

'Yes, Dad.' Robert moved closer, his eyes watering slightly from the glare of the sun.

'Now take it slowly, don't hurry it. Just straight in and up.' Robert was concentrating so hard he didn't respond. He held the knife over the vent and hesitated. He felt that the knife was at the wrong angle. Shuffling around on his haunches he tried again, plunging the knife in and ripping it forward as far as he could.

'Well done, son! Perfect job!'

'Thanks, Dad.' Robert was more grateful than he could say. The thought of not being able to do it was in the back of his mind. And the thought of doing a botched job would be harder to bear. He would have to do it again and again until he got it right.

He put the knife down and plunged his hand into the cavity and pulled at the slimy guts. They slipped through his fingers and stubbornly stuck to the abdominal cavity. He scooped them out as best he could, feeling some gooiness slide under his fingernails. Eventually the fish was clean. Malcolm helped with severing the gut.

'You've done well, Robert.'

'Thanks, Dad.' Robert was pleased. Now that the fear and challenge had been overcome, he looked at the innards glistening on the boards. 'What's that orange bit?' he said, pointing his finger at the oval-shaped roe.

'That's the roe. That means it's a female fish. That's where all the baby fish come from.' Malcolm reddened. He tried again. 'The female stores all her eggs in that organ. When she's ready to spawn, she releases the eggs and the male fish fertilises them, and they grow into more fish.' He busied himself with a tangled line.

'So the roe is full of fish eggs?' asked Robert.

'Hundreds of them.'

'And does she have a nest like a bird?'

'No, she just leaves them on a rock. The male fish comes along and fertilizes them.'

'How does he do that?'

'Oh, he just jigs about a bit. Adds his bit to the eggs and then they're fertilised. Ready to grow into fish.'

Robert had it now: the key that would get him out of any more gutting of fish.

'So he just jigs around a bit. Jiggy, jiggy, jiggy and then they become fishy, fishy, fishy!' He knew this would annoy Malcolm.

'Yes, yes. Something like that.' Malcolm abruptly put the line back in the tackle box and banged the lid shut.

'So the little fishy come from jiggy, jiggy!' Robert chanted in delight. 'The little fishy! Jiggy, jiggy!'

'Yes, Robert. You've made your point. Do you want to go and see if you can find some mussels?'

Got him! thought Robert. *I'll stay away long enough for him to finish all the gutting and cleaning.*

'Yeah… there should be some under the jetty,' he said, looking out at the silvery river as if it were all the same to him.

'Don't take them from there! Only take them if they're growing on rocks.'

Robert knew that, but said nothing, happy to give Malcolm the chance to issue commands.

'YES DAD!' And he was off.

———

Malcolm went out the back and cupped his hands around his mouth. 'Robert!' he yelled. The hills remained silent. 'Robert!' he yelled again, louder this time. Losing patience, he put the little finger of each hand into his mouth and whistled hard enough to quieten all the birds within a quarter-mile radius.

The whistle was something he was loath to resort to, as it was often heard by Spangles. The dog would come bounding down the road at a gallop with his tongue hanging down the side of his mouth. Ever since the night of the garlic sausages, Spangles had held a deep and abiding affection for Malcolm.

The whistle echoed around the silent hills. Malcolm waited to hear a cooee in reply, or the sound of sandshoes heavily flapping on the road. Nothing. It seemed to be too quiet. *Where the blazes has he got to?* He went back into the house to check Robert's room.

Louise, Jennifer, Susan and Annie heard him from Louise's bedroom. 'You'd better go,' said Louise. The four girls looked down at Robert sitting on the floor with his fingers in his ears.

'But today I'm Roberta!' he exclaimed and stood up in one quick movement and flung his arms out as if he were Al Jolson. 'Mammy! How I love you, how I love you. Myyyyy dear old Mammy!' he sang, shaking his hands wildly. 'I'd give the world ... to ... see you once more—'

'Robert, shut up! Dad'll find you!' Louise came at him with a jar of cold cream and a handkerchief. 'Keep your lips still!' Robert pursed his lips as Louise wiped the scarlet lipstick from his face.

Louise wore a satin negligee beneath an enormous bra. She'd stuffed the bra with handkerchiefs and old pants to fill it out. Around her waist she'd dangled a curtain cord.

In the dress-up box Annie had found a black velvet fascinator. Peering at the world through a hazy lattice made everything strange and contorted. It made her feel unsettled. 'Robert, you shouldn't be here anyway. We'll all get into trouble,' she said. It had been fun having Robert to play with, but after all, he was a boy and should be out doing boys' things. She felt something was wrong and wished for him to disappear, especially now that his father was looking for him. She looked to Susan for support.

But Susan was a fixer, uninterested in gender appropriateness. If there was a problem, she would find a solution. Robert needed to remove his lipstick, take off his tutu, suspender belt, stockings and feather boa as quickly as possible and report to his father, offering some lame excuse. Maybe he was asleep or on the toilet? Susan stood up out of the recliner chair, tortoiseshell cigarette holder in hand. The high heels she wore were far too big. The orange crocheted skirt came down over her ankles. She wobbled and fell.

Jennifer could not help herself. She laughed and laughed and the little dimple above her cheekbone puckered as she held her sides. Such hijinks! She'd found the greatest treasure in the dressing-up box. Right at the very bottom, where the smell of mothballs was overwhelming, she found a layer of straw that on closer inspection became a Hawaiian grass skirt. It wobbled and crackled as she laughed. She had to hold onto the coconut bra she'd wrapped around her chest.

Malcolm put his head around the door. Susan threw an arm around Robert's neck, pulling his head down and rummaging in the box of costume jewellery.

'Have you girls seen Robert?'

'No,' they all replied in unison, not looking up from the box.

Malcolm shut the door and strode off through the house.

A large trunk on the verandah stored all the outdoor games equipment. The cricket season was approaching. Malcolm was determined to teach Robert the art of spin bowling. Robert was young, yes, but he had potential. If he could get him into the practice of using the spin, by the time he was able to use a real cricket ball instead of a tennis ball he would have a superb technique. Now was the time to get started. If he could only find the damn boy! As he took out the cricket bat, tennis ball and wickets, he turned around too quickly and hit his forehead on one of Marion's macramé hanging baskets. He let out an oath. Pink and purple fuschia swung and danced and the basket lurched back and hit him again, this time on the ear. 'Stone the flaming crows!' he roared. 'What the bloody hell are these things doing here anyway!'

Back in Louise's room, the girls descended on Robert as one. They unzipped the tutu, peeled off the stockings and pulled off the feather boa, half strangling him in the process. Robert made himself as rubbery as possible, giving himself up to their ministrations, all the while continuing his Al Jolson impersonation. When he was decent, in shorts and tee-shirt, they pushed him through the door and out into the hall, slamming the door behind him. The girls sunk to the floor, Annie in fear, Jennifer in hysterics and Susan slapping her hands together: 'That's that!' she exclaimed.

Louise was quiet. She thought about her father's inability to see Robert when he came into the room. Robert was there. He had his head down, but anyone could see it was him. But Malcolm hadn't really looked. All he'd seen was *girls*. Not individuals. He might have seen her, but he didn't distinguish any of the others. He might know their names but he was unlikely to know which name belonged to which girl. Whenever she had a friend over to play, he was affable but distant. In his universe there were people, and there were girls, or females. He invariably forgot their names and had to be prompted by herself or Marion. Louise's world did not exist for Malcolm with the same ferocious urgency that the man's world demanded. She didn't mind. *Off the hook*, she thought to herself.

The concrete slab had yet to be united with its timber frame and roof. For over a year – as Marion frequently reminded him – Malcolm had put off the building of the garage. He used the slab as a cricket pitch, parking the car on the lawn in front of the house. A practice that made Marion's blood boil. 'I don't want our home looking like a car park! Every second house in this neighbourhood has bombs littering their front yards! And putting the car in the side paddock is even worse!' In the end he'd settled for round the back of the slab. This didn't look too bad and left the slab clear for cricket.

'Make a 'V' shape with your first two fingers. Now, as you follow through, flick the index finger fast around the ball. Have you got that?'

'Yes, Dad,' came the reply.

'Keep your eye on the wicket and watch the spot where you want the ball to bounce.'

'Yes, Dad.' Robert sighed. How was he supposed to look at two places at the same time? Malcolm ran down the pitch and held his foot at the halfway point.

'That's where you should aim,' he said. 'Take your time and give yourself a decent run-up. Don't rush it. Look at the wicket. Aim for the bounce about here.' Malcolm pointed to the centre of the pitch.

Robert nodded and turned his back. He took a few steps away from the pitch to get a good run-up. His instinct was to pretend to shine the tennis ball on the crotch of his shorts, the way he had seen it done on the telly. But he knew Malcolm was not in the mood for levity. They had been practising for over an hour and still Robert had difficulty with the manipulation of the ball. He couldn't quite get the spin. He took four long strides and lifted the ball high over his head. As it came down the descending arc he twisted it sharply in his hand and let go. The ball hit the bounce point then veered off to the right.

'You've done it, son! You've done it!' Robert was relieved.

At last his father sounded happy. 'Now we have to work on your aim and line it up with the wicket. You see how far off the wicket you were? Well you have to change the point where the ball bounces. We have to move that point. Right over to here.' Malcolm pointed to a spot to the left of where the ball had previously bounced. 'Do exactly what you did, but aim the bounce here. Have you got that?'

'Yes... Dad.' Robert was getting tired. He'd just managed to accomplish one task and now he had to add more to the achievement. He knew that his father would not stop until he had hit the middle stump. He steeled himself to carry on.

'Take your time. Give yourself a decent run-up. I know it seems odd to aim over here but if you put the spin on it, you'll be fine. Take your time now.'

Robert measured his paces back to his run-up position, keeping his eyes on the ground. He turned and eyed up the wicket and then the point where Malcolm indicated the ball should bounce. 'Just a minute, son.' Malcolm held up his hand. 'I'll get some chalk to mark the spot.' Robert started practising the spin, twisting the ball and letting it drop by his feet and watching it bounce in a crazy fashion. It seemed so random that he doubted he would ever be able to control it.

Malcolm realised a search for chalk would take longer than he wanted. 'Lou!' he cried. 'Lou, can you come here?'

Louise was in her bedroom. Annie, Susan and Jennifer had gone home long ago. Louise was finishing her special project on 'Australia's first settlement'. She was doing the illustrations and had just finished a male and female con-vict and was about to start on the free settlers. Putting her pencil down, she turned and opened the window.

'Yes, Dad?'

'Have you got any chalk?'

'Yes. What colour would you like?'

'White, of course!' he said. Louise had little white chalk left as it was always used when playing hopscotch on the concrete slab.

'Just a minute.' She found what was left and handed it out the window.

Malcolm deliberated as to the exact spot where the ball should bounce. Eventually he made the decision. 'There you go. About there. Now take your time. Eyes on the wicket, then on the bounce point. Have you got that?'

'Yes, Dad.' Robert took his run-up. As he did so he licked his lips and tasted the greasy cold cream. His concentration faltered and his feet felt out of rhythm. He let the ball go with a flick and saw it take off to the opposite side of the wicket, away from where Malcolm had indicated.

'No! No! No! You've got the spin the wrong way round! Weren't you listening? The spin goes outwards not inwards.'

'Sorry, Dad.'

'Have another go.'

Robert took the run-up again. 'The spin goes outwards... The spin goes outwards,' he said to himself in his chanting voice. If he wasn't careful it would become a dance. 'The spin goes outwards... The spin goes outwards.' He could feel it in his feet... *Yes*, he thought. It was a good rhythm to do a little dance to, and forgetting Malcolm's mood, he pointed his feet one way and then the other. *The spin goes outwards... The spin goes outwards.*

'Stop mucking around and get on with it!'

'YES! DAD!'

Robert's little chant had become a Mexican band in his head. It had counter rhythms and harmony. He thought of bright red boleros with gold braid. *The spin goes outwards ... yeah ... yeah ... the spin, the spin ... the spin! Spin! Spin! Out she goes! ... Big hats with wide floppy brims ... Yeah, yeah ... the spin she goes ... High-waisted pants and black moustaches ... Out! Out! Out! ... Black boots with big heels ... Olé!*

He turned, did his run-up and just as he was about to let the ball go, he had a moment of doubt. *Which way is out-wards?* he asked himself in mid-flow. His mind was confused, flooded with doubt, but his body took over and executed a replica of his last shot.

'What did I say? What did I tell you? Other way! Have you got that? Oth-er! Way!'

'Yes Dad! Yes Dad!' Robert had to rein in the free-ranging Mexican band and concentrate on the job in front of him. The sooner he got it right, the sooner Malcolm would leave him alone.

Malcolm was sick of running hither and dither after the ball. It was so unpredictable. He needed another fielder. 'Lou!' he yelled. 'Lou, we need you out here!'

Louise bit into her pencil. She was halfway through draw-ing the free settler's wife with her bonnet and shawl and wondering what colour to make her bonnet.

'Yes, Dad?' She leant out the window with reluctance written all over her face.

'I need you here,' said Malcolm. Louise left her drawing and dragged herself outside.

'I need you to stand here and field the ball. Have you got that? All you have to do is throw it back to me.' He posi-tioned her down towards the wicket on the opposite side to himself. 'You're at silly-mid-on,' he said, hoping this would lighten the mood.

With a great deal of perseverance and concentration, Robert managed to deliver a dozen balls with the required spin and even managed to hit the wicket three times.

'You've done well, Robert,' said Malcolm, relieved that he had finally mastered the skill. 'You'd better let Lou have a little hit now. But don't try any spin. Just a straight forward bowl. Spin's very confusing for the batsman. Just let her have a hit.'

Louise picked up the bat. Malcolm drew a crease in front of the wicket. 'You've got to keep one foot behind the crease. Have you got that?'

'I know that, Dad,' she replied.

'Keep your knees bent. Eyes on the ball. Face the bat towards the bowler.'

'Yes, Dad, I know!'

'Take your time. Watch the ball.'

'Yes, Dad!'

'Keep the bat close to the feet.' Louise started tapping the bat on the ground like a war drum. She said nothing.

'Take it away, son. Not too fast. No spin. Have you got that?'

'Yes ... Dad!'

As the pressure on Robert retreated, the Mexican band took up residence once more. The costumes became more ornate. The rhythms more definite. *The spin goes, the spin goes, the spin goes . . . outwards . . . yeah . . . yeah . . . yeah . . .* Unconscious of what he was doing, except aligning his internal Mexican band with the rhythms of his body, he let the ball set sail, to reach high into the air and gradually curve down towards the pitch.

Oh, Gawd! thought Malcolm. *He's done a full toss. She won't be able to hit that in a month of Sundays. I should have told him to give her some underarm bowling, at least then she'd be able to hit it.*

Louise looked up and saw the ball veering down towards her. It wasn't going to bounce, she could see that. She took three graceful steps forward, pulling the bat behind her. Angling the bat under the ball she hit it with all her might. All frustration distilled to the point in space occupied by the worn and grubby tennis ball. *Thwop!* The ball hit the middle of the bat and doubled its speed, shooting up over Malcolm's head. He was so surprised that he didn't even attempt to catch it. The force of the stroke left Louise spinning a full three hundred and sixty degrees before she steadied herself. By that time the sound of tinkling glass filled their ears. The windowpane on the back verandah shattered and fell.

'Ah! Good one Lou!' cried Robert.

Malcolm rushed up to Louise. She shrank back, thinking he was going to hit her.

'I didn't mean to,' she said with tears forming in her eyes. 'It was an accident!'

'How did you know to do that?' said Malcolm.

'Do what?' said Louise in confusion.

'How did you know to move in to meet the ball? I never taught you that!'

'I don't know,' she said, tears now falling freely. 'I don't know. It just happened.' She threw down the bat and ran inside.

Chapter 10

'THE SEA IS A MARVELLOUS thing,' said Malcolm. (Robert kept his 'Yes, Dad' in his head.) 'She can be your best friend and your worst enemy all within an hour. One minute you might be sailing along with a clear blue sky above you, the next minute it'll cloud over and the wind will pick up and you're doing twenty knots without even trying.'

Malcolm's face was alive at the prospect. He and Darryl Birchall, his mate from the office, had planned the trip. Malcolm thought the only way Robert was going to overcome his seasickness was to spend more time on the water. Darryl thought that Robert might be able to manage the trip if they stayed in the river where it was relatively calm. Marion was pessimistic.

'It's very changeable in the river,' Marion said. She was thinking of the last time Malcolm took Robert out on a boat. He'd come back as if he were the walking dead. Practically the whole trip was spent with Robert vomiting off the back of the boat. His complexion had gradually changed from his normal freckled, rosy sheen to a grey pallor and then to a deathly green. His eyes lost their shine and seemed as dull as those of a dead fish. Even his legs looked green. All the blood had been drained from his body as if the river siphoned it out of him.

'Don't go too far down the river, Malcolm. If he gets sick it can feel like an awfully long way back.' Marion, who knew what seasickness felt like, tried not to think of what Robert was about to experience. She would be cheerful and simply hope that Robert would start throwing up as soon as they hit the water. Then at least Malcolm would have no reason for taking him right out of the estuary.

'We'll be lucky if we get to Dover,' he said.

'Dover! That's too far!' Marion was alarmed. 'Malcolm you can't take him that far! Just through the canal and around Egg Island. That will be enough. Let him get used to it.' She'd be counting the minutes till he got home.

'Egg Island! Marion, that will take about one hour at the most. This is a river. It's not the Atlantic Ocean. You'd be lucky to get a wave that's six inches high. We want to make a decent trip out of it. There's a nor'-easterly that can take us down to Dover, and by then the sea breeze will be in and that'll bring us home. It'll be a piece of cake! Nothing to it! What do you say Robert? You can handle that, can't you?'

'Yes, Dad, I think so.' Robert knew he had no choice in the matter.

Malcolm's deepest longing was to share his love of the sea with his son. If Robert could overcome his seasickness, the great world of sailing would open to him. To feel the surge of a wave, like a mighty beast beneath the bow, was one of Malcolm's most exhilarating experiences. To not have that connection with the sea was to lead a half-life. Marion couldn't hack it. He knew that. Lou was good in the water. She was a fine swimmer and good on a boat. But he wanted to go sailing with his son, not his daughter. He'd seen men out sailing with their daughters: tomboy types who stripped down to their shorts and singlet. Sometimes not even a sin-glet, their ribs sticking out and their tiny breasts just a fillet of fat on their bony chests. No. He didn't want his daughter to be one of them. There was something distasteful in it.

Marion handed Robert the picnic basket in which she'd packed corned beef sandwiches, two sausages left over from last night's tea, fruit cake, apples, water bottle and a small towel in case Robert had to wipe any sick from his face. 'Off you go then,' she said in a cheerful tone. Her stomach already knotted at the thought of the boat bobbing up and down in the middle of the river.

It was early morning, and the river was flat and still. Swans were curled up asleep, floating with gentle buoyancy. Plovers were returning to the sports oval, landing as one, as if they were joined by invisible threads. Above them a sea-eagle rose on a warm current, head swivelling.

'Look out there.' Malcolm pointed to the middle of the river. 'The northerly is just coming in. You can see the waves forming.' Robert peered out across the water as if he doubted it. Little creases on the taupe-coloured river changed to flecked brown. Robert liked the effect and momentarily forgot his trepidation. The air was moist and warm. It was going to be a hot day.

'You'll need your hats,' said Marion, retrieving them from the back of the car. Malcolm pretended he didn't hear. Marion was always fussing. A couple of blokes couldn't go out on the river without being loaded down with things that she thought were essential. Robert took the hats and shouldered the picnic basket.

'We'll motor out to midway and then put the mainsail up,' said Malcolm, not looking at Marion.

'Have you got life jackets?' Marion asked, tight-lipped.

'No, Marion. We haven't got life jackets! I know this river

like the back of my hand. We will not need lifejackets.' Malcolm kept his eyes on the river and his voice even, but threatening.

'But what if a storm blows up and—'

'Marion, we will be alright!' He turned around and glared at her. Why couldn't she butt out for once? Why did she always have to go on and on? All he wanted was a bit of peace and quiet. The boat gliding over the water in the fresh morning breeze. 'I know what I'm doing,' he said as a finale to the conversation.

A Holden ute pulled up beside them with a belch of black smoke.

'Carburettor's buggered,' said Darryl. He slammed the door shut and leant into the tray to take out an old school bag. The unmistakable sound of bottles emanated from it.

'Boys' day out, eh Robert. Us men out on the river, what d'you say? Ya ready for a good time?' He ruffled Robert's hair. Marion coughed. 'Shove these in the cubby, mate,' he said to Malcolm. 'That'll be the coolest place.' He turned to Marion. 'I'll bring 'em home, love. Don't you worry.'

They exchanged perfunctory farewells and the men clambered into the boat. 'Easy does it,' said Darryl as he gave Robert a hand. 'Hats! Cor blimey! Are we on a royal tour! Did ya bring any fishing gear, Mal?'

'There should be some lines under the stern seat. But I don't have any bait. We'll get some mussels along the way. You'll be up for that won't you, Robert?'

'Yes, Dad,' said Robert. He sat on the stern seat with his legs wide apart, and his hands gripping the edge of the seat. Malcolm started the engine and they were off.

———

Marion got into the car. Her hands were trembling slightly as she turned the key. The car jerked forward and cut out. She'd forgotten to engage the clutch. She had had her licence for over a month now, but had only had the opportunity to drive the car twice. Both times only as far as Vonnie's shop. This was the first time she would be driving all the way from the river to Golden Valley. The seat was positioned back from the steering wheel. She had to stretch forward to reach the clutch. A more experienced driver would have reversed and backed clear of the jetty but Marion didn't want to risk using reverse gear. She couldn't keep the clutch down and turn around to see what was behind her unless she sat on the very front of the seat and held onto the steering wheel for balance. She simply wasn't big enough to reach the clutch and turn around to look out the back window, as Malcolm had taught her.

She was in no mood to try a complicated manoeuvre. She swung the car hard right, flattening the accelerator. The car spun round to face the road, splattering mud around the grassy shoreline. It then lurched forward at a frightening speed. She panicked and took both feet off the pedals and slammed her right foot on the brake. The engine cut out and the car shuddered to a halt. Marion looked around to see if anyone was watching. Breathing deeply, she engaged the clutch and started up the motor, and the car lurched forward in three jumps like an injured rabbit. It reached the road and cut out again.

'Mrs Johnstone, can I be of assistance?' Mick O'Connell appeared out of nowhere, his large friendly face beaming at her through the window. 'I keep telling Malcolm to get rid of that Holden. An over-rated heap of metal. What he needs is a Valiant. You can't beat a V8 engine, that's what I say. You'll have to talk him round. You wouldn't have any problems with a Valiant.' Marion wound down the window as he spoke. 'Move over, Mrs Johnstone, and I'll see if I can get her to the side of the road.' Marion gratefully slid across to the passenger seat and Mick settled in the driver's seat with a rustling of shiny suit and an overpowering smell of Old Spice aftershave. 'So how are you going in the new house? Everything satisfactory?'

'Oh yes, Mr O'Connell. We've been there over two years now.'

'Well I guess that would be about right. Now you call me Mick. We don't have to be too formal with each other.'

'Yes, Mick. We like the house very much.' Marion was breathless with thankfulness. 'Oh, and do call me Marion. Everyone is so friendly in the country.'

'Ya right there, Marion. Not so many snooty people down this way. Just good country types. You included of course!'

'Thank you, Mick.'

'Now hold on and I'll have a go and see if I can get this lump of junk started.'

Mick started the car with a gentle rumble and steered it to the side of the road. He left the engine purring like a tamed beast and turned to Marion. 'I'm on my way up to the hospital. Why don't we swap seats and I can talk you through the gear changes. I was going to walk – get a bit of weight off – but if you'd like a bit of help I'm at your service.'

'That's very kind of you.' Marion breathed out for the first time in ages. Her anxiety was lifting. 'I've only just got my licence, and there are so many things to think about at once.'

'No problem, Marion. First thing we need to do is pull the seat forward. We'll have to both get out.'

Marion hadn't known that the seat could be moved forward. It made all the difference. Her feet reached the pedals easily and there was support for her back when changing gears or using the hand brake. She wondered why Malcolm hadn't thought to adjust the seat for her. It made it so much easier.

'Now ease her forward ... little bit more on the herbs ... That's it, you're doing well ... Now you're ready for second gear. Right in with the clutch ... and up with the gear stick ... Ease her out slowly ... and you've made it. That wasn't so bad was it? You're doing real well, Marion. Real well.' Mick's slow gentle voice, rising and falling like the hills, was like a balm. 'Now you're ready for top. In she goes again ... little more on the herbs before you change. Rev her up a bit ... That's it ... Have another go ... That's it ... Won't hurt her to have a few more revs ... Yep. That's it! She's liking it ... You've got her in top! It's a bit of a haul, sometimes they're a bit stiff in top – wouldn't happen in a Valiant, mind you.'

Marion stopped smoothly outside the hospital. 'Marion, you've done real well,' Mick said with a broad smile. 'Now, will you be right to get yourself home?' She couldn't thank him enough. 'Now, you can do it Marion. Just take your time and think it through. You'll be a fine driver,' he said, as if casting a spell.

'Thank you so much!' Marion leant along the front seat as he stood outside the hospital. Mick had a clear view of a small but delightful cleavage. He straightened his shoulders and his tie and gave her a wave. The car jolted forward but didn't stall. Marion made it home but stayed in second gear once she came to Golden Valley Road.

———

Robert looked down at the lapping water: little waves that made slap and glop sounds. He felt fine just sitting there with his head hanging over the stern. Malcolm and Darryl fussed with the sail, issuing instructions to each other in gruff insults, their raucous voices uncontained by the flat river. Robert looked at the curling underside of each wave. He tried to determine the colour as it changed with the motion of the boat. There was a deep Prussian blue in the trough of the wave. And the tops of the waves were losing their taupe, the yellow leaching out and giving way to a thin sky blue with flashes of turquoise and green. As the breeze riffled the skin of the water, Robert looked deeper to determine the colour created by the river bed.

The hatching patterns on the surface looked like a net containing the darker colours beneath. His own shadow and the glint of the moving sun on the water changed the colours yet again. He looked up and saw that the blue of the sky had strengthened: the hard blue of summer dropping its colour into the river. All these colours he knew. His grandparents had given him a box set of Derwent coloured pencils for his birthday. Seventy-two colours: twelve different blues and twelve different greens. He'd memorised their names, shades and density and held them in his mind as he felt the boat slowly lift and cut into the water.

Malcolm grimaced as he watched the boy. *Daydreaming again.* 'Watch your head, Robert,' he said, positioning the boom and securing it. 'Your mother will put you to bed for a month if you get a knock on ya noggin.' He looked to Darryl and smiled: conspirators against the fairer sex. They laughed.

Out here it was a man's world, no interfering, fussing

women. No petty concerns about what might happen. No fear of the unexpected. And buggered if they were going to wear hats when you could feel the wind in your hair and the sun on your face – or eat sandwiches when you could catch a few fish and cook them over a fire on a deserted beach. Marion had no idea of the joys and freedom of the natural world. She'd go for a half-day walk all kitted out with jumpers and coats and towels and first-aid kits, something for every contingency. Everything strained and controlled. She molly-coddled Robert. They were always singing songs together. It was nice in a way, but not something that should be encouraged. Sure, Marion had a fine voice. But there was no reason to encourage a boy to sing. No. Robert had to be steered in the other direction: he had to build his physical strength and his endurance. Robert needed to see where he belonged. In the man's world.

'Sun over the yard arm yet, mate?' Darryl grinned at Malcolm.

'I reckon so,' replied Malcolm. Darryl pulled out his bag from the cubby.

'Only got longnecks mate,' he said, taking the top off a Cascade Draught and handing it to Malcolm.

'Good on ya, Darryl,' said Malcolm. He took a couple of gulps of beer and felt an immediate surge of happiness. The perfect morning was unfolding. The gentle breeze was like a soft cocoon. The boat moved slowly and smoothly. A group of swans applauded: their large wings clacking against the water, their heads angled down and their feet turned up like water-skiers slowly slicing into the river.

'Shall we do the canal first?' asked Darryl.

'Might as well,' said Malcolm. 'We'll have to motor. Not

enough wind to get us through. Robert, you can steer.'

They turned and headed for the small canal cut through Egg Island by the early British settlers. In the still morning air, the waterway was protected from any breeze. Scraggy paperbarks grew along the banks, bolstered by large clumps of tussock grass. Half-submerged logs angled into the water from the sides. The surface of the water was perfectly still and clear, as if glazed by dew. Enclosed by stillness, Malcolm felt the urge to cut the engine and just drift for a while. Robert held the tiller as the boat gradually glided to a halt. Transfixed by their surroundings, none of them felt the urge to talk, each caught in his own thoughts. Darryl was the first to break the silence.

'It's like church. Only ya can't have a beer in church. It's like that moment before all the yakking and singing starts. I'd go more often if everyone would shut up. This is the best church for me. The river. Or the bush. Marcia goes to St Alban's every Sunday. I call it St All-Bran's 'cause it gives her a good clean out. Come the end of the week she's as cranky as hell but after church she's a different woman. Does her the world of good, but I can't stand it! This is my church right here. Out in the open. Mother Nature all around ya!'

The serenity of the small, protected canal affected them all. Caught in an eternal moment of absolute beauty, they felt transformed, lifted out of themselves – more spirited, more alive. Robert gazed at the reflections. With his head to one side, beings of incredible strangeness came alive to him. The tussock grass took the form of great hairy monsters with dark black eyes where the grass flopped over into the water. The monsters were adorned with ornate headdresses of patterned bark: encoded messages from the hidden giants. The dead fallen branches formed geometric patterns, entrances to other worlds or secret coded messages: runes from the gods. And the water, so still, yet seeming to breathe, became the sky: an infinity of blue. As they rounded the head of the island and came out of the canal, the enchantment faded away. The river became opaque. A gentle nor'-easterly nudged them southward.

Robert was travelling through silken blue. Facing directly into the wind and breathing deeply he felt safe and happy. As he looked out over the stern at the purple mountains, he felt himself dissolve in the colour of the day. He was finding his balance, as the rhythm of the waves seemed predictable.

They passed Cradoc and heard the *clokk* of a farmer's axe. Soon they could see the man with his axe held high and the sound of the splitting log out of time with the actions. Darryl looked at Robert's puzzlement. 'Yeah, everything's out of whack in Cradoc. Always has been! I put it down to there being no pub. Cradoc's never had a pub. That's the reason that axe won't fall at the proper time. Isn't that right Malcolm?' Darryl laughed. A beery, burpy laugh.

Robert smiled. He liked the quirky way Darryl behaved and he loved his gravel voice that threw words out from his throat, with his head always moving this way and that. It was as if Darryl couldn't talk without his head moving, always flicking around like a chook. If something could be made into a joke, Darryl would be the one to do it. It was reassuring, knowing that the world could be seen with humour and imagination.

Marion's anxiety came flooding back once she was home.

There was cleaning to be done, and done quickly. She recruited Louise in helping to remove cobwebs from all the ceilings in every room.

'I can't see any cobwebs!' Louise complained.

'You can't see them in this light, but I know they are there.' Louise rolled her eyes. Moving the short stepladder from corner to corner, she shoved the broom in the direction that the cobwebs might be.

'You've missed one over there,' said Marion.

'Where? I can't see it!'

'Just below where you are now. To the right. No, back a bit. Further down, now up a bit.'

'Mum, I can't even see it. It might just be a shadow.'

'It's not a shadow.'

Marion had tied an old pillowcase around the broom head to collect all the dust and cobwebs and to stop the broom getting too dirty.

'Look at that!' she said, displaying the dirty pillowcase. 'Who would have thought it! So dirty! – If the phone rings, I'll get it. Or if you're closest, you get it and hand it to me.'

'Mum, they'll be alright. Stop worrying!'

'I'm not worried!' said Marion, giving a false high laugh. 'I'm just saying… if there's an accident and the phone rings make sure you get to it quickly. I'm going to do some gardening. The bulbs next to the front gate need lifting. I should have done it ages ago. If the phone rings, that's where I'll be.'

'Mum, stop panicking.'

'And if you want to leave the house, give me a yell so I can come inside.'

Marion changed into her gardening trousers, old shirt, straw hat and gumboots. Armed with paper bags and a trowel she settled down by the front gate. Every half-minute or so she looked up to see if Darryl's ute was making its way up the road.

She'd be very casual when they arrived. 'Back so soon?' she'd say in an offhand manner. She'd keep concentrating on what she was doing. She'd ask about the fishing – 'Did you catch any fish?'... and the mooring – 'You managed to moor the boat OK?' She'd gently admonish them, if they were sunburnt, for not wearing their hats.

Once the bulbs were lifted, she started on the weeding. *Still no sign of them.* But it had only been an hour at the most, and that was counting the drive home. The weeding could go on forever! There was so much to be done. All the fruit trees in the back yard needed the weeds removed from around their trunks, and mulching needed to be done. She'd do the Kentish cherry first. That was on the far side of the house . . . Louise would hear the phone, as she was inside . . . But she must tell Louise where she was . . . *If Lou comes outside and can't find me, the person ringing might hang up . . .*

Just as she was making these decisions, Louise came down the front path with a cup of tea. 'I'll come inside for it,' Marion yelled. She raced up the path and in the front door, not even stopping to take off her gumboots.

'Mum, they've only been gone an hour. They won't be back till three o'clock at the earliest. Dad's a really good swimmer, and Robert's one of the best swimmers in his class.'

'Oh, I'm not worried, dear. They'll be fine,' Marion said. Her voice was cheerful, but her eyes were blank. 'If you see them coming or if the phone rings, I'll be round the side weeding under the cherry tree.'

'Yes, Mum.'

———

'Ah! You beauty Marion!' exclaimed Malcolm. He had opened the picnic hamper and found two cold sausages. 'These'll do for bait. Robert, can you hook them up?'

'Yes, Dad.'

'We'll cut across to Shipwright's Point and have a go.'

'Fair enough,' said Darryl. 'Anything more in that basket?'

'Help yourself, Daz. You hungry Robert?'

'Not yet.'

'Food tastes better in the open air,' said Darryl, and bit into a slice of fruit cake. 'Gawd! Did Marion make this? It's bloody delicious! Malcolm, you're a lucky man. All I get at home is packet cakes. This is the real thing. Robert, your mother's a great cook! No mistake!'

Robert smiled and helped himself to a slice. Darryl was right. It tasted great in the open air.

After a lazy hour at Shipwright's Point, not catching any fish, they pulled the anchor and headed out to the middle of the river. 'Too late in the morning for any fish,' said Darryl. 'They've already had their breakfast.' It was the sort of thing Robert would say. And if he did, Malcolm would correct him and say, 'Not breakfast. Their morning feed. People have breakfast. Not fish.' But when Darryl said it, it was simply amusing.

Darryl looked downstream towards the widening mouth of the river.

'Malcolm,' he said. 'You know you said there'd be a mild sou'-easterly about eleven o'clock?'

Malcolm looked around the mainsail and followed Darryl's gaze. Darryl went on, 'What I'm seeing here is no sou'-easterly. She's a southerly and she's coming in quick!'

'Well bugger me!' said Malcolm. 'This is going to put a damper on things.'

'It's coming up quick, Mal. I can see white caps. This calls for desperate action! Robert, you're in charge of valuable cargo. Hold this beer and don't spill any. And don't drink any either.' Robert put two hands around the bottle and sat on the stern seat with it between his legs. 'What do you think, Mal?' asked Darryl. 'Sail up or sail down. It's your decision. You're the captain, I'm just ya first mate. Sometimes I think I'm your only mate.' He smiled at Robert and winked.

'Let's see how we go. She'll be on us in ten minutes. The engine won't take us any faster than what we're doing now. Bloody early for a southerly. Did you get a weather report?' he asked Darryl.

'Yes mate, of course I did. Just like you did. I put me head out the backdoor this morning and said to the black jays, "What do you reckon? Will there be any wind?" And they said, "farrrrrrk".'

Malcolm trimmed the mainsail and tacked back towards the western bank. He didn't want to be caught in the middle of the river when the southerly hit. It would be like surfing if they kept the sail up, which could be a lot of fun. But he had to consider Robert.

'You right Robert?'

'Yes, Dad.'

'Just stay where you are,' said Malcolm. Robert didn't know what he meant. There was nowhere else to go.

'Now if you get the inclination to walk on water, think twice about it, mate,' said Darryl, reading Robert's mind. 'Just remember. Looking after my beer is your priority.'

'Yes, Darryl,' said Robert with a smile. Malcolm took no notice. He was watching the approaching wind.

'It's about to hit us. Hang on!' Robert was sitting on the stern seat facing north, so he couldn't see the wave behind him. He felt his whole body lifting up into the air. He became weightless before coming down with a crash. As his bottom hit the seat the wave splashed over his back, saturating his neck and shoulders. The beer, held tightly in his hands, foamed over his knuckles. The yeasty smell of it turned his stomach. The sun needled his eyes. He felt his head beginning to throb. Another wave hit the stern. The throbbing spread across his forehead and took hold behind his eyes. His body rose once more, higher this time, his arms extended above his head as if he were offering the foaming beer to the wind god: a supplication to placate the angry elements.

'She's right, Robert,' said Darryl, taking the bottle from his tight hands. 'I reckon I'll be able to take charge of essential cargo from here on. Not too bad is it Malcolm?'

'Might be a bit bumpy, but not as rough as I thought. You travelling well, Robert?' Malcolm looked down to take a good look. Robert's eyes were wide and glassy. He was madly blinking and swallowing. He wiped his mouth with the back of his hand, trying to fend off his rebellious stomach, but the smell of the sticky beer caught in his nostrils. His spine ran hot then cold and his stomach knotted. The sun glared. He felt a great hand strangling his innards and convulsing his body. He threw his head backwards over the stern, spraying fruitcake vomit all over the seat. Another wave hit.

'Jeez, Malcolm, he's got it bad!' said Darryl. He moved towards the boy and picked him up and turned him round. 'Keep your knees on the seat. I'll hold onto ya.' Darryl's large hands wrapped around him, one on his back and the other on his chest. 'Malcolm, this boy's as thin as a rake. He wouldn't make a decent pot of soup!' As another wave hit, Robert vomited again. 'Ah! Robert. This is no good. All that lovely fruit cake going to waste.' He patted the boy on the back. 'I'm losing good drinking time ya know. This isn't what I enlisted for. How we doing, Captain? Any sign of land?'

'We're only five minutes from the jetty. Ten at the most.' Malcolm's voice was flat with disappointment. He felt let down. It had been a perfect start and now it was all mucked up. 'Hang on son, it won't be long.' His tone colourless. Robert had taken all the joy out of his day.

The waves hit relentlessly. Darryl kept hold of Robert. He offered him nonsense limericks and silly jokes. Robert was so grateful he cried. His wrenching stomach covered up any sobs. By the time they reached the jetty he was completely exhausted, and his head felt like it would split in two.

After securing the boat, Malcolm gave Robert a bucket of water and a washer. 'Clean yourself up,' he said.

———

The *Belle Brandon*, one of the last remaining ketches from the nineteenth century, was moored on the opposite side of the jetty. Clydie Clayton, the owner, stood on the deck: a rickety scarecrow with a cup of tea in his hand. His thick white hair sloped at an angle like the waves of the southerly swell. He'd spent his days sailing the windswept waters between Hobart and the West Coast.

Clydie raised his right hand like a prophet and pointed downriver. 'Take him right down to Southport,' he said in a crackling voice. 'Right down till you're off South Bruny coast, opposite the lighthouse. Down there the water's real blue. Real dark blue. Take him down there, get a mug like this, and make him drink that dark blue water. He needs to drink some ocean water. He has to have that water in him. He'll never get sick again.'

'Stupid old bugger,' said Malcolm under his breath.

'Could be something in that, Clydie,' Darryl responded, looking up into a face full of crosscurrents. 'We'll do it another day.'

In the ute Robert sat in the middle, squashed between Malcolm and Darryl. The men smoked as they chuffed along the road to Golden Valley.

'Not such a bad day, Robert? You feeling alright now?'

'Much better thanks, Darryl.' Robert's head was still aching, and he felt cold and very tired.

'You'll be right, son,' said Malcolm. 'You're none the worse for wear.'

'No, Dad.' Robert let his head drop onto his chest. Darryl opened his window to let some of the cigarette smoke out.

The ute belched out black smoke all the way up Happy's Road and spluttered to a halt on the front lawn. Marion came out the front door wiping her hands on her slacks. She stopped herself from rushing to Robert and stood exchanging pleasantries with Darryl. Robert stood next to her, not looking at her, just relieved to have her near. When Darryl had gone, she bent down to look at his face.

'Was it as bad as last time?' she asked. Robert couldn't

speak. The answer was held in his throat. He knew it would come out with a sob of misery, so he simply looked at her.

'Wasn't that bad, Robert. You survived.' Malcolm's voice was flat and bitter. 'Trouble is you take after your mother. In more ways than one!' His father marched away into the house.

Robert's eyes flickered. The words seared him more than the dreadful convulsing vomiting on the boat. Marion took his hand, but he pulled it away.

———

They don't know nothing. Clydie lit his pipe. *Always forcing things. Thinking they know all about it. Think they know the sea. Especially those navy types. They never listen to her. Never listen to the sea and the wind. If they were quiet in their heads they'd hear her, but no. They lark about, chatter, drink. You've got no time for that on a boat. Not with the sea and the wind talking to you all the time. The slightest whisper of wind can tell all you need to know. If you really listen. And they never look up. Never see the feathery winds way up high. Stuck in their own little world and then wonder why they come a cropper. The sea's got to be in you. If you're all air and hollow bones you can't hear her. The sea's got to be a part of you. There's got to be salt in your veins. You've got to have that deep blue threading through your heart. If you can feel the water in your body you know what a wave will do. Without that bit of sea inside you, without that cup of blue, you're only air. You're just a bubble being tossed around. You've got to feel that vast moving river, or sea, or ocean like it's inside you. You've got to take it into your body and start listening and feeling. And that's only the beginning.*

Chapter 11

CLOUDS OF BUTTERFLIES HOVERED ABOVE the grassland. Swallows performed pirouettes and arabesques before whirling into long, slow parabolas. A pair of eagles glided high above them. The clouds drifted aimlessly.

Halfway up the hill the mist-grass, cranberries and dandelions gave way to a straggly forest. The she-oak, tree of grace, whispered its ancient keening. The native cherry swayed its long downward branches like the arms of a Japanese kimono. Majestic white gums caught the wind in clattering song. Their lower limbs clean and pale, crossing each other like the legs of lovers. The sun was caught and tossed through the flickering leaves as the Johnstones' footsteps crackled the twigs on the ground.

From the top of the hill they could see all of South Arm. Below, Ralph's Bay was streaked with turquoise and royal blue. White sand was overlaid with water smudges and great curved runnels where the tide ran in and out. To the west lay Storm Bay, flourishing white caps kicked up by the wind. Beneath the surface great kelp forests swayed in silence. Seagulls, like dots of ocean white, scoured the purple shadows. The great Southern Ocean pounded the Tasman Peninsula, pulling the eye to its explosions of white spume. The restless horizon pulling the desires of the soul: to fly like a bird and disappear within its clean saltiness and single-minded soundscape, its great breath.

Betsey Island lay dappled with light as lengthening shadows sucked the brightness out of its emerald green, letting it fall back into the landscape. To Betsey's north lay Goats Beach, wild with surf, grinning its brilliant white back at the island. A small colonial cottage sat balanced on the hill overlooking the beach, its gates and fences and hedges pegging it to the earth.

A bluish mist from the horizon was creeping into the bay. The butterflies rested, their wings semaphoring the ending of the day.

'We'll go to the beach tomorrow,' said Malcolm. His voice soft and reassuring. It had been a long walk to the top of the hill and now they stood together, shocked into silence by the grandeur of the view.

Marion broke free, starting the descent. 'We'll all sleep well tonight! And there's jaffles for tea. Come on, you lazy lot!'

Louise wanted to linger and watch the changing light: to feel the queer change within herself. The dimming light seemed to soften the boundaries of her body, making her feel light and insubstantial, restless with a nameless yearning. She wanted to stay beneath the glory of the sunset and dress her soul in its changing forms and colours.

———

They were renting the shack from a friend of Darryl's brother's. It was used as a depot for fishing trips and *goodness knows what else*. Marion spent the afternoon cleaning while Malcolm and the children strolled along the beach collecting wood. She had brought with her cloths and scrubbing brushes, kerosene, methylated spirits, Velvet soap and Ajax.

Vonnie had warned her that Darryl's brother's friend had bachelor habits.

The first thing to be cleaned was the outside dunny. Spiders that had lazily clung to their dusty webs for years were traumatised by a hurricane broom. The toilet needed dousing with kerosene and a liberal sprinkling of sawdust from the pile next to the door. Marion gave the Huon pine seat a vigorous scrubbing with hot water and soap. A pile of magazines and newspapers dating back ten years, including several *Playboys*, was unceremoniously dumped in the incinerator. (But not until Marion had examined the centrefolds and compared the models' enormous breasts to her own modest dimensions.)

The kitchen smelt of mice and something pungent, acrid and salty. The stove had never been cleaned in its life and looking at its grease and grime, Marion decided it wasn't worth the effort for just a week. The largest hotplate had a rim of caked-on dirty yellow fat. Raising her eyes, she saw that little stalactites of fat were growing downwards from the ceiling above.

'Mutton birds,' said Malcolm, following her gaze. 'They're full of fat and taste disgusting. They've been boiling them up on the stove. You can never get rid of the smell of them.'

Windows were forced open and propped up with old cans or bottles. Curtains were shaken and pulled back, one disintegrating in the process. The children dragged the kapok mattresses outside and pummelled the dust out of them, while Marion wiped down the chairs and scrubbed the wooden table. Louise picked a bunch of marigolds, pig-face, gum blossom, wattle and Spanish heather and arranged them in a tin can and placed them on the table.

At the front of the shack was a patch of sandy garden. Cabbage bush, grevilleas, bottlebrush and pigface stretched horizontally. The prevailing wind gave all the plants the look of bowing their twisted limbs close to the ground, shouldering the southerlies with tough, thick roots. A circle of stones marked out a fireplace, with large logs of driftwood for seats. Malcolm lit a fire using bracken and twigs for kindling and added the small branches the children had collected. There was a pile of larger logs resting against the foundations at the side of the shack. No axe, but it wasn't necessary. Soon the fire was blazing. Marion spread the jaffle fillings out on a cloth on the verandah: bread, butter, baked beans, cheese, eggs, ham.

They sat around the settling blaze and listened to the hiss of the jaffle iron and the lonely call of the gulls. As the sun set, the wind died down and allowed the smoke to gently rise without blowing it in anyone's face. They looked at each other in the fire light and saw glowing eyes and blood-filled skin. *How handsome and beautiful we are*, thought Marion.

When the children had gone to bed, snuggled into sleeping bags on the lumpy mattresses, Marion and Malcolm stayed by the fire until the last ember had blackened. Wrapped in a single blanket, they chatted about the day and imagined what Darryl's brother's friend was like.

'I found a pile of *Playboy* magazines in the loo,' said Marion.

'You beauty, Marion! Where did you put them?'

'I threw them in the incinerator!'

'That's a bit harsh isn't it?'

'You wouldn't want the children looking at them, would you?'

'Well, I'd have to look at them first and decide...'

'Malcolm, you're wicked!'

'I know,' he said, pulling gently on her bra strap. 'Did you throw them all out?'

'Yes!'

'You're going to pay for that, my girl! Do you want to be my centrefold?' He slid his hand across her breasts and kissed her cold nose. 'Inside with you this minute!'

The morning seemed to arrive late and lazy. Time was stretching and slowing. Marion wanted to be up early to make the most of the day but, like the others, she slept in. Now, feeling that something had been lost, she busied herself with picnic baskets, hats, suntan lotion, towels and the beach umbrella. There were walks to be walked. Swimming to be done. Shells to be collected and examined. Rock pools beneath the cliffs to be discovered. She'd even brought a sketch book and crayons. But the languid night had turned her head and she had to fight against lethargy. Trying to invigorate the children with a sense of crisp energy was proving fruitless. They too had caught the mood of inertia.

'Just let the day happen, Mum,' said Louise, emboldened by the change of environment.

'Yes,' said Robert. 'LET. THE. DAY. HAPPEN.' He rapped his knuckles against an imaginary blackboard for emphasis. Malcolm smiled quietly.

The bay was a murmur of pale satin. Without the wind, each wave formed a clear green membrane that trembled as it crested and fell. White foam marbled the wet sand where seagulls picked crabs too sluggish to scurry away. Behind the break-line, a group of surfers sat on their boards waiting. Waiting to be chosen. Waiting for the moment when the surge beneath the board had the feeling of rightness.

When that moment came, with his heart lifted in his chest, the lucky surfer would eye his fellow surfers. *It's for me? Yes?* The quick paddle and then the triumphant stance while cutting through the curling lip of the wave. A complete moment of unity with nature: of exhilaration, judgement without thought, skill in the body, the mind in suspension. No thought would interrupt the oneness of physical life. In the sea, a moment of timelessness would hold him erect and the ongoing rush of adrenaline pull him into the shore with outstretched arms. Then the long slow paddle back out to the break-line to do it again, and again, and again, till all thought was obliterated. Conversation was an unwelcome distraction. The surfers were one with each other, and one with the waves. Like gods, they held their great knowledge in silence.

'Bunch of dole bludgers,' said Malcolm. 'You don't want to end up like them, Robert.'

'No, Dad.'

By midday the sun had some real heat in it. Families made little camps for themselves, marking their territory with towels and beach umbrellas. Two girls in their late teens promenaded along the beach in front of the surfers, beehive hairdos and skimpy bikinis making no impact on anyone but Malcolm. 'Cor! Would you look at *that!*' He rolled over onto his back. The children had been playing in the breakers for some time but neither he nor Marion had ventured near the water.

'Time for a dip?' He placed his hand on her ankle and pulled her leg gently towards him. She peered over a pair of sunglasses.

'I'm willing if you are.' She pulled her shift over her head, revealing her swimsuit. It was the same one she'd worn on the ship coming out from England. It still fitted. It had lost the decorative buttons at the neckline and the colour had faded from the original turquoise to a pale peppermint green. Nevertheless, she felt comfortable in it. She'd purchased a bikini for sunbaking, but dared not wear it just yet. Besides, the old swimsuit filled Malcolm with nostalgia.

———

Louise, on the other hand, had grown so much that they'd had to make a quick trip to Mrs Vonnie's shop. The pretty seersucker bathers, with the print of mermaids and seashells, no longer reached over her chest. She could have rolled the top down and just worn them as pants, but she was too old for that now. Vonnie had the new Speedos, the ones all the girls wanted. Louise picked some out and held them against her body, looking up at her mother with wide, unblinking eyes. Marion thought the maroon colour was too old for her. 'That's the only colour I got, duck,' said Vonnie. So they bought the maroon bathers and a new pair of plastic sandals to match.

Louise tried them on when they were back at the house. After the heavy cotton seersucker, the nylon was so light it made her feel naked. She raced to her mother's wardrobe mirror. The modesty panel that ran down the centre of the bathers made her look taller and skinnier. She flicked her auburn curls back over her shoulders and pouted with her hands on her hips. 'Can I wear these to school under my uniform?' Marion tied the shoulder straps together at the back to make them a better fit.

'No!' she said, laughing.

———

Robert saw his parents getting up to go for a swim and made a judicious decision to leave the water. Louise could take the heat for once. He stumbled up the shore and collapsed in mock exhaustion on his towel.

At the water's edge, Marion let the water lick her feet and jumped back in predictable surprise. It was freezing.

'Come on Marion! It's great once you get in!' Malcolm took her hand and urged her into the water. With much cajoling she eventually waded in up to her waist. Malcolm dived under and came up in a surge of water.

'Just go under!' Louise swam up to Marion. 'Come on Mum! Go under. You can do it!' She was made brave by her mother's reticence. 'It's much warmer when you're under. You've got to move about more.'

Marion slowly lowered herself, keeping her neck straight and her head above the water. She tried a few strokes and stood up.

'That's it for me, darling. It's far too cold.'

Malcolm watched her as she waded to the shore. Marion was so afraid of things! She was scared of the river and of mountains: all the creepy crawlies of the bush. She was fastidious about housekeeping: waging a continuous war against germs, mould and dust. She could never just throw herself into the physical world.

He turned to Louise, and dived like a whale to rise up, lifting her on his back. She slid down, turning in the water, her eyes and mouth circles of surprise. Malcolm laughed and picked her up in his arms, twirled her round and round and threw her into the foam. He came under her again, this time pulling her by the arms and dragging her through the shallows. 'Kick! Lou, kick! Faster now. Come on! Kick harder! Faster! Now both together... That's it. Feet together. You'll be doing the butterfly in no time!'

Louise stood shakily and blinked the water from her eyes and pulled her hair back off her face. He grabbed her hips and turned her around facing the oncoming waves.

'We'll go out to where the waves are breaking. Don't be scared, I'm with you. You swim out and I'll show you how to bodysurf. Don't worry. I'm right here. Just breaststroke. Breaststroke will keep you above the wave and you can see where you're going. Nice and easy, take your time. Have you got that?'

———

Louise had no time to think. Pleased to be the focus of his attention, she started out with a frog-like stroke. She wasn't out of her depth, so she didn't feel frightened. But the waves seemed very big at eye level.

'You're doing well, Lou. Go under the next one ... Big breath!' She filled her lungs with air and dived into the green muscle of the wave. She could feel her bathers fill-ing with a rush of water. Coming up, Malcolm was by her side. 'And another one ... Big breath, under you go!' The next wave was bigger. She felt a rush of adrenaline and gulped in air. Diving deep into the wave she felt it ripple across her back. 'One more, Lou. Same again. Big breath. You can do it!' Louise waited for her feet to touch the sand. The sand wasn't there. She scissored her legs as fast as she could. 'Don't panic, I'm here. Just duck into this one. Big breath.' She crouched down and pulled herself towards the ocean floor. The wave caught her head and sent her tumbling backwards. Malcolm grabbed her. 'Well done! That's the last of them for a while. They're coming in four waves at a time. See, it's all flat now.'

Louise wrapped her arms around his neck for support. Looking back towards the beach she could see Marion. She was shading her eyes and looking in her direction. *She's worrying*, thought Louise. Robert was bucketing wet sand and making some sort of castle, leaping around, dancing and probably singing, although she couldn't hear. They were so far away. No sound could reach them. They were in their own world. She could smell the suntan lotion on her father's shoulders and his cigarette breath close to her face. She held on tightly. 'Not too tightly round the neck.' Malcolm moved her hands onto his shoulders. 'Just hold on and we'll take the next wave.' He turned and faced the beach. 'Hold on.'

A great animal seemed to take shape beneath her. She kept her elbows bent and her head up close to Malcolm's. The first thing she noticed was the speed. They shot through the water, creating their own channel. Malcolm lowered his head and straightened his arms. His face disappeared into the breaking wave and he became only body. He was all limbs and shoulders, hunched like a beast. Louise felt alone. *I'm on my own now*, she thought. *He's gone. Disappeared into the wave. I'm no longer his focus. For him, I'm not here. The wave is all that he is thinking of.* She loosened her grip and slid off his back. Letting her legs fall, she realised too late that she was out of her depth. Water filled her mouth and she gulped and bobbed.

'What did you let go for?' Malcolm seemed surprised and a little angry. She couldn't reply through the coughing and gagging. Besides, she didn't know why. 'Come on,' he said, his voice encouraging but showing disappointment as well. 'Up you go. We can make it in a little further. Then we'll go out again.'

Louise became used to it after a while: the sovereignty of being on his back, the reddening skin and the hard, strong muscles beneath. But the biggest challenge was swimming out to the break-line. They dived together under each wave. Gradually she allowed the thrill of the act to overcome her fear. His face was there after each dive. 'You can do it! That was a good one! One more! Under we go!' It was fun. She felt safe. But something disappeared when he turned his back. 'Up you go,' he'd say and fling her onto his back. It was as if he had changed into some fish-like creature. He was unfamiliar to her. She felt solitary, bobbing on the back of the strange creature as it churned through the waves.

Marion ran to the shoreline, her heart in her mouth. She saw Malcolm leading Louise out through the breakers: a sea-demon stealing her child. She stood rigid in the shallows and watched until they turned and headed in towards the shore. She felt a rush of relief and realised she'd been holding her breath. Back under the beach umbrella she thumbed through the *Women's Weekly*. She crossed and uncrossed her legs, sat up, lay down. Shading her eyes, she looked out to the waves. They were going out again! Surely once was enough! What did Malcolm think he was doing? *She's only a little girl! She hasn't the strength to swim that distance.* Then she saw Malcolm twirl her around and laughingly dump her in the water. She watched Louise, a water-sprite, a changeling, lording it over him and riding his back into the foaming sea, holding on tight to the world, the joy of childhood racing through her body.

There was little time left for the simple playfulness of childhood, thought Marion. Within the next eighteen months Louise's menses would start and the kingdom of childhood would banish her. *Let her frolic now*, she thought. *Let her enjoy every moment.*

'Look! Mum! Come and see.' Robert pulled her by the hand to the water's edge. He made her shut her eyes. 'Now. Now you can open them.' She looked down and saw a magnificent dragon. Robert had heaped sand into a large pile and then cut and moulded it using the spade. He'd used cockle shells for outlining the scales on its long back. Its fiery nostrils were two mussel shells. He'd even moulded its fiery breath with curling patterns of wet sand. He'd let the tail end sink into the sand but the very tip emerged a little way off, giving the effect that the dragon was coming out of the earth. Its talons were being threatened by the rising tide. 'I should have started further up. You can see how he's coming out of the sand. His name's Puff, of course.'

'It's marvellous, Robert!' Marion was very impressed. 'I love his scaly back. Are there any more shells around that we can use?'

'There might be, but it would be better if they were a bit smaller. The big shells should go right on top of his back and the smaller ones underneath, on his belly.'

'I think you're right. Shall we look for some pipis? They should do for his belly. I'm afraid the tide will be in soon and Puff will go back where he came from.' Taking the bucket, they wandered along the high tide mark looking for pipis and other treasures.

———

The afternoon was growing cloudy. An offshore wind began lifting spray from the tops of the waves. Malcolm and Louise were still in the water frolicking like dolphins. Louise had lost all fear of the waves and felt perfectly confident in staying afloat in the troughs and diving beneath the peaks. She could dive into the wave now without her feet having to be on the sea floor. It took strength and concentration, but she'd proved herself to her father. She'd become his companion, his pupil, his delight. She saw his broad smile every time she came up from beneath a wave. He saw her hopeful look of devotion.

'Time to call it quits, Lou. Come on. I'll piggyback you in.' Louise was near exhaustion. She flung her arms around his shoulders and climbed onto his back feeling the heaviness of her body. Like heroes from the depths of the sea, they made their triumphal march up the shore, across the wet sand.

———

Robert felt the warm breeze on his face. He looked at Marion and smiled. It was a perfect moment: together, working on his grand project. The bucket was full of pipis, enough to finish his dragon. Hand in hand, they turned back just as Malcolm and Louise, laughing with the exhilaration of their swim, came out of the waves. Robert cried out as Malcolm ran carelessly up the beach and stomped right across the head and neck of his beautiful dragon. The decapitation of Puff.

Robert ran towards Malcolm, his hands in tight fists and his face a tight, red ball. 'Look what you've done!' he cried. 'Look what you've done!'

Malcolm let Louise slide off his back. 'What's the matter, Robbie? What have we done?'

'Look!' exploded Robert. 'My dragon!' Malcolm looked to where Robert was pointing and saw a pile of kicked sand. Marion caught up and explained.

'I can tell it was a wonderful dragon, Rob,' said Malcolm. 'You've got a good eye for detail.' They all looked down at where the head had been. Just a few of the strands of smoke, carefully carved from wet sand remained intact. The talons were already dissolving with the incoming tide.

'It's just a mess now! It's all messed up!' Tears streamed down Robert's reddened face. 'You wouldn't like it anyway! You never like anything I do!' He threw himself down on the dragon and started throwing handfuls of sand at it. He picked the cockle shells off its back and hurled them into the water. He stood and tried to rub the dragon out with his feet, stomping on its belly and kicking its tail. Every muscle in his body was tight with rage.

'I'm sorry, Robert,' said Louise. 'We just didn't see it. I'm so sorry we messed it up. I'll help you make another one.' But Robert was wretched beyond consoling.

'Come on, son.' Malcolm was shocked by the intensity of Robert's rage. 'We honestly didn't see it. It was an accident. We didn't do it on purpose. I tell you what. Tomorrow I'll help you make another one.' He emphasised the *I'll*, knowing that they'd all think it a great joke.

'Dad, you can't even draw,' Louise said in mock scorn, hoping it would pacify Robert and pull him out of his tantrum.

'No, but I can have a try can't I? You never know what hidden talents I've got. I just keep them under wraps. Isn't that so, Mum?'

'Yes, dear,' replied Marion.

Robert thought his father was trying to sound like Darryl. 'You've destroyed him!' he shouted. 'You've destroyed my dragon!' He threw himself on the sand again and pounded it with his fists. He felt his anger consume him, as if it would splinter his very bones, and his mind was filled with shrieking clouds of fury to the exclusion of all else.

There was no stopping him. Malcolm took Louise back to the shack. As soon as they were gone, Marion sat down next to Robert. She placed her hand on his rigid back, simply holding it there as his shoulders continued to heave with gasping sobs. She sat with him for what seemed like hours, as the day grew cold and cloudy and all the other picnickers and swimmers left the beach. Gradually his body grew soft, and the wrenching sobs faded. Eventually he turned to face her. His eyes were red and swollen. Mucus and tears were mixed with sand and smeared all over his face. He looked up at her and said in a frozen voice: 'He'll never love me.'

———

When Malcolm went to check on the children that evening, they were both so profoundly asleep it was as if they were drugged. Marion had closed the louvre windows in the children's bedroom to stop the mosquitoes from getting in. The low ceiling made the room stifling. It smelt musky and damp despite the heat. Robert lay with his neck fully extended and his head tilted back across the pillow, as if his mind was trying to separate itself from his body. His thin ribs, knitted across his raging heart, rose and sank. Malcolm wondered what he could do, how he could make it up to him. A good night's sleep, he reasoned.

Louise lay on the top bunk. She hadn't taken off her bathers, and her hair was matted and damp. She looked wild and bedraggled: a sea creature stranded on land. Her feet were dirty, crusted with the grey sand. A trail of sand lay across the top of her leg where the bathers had lifted away from her thigh. Underneath the stiffened, salt-encrusted fabric Malcolm could see the mound of her sex, sleeping like a white moon against a maroon sky. He lifted his eyes to her chest and saw the dots of her nipples riding on the soft curves of tiny breasts. To his horror he felt his penis fill with blood.

He bolted out of the room and stood in the kitchen away from the fetid air. He lit a cigarette, drawing the smoke hard into his lungs. Earlier in the day his mind had wandered playfully: fantasizing about the nature of relationships.

He knew he loved his wife. Marion could be a nag and critical, but she always gave way to him. Even in the bedroom she'd make the effort; even if she wasn't feeling like it. She was a good cook and good at making clothes for the kids. But she was always afraid of the natural world.

On the other hand, Louise was willing to give anything a go. More spirited, more adventurous. She was becoming feistier by the day. The next few years could be a bit of a battleground. But for now he still had power over her. When she was diving through the waves he saw the adoration on her face and felt himself a god: saw the determination in her whole body as the waves came crashing down on her. He knew she could handle it. She was fearless. Marion could never do that.

Somehow, he had thought, there had been a cosmic accident. He should have been partnered with Louise rather than Marion: like there had been some terrible mistake in heaven and Marion had been sent to him instead of Louise. It was all nonsense of course, just a playful game of the mind. But still, he couldn't help thinking that Lou was a better match for him: the way she'd jumped on his back and rode him into the shore and let him twist her round and throw her into the waves. She was lithe and light, giving and playful. You couldn't do that with Marion in a month of Sundays! And Robert would be moaning and teary if he got water in his ears. No. Lou was made for him and Robert was made for Marion. It all made perfect sense. Except it was nonsense.

And now his body was showing signs of an unforgivable betrayal. He'd have to change. He'd have to rethink what he had so carelessly thought in the afternoon. Louise was only a child. He'd watch his mind for careless thoughts. She was his responsibility until she was married and he would love and protect her. But it would mean distancing himself from her. He couldn't risk this reaction happening again. As he butted out the cigarette he vowed to keep physical contact to a minimum: to only look at her eyes and not look at her body and to keep his affection chaste and his thoughts pure. He regretted the impulse that made him lift his gaze from her legs to her sex, to her breasts. It was a ghastly mistake. In his imagination he relived the scene, this time drawing a blanket up over her body, only looking at her sleeping face.

He lit another cigarette and looked desperately around the kitchen for something to distract him. There were two bottles of beer in the fridge. He quickly took one out and rummaged through the cutlery draw for an opener.

Eventually he found it and whisked the top off. He grabbed two glasses and went outside.

'What kept you?' asked Marion.

'Smoking out the mozzies.' Malcolm blew out a puff of smoke and placed the beer and glasses on the ground.

'We don't normally have a drink after supper?'

'Today's not normal. We're on holiday.' Malcolm poured the beer into the glasses and held one out to her. He was hoping the beer would fog his brain and dull his body.

'Thank you,' she said. She felt like a beer: felt like being a little more relaxed. She took a sip and gazed at him. Drawing her knees together she straightened her spine and brushed her hair away from her neck. It was her coquettish, Audrey Hepburn look.

Lord have mercy on me! thought Malcolm. *Marion's feeling frisky and all I want to do is cut me dick off and howl at the moon!*

'I think I've done something to my back,' he said. 'In real deep.' He twisted and stretched and just managed to feel a twinge in his lower back. 'I must have overdone it today.'

'You certainly did!' Marion maintained her posture and thought of the centrefold from November 1965, now slumped in the incinerator. It was a blonde girl in a check shirt provocatively unbuttoned, with her breasts bulging out towards the reader.

'Would you like me to rub it?' she asked.

'No, it's alright. I'll just walk around for a bit.' Malcolm wandered around the camp fire, stretching this way and that. 'Ow! There it goes again!' he said as he twisted his spine around the kidney area. He could really feel it now. There was definitely pain in that area. He limped to the fire and poured another beer. 'I'll have to take it easy tomorrow,' he said, meaning that he'd have to take it easy tonight. Marion looked a little disappointed. It wasn't every day she felt like this, warm and soft and sexy, fuzzy with the alcohol hitting her bloodstream. Never mind. There was always tomorrow.

———

The next day was overcast. It was still warm and muggy, but no wind. A thunderstorm was forecast for the afternoon. The south-easterly swell kept the surfers happy, and the teenage girls with big hair were grateful for the lack of wind. Even though there was no sun to be had, people came to the beach. It was a good day for cricket on the wide wet sand, or for tossing a beach ball. The cliffs and the rocky shore beneath held a host of treasures for exploring children. There were books and transistor radios to keep the more sedentary holidaymakers happy.

Louise was in the water, jumping up and down and splashing the surface. She dived beneath the waves and came out looking towards the beach.

Yesterday, before Malcolm had joined her in the water, she had had no thought but to drift on the surface of the water and watch the sky. She'd been content to perform some lazy strokes and let the waves wash over her in the foaming shallows. She'd been self-contained in her reverie, with no need of companionship.

But now her eyes were hard and searching. She was looking for her father. He'd gone back to the shack to grab another towel. She waited and waited, watching the path that led to the shack. *When he comes back, we'll go out together and it will be like yesterday.* She was confident now that she could be even better at negotiating the waves: going over the top with a high leap, or slicing underneath. She'd know how to ride him into the shore. She was even willing to try bodysurfing by herself. Malcolm would tell her what to do and she would show him how good she was.

But when he eventually returned, he simply sat down on the towel and opened a book. He'd found a Raymond Chandler in the shack. He groaned convincingly as he shifted his weight from one elbow to the other. Marion smiled in sympathy.

Louise came running up the beach.

'Are you coming in, Dad?' She stood over him, water dripping on his shoulders and head.

'Don't stand there!' he said. 'You're getting me all wet!'

Louise moved impatiently. 'Are you coming in?'

'Lou! You're dripping all over my book! Go and play with Robert,' he said, changing his posture, keeping his eyes on the book. Dismissing her.

'I don't want to play with Robert!' She was flabbergasted. 'I want to do bodysurfing!' It sounded like nagging.

'You don't always get what you want, my girl. Look what you're doing! Don't stand on the towel! You're getting sand all over it!' Malcolm could feel his self-righteousness growing with every clumsy move she made. She was a petulant, demanding girl that needed putting in her place.

'Daddy has a sore back, darling. Go and find Robert. I think he's over there with those boys.' Marion pointed to some boys tossing a beach ball towards the water's edge. Louise turned back towards the water, head down, dragging her toes in the sand as she went.

She didn't think that the rejection might be permanent. She thought at first that he would eventually make his way to the water. After all, he loved the water, loved the sea. Soon he would come. Soon he would make it all right, like it was yesterday. She looked out to the surfers on their boards. Their bodies were muscular and tanned. Imagine holding onto one of those men, she thought. Or imagine going on a surfboard and riding the tops of the waves.

The afternoon wore on and Malcolm remained on his towel, nose in the book. In the evening he was polite but contained. Even Marion felt the chill in his behaviour. She put it down to his sore back: he was trying to control the pain. It would pass. Louise felt the brunt of his coldness. With Robert he was jovial and considerate. With her, he was brusque, offhand and rude. If she put a log on the fire, it was in the wrong place. If she did the washing up, she forgot the cups on the verandah. If she filled up the billy for tea, it was too full and spilt on the fire. When she went to kiss him good night he moved quickly to stand and stretch his back, avoiding her lips. He let Marion check on the children when they were asleep and didn't go into their bedroom.

———

Malcolm felt proud. He'd achieved self-control. He'd acted properly and with restrained decorum. Louise would get used to his reserved behaviour and keep a respectful distance. With yesterday's incident behind him he was ready to start a new phase in his life. There would be no looking at the teenage girls in their ridiculous bikinis. He'd refrain from joining in the dirty jokes at work, or participating in the sly, sexual innuendo directed at the women in the typing pool. He would no longer look at ankles, legs or breasts. He would not flip through the *Playboy* magazine in the newsagent. Cleansed and resolute, he went to bed with a clear conscience and said the Lord's Prayer for good measure.

Sleep eluded him and he tossed and turned in the stultifying air. When it eventually came, he dreamt fitfully. He dreamt of a naked girl, a Snow White figure, lying on a sandy bank. He had been given a task. He was to pull a white sheet over her sleeping body. As he did this, the sheet disintegrated. By the time he had the sheet up to her chin the material had frayed into threads, falling away to reveal her body. He tried again and again but every time the same thing happened and her sex grew and became alive like some strange sea creature with many floating tentacles. The Snow White figure woke and pulled the sheet off with a hand the shape of a claw. It scratched at the writhing monster between its legs, sending its tentacles into a frenzy.

———

'I'm peeling,' said Robert.

'So am I.' Louise pulled a dry flaky piece of skin slowly off her nose and held it out for Robert to see.

'Look at my back,' he said. 'And my shoulders. Watch this.' He brushed his hand over his shoulder, sending tiny flakes of dead skin floating through the air.

'You'll have to wear shirts today,' said Marion.

'That'll make it worse,' said Robert. 'It'll itch and sting.'

Marion dabbed them both with calamine lotion and smeared greasy zinc cream on their noses. Robert reluctantly put on a short-sleeved shirt and Louise pulled a shift over her beloved bathers. It was a morning for exploring. The children disappeared down the track to the beach. Marion and Malcolm would meet them later at their usual spot.

They were free to explore the cliff and the rock pools, after much instruction from Marion. 'Don't touch anything that's alive, it could be poisonous, and dead birds are covered in diseased fleas. Don't go too close to the water because of rogue waves – a boy in Sydney was swept to his death the other day! Don't talk to any of those surfers. If they say anything to you just walk the other way. Don't climb up the cliffs, and don't be too long.'

The children answered 'Yes, Mum' in unison and ran to freedom.

They set off in chattering delight, racing along the wet sand, kicking the foam left behind by the receding tide. Robert picked up a handful of the wobbling foam and made a beard of it. Louise laughed and put some on her head.

Stray pieces of bull kelp had washed up on the sand in sculptured mounds. Louise picked up a string of seed pods and strung it round her neck. 'I'll need a dilly bag,' she said. They pulled a large strand of kelp free from the tangled mound and wrapped it round and round till it formed the shape of a basket. 'I don't think it'll last,' said Louise as the structure fell back to its amorphous mass. Laughing, they abandon the whole idea and headed off again towards the cliffs.

Stringy bits of rotting seagrass carpeted the sand at the end of the beach. The smell of methane filled the air.

'Aw! Lou! You farted! Aw! That's disgusting. A rat's crawled up your bum and died!'

'It wasn't me, it was you!' Louise laughed. 'You're the champion farter.'

'This is even worse that Dad's farts!' Robert held his nose.

'It's even worse than Mum's farts!' said Louise.

'Mum doesn't fart.' said Robert. 'She's trained her bum not to fart.'

'She'll train you not to fart.'

'Then it'll stay inside till there's a huge explosion and I'll die of exploding farts!'

They picked their way through the seagrass and found themselves on the rocks. There they sat and rested for a while, looking across the beach. Robert was the first to break the silence and scramble down to the shoreline. Louise followed. The first rock pool was ringed with sea anemones. Orange, pink and green, they lay with their tentacles stretched towards the surface.

'Which one do you like the best?' asked Robert.

'I'm not sure. The green one is beautiful but it's very small. It's a lovely colour. The pink one moves around the most. Its tentacles are fatter. The orange one looks thinner.'

'I like the orange one,' said Robert.

'I like the little green one,' said Louise. Robert leant over and put his finger in the centre of the orange anemone.

'Ah! Lou, help! It's got me!' Louise looked at the tiny green anemone. She placed her finger in its sandy centre. The tentacles grabbed around her finger with a gentle sucking sensation.

'It doesn't hurt. It feels tickly,' she said.

'But mine is the DEADLY ORANGE ANEMONE!' said Robert. 'I'll probably die any minute now.'

'Don't be silly,' said Louise. 'Look at this.' She lifted a rock as big as her hand and watched the crabs scuttle for shelter.

In another rock pool they found an abalone shell. There were several in the shack that were used as ashtrays. It was nice to see one with its mother-of-pearl shiny and intact.

Louise put it in the pocket of her shift.

'If we found enough of them we could make a giant necklace... A necklace for a giant... A great big mermaid the size of that rock out there,' Robert said, pointing to a solitary boulder at the very point of the bay.

'Or it could be a bed for tiny people to sleep in,' said Louise. 'They'd just curl up and fit exactly into the shell. They'd wake up every morning to a glorious pink and blue shiny sky and then they'd crawl out and fall off the edge and find the world was nothing but sand.'

'Look at this!' cried Robert. 'It's a scale from a mermaid's tail.' He held up a scallop shell.

'And this is her hair,' said Louise picking up a clump of black dried seaweed.

'And these are her teeth,' said Robert, holding out two large cockle shells. 'And these are the pimples on her bum!' He pointed to the barnacles on the rocks.

The game faded away as they drifted among the rock pools. Gradually they moved away from speech to a land beyond words, where observation and sensation bypassed the naming of things. Everything was felt: colour, shape, movement, density, lightness. Their feelings and reactions became synchronised as language left them and words were washed away by the relentless susurration of the waves. They were enveloped by a primitive, holistic experience of sensation without words, without labels and explanations, without past or future. Just being. By a signal of the hand Robert could alert Louise to a dried crayfish claw or the skeleton of a seagull. When Louise found a pygmy octopus stranded in a rock pool, she held her breath and stretched her hands out. Robert saw the sign and came running.

Neither of them spoke. They simply looked at the creature. Its bulbous eyes were sinking back into its head. White eggs skirted its body. It raised one tentacle at a time, testing the water, the air, looking for an escape.

When eventually they spoke, it was in whispers. 'Do you think we should help it back to the sea?' asked Robert.

'We'd need a bucket or a shovel or both,' said Louise. 'The tide's coming in. It'll be alright.'

The words had broken the spell. Clouds were forming angels' wings high above them. The pristine part of the day was over. Soon the sea breeze would round the point and kick up the waves. They had treasures enough to take home. To have seen an octopus was the greatest of them. Louise's pocket was full of shards of kelp shells in iridescent greens and purples. She thought she might make patterns with them on the kitchen table. The abalone shell only just fitted into her pocket, but it served to cradle the shell of a crab that was entirely intact.

'You kids having a good time?' A tall surfer with golden skin smiled at them from the top of a boulder. He held a surfboard under his arm and wore a pair of cut-off jeans. Prehensile toes gripped the boulder. His body was lean but muscular, and the fine blonde hairs on his legs and chest gleamed in the sun.

'We found an octopus!' cried Robert.

'Yeah? Whereabouts?'

'Over there,' said Robert, pointing to the water's edge. 'It's stuck in a rock pool.'

'You ever eaten one?' The surfer smiled again, showing a mouth cluttered with white teeth.

'Yuck! No! I'd never eat one! We were going to put it back

in the water, but we didn't have anything to put it in.'

'It'll be right. The tide's coming in. That'll wash it back out.'

'That's what Lou said,' replied Robert.

Louise heard her name. A crimson blush enveloped her like a hot wind. Her hair had blown across her face. She let it stay there. She had been looking at the surfer, his handsome face and his dried-out blonde curls. Her voice disappeared. The pocket of her shift felt heavy and awkward, bulging out from her dress.

'You got some treasures there Lou?' the surfer asked good-naturedly. He waited for a response, his blue eyes sparkling. Louise dropped her head, letting her hair obscure her face entirely. Her voice would not respond and the blush would not leave.

'She's got an abalone shell and a dead crab. But what I really, really want is a nautilus shell,' said Robert, moving closer to the surfer.

'Have a look at the high tide mark,' the surfer said, nodding towards the beach. 'Sometimes you see them there.'

'Gee, thanks,' replied Robert. 'What's wrong with your board?' He pointed to a gaping hole at the base of the board.

'The skeg broke off. I got stuck on the rocks. Lucky I didn't get smashed up.'

'What's a skeg?'

'The fin. The skeg's the fin. It helps you steer. If you see it, can you bring it to me? It's about this big,' he said, holding a hand out from the surfboard. 'It's already got nicks out of it, but I might be able to fit it back in. One of me mates has got some fibreglass. He says he'll be able to fit it.'

'If we find it where do we take it?' asked Robert.

'Just over there.' He pointed to the cluster of surfers on

the beach. 'They all know me. My names Dinger, by the way. Well, it's not really, but that's what me mates call me.'

'My name's Robert. But I like Rob. I used to like Robbie, but now it's just Rob. Sometimes Dad calls me Bozo. I hate that.'

Dinger laughed. 'That's what my dad used to call me!'

'Does he call you Dinger now?'

'No. That's what me mates call me. They call me Dinger 'cause when we're out on the waves me board dings into other blokes. I don't mean it to happen. I'm just naturally clumsy.' Dinger laughed again. Robert thought it must be wonderful to have so many mates and a special nickname.

'Did you smell that stink there on the beach?' Robert pointed to the wide pad of seaweed at the water's edge.

'Yeah. It's really off, isn't it!' said Dinger, laughing again.

Louise couldn't believe that Robert would mention the dreadful farty smell to the stranger. She was already hot and flustered and now mortified at the thought that he would continue a conversation about it. She looked at Robert, hoping the deadly glare underneath her mop of hair would stop him in his tracks.

Dinger lifted each foot one at a time. The rock was hot and he was drying off fast. 'I better get going,' he said and switched the surfboard to the other arm. 'You two have a nice time out here.'

'If we find the skeg we'll bring it over to you,' said Robert.

'That'd be great. Thanks Rob.' He lifted his voice a little louder and looked at Louise. 'Bye Lou.'

She looked up at him through her hair. Her voice box allowed a soft 'Bye,' then she dropped her head again, waiting for him to go.

When it was safe, she looked up to see him moving quickly

across the hot rocks, his feet moving as if they had suction caps beneath them. Now she was free from the hot cloying feeling, but nothing was normal anymore. She felt resentful of Robert, his easiness with the surfer. The strength and straightforwardness that she could muster at times had deserted her, leaving her body feeling as soft as a jellyfish.

'You're really dumb sometimes Lou.' Robert sounded annoyed.

'Mum said we shouldn't—'

'I don't care what Mum says!' Robert's voice was loud, carrying only a short distance before being smothered by the wind. He had seen a dream of a life ahead where he would have mates, not a family. 'I don't care what Dad says either,' he said defiantly.

Sullenness took over as clouds darkened the water. They made their way back to the shack in silence. Robert didn't find the skeg, or a nautilus shell, but he vowed to himself that he would search again tomorrow. They told their parents the story of the octopus, its tentacles growing in the telling. A silent pact prevented either of them mentioning Dinger.

The trip back to Golden Valley was uneventful. In the morning the children had their last swim. The water was flat, the sky overcast. Marion cleaned the shack while Malcolm finished his book. After lunch, they went for a final walk along the beach.

Packing the car took longer than expected. Marion jettisoned Robert's large piece of driftwood and insisted that Louise change out of her bathers and into a pair of shorts and a blouse. She tied Louise's hair back with a rubber band. Louise untied it as soon as they got in the car.

Malcolm lit a cigarette, pulled out the choke and started the car. As it lumbered over the uneven sandy drive, Robert knelt on the back seat to look out the window. The little shack that had been greeted with disdain when they first arrived had become charming, familiar, and homely. Even the camp fire site looked welcoming. They'd set the fire for the next lot of visitors.

Once the monotony of the drive had established itself, Marion started humming 'Lara's Theme' from *Doctor Zhivago*. Soon the children joined in. Once the tune was entirely saturated with sentimentality, Robert lampooned it by adding an accompaniment with comb and tissue paper and making it go twice the speed.

The children knew the soundtrack to *The Sound of Music* off by heart. Malcolm listened with pride and envy. How could they remember all those words? And to hold the tune as well! It seemed like a miracle to him. The words of that 'Do re mi' song didn't make any sense to him, but he loved hearing it. The most he could do to join in, was to tap his fingers on the steering wheel. The world of music was a closed door to him, but it moved him more than he could say or explain. Marion would start singing and he'd just melt, be totally swept away by the sound of her voice. He would be transported to another world. For her it was simply second nature. She'd sing while she was doing the dishes or out in the garden. She was like a little bird. Music was part of her, but it didn't move her the way it moved Malcolm. He would be almost in tears, and all she was doing was singing while doing the dusting.

As they approached the Tasman Bridge, Louise started singing 'Sixteen Going on Seventeen' in a slow, self-conscious way. 'Yuck!' said Robert. 'You're not sixteen going on seventeen! You're eleven, so don't pretend you're grown up!' He refused to sing the song and waited till Marion and Louise had given it a decent run. Then it was his turn with 'High on a hill was a lonely goatherd'. In his piping voice it was loud and shrill. When he got to the yodelling part it was even louder.

Malcolm slowed the car to a halt. Traffic on the bridge had stopped. He cut the engine and they opened the windows to let in a bit of air. Robert, revived by the fresh air, resumed the yodelling chorus of 'The Lonely Goatherd' with renewed vigour. Three children with big eyes and small mouths turned around in the car ahead and stared at Robert with expressionless faces. 'Keep it down a bit son,' said Malcolm.

A bright yellow Volkswagen with twin carburettors sidled past in the outside lane, the radio blaring out 'Little Girl' by the Beach Boys. Surfboards were piled on the roof rack. One of them was missing a fin. Dinger was resting his elbow out the window of the passenger seat. He was laughing at something. Robert punched Louise lightly on the arm and pointed. He leant out of the window and waved at the car. Louise saw the conspicuous Volkswagen and heard snatches of the lyrics, about a little girl with movie-star lips. The dreaded blush swamped her body. She slunk down in the seat and pulled her hair over her face. Dinger and his mates glided slowly past, absorbed in their own world.

The story of Dinger and his surfboard was one that was growing with embellishment in Robert's mind. When school resumed he would nonchalantly refer to his mate Dinger and the missing skeg. (*That's a fin! Didn't you know that?*) It was just possible that a shark might have taken it. Oh! He wished he'd asked Dinger about sharks! He might have even seen some. *Well, he must have, really, being in the water so long.* Sharks would add extra excitement to his story. And of course, Dinger would call him 'mate' like he did all his other mates. It was such a friendly word. He'd try it out when they got back home.

Chapter 12

HEADMASTER NORMAN DILLON STRODE ALONG the path to E block. His academic gown billowed outwards, revealing a well-tailored three-piece suit. It was brown. A colour his wife informed him was fashionable. He would have preferred a classic navy blue, but she insisted that brown would give him a friendlier look. He had capitulated. He wasn't quite sure why. There seemed to be a growing confidence among women these days. He would have said unrest, but that seemed too severe. It was hard to tell. His wife was approaching the menopause and he knew it was a stormy time. Maybe her restlessness was purely biological, or maybe it was a sign of the times. At any rate, it was prudent to don the brown suit.

An observer would have thought he was pursuing a task of some gravity. But in truth it was levity he was seeking. The beginning of the school year always provided a wealth of new experiences for students, but none so entertaining as their initiation into the school band. In his mind he justified the visit to E block as a preliminary encounter enabling him to monitor progress throughout the year. But even as he approached the single-storey wooden building, he was beginning to feel the mirth rising. He straightened his shoulders and put on his friendly, jolly face, and swung the glass doors open.

In the main hall, he knew, Ron Joliffe was taking the brass

section. Ron was one of Norman's favourite teachers, and popular with the students as well. He was a short, round, meaty man with an oversized head that swivelled on his thick neck. Dark, curly hair surrounded his face and glasses. It was lovely hair and as it grew, girls would find themselves thinking he was attractive. Crushes would develop among the first and second years. The hair made him look like a pop singer. But he was not a vain man. Every now and then he would have the hair cut ruthlessly short and the girls with crushes would fade away. They would migrate to the science department, where a young physics teacher with startling blue eyes was growing a moustache.

Ron was explaining something to the students. The long, round vowels of his speech and the blunt upended turn of phrase lost definition and meaning as it filtered through the door and became a form of music in itself. The lovely ups and downs of his voice, its give and take, its gravity and lightness, all seemed exaggerated compared to the monotones of Australian speech. The Lancashire accent was mesmerising. When Ron filled his lungs and put the trumpet to his lips, the air around him seemed to move in line with his intent. And his music was golden.

Norman hesitated, listening to Ron's lilting voice. Before he realised it, the class had taken its collective breath and pursed its collective lips. The headmaster held his breath, knowing that what he was about to hear would give him a moment of pure delight. It was his chance to become a carefree schoolboy once again and delight in rude sounds and the raw slapstick of life.

It came in dribs and drabs and splutters. The trombones released a wavering flatulence of indeterminate pitch. Irregular bubbles of sound seemed to dribble out of the instruments and roll along the floor. Norman released a guffaw and put his hand over his grinning mouth. Euphoniums strained and pushed, trying vainly to take hold of slippery harmonics. Skittish trumpets reared like elephants, overstretching themselves and stopping dead as if their notes were cut short by a meat cleaver. He heard Ron call out over the din. 'AND AGAIN!' Norman chuckled, enjoying the raucous dissonance: the blubber of chthonic sound. In a day filled with tedium and diplomacy it was a simple, welcome joy: the release of so much pent-up wind. The hilarity of it overwhelmed him and he gave way to a rolling belly laugh.

He pulled a monogrammed handkerchief from his trouser pocket and wiped his eyes. An extraneous thought about his wayward niece, who had given him the handkerchief as a Christmas present, passed like a cloud. He quickly folded it and placed it back in his pocket. Straightening up, he pulled his waistcoat over his burgeoning paunch with both hands. All mirth expelled, he was ready to enter the classroom.

Suddenly he hesitated and his face lost its prepared countenance. His eyebrows shot up of their own accord and he bent his ear to the door. Amid all the cacophony – the unruly instruments, the laughs and chatter of the children – sailing free above the noise he heard a single, pure note with a life of its own. At first he thought it was Ron, but then he heard Ron's voice while the note was being played. Forgetting to knock, he barged into the room.

'Ron!' he exclaimed.

'Ooh aye, sir. And it's his first time!' replied Ron. The class had automatically risen. The headmaster glanced towards the children.

'Class be seated,' he said distractedly. 'Stand up the boy who played that note.' The statement made no sense but the class knew what he meant.

'Up now, Scotty,' said Ron in a slow, kindly voice.

Scotty reluctantly got to his feet. In all his school years he had never been asked to stand without expecting some form of humiliation to follow. His shoulders drooped and he looked at the floor. He held the trumpet as if he'd stolen it.

'Hold your head up, lad,' said Ron.

'Scotty, is it?' asked the headmaster.

'Yes, sir,' said Scotty.

'And your surname, Scotty?'

'Donohue, sir. Scott Donohue.' Scotty made an attempt to lift his head and look at the headmaster, but his eyes brushed past and rested on Mr Jolliffe, then fell back to the floor. His gaze had no grip on adults. He didn't want to see the look in their eyes: the anger, frustration, the disappointment and sometimes the intimidation. He remembered the Basher Barwick days and felt fear crawling on his skin. His stomach knotted and his throat grew hollow and dry.

'Well done, Scott!' exclaimed Norman. He said it with his whole body facing the boy. 'Well done! I thought I was listening to Mr Jolliffe when I heard that note. That was a very well-played note! I congratulate you! And you've never played the trumpet before?'

'No, sir. Never!' Scotty replied as if he had been accused of stealing sweets.

'Mr Jolliffe, I think we have a musician on our hands!'

'Right, sir. No doubt 'bout that, sir. He's a natural.'

'And the rest of you are doing extremely well.' Norman

was anxious not to show any favouritism. 'Thank you, Ron. Well done, Scott. Well done, class. Carry on, Mr Jolliffe.'

The men nodded to each other: generals on the field of battle. Ron hitched his trousers up and Norman pulled his waistcoat down: fighting the good fight and winning, by Jove! Galvanised by enthusiasm, Norman left in a cloud of elation. The beautiful sound of Scott Donohue's first note was something that he would hold in his mind long after the boy left school. He must look up his record and see what he was like academically.

———

Scotty kept his eyes on his feet. 'You can sit down, lad,' said Mr Jolliffe. 'You've impressed the headmaster and that's something to live up to.' Scotty suddenly felt afraid. What if he couldn't live up to expectations? What if he was just a one-note wonder? He'd never been able to do something other people couldn't do. A smile that had been shyly hovering on his lips suddenly flew away. Ron Jolliffe sensed the panic. 'You'll be right, lad.' He raised his voice to address the whole class. 'All of you will get the hang of it. Some get it quicker than others and that's alright. You've all made a good start, but now it's time to pack up.'

Ray Brown, who was sitting next to Scotty, formed a fist and punched him hard on the bicep. 'Yeah, go Scotty! You're a champ!' Bruce Fazakerley hit him on the head with a tutor book.

'You're a wonder, Donohue!' he said as he collected the other books strewn around the room.

'The beautiful note! The beautiful note!' chanted Andrew Wallace and he slid the slide of his trombone out as far as it would go in order to hit Scotty on the bum. The children clambered over seats to pat him on the back or ruffle his hair, punch him on the arm and accuse him of being 'a suck'. Still doubting his success, Scotty put the trumpet to his lips and let his breath squeeze out of his vibrating lips. It was there. It was still there. Crystal clear and beautiful. He felt the roundness of it: its golden timbre. It was like a magic shield: a huge bubble of sound that enveloped him and was him, that rose from his heart and lungs and pulled his very being out of dark hidden places. He felt light-headed and dopey.

For the first time in his life Scott Donohue experienced success in the classroom. It felt good and unbelievable and scary all at the same time.

Chapter 13

SUNDAY. A CREAM-COLOURED FORD FALCON swung through the gate onto the lawn. Marion flung her apron onto the draining board. 'Why can't people use the driveway? That's what it's for!'

'Marion,' said Malcolm. 'That's the mayor. And that's his new car. The Falcon XR! That's Cliff Bumford!'

'I know who it is! I'm just saying... there's a perfectly good driveway to park in and people insist on parking on the lawn. I'm going to put up a sign. Or a fence.'

'You'll do no such thing. He's the mayor, he's my boss and he can park in the kitchen if he wants to.' Malcolm opened the front door and hesitated.

'What's her name again? The girl? What is it... Veronica?... Vera?'

'Malcolm, you're hopeless! Her name is Vicky!'

'Vicky! Vicky! I've got it. Where's Louise?'

'In her room.' Marion straightened her shoulders and flounced her hair, giving it a bit of body. There wasn't time to put on lipstick. Her new halter-neck dress was the latest fashion. It drew attention to the shoulders and collarbones.

'Louise!' Malcolm yelled down the hall. 'Vicky's here!'

'Dad's learnt a na-ame.' Robert swung half his body around the doorway into Louise's room. 'And the name is...' He swung back the other way and poked his buttocks in the doorway. 'Bummmmford!'

Louise rolled her eyes. 'Well at least looking after Vicky for the day will get me away from you!'

It had been Malcolm's idea to invite Vicky. 'Make her feel welcome and help her settle in,' he'd told Louise. 'She's had a hard time and will appreciate making new friends.' He made it sound as if Vicky was a poor put-upon waif who had suffered things far beyond what could be expected of an eleven-year-old girl. In reality she was a surly, belligerent bully who had been moved from the Catholic school for bad behaviour and had no qualms in using her father's position as a bargaining point in relations with other children or with teachers. 'My father's gunna get youse!' had been her catchcry for most of her school days. She was an expert at Chinese burns, and her weight gave her an advantage in any physical situation where she might be required to sit on someone, or pin them to a fence.

Louise pulled herself off the floor and went into the kitchen.

'Good girl,' said Malcolm in a rush of enthusiasm. 'You two stay here and I'll go and greet them... make them feel welcome. Have you got the pikelets ready, Marion? Has the kettle boiled? Have you got all that under control, Marion? Where's Robert?'

'Malcolm, just go!' Marion, too, was excited.

———

Malcolm had planned the whole campaign. He'd usher Mr Bumford into the living room, past the frosted glass doors. Marion would enter after a discreet time, with the tea tray and pikelets – she was very good at pikelets. Then she'd disappear and leave the men to discuss political issues at work or whatever Mr Bumford (Cliff as he might be called after this visit) wished to discuss. Robert could make a quick and polite entry and talk about cricket or football and then go. Louise would take the girl – Vicky – under her wing and they would go off together and enjoy the day doing whatever it was that girls did. It was all planned. Marion had prepared a picnic basket, and the girls could go for a walk. Rafferty's Falls was not very far away, and it was a fine, hot day. They could picnic by the falls and be back in the afternoon. Mr Bumford (Cliff) would pick up... Valma?... sometime after three o'clock. Yes, it was all planned. And having presented himself as a trustworthy, family man, Malcolm would be in good position when the office of Senior Clerk became available in the Council Chambers.

Malcolm strode across the lawn with his right arm extended. 'Mr Bumford, sir!' Cliff Bumford gave the proffered hand a limp, perfunctory shake.

'What do ya reckon, Mal!' He ran his hand along the sleek line of the bonnet. 'She's trim, taut and terrific! Just like they say in the ad. Great suspension. I took 'er up the top of Gunner's Road. Rough as guts up there. No problems at all. Smooth as glass all the way. Ya know I had to go right up to North Hobart to get 'er! Nearly to Moonah! By jingo she's worth it, though. Not another one in the valley.' He grinned and nudged Malcolm with an elbow. 'I won't let the Missus near it. She can't drive for nuts. She'd ruin the gearbox. Always crunching the gears. She can't stay on one side on the road either. Always in the middle. Women can't drive. Stands to reason. They don't understand logic.' Cliff paused to breathe. 'Come on girl! You gettin' out or what? Come on ya tub of lard! Trim, taut and terrific she ain't, Mal.'

He thumped his hand on the bonnet. 'Vicky! Move yerself!'

The front passenger door opened, and Vicky slowly emerged. She was not what Malcolm had imagined. Her face was a tight ball of obstinacy. Her eyes narrowed at her father. She held a pink handbag looped over her forearm as she pulled her dress free from clenching buttocks. Malcolm eyed her with quiet disdain. *Gawd struth! She's only eleven and she's dressed like a tart! Not even wearing proper shoes. How's she going to walk through the bush in those sandals?*

Louise skipped across the lawn and rounded the Falcon. 'Hello,' she said and smiled at Vicky. Vicky looked up and down at Louise's dirty white sandshoes, white socks, dark blue Bermuda shorts and white blouse.

'You had that blouse on for sport on Thursday,' she said. Louise lifted her arm and stuck her nose in her armpit.

'Yes I did!' She took a good whiff. 'Ah! It brings back memories!'

'You're sick!'

'Wait till you meet my brother,' said Louise.

———

Cliff and Malcolm headed for the house, heads bowed in seriousness, hands in pockets.

'I'm very pleased to meet you, Mrs Johnstone,' Cliff said with practised formality.

Marion nodded and smiled. 'How do you do, Mr Bumford? Would you like a cup of tea?'

'Er... yes... that would be lovely.' More of a beer-in-the-garage man, Cliff, but he rallied at the sight of Mrs Johnstone and her bare arms. Unfortunately, the dress was a halter-neck with no cleavage anyone could discern.

Going to plan, going to plan, thought Malcolm. *Here we go . . . The frosted double doors . . . the comfy armchair . . . my comfy chair . . . He's going to sit in my chair! . . . I hadn't thought of that . . .* Cliff seated himself heavily. *He can have my chair. Of course he can have my chair!* Malcolm felt a frisson of discomfort as he sat down in Marion's chair. It was strange. He'd never sat in Marion's chair before. It felt so hard and low.

Cliff moulded himself into Malcolm's chair as if he did it every night. 'It's a nice place you got here, Mal,' he said. 'Nice and open. Not too near the mountains. Kiddies like it do they? Settling in alright?'

'They love it,' replied Malcolm, feeling that the time when they were newcomers was long gone. 'I loved coming down here as a boy, staying with my Uncle Ron.' He added his claim to local roots. 'And my grandfather lived here all his life.'

'Yes, it was different in them days,' said Cliff. 'I'm not saying it's any better or worse now. Just different. Well, ya can get around more easily. Look at that Falcon of mine. I mean, she's a V8, she goes like a bomb on the straight. Stayed in top all the way up the mountain road. Cuts twenty minutes off the trip to the big smoke.

'Roads! Roads is me priority this term, Mal. We've got to have good roads. Then we'll have progress. Ya can't stop progress. More roads and good roads, not to mention the bloody bridges. Do you know that there are fifty-four bridges in this municipality? Fifty-bloody-four! They suck up money like a vacuum cleaner.'

Marion came in with the tea tray. She placed it carefully on the coffee table. Cliff casually gazed at Marion's legs as she bent forwards.

After serving the tea, Marion returned to the kitchen to

get the pikelets. She'd spread some with butter and apricot jam and left some plain, simply buttered: he might be on a diet of some sort. She arranged them carefully on the oval sandwich plate with the raised edge and the pretty autumn leaf pattern. Once she'd delivered them to the living room, she smiled and excused herself.

'You've done well there, Mal,' Cliff said, cocking his head towards the door. 'Ya won't find many women in the valley worth lookin' at after they've had a few kiddies.' Malcolm bit into a pikelet. 'She's got a spark in 'er. Your missus. You can tell. And that's a good thing, Mal. A woman with a bit of spark.' Just how much spark, Malcolm hoped would remain unsaid.

Cliff shifted his weight and leant forward. 'Oh, I'm a happily married man, Mal. Don't get me wrong. Beryl's a wonderful woman. She's a good breeder and she's worth a bob or two. Her father owned four sawmills between Geeveston and the Arve. Only had girls the poor bugger. But Beryl's worn out! Seven kids. Vicky's the last of them.' He picked up a pikelet, rolled it into a ball and placed it whole in his mouth. A dribble of jam stuck to his cheek. He washed the pikelet down with a slurp of tea and wiped his face with the back of his hand. 'You got other kiddies haven't ya Mal? Apart from ... Lorraine?'

'Louise,' Malcolm quickly corrected. 'Yes,' he went on in a hurry. 'Robert's around here somewhere. Robert's the family clown,' he said, giving what he thought was a jovial laugh – hoping to cover all bases, pending Robert's eventual appearance.

―――

Marion looked down the hall from the kitchen as Robert sauntered up the passage towards the living room. 'Just a minute!' she said. 'Robert, let me have a look at you.'

'Mum!' Robert groaned.

'Why are you wearing those ridiculous shorts? And why the football jumper? It's the middle of summer. You don't need to have that jumper on. Turn around.'

'Mum! I'm just going to say hello and then go. Alright?'

'Turn around!' Marion was not to be conned.

'Mum!'

Marion pulled him by the shoulders and spun him round.

'What in heaven's name do you think you're doing?' The shorts were stretched tight at the front and the back was bulging obscenely. 'Robert, how dare you!' She plunged her hand down the backside of the shorts and pulled out a fluffy teddy-bear and a hot water bottle. 'Wait till your father hears about this!'

'Mum, it was just a joke!'

'Yes, and a ridiculous joke at that! Do you think your father would think it funny?'

'No. He wouldn't even get it. He probably wouldn't even notice.'

Marion fixed him with a stare that would hypnotise a rhinoceros. 'Just go in there, say hello and be polite. Answer questions correctly. Take one pikelet and then go. Is that understood?'

'Yes, Mum.'

Robert dragged himself to the frosted glass windows and looked back at Marion with a look of utter abandonment. Tight-lipped and scowling, she dismissed him with a wave of her hand. 'Go on!' she mouthed. Robert turned and faced the doors. He straightened his shoulders and made his face as blank as he could.

Knocking with what he hoped was military precision, Robert quickly opened the door and stood to attention. 'I've come to say hello, answer questions correctly, be polite, eat one pikelet and then go.'

'Ah! There you go. What did I tell you! He's a clown alright!' Malcolm produced an artificial laugh and slapped his thigh for good measure.

'Robert, come and shake hands with Mr Bumford.'

'Before or after I have the pikelet?'

'Robert!' There was an edge to Malcolm's voice.

'Yes, I'll do the hand thing first.'

'G'day Rob,' said the mayor with a generous smile on his face. He leant forward and extended his hand. Robert thought of taking it and kissing it, but the look in Malcolm's eye told him that enough was enough. 'Yer better have yerself a pikelet, Rob, before I eat 'em all.'

'Thank you, sir,' he replied and immediately commenced some military-style chewing.

'Robert's in the cricket team.' Malcolm made an attempt to keep it plain and simple.

'You a batter or a bowler, Rob?' asked Cliff.

'I'm better at bowling.' Robert played it with a straight bat.

'I was a bowler. Couldn't do it now. Me shoulder's too crook. What about you, Mal?'

'Yes,' said Malcolm with a little cough. 'I played first grade for Hobart before I joined the navy.'

'Well there ya go! You've got yer coach here at home, Rob. Makes a lot of difference if yer father's got some interest in it.'

'Yes, sir!' replied Robert, focusing his eyes on the middle distance.

Cliff laughed. 'Don't ever let go of yer spark, lad. You hang onto that spark of yours!'

Robert looked at him for the first time.

'Go on, Robert. Out of here. Go and do something useful,' said Malcolm.

'Yes, Dad,' replied Robert: the automaton.

Robert gave Cliff a broad grin and pinched another pikelet. 'Bye then.' He turned and made it out of there.

'The spark, Mal,' said Cliff, laughing. 'He's got the spark!'

———

Louise picked up the picnic basket and felt its weight. 'It's too big and clumsy.' There seemed to be a lot of food.

'I think it's very pretty,' said Vicky.

'I want my hands free. You need to use both hands when you're climbing up to the top of the falls.'

'You won't be going that far. The bottom of the waterfall is quite far enough,' said Marion.

She'd taken a lot of care in packing the basket. She imagined the gingham tablecloth that she'd folded neatly on top, being spread out on a shaded boulder beneath a large tree.

'I'll put everything in Robert's knapsack,' Louise said, and ran off to find it.

'I've never been on a picnic,' said Vicky. 'Not one that you had to walk to. I thought it would be like... going in a car somewhere.'

'It's not very far. Don't you like walking?'

'Not much.'

'You might like to wear Louise's gumboots instead of those lovely sandals.'

'Oh, no!' cried Vicky. 'I'm not leaving them here!'

Marion was slightly shocked. She hoped Louise would never be so rude in someone else's home!

Louise came back with the knapsack. 'It'll all fit in here,' she said and proceeded to unpack everything and repack it in the knapsack. Marion pursed her lips at this, but made no move to stop her. 'It's probably better in the knapsack,' she said. 'It'll leave your arms free. Don't forget the tablecloth.'

'I'll check on the men,' she said. 'See if they need any more tea.'

———

Louise wound her arms into the shoulder straps of the knapsack and hefted it onto her back. The weight of it pulled her blouse tight, accentuating her small breasts. Vicky clung to her handbag and puffed out her chest to show her own.

'Are you ready?' said Louise.

'I want to go to the bathroom first,' replied Vicky. Louise led her down the hall and showed her the bathroom and toilet and then returned to the kitchen.

Vicky placed her handbag on the sink and took out a lipstick. She made her mouth into a wide 'o' and generously applied it. She felt a rush of delight. Now, her pink lips matched her new sandals. Her new sandals! The beautiful soft, pink leather straps stretched out from a large white and yellow flower. The thin delicate straps encased little bulges of puffy flesh. Her toenails shone with the lustre of matching pink varnish. Nothing could take away from her the pleasure of the new sandals and handbag. None of her father's badgering or insults, none of his aspersions and derogatory comments could dent her feelings of fulfilment at having new things. Especially new things that no-one else would have. This 'Louise' person, who sat up the front of her new class, would not have sandals bought for her at White's in Hobart. And the 'Louise' person certainly wouldn't have a handbag, at least not a grown-up's handbag.

'You took your time,' said Louise. 'Are you feeling alright?'

'I'm fine.' Vicky lifted her nose into the air and clutched the handbag to her side. 'Are we going then?' she asked.

'You've got pink lipstick on. You've missed a bit.'

Vicky pushed her lips together and rubbed them backwards and forwards.

'Does that look better?'

'Yes, only you've got a bit up near your nose.' Louise produced a hankie and wrapped it round her index finger. 'Stay still,' she commanded. Vicky froze with her face and lips protruding out towards Louise. Louise gently wiped the offending smear off her face and folded the hankie. 'There,' she said. 'It's a nice colour. Mum's got one like that. Come and I'll show you.'

They entered the quiet of the master bedroom. Louise picked up a silver-coloured lipstick from the vanity table. 'Mum hardly ever uses this one.' She quickly took the cap off and rolled the stick forward. Bending close to the mirror she applied a liberal slash of colour. They both stood there gazing in the mirror, comparing the different size and shape of their lips.

'Won't we get into trouble?' asked Vicky.

'Not if we move quick enough,' replied Louise. 'Come on. Let's get out of here!'

Moving quietly out the back door Louise saw her mother's sunglasses on the windowsill. 'Mu-um! Can I borrow your sunglasses?'

'Yes, dear,' came the reply from the living room. 'Don't lose them.'

'We're off now.' She let the screen door flop into place. They rounded the side of the house and headed for the dusty road.

Chapter 14

I<small>T WAS A GLORIOUSLY HOT</small> day. Wattle seedpods were beginning to open with a sudden *klak*. Crickets sung in unison in the long grass. Willy-wagtails fluttered from one fence post to another, leading the girls forward along the road. The river winked between the trees.

As they came to the Saltmarsh shack they could hear chaotic sounds of the children playing. The long grass below the verge started shaking. A peacock feather popped up, its eye focused on the girls.

'This is the home of the evil Sally Saltmarsh. None shall pass this way!' The peacock feather gave a shimmer.

'Aw come on, Sal, I know it's you,' Vicky said in a flat voice.

'How do you know its Sally's place?' asked Louise.

'She's my cousin... sort of.'

'A second cousin twice removed on my father's side,' said the vibrating peacock feather in a deep monotone.

'I never knew that,' said Louise.

'Why should you know it?' said Vicky.

Sally popped her head up. 'What's going on with you two? Oh my God!' she cried in mock horror. 'Your lips have been eaten away! How did that happen to you poor darling girls?'

Vicky and Louise pouted in high fashion mode. 'Come here and I'll do yours,' Vicky offered. She opened her handbag with a practised click.

'Come here,' she commanded. Sally scrambled up the bank,

eager to see how this was going to play out. The lipstick lurched from side to side as Vicky smeared it onto Sally's lips. 'That looks great,' she declared. She felt triumphant, having introduced a bit of style to the otherwise boring country bumpkins of Golden Valley. 'Now imagine we're in Hobart,' she said and strode along the dusty road with her nose in the air. Sally and Louise fell in behind her, mimicking her stride.

After a while Sally stopped. 'It feels awful and smells disgusting!'

'What does?' Vicky turned around and gave Sally a challenging stare.

'The lipstick. It's disgusting!'

'You have to learn to wear it,' Vicky stated. 'That is, if you ever want a boyfriend. It's only 'cause you can't see yourself. You've got to know what you look like. How boys'll see you.'

Louise knew how Sally felt. Her mother's lipstick had an overpowering smell. Sweet and sickly. Vicky's was the same.

'It's so smelly!' said Sally. The lipstick had curtained the sensations of the outside world. She couldn't feel the soft warm air or smell the dusty bush. Her nostrils were filled with the chemical, saccharine smell. 'Yuck!' she declared. 'I'm getting rid of it!' and she wiped it off on the inside of her dress.

'Well it's your loss,' Vicky replied. 'If you want to stay a kid forever, that's what'll happen to you and all the good boys'll be taken.'

Sally giggled and looked at Lou. A conspiratorial grin flashed across her face.

'Do you want to come with us?' Louise asked Sally.

'Where're you going?'

'Just up to the falls. Mum's packed a picnic.'

'Yeah, that'd be great!' Sally shook the peacock feather, tickling Louise under the chin. Lou jumped out of the way, laughing. 'I'll just go and tell Alice where I'll be.' And she raced off to the shack.

Vicky turned on Louise. 'What did ya go and do that for?' Her face became a tight ball of muscle and her neck disappeared.

'Do what?'

'Ask her to come with us!'

'What difference does it make?'

'She's such a kid. She doesn't belong with us.' Vicky hooped the handbag over her arm and clasped it to her side again.

'I thought you were cousins. Don't you like her?' Louise looked at Vicky's inflating shoulders.

'Like her!' she exclaimed. 'Like her! Do you know how poor they are!' Vicky spat the words out as if they were the only answer to a stupid question. 'What if someone sees us with her!'

Louise was nonplussed. On the one hand, she wanted to make the picnic fun and amusing and enjoyable by having Sally along. On the other hand, she didn't want Vicky to have an unpleasant time. It would reflect badly on her and eventually get back to her father. Vicky could also attempt to make her into a social pariah. But Louise wasn't one of the 'in' crowd at school so she hardly thought that it mattered.

Louise imagined her father's displeasure if the outing didn't go well. All his affection seemed to be directed to Robert these days. He would sidestep her in the hall, keeping his eyes on the wall or the floor. He'd greet Robert with a ruffle of his hair or a poke in the ribs. For her, he offered a nod and a quick smile and then it was back to Robert. When he talked to her in was often an instruction: do this, do that. There was no conversation. The need for his ever-diminishing approval and affection weighed heavily on her. This was a chance she had to make him see her in a different light.

'She'll be alright,' she said.

Sally came bounding back from the house wearing a pirate's hat. 'OK, me hearties! Let's venture forth!'

Vicky gave a sneer and looked at Louise. 'What did I tell ya?' Louise smiled with little sincerity. She thought of deliberately wiping the lipstick off her face as a sign of her true allegiance. But she thought better of it and gave herself into the day.

Come what may, the sun was shining and the day was young. The road felt soft and dusty. She hoped Vicky's sandals wouldn't get ruined on the track.

'Allow me to be your guide,' said Sally. She took the peacock feather from where she'd stowed it in her sock and held it aloft. Walking ahead of the other two she strode in the middle of the road and then turned to face them. 'You are strangers in a foreign land.' She used her heavy monotone voice. 'You will need guidance and help.' She waved the peacock feather around while walking backwards. 'And it is I, and only I, that can save you from the head-hunting Apache. For I am Minnie! Minnie-Ha-Ha. HA! HA! HA! HA! HA!'

Vicky rolled her eyes. 'Are you ever gunna grow up?'

'I hope not,' replied Sally.

'We're nearly at the track,' said Louise. 'Just past these two houses.'

'Where?' demanded Vicky.

'Just through here, across this paddock.'

'There's a fence. You didn't say nothing about no fence!' Vicky looked belligerently at Louise.

'Well, there's this fence.' She indicated the roadside fence. 'Then there's another one on the other side of the paddock, and then there's no more fences.'

'No more fences,' Sally echoed. Louise tried not to look at Sally.

'Look,' said Louise. 'I'll show you how it's done.'

'I know how to get over a flaming fence!' Vicky was indignant. With bovine strength she pushed the top run of barbed wire down and thrust her right leg over it. Suddenly she was screaming. Her hands cleaved to the barbed wire fence and her handbag dangled down. Her legs were rigid.

'Where is it?' asked Sally, presuming it was a snake. 'Just stay still and don't move.'

'It's not a bloody snake!' yelled Vicky.

'Have you caught yourself?' Louise was trying to be helpful. She imagined the top of Vicky's leg being scratched by the barbed wire.

'No I haven't, stupid! Just lift it up! Move it! It's gunna get scratched! Me bag, you idiots! Move me handbag.'

The handbag hung from her wrist, nonchalantly swinging against the second and third runs of the barbed wire fence. In her panic, Vicky couldn't think how to alleviate the situation: which hand to move to release the bag and save it from being scratched. And she couldn't release both hands and allow the wire to spring up and lodge in her crotch. The grand fantasy she had, of parading down Liverpool Street in Hobart with the handbag clasped to her side in its pristine glory, was being ruined. If the pink leather was scratched, that would be the end. The fantasy would die and those two idiot girls were to blame. Her elder brothers had ensured she had a working vocabulary for such situations.

'You stupid bloody idiots! Hold my bag. Get it off the friggn fence. Have you got shit for brains or what!'

Louise felt indignant and wanted to cry. Sally just felt like hitting Vicky. She laughed instead.

'So, it's your stupid friggn bag that's got caught on the friggn, damn, bloody, Jesus, crikey, useless, flamin' fence!' Sally lifted the bag with both hands, away from the barbed wire. 'Now move ya leg ya great tortoise!' Vicky recognised an equal and slowly and silently lumbered to the other side of the fence, with Sally still holding the handbag as if it were an offering at a ceremony. 'There,' she said in a mothering tone. 'Now what was all that fuss about?'

'Youse wouldn't understand.' Vicky sniffed. She was close to tears.

'Now come along,' admonished Sally. 'Let's get the party moving!'

Louise looked admiringly at Sally. How did she manage to handle Vicky so well? Louise could never be so quick and hard. Mrs Burton at school always called her 'kind Louise' and 'clever Louise'; but kind and clever was no defence against bullies like Vicky. They'd leap into the gap while she was still considering, and hurl abuse at her. Thank God she had a guide like Sally, who saw the fun in every situation.

Sally held the fence down for Louise, and then Louise did the same for Sally. 'There!' she said. 'Now we've managed one fence, let's have a race to the second one. Follow me, me hearties!' She cocked her hat at Louise and went racing across the paddock. Halfway there, she feigned a fall and disappeared into the long grass.

'You can go if you want,' sniffed Vicky.

'No, I'll walk with you,' replied Louise, to make amends. It was all her fault. 'We don't have to hurry. We can take our time.'

'If you were gunna bring her you should have said.' A dog with a bone.

'It'll be alright,' said Louise. 'She's just not as mature as you.' She felt the insidious betrayal sticking to her like the clag glue from school.

Vicky brightened. 'You're not wrong there,' she replied. Louise felt the payoff and loathed herself. The peacock feather shot out of the middle of the paddock as they trudged towards it.

The shimmering eye spoke to them. 'And so I spy the Pink Princess and her ne'er-do-well slave Louisa the Sprod. Up to no good are we?'

'What do you mean 'sprod'?' said Louise, laughing with the salvation of the lightening mood. 'Where did you get a word like that?'

'You're just so stupid!' Vicky said.

'A Sprod is a sprout that is odd. Therefore, a Sprod!'

'You're a real dead-flog, Sally,' said Vicky.

'Sprods can be very handy when you're in a throcket,' replied Sally in a lighthearted, sing-songy voice. Louise was holding her sides with laughter. 'And if you find your-self in a throcket without your Sprod, you are bloody-well frobbled!' Sally leapt up and started dancing her way to the other side of the paddock.

'Wait for us, my feathered friend!' cried Louise. 'If I'm

Louisa the Sprod, you are Sally the Feathered Wauhoo!'

'That's a fish!' said Sally.

'Well you are a fine feathered fish!'

'Am I a dish of a fish?'

'You certainly are, if you wish!'

'Youse two are really stupid,' the Pink Princess insisted.

'Why thank you, cousin. You say the nicest things!' Sally shimmered the feather at Vicky.

The Feathered Wauhoo took off at a sprint to the fence on the far side of the paddock. The Sprod followed at a gallop and the Pink Princess waddled after them.

No mishaps occurred at the second fence. The Pink Princess allowed the Sprod to delicately and reverently hold the handbag (now known as the Pink Object of Devotion) while the fence was being stretched and trodden on. They made their way up a gentle incline as the grasslands gave way to scrubby bush.

'It's quite nice here,' said the Pink Princess.

'There's no time to stop!' replied the Feathered Wauhoo.

'Let's just get to the top of the hill and have a rest,' the Sprod offered as a compromise. She said it in such a way that it sounded final. A decision. A sign of leadership. No-one disagreed. Louise had indeed found a grain of assertiveness.

They rested at the top of the hill and Louise opened the cordial bottle. Although Vicky sneered at what she described as kids' cordial, she nevertheless drank more than half of it, reasoning that Sally wasn't supposed to be at this so-called picnic, therefore she wasn't entitled to have any of it. But nothing could dampen the Feathered Wauhoo's spirits. 'I only drink the crystal waters of the sacred pool,' she said when offered the cordial. 'Keep your tainted beverage. I will not let it pass my lips!' And in a haughty huff, she stood to go.

'Suit yerself,' said Vicky and took a few more glugs. When Louise had re-packed the knapsack, they turned their backs on the dry grasslands and entered the magical rainforest.

———

The weather seemed to change immediately. It became cooler, the foliage greener and thicker. The native laurels spread their thick, shiny leaves out among the understorey of tree-ferns and dogwood. Tiny orchids lined the path. Fallen logs of giant eucalyptus barred their way. They had to scramble over the top or roll underneath on the soft moss. Straggly leatherwood and sassafras made the forest look chaotic and wild. Everything in the forest, whether it was a dead branch or the trunk of a tree, had some new growth attached to it: filigrees of pale lichen, bright green lace-patterned mosses, tiny croziers of ferns angled out of crevasses, strings of pearled raindrops barring the way to kingdoms of fungi.

As the valley grew darker the vegetation towered above their heads. Tree-ferns stretched their fronds into the sky. The girls could only see the trunks of the gums, their tops disappearing far above them. The sky was a thin patch of pale light high in the trees. The quiet, still air, moistened with the damp spores of moss, took away their chattering selves. They were explorers venturing into unknown territory, alone in a primordial forest, open to any surprises.

Even Vicky was feeling the magic. 'Look!' the Pink Princess exclaimed at the leatherwood flowers. 'Look at all the petals on the track. It's like confetti at a wedding!' Their footsteps became slower and more deliberate as they moved among the delicate white petals.

Sally had an eye for the tiny fungi: miniscule blue dots rising on long stalks like pairs of eyes amongst the leaf mould, or frilled layers of soft brown circling a tree. 'Look there! That's our wedding cake!' she said pointing to the ruffles spilling out of a crack in the bark of a fallen log.

'And there's our veil,' said Louise, stopping suddenly. From one side of the track to the other, a massive spider's web shimmered with drops of moisture.

'I'm not gunna wear that!' said Vicky. Louise and Sally stood mesmerised by its beauty. Its threads were taut at the top, sagging into loops at the bottom where moisture gathered. 'Let me through!' said the Pink Princess, armed with a long stick. She took three great strokes and the web, a fairy's veil of air and gossamer, a testament to the engineering genius of the patient spider, was reduced to a grey, sticky coil around the stick. Satisfied, Vicky threw the stick into the undergrowth. 'There!' she said and took the lead, proud of her practicality.

After some time, they could hear the tinkle of running water. A creek appeared on the lower side of the track. The rush of water became louder. Sally left the track and made her way through the tree-ferns. She slithered across a low boulder and scooped up the water in her hands. It was cold and refreshing. Taking off the pirate's hat she filled it with water. 'The crystal waters! At long last!' she exclaimed. She stood up with feet apart. 'I am now blessed with immortality!' she cried and emptied the hat over her head. She laughed and did a little dance as the water trickled down her body. 'Come, Princess and Sprod,' she commanded. 'Come and be blessed by its purity!'

Vicky gave Louise a severe look. Her eyes narrowed. 'Yer lipstick'll come off if you get water on it,' she warned. Louise thought it best to side with Vicky.

'My immortality can wait till we get to the top,' she replied.

'Fair enough,' replied the Feathered Wauhoo. 'We're nearly there.'

Although Marion had told them not to go to the top of the falls, there was no discussion about violating the prohibition. It was a natural thing to do. They clambered up the steep incline to spreading flat rocks where the creek broadened out before spilling over the edge. The sun hit them with a jolt as they came out from under the tall trees, and it took a moment to adjust to the harsh light. The deafening rush of water heard at the base of the waterfall was now only background noise.

In no time they had lunch spread out on a large dry rock. Vicky, taking the role of leader after the victory over the spider's web, helped unwrap the sandwiches. Seeing that there were three packets, she kindly offered one to Sally. She pulled her pile of sandwiches close to her body. 'Dad always says food tastes better outdoors,' she said as her cheeks bulged. Louise and Sally took a contrary attitude and ate like mice, nibbling at the edges of their sandwiches and taking an inordinate time to finish.

When all the sandwiches were gone, they started on the biscuits. Sally stood up with one of the biscuits in her mouth and lifted her dress over her head. She spread it out on the boulder to dry. Underneath her dress she was wearing shorts and a threadbare singlet.

'Do you still wear a singlet?' asked Vicky with disdain.

Sally took a bite of the biscuit and then pulled the singlet off.

'Not anymore,' she said. And with that she lay down on the large warm boulder and gave herself to the sun.

Vicky's eyes slowly moved over Sally's body. 'Mum's getting me a bra,' she said.

'A bra?' exclaimed the Feathered Wauhoo. 'How disgusting!'

The Pink Princess was satiated with the food and the sun. She smiled a knowing smile. 'You'll never get a boyfriend, Sally, if you don't wear a bra,' she said. Unclasping the handbag, she took out a clean hanky and deftly wetted it. Then she removed her sandals and proceeded to clean off the mud that had built up on the soles. When they were clean, she turned them on their sides to dry. 'You'll need a bra when your bosoms grow.'

'I tried one on once,' said Sally. 'It was like being cut in half. I could hardly breathe!'

'You'll have to get used to it,' insisted the Pink Princess.

Louise felt she had something to add to the conversation: a shared intimacy. 'I've got the top of a bikini that was Mum's. Sometimes I wear that as a bra.'

'That's not a proper bra.' The Pink Princess sneered all the more for knowing the cost of the revelation. 'You need to be fitted. You need to go to Myer's and have a fitting done. That's what I'm gunna do.' She smoothed her dress close to her chest.

Sally propped herself up on her elbow. The sun was already reddening her skin. 'Are there any more biscuits?' she asked. Louise offered a handful of pikelets.

'Here,' she said. 'Fill up on these.' Sally took the pikelets and spread them out on the rock arranging them in order of size. Then she picked out the two most similar.

'There,' she said. 'Here's my bra.' And she lay back down on the rock and placed the pikelets on her breasts. 'At least I won't get sunburnt nipples!' Louise laughed and grabbed two more pikelets and placed them on Sally's eyes.

'Youse two are really dumb,' said the Pink Princess. But she nevertheless entered into the play and placed a pikelet on Sally's navel. Then she laughed. They all laughed. Pikelets were distributed and placed over various body parts. Sally held one between her legs and picked up a carrot stick. She pierced the pikelet with the carrot. 'I've always wanted to be a MAAAN!' she cried in mock hysteria. Louise took off her blouse and devised a bra using pikelets and a vine from a native clematis. It soon fell apart, causing more hilarity. Bits of broken pikelet were thrown over the waterfall where the black jays gathered. Even Vicky was laughing without constraint. She took the one remaining chocolate biscuit.

'Watch this,' she said. Lifting her dress she peeled off her pants in a slow, sexy movement, knees together and hips wagging. Then she arranged herself on the rock in a film star pose. 'I'll need the sunglasses.' She clicked her fingers at Louise. Louise looked through the knapsack and found them. She'd forgotten all about the glasses and now realised that they added a touch of sophistication. Vicky put them on. Stretching one arm behind her head, she pulled her dress slowly up to her waist and delicately placed the chocolate biscuit on her crotch, keeping her legs crossed at the ankles.

'Very sexy!' said Sally. 'But I'd be careful if I were you.'

Sally pursed her lips and held her pikelets in place. 'I think that biscuit is melting!'

Vick let out an exaggerated, raucous scream. The black jays lifted into the air. She gobbled up the biscuit. Seeing the chocolate smear on her crotch, she stood up holding out her dress. 'Aw, yuck!' she cried. Sally and Louise laughed all the louder. Vicky knotted her dress at the waist and lowered herself into the water. 'Ah! Gawd! It's so cold!' Sally placed her pikelets in the brim of her pirate's hat and jumped in beside the Pink Princess.

They laughed and laughed and squealed and giggled. On the warm boulders they'd felt the heat daze their senses – as if they too, were chocolate biscuits becoming warm, sweet liquid in the noonday sun. Now the cold caught their breath. 'Are you coming in, Sprod?' asked Sally.

'When I'm ready,' said Louise. She stood above them, looking down into the pool. Imitating the slow monotone voice of the Feathered Wauhoo, she crooned, 'Water babies! I will serenade you to sleep in your mystic pool.' She rolled down her shorts and kicked them off, and gently took the sunglasses off Vicky, aware that this could cause an upset. But Vicky was open to the play. Louise picked up the somewhat bedraggled peacock feather. As she started singing, she used it to beat time. Feeling safe behind the sunglasses, she rolled her index finger around the elastic leg of her underpants, lifting the back of the pants to expose one buttock. She changed hands and did the same on the other side. She drew the feather slowly up to her bare chest and circled her breasts. Then she let it drift down between her legs. Finally she lifted both hands above her head and looked skywards in a dramatic gesture that she thought resembled her grandfather's desk lamp: a naked nymph holding an eternal flame. She'd seen his dry, old hand caressing the lamp, his thumb lingering on the solid brass nipple. In a soft, light voice she sang:

'Deep in the forest, I know a fairy glade.
There in the cooling shade, peace doth dwell.
Softly a streamlet sings.
Peace to the heart it brings.
Clouds drift on silver wings
Far o'er the sky.'

As if on cue a fat, puffy cloud obscured the sun. They were silent and spellbound, feeling a moment of transcendent beauty: amazed at themselves. Louise felt absolute delight as the wild sun caught her blood, pulling it into a knot at the groin. In that moment of glimpsing an unknown world, of feeling the blood hijacked by the throbbing sun, she felt her life force as nothing but beautiful, extraordinary sensations. But the sharp feeling of shadowy cloud threw a pall over what had been too hilarious, too out of the ordinary. The shadow brought heaviness and doubt.

The bush was quiet... too quiet... A TWIG SNAPPED.

'Geronimo!' Ralph Schiller rushed forward out of the bush with a large rock held above his head. War cries filled the air with high-pitched hollering. 'Lezzos! Lezzos! Lezzos! You're a bunch of Lezzos!' the cry went out all around the girls. Ralph threw the rock into the pool, making a chaotic splash. The girls screamed.

'You bloody bastard!' yelled Vicky. 'I'm gunna get you! You little Kraut!'

Louise froze, her mouth gaping – no longer a sensuous desk lamp, but a near-naked girl caught in a vulnerable position with her pants stuck up her bum. At least the other two were in the water, their modesty protected. She abandoned the feather and quickly pulled her pants into a more orthodox position. She turned around to find her clothes. But it was too late. Raucous jeering and hysterical laughter filled the air as Ralph Schiller, Ronny Cracknel, Scott Donohue and Carl Saltmarsh slithered away behind the trees, the girls' clothes in their arms.

'Typical!' said Sally. 'That little rat of a brother of mine! Wait till I get hold of him!' She pulled herself out of the water and sat on the rock. Not yet realising that her clothes were missing, she looked around then stared blankly at Louise. 'Those bastards!' The audacity of the raid dawned on her.

'What are we going to do?' whined Louise. 'How are we going to get home like this?'

'At least we've got our pants,' said Sally, looking at Vicky.

'Those filthy mongrels will be made to suffer!' Vicky leapt out of the pool. She was all for chasing them down the track, pants or no pants, and started off in their direction but soon realised they were too far ahead.

The fat, puffy cloud decided to be on its way and allowed the sun to shine down on the scene of devastation. They sat in despairing silence for a minute or two. Then Sally lay back in the sun. 'Oh, for a pikelet or two to cover my nakedness!' she moaned. Frivolity was back. Despair disappeared and they laughed again as they made plans for revenge. Vicky listed all the dreadful things she could do to the boys. This included tying them up with barbed wire and cutting off their dicks, holding their heads under water till they were near dead, and putting them in a cage with an angry Rottweiler. Louise and Sally were glad she was on their side.

Sally emptied the picnic basket and found the gingham tablecloth. 'Here,' she said to Louise. 'You can wrap this around your chest. It'll hide your mosquito bites.'

Louise, although desperate to be clad, said 'No. You use it, Sally.'

'No,' said the Feathered Wauhoo. 'You have it. I insist!'

'We'll find something for me. You have this for now.'

'Sprod! I am absolutely certain that your need is greater than mine. Come here and I'll wrap it round you.'

Vicky looked up from buckling her sandals. 'Tear it in half,' she said. Louise thought of arriving home wearing half a tablecloth. She thought of the wicker basket her mother had packed, the time she'd taken with it, the neatly folded gingham cloth sitting on top.

'No,' she said. 'I can't do that.'

'Suit yerself.' Vicky couldn't see a problem. 'You might get into a bit of trouble. You'll git a belt or two, then they'll just forget. Or make it into a funny story. Mums and dads are always doing that. You think you've done the worst thing in the world and the next minute they're making a joke of it.'

Louise wasn't sure Marion would ever see the joke.

'Come on,' said Vicky. 'It's not as if it's our fault. Them's the ones that'll really get into trouble.'

Sally had wandered off into the bush, and came back with some stringy vines of native clematis and branches of laurel. The laurel leaves were thick and lush. 'I can cover up with these!' she said. 'I'll weave them together and tie them around with the vine.'

'Oh, that's great, Wauhoo. I'll do the same.' Louise was

full of enthusiasm for the idea. 'I really don't want to get the tablecloth dirty. We can wrap leaves all over our bodies and we'll look like aborigines!'

Sally and Vicky looked at her blankly. 'You'll need a few dead possums if you want to look like an aborigine,' said Vicky.

When they'd finished encasing themselves in leaves and vines, Sally picked off some of the remaining laurel flowers and arranged them in Louise's hair. 'And now I crown you Princess Louisa the Sprouting Sprod!' she declared and placed a final cluster of white flowers on Louise's auburn hair.

'Feathered Wauhoo,' said Louise. 'I accept this crown only if you too will become Princess of the Waterfall.' The laurel flowers didn't have as much holding power on Sally's straight brown hair, but the gesture was appreciated.

'What does that make me?' asked Vicky, feeling left out.

'That makes you the Pantless Pink Princess,' said Sally. It was so funny they daren't laugh. They heaped laurels on Vicky, taking them off their own heads, making the gesture abundant.

United in distress, they packed up the remains of the picnic. 'What are we gunna do with these?' Vicky said, holding up the carrot sticks and mandarins.

'Watch and learn,' responded Sally. She took two of the mandarins and placed them side by side. Then she picked out the longest of the carrot sticks and laid them in between the mandarins, forming a phallus. 'There ya go! That's a man's THING! What do you think, Sprod?'

Louise looked at the unlikely arrangement. 'I don't know,' she admitted. 'I've only ever seen Robert's and its nothing like that.'

'Cor… I've seen my brothers' lots of times. And I've seen my dad's through the keyhole in the bathroom door.' Vicky was quick to claim another first. 'And it's about that size too, or even bigger.'

'Hmm… I don't know,' mused Sally. 'I think it's too long.' And with that she picked up the carrot and bit the top off it.

'Aw! You're disgusting, Sally!' Vicky picked up a mandarin – 'These are too big anyway' – and she deftly peeled one of them.

What's it like, Princess?' asked Sally.

'Very juicy,' replied Vicky with her mouth full. The juice dribbled down her chin. Sally laughed.

Louise was getting anxious. 'Let's go,' she said.

'Hi ho! Hi ho!' Sally lifted the bedraggled peacock feather. 'Come on, me hearties!'

'Wait a minute,' said the Pantless Pink Princess. 'I haven't finished yet.' She quickly forced the remains of the mandarin into her mouth and bent over to pick up the handbag. As she did so she felt anew the dreadful vulnerability of a bare bottom. Bending at the knees, she kept a straight back and slowly lowered herself to the ground. With the handbag firmly in place they made their way down the path.

———

The track by the side of the falls was steep and wet. It was more difficult to get down than it had been to climb up. Louise abandoned her floral adornments. The laurels were falling out of place and scratching her skin. She kept the vines, figuring she would pick some more laurel leaves when the track evened out a bit.

Sally was feeling equally uncomfortable. 'Bugger it!' the

Feathered Wauhoo cried as she reached the flatter section of the path. 'I can't go on like this!' and she pulled the branches off and threw them away. 'And my shorts are sopping wet!' She opened the knapsack and took out the gingham table-cloth. 'I'm sorry Sprod but I think my need is greater!'

'That's quite alright,' said the Sprod.

Just as they had the tablecloth firmly in position, sarong style, Vicky yelled from further up the track. 'Louise! Louise! Here are your shorts!' They ran ahead to join Vicky. Hanging on a myrtle branch were Louise's shorts, just out of reach. After exhausting her vocabulary of expletives, Vicky lifted them free with a stick and handed them to Louise. 'There ya go!'

'Thanks, Vicky.' Louise was truly grateful and quickly pulled the shorts on. Vicky was elated to have been the one to spot them. She took the lead, using the stick to beat the foliage on either side of the track.

'What's that?' she said, pointing the stick at Sally's sad lit-tle singlet dangling from a tree-fern. They gathered round. Sally was feeling quite exotic in the tablecloth.

'It's pathetic, isn't it?' she said. Vicky and Louise answered together. Vicky said 'yes' and Louise said 'no.'

'Thanks chums,' said Sally. 'I suppose I should put it on.'

Louise had an inspiration. 'You don't have to,' she said. 'Keep the tablecloth on and I'll wear the singlet!'

'Ah! Brilliant Sprod! You don't mind?'

'No not at all. I'd rather wear your singlet than nothing at all.'

'Thanks, Sprod.'

'Not at all, Wauhoo. And well spotted, Pink Princess!' Louise was learning the value of inclusiveness.

Vicky beamed and continued in the lead.

Soon they came out from the cover of the forest. The wide, open sky and the grasslands made them feel less confident. Sally's tablecloth billowed out in the afternoon breeze. Her damp shorts felt cold and scratchy. Vicky felt the breeze in her nether regions. 'Ooh, that's nice,' she said. 'It tickles your bum.' Louise gathered some foliage from the last of the tree-ferns and laurels. To disguise the forlorn singlet, she arranged the branches so that they sprung out of her shorts up to her face at the front, and past her head at the back. She put on the sunglasses to add flair to her ensemble.

They made their way down the hill. 'Walk confidently,' Sally said, holding the sarong-tablecloth in place. 'No-one will notice anything if we look as if we've dressed like this on purpose. We'll say we're practising for the school play. Heads up me hearties!' Louise and Vicky straightened their backs and marched down the hill.

When they got to the first fence, the Pantless Pink Princess handed over the Pink Object of Devotion to Sally and hesitated. 'Don't look!' she commanded. Louise was holding down the wire. Vicky did a little dance, trying vainly to keep her dress covering her bum while legging it over the fence.

'Come on, Princess,' ordered Sally. 'Get a move on!'

'Oh, bugger it!' And in a flash she was on the other side.

Louise, feeling disorientated by her camouflage, lost her balance as she mounted the fence. The sunglasses fell off and she tumbled to the other side. This caused a mad scramble to find the glasses. Eventually they were found and placed ceremoniously on Louise's nose. The Wauhoo had no trouble with the fence and led the others across the paddock to a rousing chorus of 'The Road to Gundagai'.

The second fence proved no difficulty. They found themselves on the open road. Striding along, they kept up their
singing as they passed an old Federation-style house. At
the side was a very productive vegetable garden. Clarrie
Percival stood motionless in among his potatoes. The sight
of the three girls had him grinning from ear to ear. 'What
have we here?'

The girls looked to the left without losing step.

'We're practising for the school play,' said Sally, confidently.

'Of course you are!' he replied. 'There may be something
of interest to you over in the far paddock.' He pointed with
the garden fork. Halfway across was an old bath, used as a
watering trough. The pipe leading to it stuck up in the air a
good foot above the bath. Draped around the tap was Louise's
blouse. 'Watch out for Bessie. I think she's got something
one of you will be needing.' And with that Clarrie laughed
and returned to the spuds.

The girls performed another awkward fence-hopping
and retrieved the blouse. Louise lay down in the paddock
and put it on, out of sight Mr Percival. Or anyone else. It
was slightly grubby but undamaged. They looked around
the paddock.

Bessie was a Jersey cow. She'd been a good milker in her
day but now she was old. She was good-natured and used
to people but sometimes she got a little cantankerous. As
was the case when a gang of rowdy boys plied her with
apples, then hooked a pair of Bonds size 14 underpants
over her horns. Vicky saw the pants first and let out a
wail. 'Ah!...The thieving bastards!' Clarrie Percival looked
up from the potato patch. The spectacle of Bessie being
chased around the paddock by the hapless three reminded

him of the silent movies. There was another yell and then gut-wrenching sobs. Big, unrestrained boo-hoos. He saw Vicky shaking with sobs and holding one of her sandals by the strap. It was covered in cow poo. He could imagine the squelch as her foot had seeped into it.

Vicky was inconsolable. It was all too much. Her lovely sandal was covered in shit, and her underpants were being displayed to the entire world by a crazy cow. Neither of her companions seemed to take her seriously. Sally and Louise continued their pointless chasing of poor old Bessie until in agitation the cow rubbed her head against a fence post. The pants fell to the ground. 'Hooray!' they cried. Vicky had no more sobs to give to despair. She shoved her legs through the pants and marched off to the water trough and cleaned her sandal.

There was still one more item to find: Sally's dress. 'I don't much care if we don't find it,' she said. 'It was really old, and the hem was always coming down. I think I'll take up wearing a sarong-tablecloth permanently. It's quite comfortable except for the split up the side.'

'You're such a dag, Sally,' said Vicky. Things were returning to normal.

'Yoohoo!' Clarrie called from the garden. 'Take these with you, girls. I've got far too many.' He leant over his fence and held out three bunches of radishes. 'These'll keep you going till you get home. I've already washed them. They're quite clean.'

'Thanks, Mr Percival,' said Louise.

'Yah! Thanks Mr Clarrie!' said Sally.

'I don't like radishes,' said the Pink Princess.

'I'll eat yours,' offered Sally. And with cheery waves and

thankyous they continued on their way.

Clarrie rested his arm inside his overalls and took a good look at them. On the cusp of maturity, they were the most beautiful mixture of child and adolescent. Louise was going to be a beauty, he thought. You could tell that already. Although she was skinny and shapeless now, she'd fill out and be lithe and svelte like her mother. Her auburn hair and clear complexion and startling blue eyes would cause no end of bother among the boys. Sally had personality but was not without physical charms. If you took that lank hair and gave it a good wash and pinned it up, you'd see her lovely heart-shaped face. And as for Vicky, well Vicky had comfortable looks and a straightforward personality. Common sense was the driving force behind many of the women in the valley, and Vicky would carry on that tradition. Clarrie sighed with the pleasure of it all. It was time for a cup of tea. Maybe a little lie down. He'd see what his wife Lizzie was up to.

Down the road from Clarrie's house, the girls came to another dwelling. As they sauntered along they heard a knock, knock, knocking coming from inside the gabled room at the front of the house. The paisley-patterned curtains trembled. The knocking increased in frequency. Sally looked up. 'Alice says they're always moving the furniture in that house.' Louise looked in puzzlement at the nervous curtain. The knocking increased in intensity, volume and pace. 'She says they won't be doing that once the stork arrives.'

'Why are they always moving the furniture around?' asked Louise.

'I don't know,' said Sally. 'Some people are never happy with the way things are.'

From inside the house a drawn-out yell of agony was heard. 'That's the other thing,' said Sally. 'He's always stubbing his toe on something. You'd think he'd be more careful.'

Louise and Sally pondered the necessity to be constantly moving couches and beds and dressing tables from one part of the house to the other and the terrible exertion it was costing the poor man who seemed destined to be forever stubbing his toe. Vicky looked at them and laughed.

'Youse don't know nothin' do you? That's not furniture moving. That's him doing IT to her.'

'Doing what?' asked Louise.

'You know!' said Vicky. Sally said nothing.

'Doing IT.'

'What?'

'IT!' said Vicky in an exasperated tone. 'Poking her! Giving her a F. U. C. K. Making a baby, you idiot!'

Louise thought that this couldn't be right. How could such a hideous sound and such gross noises be anything to do with babies?

'You don't know anything about it do you!' Vicky looked at her with a sneer on her face. At last an opportunity to get even.

'They're making love,' said Sally. She'd just worked this out. It all made sense now. She'd heard the rhythmic knocking often enough and she certainly knew about the stork. She was a little bit hazy on the details in between but it was all beginning to make sense. 'The carrot visits inside the pikelet then nine months later . . . you've got a baby! Easy!'

'Yeah. My mum says it really hurts,' said Vicky.

What?' asked Sally. 'The carrot or the baby?'

'You're such a dead-flog Sally. They both hurt.'

'Why would anyone do it if it hurt?' Louise was ready to admit ignorance to attain more information.

''Cause they're really stupid,' said Sally. 'Or they're IN LURVE!!!'

'Mum says that a secret passage opens up inside you when you're in love,' said Vicky, the keeper of secret knowledge. 'But it only happens when you've got a husband.'

Louise was pretty sure none of this was ever going to happen to her. The frightening sound of the man yelling, and the shifting of furniture, seemed in no way related to babies descending from heaven on pink fluffy clouds.

They trundled along in ponderous silence for a few steps and then heard a loud burp. In unison they turned around and saw the man with the stubbed toe standing on the verandah. He took a swig from a bottle of beer. He offered them another minor burp and raised the bottle in salute. The girls turned and quickened their pace. Louise felt a blush wipe over her entire body.

Sally was affronted. 'Surely they could do it at night when nobody could hear them!' she said indignantly. 'It's really disgusting!'

'Yeah, and he looks like such a drop-kick,' offered Vicky.

'Come on, Pink Princess,' said Sally, striding out into the middle of the road. 'This is no time for baby talk. Get a move on, Sprod!'

It was getting late. Four o'clock.

Californian poppies were slowly closing their petals, wrapping their simple folds around a shy stamen. Fireweed was looking anxious and bedraggled, roughening in the afternoon breeze. A flock of green rosellas flew overhead, squawking disorder. The girls tried not to amble. Lethargy was gathering round them.

The hiatus of the day had arrived: the moment before the earth's energy diminishes; the suspension at the top of the in-breath before the long, slow sigh of the dying afternoon. It was a palpable force, heavy and slow. Golden Valley filled with golden light: the languid touch of summer air brushing over bare skin; the afternoon haze invading the senses; the scent of natives and exotics mingling – honeysuckle and jasmine, wattle and eucalypt. And behind the late afternoon breeze, the faint tang of the salty sea, like a memory just out of reach.

———

All over the valley people were putting down their gardening tools or folding the newspaper; bringing in the washing or returning home from fishing; letting go of a daylong argument; maybe taking a lemon meringue pie out of the oven ready for tea. The minutiae of life fading away. The Sunday chores completed or abandoned. It was time for '*a little lie down*': a time for Mummy and Daddy NOT TO BE DISTURBED.

Sunday afternoon: the licensed time for licentiousness. Farmers with impatient, calloused hands, kicking off boots, arms swimming out of braces, unbuttoning flies with a flick, flick, flick. Diving between cool, white sheets and feeling blindly for soft, warm flesh.

Young couples new to Sunday afternoon rituals were surprised and delighted by their bodies. No need for stimulation outside the lithe body of a husband or wife; the astringent sweat of a man, or the salty musk of a woman. Older women lay back with the radio playing, allowing the harmonies to coalesce in a fine aural cloud accompanied by the vision of Paul McCartney's shiny bobbed hair. Others imagined being one of Dean Martin's chorus girls: exaggerated busts and golden smiles. The Marlborough advertisement for cigarettes featured heavily among fantasies, with its thundering horses and winking cowboys. For some women it was the horse with its rippling muscles and fine tawny hair, not the cowboy, that brought on the ecstatic sigh. Old cynics felt like heifers in the paddock, waiting for the show to be over. *I could be doing the ironing.* Counting the thrusts before the mournful cry and thinking about a nice cup of tea. And in the golden rays of the closing afternoon, even Madame Courte and Frau Breukel took time out from their bulb farm, secretly smiling as they put up the 'closed' sign and went inside to spank each other with the wooden spoons.

———

As the afternoon released its breathless sigh, the girls sank into a puzzled silence each in their own world, trying to connect the dots to make a picture of the grown-up world. Vicky kept her handbag clutched to her side. For all the wear and tear of the day, it was surprisingly unscathed.

From a distance they heard the revving of a powerful engine. Cliff Bumford came zooming towards them in the Falcon. The car screeched to a halt.

'Hop in girls! I thought I'd find you down this way.'

'Thanks, Mr Bumford,' said Louise.

'Yeah, thanks Uncle Cliff,' said Sally.

'You girls had a good day, have you?'

'Yes,' they all responded in noncommittal unison. Vicky

got in the front seat and immediately opened the glove box and removed a packet of marshmallows. She took one, then offered them to Sally and Louise in the back seat.

'I'll have one too, thanks darl,' said Cliff. He was in a good mood. Vicky took one and popped it in his mouth. 'That's a nice dress you've got on, Sal,' he said looking in the rear vision mirror. 'It reminds me of a tablecloth.' The girls laughed.

They came to the corner where the Saltmarsh house leant into the bank at the side of the road. 'I'll get out here, Uncle Cliff,' said Sally.

'Nah... it's alright, love. I've got to come back and talk to Salty. There's a boat down at Shipwright's Point that I want his opinion of. We'll drop off er... Louise first. Then pop in and see your old man.'

Sally looked at Louise and sank back into the seat. There was no time to make a plan or discuss strategies. Cliff wheeled the car to the right and they were on Happy's Road. In less than a minute he'd swung the car onto Marion's lawn.

Malcolm came marching around the side of the house wearing a radiant smile. He'd been turning the compost. Man of the soil. Mr Bumford (Cliff) seeing him in his natural habitat. Engaged in physical activity. Cliff would see him as a man of the land, not just a pen-pusher in a shiny suit waiting for the day when he could get away with wearing a grey cardigan. Marion left her apron on as she came down the front steps, ignoring the voice in her head that said *get off my bloody lawn!* She arranged her smile to fit the occasion and, wiping her hands on her apron, she tilted her head to the side in a posture of genteel enquiry.

Cliff wound down the window. 'There ya go, Mal. I found them dawdling just up past Clarrie's place. Looks like they've had a good time. I went up to Willows Marsh to see Mick about a block of land. By crikey there's some good land up there! Going for a song. Doesn't know what he's got, funny old fella. I asked him what he wanted for the block and he says, "Whatever you think's a fair thing." What do you do? You dunno what to say to a question like that! Anyhow. We best be off. Got to see Salty about a boat down at Shipwright's Point. I reckon it's one he's been on. You wouldn't guess we were cousins. He got the black looks and I got the white. Same grandmother. Nan Ethel. She was real dark. Do you remember her, Sally? No, you wouldn't. You'd be too young… Most of us got a lick of the tar brush down this way… Isn't that so Sally?' He looked around and smiled at her. 'Salty's got quite a tribe down there but you're the pick of them, aren't you Sal!' Sally squirmed, and Cliff straightened. 'You say thank you to Mr and Mrs Johnstone, Vicky.'

'Thank you for inviting me,' said the Pink Princess.

Louise got out of the car and swung the knapsack onto her shoulder. 'See you… everyone,' she said, not wanting to name Sally in case naming her would attract attention. Sally wound down the window and glared defiantly at Marion. The benevolent smile fell off Marion's face as she looked at the girl. Sally's hair was tangled and knotted, with bits of vegetation hanging around her ears. The tablecloth was pulled tightly round her skinny frame.

'I'll wash it and give it back!' she yelled at Marion, and quickly wound the window up. Then she sat back with tightly folded arms and stared at the back of Cliff's seat.

Cliff's revelation about his relationship to the Saltmarshes was gradually dawning on Malcolm. He held his smile as the ground shifted beneath his feet. With unwarranted urgency, he thrust his hand into the car. Whatever all this was about, he'd make sure he acted like a gentleman. A handshake was the thing. Cliff couldn't see the need for it and awkwardly lifted his arm out the window.

'Alrighty,' said Cliff. 'Thank you Mrs Johnstone.' He nodded at Malcolm. Then he turned to look at Sally. 'Let's go see what your old man's up to, Sal. I hope he's got a bottle of beer in the fridge.'

⸻

The Johnstones were left with the feeling that Cliff Bumford was on his way to where he wanted to be. Not eating pikelets with one of the clerks from the office but down at Salty's shack having a quiet beer and a yak. They felt somehow snubbed and isolated. It was as if all their efforts had been to no avail. *Surely there must be moral standards he has to live up to*, thought Malcolm. It was all very well for the likes of Flo to go socialising with half-castes. She and Barry were radical university people. But the mayor! Wouldn't he try to distance himself from his darker relatives? It made no sense at all.

Marion went quietly back to the kitchen. *It'll take a while for all this to soak in*, she thought. The best she could do was keep quiet and keep out of his way. She heard him go back out to the garden. After an hour the screen door yawned, and he was in the kitchen. 'Might as well scrub up for tea,' he said. 'Here's some of the last of the kennebecs.' He plonked them on the sink.

'Is Robert around?' he asked. 'Might be a chance for a bit

of a hit before tea.' A little bit of occupational cricket might help absorb the changing situation.

'I don't know where he is,' said Marion.

'Where's Lou?' Lou might be able to give a clue or two, he thought. Did she know about this? Did she know about Cliff Bumford being related to the Saltmarshes? Had he been set up in some way? She probably had something to do with it: her and that wayward Sally.

'She's in the bath,' Marion said quickly. She busied herself with preparations for tea. Sunday night was toasted sandwiches in front of the telly. 'Disneyland will be on soon,' she said in her bright, efficient voice. Malcolm loved Disneyland. But for Marion it had been spoilt by Flo's off-hand comment that Disneyland was for mature children and immature adults.

Robert turned up in time to have a bath before Louise pulled the plug. Malcolm and Marion sat on the couch and the children sat in their dressing-gowns on the floor, resting their backs against Malcolm and Marion's legs. It was a Sunday night ritual. Halfway through Davy Crockett's adventures in the wilds of Kentucky, Malcolm reached down and stroked Louise's head. He didn't know why he did it. He was still confused and felt betrayed. He didn't know what the answers to anything were. All he knew was that he loved her with the whole of his being.

Louise felt the gentle warm hand. The same hand that had foolishly thrust itself at Cliff Bumford. The same hand that had delivered the stinging blows of his belt; the hand that had kept her buoyant in the waves of South Arm. Her bones seemed to melt in an agony of love, fear and hope. Tears silently ran down her face.

A week later, Clarrie Percival was leaning on his garden fork contemplating the possibility of digging up some of his wife's dahlias to make room for another patch of spuds. He didn't like his chances. He wondered if she'd notice if he just took a little of the patch at a time. In his indecision, he lifted his head to the horizon and stared at the hills all around him. There was no relief from the hills except down in the flat of the valley. Perhaps he could use the narrow strip of land against the side fence. He walked over to the boundary and as he did so, he heard a queer, high-pitched sound. He cocked his head and cupped his ear.

The sound came in fragments: high and jittery like a bird-call, then swooping low in a sing-song way. It could even be singing. Maybe the wind was playing with it, stretching some notes and obliterating others. He looked around to find the source. In the paddock opposite, where the girls had been chasing poor Bessie for their clothes, Clarrie could see a figure dancing under the trees.

Yes, that was indeed the source of the sound. Now he knew it must be singing. It was Robert. Everyone knew that Robert had a fine voice, but it was his sanguine personality that really shone: people would mention Robert, and then a smile would lighten their faces as they thought of his hijinks or stories or his unique turn of phrase, or his ability to see what other people only had a vague feeling about.

Yes, it was Robert alright. But Clarrie didn't smile. Robert's singing seemed wayward. Snippets of sound came to him in a disorganised way. Clarrie couldn't make out the tune. Maybe it was the wind. Maybe he was going deaf. But somehow the sound seemed to be in tune with the wind:

Robert was singing a wind song. Perhaps making it up as he went along. He was by himself, and he was dancing: lifting his arms up towards the gums by the creek, swaying into the wind as if he were a tree himself, and then crouching low and moving his hands in circles over the long grasses as if he were commanding them to twist and wave with the wind. Then he spread his arms and lifted them as high as he could, like some Old Testament prophet calling on God, throwing his head back and shouting his song to the clouds.

Clarrie found it odd and a little unnerving. Then again, he'd seen a lot of strange behaviour in forty years of teaching. But the oddest thing, or the most worrying thing to Clarrie, was that Robert was wearing a dress. *If he's taken to wearing dresses, he's in for a rough time!* he thought. *No . . . he'll grow out of it . . . it's only a stage.* He stood watching for a little longer, feeling like a voyeur. The movement of the dance and the cry of the song filled the rushing wind. He *was* the wind, thought Clarrie. He looked up at the gusting clouds and back to Robert. And he smiled to know that he was a witness to the synergy of elements in this unique performance. He was the only audience to this embryonic art form particular to Robert. The boy was a great conductor weaving a symphony with the raw elements, making music and dance in a constantly moving stage: calling the strength of the trees and the flightiness of the clouds and the rushing of the creek, commanding the grass to bend and challenging the sun to pierce his eyelids. He was like a primal soul talking to the spirits in the natural world, filled with a great love and joy of being.

Clarrie's feelings changed from the condescension

reserved for children, to a great sense of wonder and awe. He was witnessing the joy of the world, and it lifted his spirits. The dahlias could stay where they were.

Chapter 15

Tuesday 7 February 1967

MALCOLM WAS SWEATING. HE COULD feel his shirt sticking to his back and armpits. He looked out the office window. Sleeping Beauty was nowhere to be seen. The smoke was so thick he couldn't see beyond the Golden Valley turn-off. The wind was picking up by the minute. The Council Chambers were in chaos. Malcolm was dismissed from work at eleven thirty and made his way to the fire station. Darryl was already there.

'Mal, mate. We've got to do the western side of Golden Valley.' Malcolm looked confused. 'There's fires out of control all over. We've got to get them out, Mal! Everyone! From Happy's Road through to Willows Marsh. Tell Roj you're coming with me.'

Malcolm found Roger Grogan looking anxiously at a map of the valley. Roger was the fire warden for the district. The logistics of moving people out of their houses in a scattered, thinly populated community were a nightmare. There was too much terrain to cover, too many isolated farmhouses, shacks and one-room huts. No-one knew for sure who lived in some of the places. Few people had telephones.

'Take the truck, Mal,' he said. 'I'm sorry but it's the last one left. It's the garbage truck. We've cleaned it out. You know the area. Get everyone onto the truck and get them back here. If you can't get through, take them down to the river. There's plenty of spots on the lower side of the road. Opposite the dairy's a good spot. It's sheltered. No big trees. Can you and Darryl manage that?'

Malcolm felt a huge surge of adrenaline.

'Come on,' said Darryl. 'Let's get moving!'

The truck didn't smell too bad. It had been hosed down, and a stained tarpaulin was folded in one corner. Darryl took the wheel and they headed up Golden Valley. At least all the children were at school – one less responsibility. They'd have to start high in the hills if they were going to cover the entire western side of the valley. Happy's Road could wait till last. It was close to the river and not too far from town.

They passed Logger's Road and Jeffrey's Road and headed up to Willows Marsh. Paddy's Turn-off was the last road in the valley. Paddy was long gone, but the Donohues lived there these days. Scotty was the youngest. Malcolm didn't know them, except for a friendly 'G'day'. Old man Donohue was said to be a bit of a whinger, but he was a logger of some renown. His name was Mert. Short for Myrtle.

It was a long haul up Paddy's Turn-off to the Donohue place. Malcolm was worried that they mightn't have enough petrol in the tank. 'She's right,' said Darryl, seeing Malcolm look at the gauge. 'She's on full at the moment.' Malcolm relaxed.

They got to the Donohue place and the truck was nearly boiling. They scouted around and found a jerry can inside the back door and filled it in the laundry. There was no-one around. Malcolm found a note on the front door that simply read 'weev all gon to town'. Malcolm kept the engine running as Darryl filled the radiator. They filled the jerry can again and took it with them. Malcolm looked back at the dingy little house set in a garden of old rusted logging equipment, wrecked cars and farm implements. A clothesline was strung up between the open bonnet of a 1940s Chevrolet truck and the side post of the verandah. All the washing looked grey. How could people live like that? he wondered, and vowed never to park on Marion's lawn again. He'd seen the Donohue children round the valley: smiling, happy-go-lucky kids. He'd heard that Mert was a drinker.

They settled into a routine as Darryl kept the engine running and Malcolm checked all the houses. The truck was filling up with disgruntled residents. 'So now we know the council think we're rubbish!' quipped one burly matron as she manoeuvred her haunches onto the tray. Malcolm became immune to the jibes after a while. As a council employee he was fair game. Everyone who cared to, had a shot at him. 'Moving up in the world are you Mr Johnstone? Is this another cost-cutting measure? Pen-pushers having to do the garbage run?' Optimism had moved out of the valley with the declining apple industry. Most people were stoic and prompt, taking only a handbag and a coat.

Darryl's hands shook on the wheel. 'I don't like fire, Mal. I just don't like it. Give me a good clean flood any day!' Every five minutes he had his head out the window, checking the wind to gauge its direction and strength. 'If this changes to a westerly we're buggered!' he said. 'Willows Marsh will go up like a cracker. It's as dry as buggery up there. If it takes hold, it will head down the valley like a tornado. There'll be nothing stopping it!'

Malcolm kept his concentration on the residents. He didn't want to think about the wind or the fire. It was enough for him to make sure everyone was out. He didn't want to leave anyone behind, and begged and pleaded when people got stubborn. But once the truck was half full, the job was halved by agile mums jumping off the tray to help check houses and convince people to leave their homes.

They'd cleared right down to Logger's Road. The truck was three-quarters full. There was only the shop, the dairy and Happy's Road to go. Malcolm checked the dairy. It was deserted. He could see the cows down by the river, the black-and-white figures moving restlessly along the bank.

When they got to the shop, things were different. 'I'm not going,' said Vonnie. 'There's no need. We'll be right.' She stood firm with her hands on her hips. 'This'll blow over. Youse'll all be wondering what the fuss was about.'

'Vonnie! You and Merv have to come,' said a young woman. 'Mr Johnstone's responsible. If you don't come he'll get into trouble!'

'Nup!' Vonnie folded her arms. 'You're making a fuss about nothin'. Merv and me are staying put. This is our home and we're not leaving!'

'Please, Vonnie,' said the young woman. 'We've all had to leave.' They managed to talk Vonnie into coming out onto the road so she could see the clouds of thick yellow smoke. The wind nearly bowled her over.

'Jesus! Mal!' cried Darryl. 'The wind's changed! She's swung round! We've got a full-on westerly on our hands!'

Merv came out to the entrance of the shop. No-one heard him. The wheels of his chair made no sound. 'You go darlin',' he said to Vonnie. 'You go. I'll stay here and mind the shop.'

Then with tears in his eyes he looked down at the ground. 'I've had enough, Vonn. I've had enough... of this!' and he hit the arm of the wheelchair with all his might.

There was silence. Even the wind seemed to stop. Everyone on the truck felt his sorrow, his deep despair. Then Vonnie yelled at the top of her voice. 'If I'm going, you're coming with me! I love ya, you silly old bugger!'

People got off the truck. They crowded round Vonnie and Merv. Someone gave Vonnie a hanky. The young woman gently stroked Merv's hand. 'Come on, love,' she said. 'We can't leave you here.'

'We're all in it together, mate,' said a young man in a check shirt.

Merv shook his big, bull head and cried out. 'I've had enough! Just leave me be! I've had enough! Let me alone!'

'Oh, Mervy love. I can't do that!' Vonnie said through tears.

Malcolm and Darryl had been holding back behind the crowd. 'Now!' said Malcolm. Both of them rushed forward and positioned themselves on either side of Merv, lifting him from the shoulders. Malcolm automatically put a hand under Merv's knees and then realised, with horror, his mistake. Merv had no knees. He'd left them back in New Guinea in 1944. It was an awkward manoeuvre to get him onto the truck. Merv's face had set to stone. Vonnie hoisted herself up and sat quietly beside him. The young man in the check shirt helped with the wheelchair. There was a grim silence as they headed up to the top of Happy's Road.

It was so narrow at the top that Darryl had to do a three-point turn. Malcolm ran up the track to check on Snakey's shack. Snakey often used it as a base to go wallaby shooting, but no-one was there. While he was gone, Darryl filled the radiator again just as a precaution. The young bloke kept the engine running.

The next two houses were empty and then they were at Flo and Barry's place. Barry was at work. Flo was there, looking after the Saltmarsh twins. Alice had gone to Hobart. Flo came down the steps with both children in her arms. Shaken and frightened, she was relieved to see the truck. She tried to say something to Malcolm but the wind took it away, throwing her hair around her face and plastering her dress to her body. Neither of the twins was wearing shoes. She lifted them onto the truck. They made a beeline for Merv and sat down in his lap.

Malcolm's place was next, but he knew no-one was there. Marion was in Huonville helping with the fire brigade auxiliary, and the kids were at school. He was starting to feel relieved. He turned to Darryl in the cabin. 'Nearly over, mate.'

'Bloody oath, Mal. Let's get out of here!' Darryl couldn't wait. He pulled on the gear stick and revved the engine. The engine cut out. 'Oh, cripes!' He turned the ignition. The engine turned over and then stopped. 'Bloody hell! What's wrong with the bloody thing?' He tried again.

'What's the petrol gauge say?' asked Malcolm.

'It says bloody full! And it's been saying that all day! Mal, the gauge is buggered! We're out of bloody petrol!' Darryl was nearly hysterical. The tall gums on the lower side of the road from Flo and Barry's house exploded. The westerly had taken the fire up the road and was facing them head on. They could hear the roar of it getting louder and louder, a great crescendo bearing down on them. Visibility was virtually nil. Even with the headlights on, the road could hardly be seen in the swirling smoke.

'Let me have a go,' shouted Malcolm against the roar of the fire. 'You get in the back and cover everyone under that tarpaulin.' Darryl was shaking all over. He managed to get in the tray and spread the stinking tarp. Malcolm raced round to the tray to warn them. 'Keep your heads down and cover your ears. I'm going to put her into angel gear. It's the only way we'll get through.' He had to yell at the top of his voice to be heard. The young bloke and Darryl pushed the truck to get it moving then jumped on the back. Just as they made it onto the tray a huge branch lit up like a Christmas tree and crashed to the ground, sending sparks and flames in all directions. Three seconds ago they'd been standing right there. They looked in disbelief at each other and crawled under the tarp.

Malcolm knew what he had to do. He had to go as fast as he could through the wall of the fire. He'd heard about situations like this. Robert had done a project on firefighting and had been obsessed by the 'wall of fire'. Malcolm wished he'd taken more notice. At least there was no petrol in the tank, nothing to explode. He knew the road, even if he couldn't see it. It was downhill for two hundred yards and then a flat stretch leading to a wide corner. Then on the left, set back from the road, was his home. He didn't think about it. All his attention was focused on the truck and the twenty-three lives huddled under the tarpaulin in the tray.

The truck was gaining momentum. He didn't want to use the brake at all – speed was what he needed. Although he couldn't see the road clearly, he knew what to expect. Relying on kinetic memory: when to turn the wheel, when to keep it straight. The roar came at him like a great opening mouth. He gripped the wheel with all his might, holding the truck straight down the hill. *It's nearly over*, he said to himself. Then it was upon him. The deafening roar seemed to explode his head. All oxygen disappeared from the cabin. Nothing but red all around him, no air to breathe, only sound and fury and heat. He held every muscle in his body tight to keep the wheel steady as his mind reeled from the enormity of the risk he was undertaking. His heart seemed to want to break free of his chest. There was no possibility of losing his nerve now. There was no shelter outside the truck: a thin tarpaulin, on a set of wheels hurling itself towards hell. The roar was like a physical assault, as if it would leave bruises and gashes on the skin. The sounds exploded in his head. Before he had time to think, it was over. The sound was dissipating. The red glare was behind him. *I've pulled it off*, he thought with relief. *Thank Christ! I've pulled it off!*

Just as he relaxed, a tree crashed down on the engine, hitting the windscreen and smashing through it. Flames were everywhere. Malcolm yelled and tried to cover his face. He pulled on the brake, wrenched the door open and ran around to the tray. 'Everybody off! Now! Quick! Everybody off!' The branches ignited the cabin, licking the inside lining of the bodywork, looking for more fuel to feed on.

People scrambled off the tray as quickly as they could, the more able helping the older residents. Darryl and the young bloke organised Merv's chair and sat the two Saltmarsh boys in his arms. Everyone ran downhill as fast as they could. Malcolm came last, making sure no-one was behind him. As they rounded the corner they felt the danger lessen. He looked back and saw the truck engulfed in flames, the fire leisurely feeding on the wooden sides of the tray. A bright orange flare leapt up as the tarpaulin ignited. The main front of the fire strode up the hill like an angry dragon, its curtains of power whipping the vegetation to nothingness, stomping fury on the earth and stretching red tendrils far into the blackened sky.

Flo came up beside him. She touched his arm. Her lips were trembling. 'I'm so sorry Malcolm,' she said. He turned away from the burning truck and the retreating fire. He looked across the road to where his house should have been. The roof had twisted and buckled and most of it had collapsed into the remaining shell of the walls. It was a pile of rubble. Ash and smoke clouded his view but he knew that nothing was salvageable. Intense heat was still radiating from the collapsing brickwork.

'People are more important,' he said, brushing her hand away. But his nerves were shot to pieces. He started marching down the road as if he were on the parade ground, legs swinging and hips rolling, his jaw clenched shut and his mouth turned down, his navy training overriding the immense shock. There were no thoughts in his head now. Left, right, left, right. Everyone was safe. He'd done the right thing. Left, right. Left, right. His lungs hurt with every breath, and the tip of his nose and his ears felt blistered. Adrenaline was still racing through his body: a crazy frenzy of energy looking for a way out. Left, right, left, right. The women gathered around him as he marched, waiting to support him when the crash came. But he held it all together, marching down to the river: a scarecrow figure accompanied by a band of pilgrims – sobbing women, bewildered men, scruffy children, and the wayward wheelchair lurching up and down across the paddock. The Saltmarsh twins couldn't help themselves but laugh, as every bump threw their small bodies into the air and Merv anxiously caught them in his huge hands.

'Precious cargo, Mal,' he said as he looked up at Malcolm for the first time. 'Precious cargo.'

Chapter 16

ROBERT KNEW THAT HIS HOME had burnt down. He had held onto Marion as she cried and cried. He'd witnessed his father's lower lip trembling. He'd watch Louise howl in despair. But for him, it wasn't quite real. This was a tragedy that didn't quite touch him. Part of him felt extraordinary; exempt from the ordinary world. There was a special god looking after him.

The wall in his bedroom, that Marion fondly referred to as his art gallery, remained standing in his mind's eye. This wall would have resisted the flames. All his wonderful creations would still be intact. The maps he had made of Golden Valley with pathways to hidden realms, the painting of the willow trees down by Clarrie's creek, the bright crayon sunset and mountain ranges, his pencil drawings of cows, sheep and dogs. All his great works. They would still be there. His Sunday school god would be looking down, protecting his work. His specialness, his passion, would make him immune from ordinary tragedy.

It wasn't till they returned to Happy's Road that reality struck. Robert looked out the car window to locate his bedroom wall. It wasn't there. *Not to worry*, he thought. *God's protecting it*. A layer of bricks, protecting his art gallery.

During that first dreadful day, Robert searched and searched among the bricks. Everything had turned to ash. Sometimes he'd lift his head quickly in the hope that he'd somehow missed seeing the wall. But the wall had vanished. He became silent and steely.

Marion would have liked to suggest he go for a walk by the river or up into the bush. But the bush and the river offered nothing but dead sticks and stagnant water.

———

'The bones of the earth—'

'Louder please, Louise. Lift your head. Loud, clear voice, now.' Louise lifted her head and held the piece of paper in front of her.

'The bones of—'

'Not so fast. Make sure you enunciate the words carefully. "The *bones* of the earth." Bring out "bones". It's such an unusual turn of phrase.' Mrs Burton stood facing Louise. The class formed a mass of faces behind her.

'The bones of the earth lie bare to the sky.
The dark, sullen rocks litter the ground.'

'Try lowering the paper, Louise. Don't lift it in front of your face. We still can't hear you clearly.'

Louise lowered the page. She started again.

'The bones of the earth lie bare to the sky.
The dark, sullen rocks litter the ground.
No cry of birds or rustling of leaves
Are heard in the wastes of the grey silent land.'

'Can you hear her up the back?' Mrs Burton turned around to look at the class. The back row nodded. The class was quiet. They were all exhausted. Those who had lost their homes were still in shock. A week had passed. Mrs Burton allowed creative writing every day. She hoped that the writing of the experience would help heal the children. There was such a hush in the classroom: they weren't banging lids of desks or flicking rubber bands at each other. They looked bored and withdrawn.

'On you go, Louise.'

'Where once was a forest, cool greens of the earth,
Now dry ash has fallen.
The land waits for—'

'Louise, you need to project. Keep your head up. If we're going to do this in the assembly hall, you'll need to almost shout it. Come on. From "The land waits for rebirth".'

Louise blushed and her eyes watered. She had not wanted this attention. Mrs Burton came closer and spoke in a soft voice. 'You don't have to do this if you'd rather not.'

'No, Mrs Burton. I can do it.' Louise straightened up.

'The land waits for rebirth.
As quiet as stones we're numb to the pain.
We sift through the ashes to find what remains.'

'Well done! Let's give her a clap, class.' Mrs Burton nodded and clapped. The mocking boys in the back row clapped slowly and loudly.

Louise quickly returned to her seat. She hadn't wanted to be chosen to read her poem in assembly. She didn't want to be made a fuss of.

When the bell rang for lunch the children filed out. One of the boys mumbled, 'The bones, the bones!' Vicky and a few others sniggered.

'So unusual!' someone said.

Louise ran to the toilets. She stayed there quietly crying and vowed never to show her poetry to anyone ever again.

———

After three days, Malcolm's hearing began returning to normal. The high-pitched sound in his head receded to an occasional whistle. It seemed to him that he had been caught in a net of sound that not only seared his brain, but stuck to his skin. There was nowhere he could turn, nowhere he could be, that the dreadful sound didn't follow him. He'd move his head and momentarily think the sound had disappeared, but then it would be back as strong as ever. Marion would see him shaking his head this way and that, quick little shakes like a nervous tic, and wondered if he was going mad. And he might have been for those three days. Everything was a blur.

Several times during those early days he woke the whole family with a roar of terror in the middle of the night. His body was covered in sweat and his hands were holding fast to an imaginary steering wheel. Marion rocked him gently when he let her, but sometimes he'd throw her off. The children lay terrified, each in their own cocoon of mourning, waiting for the sun to rise so they could escape to school.

Chapter 17

THE FAMILY SLEPT ON MATTRESSES in Darryl and Marcia's living room. Marion couldn't stand being in Darryl and Marcia's house. If one of them wasn't talking, the other was nattering on about nothing in particular. As if the air needed filling with their constant jabbering. Wasn't it enough that she'd lost her home? Couldn't they give her any peace and quiet? Darryl couldn't take two steps without opening his mouth, and his wife accompanied every gesture with a sigh and a saying. Every action had its little quip or homily. 'Once when I was...' she'd start, and Marion would know with a sinking feeling that she'd be forced to feign interest for the next fifteen minutes.

It wasn't conversation. There was no give and take. No exchange of ideas and experiences, no listening and appreciating the other's point of view. When Marion tried to break into Marcia's soliloquy, Marcia simply talked over the top of her.

There was no escape. If your house had burnt to the ground, Marcia knew someone who'd had their house burn down twice! If it was the worst bushfire ever, she knew that the worst was yet to come. If you knew how to cook pikelets, Marcia knew a better recipe. If Marion offered to buy some vegetables or meat for dinner, hoping to get away for an hour, Marcia gave her a list, as if she were a child.

And Marcia explained everything she did in the house:

every action was spelt out to Marion. The proper way to peel onions, the proper way to cut out the eyes of potatoes, the best way to fry steak, how to crack eggs without getting sticky hands, how to make an invisible join in yarn, how to heel in bulbs at the beginning of winter. There was no end to Marcia's expertise.

Marcia needed an audience. She wanted to be able to explain all the little chores of her household and how she performed them with a clipped economy of movement. She wanted to place so much meaning into each little chore that it became a sacred act. Cleaning the bath became a religious ceremony – a cleansing act of redemption. The shower curtain had to be arranged with the folds in uniform columns as if it were the skirts of the Virgin Mary herself. Even the way she trod on the carpet had a self-consciousness about it: measuring the strides of her life, her footfalls on the earth, pacing through her life with a constancy that had taken her from mindless drudgery to symbolic ritual.

Marion felt she was being punished for something. There was no escape. They could go up to Hobart and stay with Malcolm's parents in Battery Point – but that would be jumping out of the frying pan into the fire. The last thing she needed was to be confined in her mother-in-law's house. Besides, it was too far away for Malcolm to travel, and the children shouldn't be traumatised further by changing schools. No. They were staying in the valley. Marcia might be a pain, but Mother-in-law was a lot worse. They would stay in the valley and rebuild. They were 'valley people' now and that was where they belonged.

Cliff Bumford came up with the perfect solution for Malcolm and his family. There was a flat above the police station that hadn't been used for some time. It was built on top of the cells that held the occasional drunk. Most of the time the cells were empty, and Cliff promised that if there was a case of having to use them, he would wield his power and have the miscreant sent up to Hobart so that Marion and the children wouldn't have to put up with the filthy language of half-mad drunks. Marion jumped at the chance. The relief was instantaneous. They had their own space. The front room overlooked the main street, and the two bedrooms were at the back where it was quieter.

At the end of the first week in their new accommodation, Darryl took Malcolm to the pub to consolidate the friendship that had come close to breaking point. They got blind drunk together. Marion threatened to lock them both in the cells, but the truth was she was relieved.

'He needed a blow-out,' she said to the children.

—

Marion took the lid off the casserole dish. 'Oh! Flo! It smells divine!'

'Chicken and apricot. It's the only thing I can successfully cook. And I bought this.' She lifted a bottle of Mateus out of her bag. 'I know. Malcolm won't drink it but I'm sure you'll like it. You need to celebrate your release from Marcia's prison.'

Marion laughed. 'Oh, it wasn't that bad. Well at least here, I'm above the cells not actually in them. She was very kind, but there's nothing like your own place. I really love it here. Look! I've got a bird's eye view of the street. I can spy on everyone.'

Flo looked out the window down to the bustle below. 'Yes.

It does have its attractions. Sometimes I wonder if Barry and I are really suited to the bush. It's very romantic. And very cheap. But… I don't know. It's so dreadful now. Everything's so ugly. There's not a bird in sight. It's so depressing, Marion. I wish in a way that it was our house that got burnt down. Then we'd up stakes straight away. Move to somewhere new.'

'Oh, but you've really made a home for yourselves here. You're part of the valley.' Marion thought of Malcolm's sobriquet for Barry and Flo: 'Barry the Book Man' and 'Flo ON and ON'. She moved the casserole dish to the stove.

Flo sat down at the table. 'Marion, I saw a side of Malcolm that I hadn't seen before.' Marion sat down. 'He was so clear about the situation. He knew exactly what to do and how to do it. And the risk he took … It was breathtaking. But he knew. He knew exactly what to do and how to do it. He saved our lives, Marion!'

'Yes, he's paying for it now, but I'm very proud of him.' Marion poured the tea. 'His ears haven't stopped ringing and he's got this horrible nervous tic. How's Barry doing?'

'Oh, Barry's fine.' Flo thought of Barry's soft sluggish body. 'He'll get over it pretty quickly. Most of Barry's life's in his head.' Flo remembered the visceral reaction she'd felt when Malcolm herded everyone under the tarpaulin, Malcolm moving with muscular authority, wiping the sweat from his eyes, yelling at everyone to keep themselves covered.

Chapter 18

ON WEEKENDS MALCOLM AND MARION, Louise and Robert would pack the car with a picnic lunch, fill the boot with shovels, garden forks, wire sifters, work gloves, empty cartons (for moving rubble) and any other tools they thought might be useful, and head up the river to where their house used to be. Flo would come down with the wheelbarrow and a thermos of tea. They'd work through the day: cleaning and stacking bricks, dragging the corrugated iron into piles. They spent hours sifting through the ashes hoping to find some intact possession that hadn't been destroyed.

Robert found his box of treasures. It had been flattened by the falling ceiling. He spent half a day trying to open it. The top lip of the box had become welded to the base by the heat and pressure. Eventually he used a can opener and prised the lid off. Inside, the false teeth that he had found when they first came to Happy's Road were still in one piece. It was a great moment of merriment. He danced around singing 'I've still got the teeth! I've still got the teeth!' Malcolm would have liked to point out that it was a bloody useless find, but somehow the absurdity of it lifted them all to a level of carefree hilarity. Jokes came thick and fast as Malcolm instructed Robert to 'get his teeth back into it'. Robert countered by holding them high, as he balanced on a pile of rubble.

'Look at me! I'm teethering on the edge!'

'I'm going to teeth you a lesson!' Louise pulled at his shirt.

The children looked around to find Marion, knowing she'd have some witty repartee to add. She was further away towards the back of the block where the verandah used to be. She'd removed a tangle of wire that once held her macramé pots. There was buckled iron, and handfuls of molten glass from the verandah-sill. It had set in random clumps like marshmallow on a baking tray. The children saw Marion stiffen and place her hand over her mouth. Among the debris she'd seen a brass stud.

Spangles, Flo and Barry's dog, had been missing since the fires. They assumed they would never find him. Spangles had spent a lot of time hanging around the Johnstones' back door, waiting for Malcolm, his favourite person, to come outside and throw him a stick or rub his ears. He was indeed more Malcolm's dog than Flo and Barry's.

Marion gasped in horror at the tangle of bone and hair and shrunken sinews inside the studded collar. The smell of rotting flesh was overpowering. Malcolm came rushing over. He let out a soft cry. The dear sweet dog that'd made a friend of him at the crazy party up the road, who was always there for a pat, always dripping slobber all over his trousers, was now a fetid, rotting corpse. His death was gruesome, horrible and undeserved. Determined not to cry, not to show any weakness in front of his children, Malcolm grabbed the spade and attacked the hated earth, pushing the blade deep into the charred soil in a frenzy of agitation. 'You stay back!' he yelled at the children. 'Stay back! I don't want you see this.'

Marion and the children drew back and watched as he cut into the ground with all his might. The sweat was coming off him, and with it tears. He kept going, down, down, down till the earth looked cold and damp. Louise looked around for some flowers to put on the grave. There were none to be had. Eventually she settled for some new shoots pushing out of the trunk of a eucalypt. Robert collected some of the dollops of melted glass that had once been the frosted windows, and made a circle around the grave. With infinite care, Malcolm shovelled the remains of Spangles onto a sheet of iron.

'Robbie, I'll need you now,' he said. Robert knew what he had to do. He had to swallow his feelings of nausea and disgust and take the other end of the iron sheet and tip poor Spangles into his final resting place. It was more than he could bear. The sight and smell was so hideous he felt out of control. He felt like laughing. The horror of the corpse was beyond anything he had ever seen before.

Marion pushed him out of the way. 'I'll do it,' she said and grabbed the other end of the iron sheeting. They moved in cooperative unison to the grave side and poured Spangles' rotting remains into the hole. As quickly as he could, Malcolm filled in the grave.

On the following weekend their mood was lighter as Malcolm swung the car into Happy's Road. They could see from a distance an old Chevy truck parked on the block. Two men were loading bricks onto the tray. Malcolm and Robert had stacked and cleaned those bricks a few weeks back. Malcolm pulled up on the road beside the block. 'Stay here.' His voice was shaking. Marion, Louise and Robert watched as Malcolm's naval march clicked into gear. He took mighty strides across the front yard. He wasn't going to run. His head was up and his fists were ready.

One of the men looked up and mistook Malcolm for another pilferer. 'There's some good ones here, mate. But this pile's ours.' As Malcolm marched up to him, the realisation of his mistake dawned on him. He opened his mouth to speak and Malcolm shut it with a well-placed right hook. The other man ran towards the front of the truck but Malcolm swung round, his flying fists landing on the man's throat.

'You put every single brick back where you found it! Then get off my land you thieving bastards!' Malcolm was shaking with fury. He grabbed the first man by the shirt front. 'Did you hear what I said?' The man could feel the strength of the rage pulsing through Malcolm's body.

'Jesus Christ! You don't have to kill a man!' There was blood dribbling down the side of his mouth. 'Awright! Awright!' He leapt onto the tray and flung the bricks to the ground. When the pile was low enough he pushed the remainder with his foot, sending them crashing in a dusty pile. 'We're off. Come on, Blue. Do as the man says. Let's get out of here!'

'Don't you ever come back here again!' Malcolm yelled. The men got in the Chevy and sped down the road.

Malcolm was still shaking when he came back to the car. 'Dad! That was amazing!' said Robert. 'Cor! You were like John Wayne or Clint Eastwood! They didn't dare fight back!'

'They're cowards! That type of men always are!' said Marion. 'They belong in jail. I took down their registration number and I'm going to give it to the police.'

'I don't think they'll come back, Marion.' Malcolm was nursing his right hand in his left. 'Never fight bare-knuckled if you can help it, son. You can break your hand if you're not careful.'

Louise was flushed and breathless. Her hand was shaking as she opened the car door. Robert was already out of the car punching the air and kicking an imaginary foe. 'Can you teach me to box like that, Dad?'

'You've got to know how to defend yourself,' said Malcolm, warming to the task. 'You never know when you might need it. You'll need to learn some self-defence too, Lou.'

Louise heard the words. She didn't want to look at him. She was used to being ignored. He rarely spoke directly to her unless it was a command of some sort. She didn't want to be included in his plans. The violent outburst made her feel sick. Not like Robert, who seemed to want to orbit around Malcolm, feeling the power and energy radiating off him.

Marion was tight-lipped and crisp. 'Let's hope that you never have to use it,' she said, and marched up the road to borrow the wheelbarrow from Flo and Barry.

———

Slowly, little by little the block was cleared. The bath was the last item to be removed. It was cast iron, big and heavy, with clawed feet. Malcolm hated looking at it. When he first saw the ruins of the house, the bath was the only solid thing left. It lay open to the sky with a twisted piece of corrugated iron lying inside it. It made him feel exposed: the whole world could see his bath. His privacy had been invaded. Initially, Marion thought it might be worth saving, but the enamel was blistered, and a large crack had formed on the base of the inside. It didn't go right through, as Robert proved by pouring water into it. In the end they decided to give it to Clarrie Percival. Clarrie and Lizzie's house had escaped the fires, although all his fencing was gone. Clarrie was going to use it as a water trough in his back paddock. (Lizzie thought it would look nice in the garden filled with bulbs.)

Clarrie brought the tractor round to the Johnstones'. He had a trailer attached; his only problem was getting the bath from the ground up onto the trailer. He'd brought with him some planking, chocks and ropes. As he proceeded down the main road at five miles per hour, Mert Donohue had come up behind him in his truck. Mert was in no hurry. He'd lost his shed but not his house. At some stage he wanted to borrow Clarrie's tractor to push all the rubble over the escarpment at the back of his property. He followed Clarrie up Happy's Road.

'Need a hand, Clarrie?' he said as he pulled the truck to the side of the road.

'I reckon I do, Mert.'

Mert sprang into action. He gave Malcolm a crushing handshake and ignored Marion and the children. He strode over to the bath and lifted the corner of it with one hand, testing its weight.

'You'll need to get as close as you can, Clarrie. That pile of bricks there is in the road.' Mert pointed to a dozen bricks that Robert and Louise had been cleaning.

Well! Full marks for stating the bleeding obvious, thought Marion. Nevertheless, she helped the children move the bricks. Just as they were dusting themselves down, Flo and Barry arrived to help. Barry approached Malcolm.

'There are several options, old boy,' he said to Malcolm. He produced a piece of paper and began explaining the various diagrams he'd drawn up. There were pulley systems and counterweights, scaffolding, ditches and harnesses. Mert wandered over to have a look. Barry flowed on, mentioning something about Egyptian pyramids. Flo flushed bright red.

'We'll just lift the bloody thing,' said Mert. 'You right to do a bit of lifting, Clarrie?'

'Not if I can help it, Mert. My back's not what it used to be.'

'Nothing wrong with mine,' said Malcolm, pitching his voice as low as he could. Malcolm was strong and muscular, but Mert was a giant. His bicep was the size of Malcolm's thigh. Malcolm had a natural reverence for big fellas. Best to stay on their good side, he thought. And be thankful for their help. He made a mental note to buy Mert half a dozen longnecks.

Barry pushed his glasses back up his nose and looked around, seemingly for the first time. 'I think option C is the best for this situation given that—'

'Yer bit of paper's not gunna move that bath, mate,' Mert said.

Clarrie took matters in hand and moved the tractor into position. He lowered the tray and had ropes ready. 'Alright!' he said. 'Mert, you get the low end, everybody else on the other. Come on kids, we need you too.' Everyone lined up, happy to let Clarrie take the lead. Barry folded his piece of paper and put it in his pocket, but by the time he got into position, Clarrie had counted to three and the bath was safely on the tray. Marion and Flo didn't dare look at each other in case they burst out laughing. Robert ran around with the ropes. Malcolm secured it, showing off his knotting skills.

———

The block was ready. They were starting again from the ground up. The smell of ash had given way to the raw smell of the earth: the underground sullen smell that pulls expression out of curious faces and fills the lungs with dampness. Robert and Louise had made a collection of souvenirs from the rubble. Louise had some bubbles of glass from the frosted windows and a small china koala that had been in her shadow box. Robert had his teeth and the remains of his money box. All the pennies had curled and stuck together. Some of the dates on them were still clear. Altogether he counted fifteen pennies: fifteen cents in the new currency. Marion had found some knives from the kitchen. The bone handles had cracked and splintered but the steel looked good, although when Malcolm handled them he said they'd lost their temper.

On the Bus

Sean strides down the aisle, cigarette in hand. He swings himself into the seat behind Louise and Sally. Louise and Sally eye him with beady little possum eyes. They giggle. Sean smirks. Louise and Sally lower their heads.

'Let's give him the "chook face",' whispers Sally.

'I will if you do.'

'On the count of three.'

'Wait! Wait! I'm not ready.' Louise tries to control her facial muscles as another bout of giggles takes hold. 'Let's practice. How does this look?' She sucks in her cheeks as far as they will go, crosses her eyes and elongates her neck. She leans forward. Clunk! Her forehead bangs into Sally's.

Sally collapses in laughter. 'How about this?' She does the same. Her fringe is so long you can hardly see her eyes. She pulls the offending hair back behind her ears. 'That better?'

'Better.'

'Ok. On the count of three!'

Unison chant: 'One, two threeeeee!'

They swivel around. Two chook faces appear above the seat in front of Sean. The effect is wasted. He's butting out his cigarette and doesn't see it. Hoots from the back seat. Carl throws a ball of paper at Sally. Robert rolls his eyes: embarrassing sister. The girl with the high forehead stops counting telegraph poles and smiles. The Schiller children sit rigid. Gert rummages in her handbag for her glasses.

'That was hopeless,' says Sally.

'Let's try again,' says Louise.

A scrunched-up ball of paper bounces off Sally's head. Sean straightens up. He knows he's in for some entertainment. *Bring it on*, he thinks. *They're cute. They're harmless. How old are they? . . . Salty's eldest . . . must be about twelve? They're jail bait . . .* He can take his eyes off them any time he chooses. They're practising flirting. He sees them huddle down on the seat.

They're counting. Up they spring.

Chook face!

It's even better than the first time. They hold it for as long as they can. But you can't laugh and keep your cheeks sucked in at the same time. Oh, the joy of silliness! They look at each other then back at Sean. He's suddenly smiling. He's actually smiling. No-one has seen that smile before. It's a broad grin. It comes upon him like a shock. Involuntarily.

Sally drops the look. 'Hello, Mr O'Hara!' she says. All innocence.

'Hello. You can call me Sean.' He doesn't believe in old-fashioned servility.

'Hello, Sean!' Sally and Louise say together. He smiles again. This is unbelievable. He's putting them on equal footing.

It's a new age. He's not one of those old-fashioned 'squares'. Louise and Sally bask in the glory of his smile. Gert fixes thick glasses onto her proboscis.

They smile at him, resting their chins on their hands, arms sprawl over the back of the seat, staring gormlessly at him. They do gormless really well. He laughs.

'I'm Sally, and this is Louise.'

'Yes, I know you're Sally. I know your dad.'

'Oh! Everyone knows my dad!' Sally is a bit exasperated. How come Salty is known to all the odd bods?

Sean takes out his tobacco.

'Didn't your house burn down?' asks Sally.

'Yes,' says Sean. 'I found a caravan.'

'Lou's house burnt down. She's in the police station. She's very wicked!'

'I'm sure she's not.' Sean smiles at Louise.

Louise turns red.

'Can I roll one?' asks Sally.

'If you like. But you can't smoke it.'

'No worries... Sean!' Sally's revelling in the intimacy of the conversation.

Sean hands over the tobacco. Louise and Sally each take a paper of Tallyho and hang it off the lower lip. Very professional. They take a wad of tobacco and rub it in the palm.

Sean watches.

'Are you impressed?' Sally asks.

'Very much so,' he responds.

There is much giggling. Louise pulls the paper from her lip. The lip comes with it, extending out like a great lozenge. They're laughing so much, they're crying.

Sean can't help himself. He smiles, then tries to look away: maintain some distance. It's impossible.

Eventually Louise and Sally humbly present Sean with their finished handiwork. Sally's is bulging in the middle. Louise's is thin with strands falling out of each end.

'What you need to do,' – he's addressing Louise with avuncular authority – 'what you need to do is just break the last few strands off.' He takes the cigarette and clips the ends with his fingernail. He looks at Louise.

She gives him the gormless look. She's just realised she can use it as a mask. As irony: what was once for real, can be turned around and used in a mocking gesture. How sophisticated. It means that she doesn't have to succumb to his amazingly handsome face and his glorious smile. She's too busy concentrating on herself.

Sally's found her own level of feigned indifference: no friend of her father's is going to make an impact on her.

'There!' she says. 'I'd give myself nine out of ten for this one.'

Sean takes it and examines it. 'Seven. There's a big lump in the middle.'

'It's pregnant!' she cries. 'It has a little baby cigarette growing inside. That's extra points!'

Sean takes the rollies and puts them in the tobacco pouch.

'Oh . . . can't we keep one?' Sally whines.

'No.'

Oh . . . just one?' They revert to gormless, possum eyes.

'What would your father say?' says Sean.

'Salty? He wouldn't care. I light his cigarettes all the time.'

Sean contemplates what it would be like to have a twelve-year-old daughter. 'Then ask him for one.'

'Mum won't let him give me any.' Sally puts on a sulky

voice. Louise wonders how many voices Sally has. She's a good actress.

The bus slows to a halt. It's his stop. Sean smiles once again. Time to be a gentleman. 'Goodbye Sally,' he says. 'Goodbye Lauren.'

'She's not Lauren! She's Louise!' Sally exclaims in mock outrage. Another character, thinks Louise.

'My humble apologies.' He bows slightly. 'Goodbye, Louise!'

Louise doesn't cope well with the attention. She looks to Sally to take the lead. 'We won't stay here a moment longer! To be insulted in such a way!' Sally puts her nose in the air. 'Come, darling Louise! We'll go and talk to Auntie Flo.'

———

Flo slouches in her seat. She flips open a packet of Alpines. Rummaging in her handbag she eventually finds her lighter. Flicking the flame to life, she draws the smoke deep into her lungs. The relief is instantaneous. Smoke curls towards the ceiling. She sits up straight and stashes a letter into her handbag. She smiles, turns around to face Sally and Louise. 'Hello, you scallywags. What have you been up to?'

'Nothing.' Innocent unison.

The bus pulls to a halt. Clancy turns around to face them.

'Youse all forgot your stop?'

'No! Yes!' Flo exclaims.

They all clamber down into fresh air.

Chapter 19

'Listen to this.' Flo leant forward. '*Please bring the following: paracetamol, quinine, a mouth organ and two sets of playing cards. If for any reason you're held up at the border, offer money straight away. Keep wads of cash, in your underwear. Any currency; English pounds are best. If you see any nuns they're from the mission. So attach yourselves to them. The military will leave you alone. Keep in mind that the hospital has, on occasion, removed bullets from members of the opposition. Don't take any chances.*'

'Struth!' said Malcolm.

'You can't be serious, Flo,' said Marion. Barry shifted in his chair looking pale.

'Where is this place?' asked Malcolm. 'Rob, go and get your atlas.' Robert raced out of the room.

'So, what if these ning-nongs can't speak English? What are you going to do then?'

'Speak French.' Barry said. 'Flo and I have high school French. It'll have to do for starters.'

Flo looked at Barry. This was the first sign that the trip was a possibility.

'What else does she say?' Louise looked at the letter. The writing was small, with no margins or paragraphs.

'She says, *The school is overflowing and the orphanage is filled to capacity. Children are sharing beds. There's not enough linen, or toilets and bathrooms. We usually go into ration mode at the end of each month. The children are wonderful! You won't have any trouble* – Oh, I'll skip that part.' Flo gave Barry a quick look.

'Who's the letter from?' asked Louise.

'My cousin. Her name's Janet but she's Sister Angelica now. She's been a Sister for ten years or so. I haven't seen her since she went to Africa.'

Robert came back into the room and slapped his school atlas on the coffee table. 'It's in the middle.' They all looked at the map.

Malcolm shook his head. 'You won't get much fishing done. There's no coastline.'

'There's a huge lake,' said Barry. 'Fishing is one of the main industries.'

'Ah, well. There ya go,' said Malcolm.

'More tea, Flo?' Marion lifted the teapot.

'No thanks. We'd better get going. Just wanted to share the news. Nothing is organised yet, and it will take months and months.'

'If I hurry up my PhD we can get there in two years' time,' said Barry. He held a steady gaze on Flo and smiled.

'That's ages away!' Robert said. Flo laughed.

'It'll go very fast. Would you like the stamp?' Robert looked at the wild flamingo coursing over a jungle, CHAD written in black across the top.

'Cor! Would I ever!'

Louise leant over to have a look. 'You're not getting it!'

'Don't worry. There'll be plenty more. You can have the next one, Lou.'

'Thanks!'

'We'll see you up on the block on the weekend.'

———

Marion looked out the window of the policemen's flat. The sky was a luminous turquoise stretching to a pale dusty blue towards its dome. High scattered clouds were turning pink, orange and red in the lingering twilight. Heavy clouds, closer to the earth, held their gunmetal grey until the last rays of sun inflamed their edges to a soft pink. The sky shone like the inside of an abalone shell. Folk felt the extra light buoying them up, giving them extra energy and making them feel light-headed. Marion felt it too. From where she stood at the kitchen sink, she could see all the way up the main street from the butchers' shop to the pub. She was looking forward to having a shandy with Malcolm. Even the diesel fumes, wafting up from the belching lorries, seemed benign and jolly.

Dinner was in the oven. Roast chicken and potatoes. King Edwards, the best for roasting. She'd peeled the carrots and opened a can of peas. Everything was ready. She had time to luxuriate in the soft closing of the day. The streetlights came on and added a gentle amber light to the scene below. It seemed quieter than usual.

Since leaving Marcia and Darryl's house and moving into the flat, she'd had time to mourn the loss of her home. She hadn't realised how much of her identity was associated with it. People spoke of the house as an entity in and of itself. Vonnie knew its history going back before Dr and Mrs Cunningham lived there. It had originally been built and owned by Happy Heywood, who had had the good fortune to win the Golden Casket. Vonnie said that Happy was born with a smile on his face and a genial personality. It wasn't the winning of the lottery that made him that way. His smile had always been there. Some people had taken offence at his luck and referred to him as 'Happy Wayward', implying that a person with such a benign personality obviously was not capable of recognising the true nature of reality. But Happy smiled from the cradle to the grave. He never married or had children. He simply lived, giving his smile to those he met and usually receiving one back.

Now the house was gone and the only reminder of Happy's existence was the hand-written sign that Malcolm had nailed to the stump of the large gum at the turn-off to Happy's Road. The original sign had, of course, gone with the fires. Malcolm had done the best he could as a temporary measure: his stolid handwriting marking out the lettering. It irritated Marion that he hadn't spaced the lettering correctly and that the last two letters were cramped together. *Robert could have done a much better job.* But Malcolm thought it was his duty, as a council employee, to do it himself. It was only temporary, he said, until the council could afford new signage throughout the district. Marion reminded herself of this every time they drove to the block.

Marion hadn't seen herself as part of the history of the house, although she'd felt its pull. Without it, she felt different: not tethered or mired in the history of the place. And with that feeling came an energy to redefine herself. The new house would give her the opportunity to make her mark. Malcolm had always been the decider in their living arrangements. She would have her say, but there was a tacit agreement that his opinion was weightier than hers. Now it was her chance. She would design the new house the way that would suit her. Here was an opportunity for self-expression that she had never dreamed of. There were building materials to consider: brick or weatherboard. Of course she would prefer brick, but weatherboard could look attractive given the right coat of paint. The size of rooms and height of ceilings, the soft furnishings, curtains, lounge suits, cushions, bedding. And there was light to consider. The natural light in the changing seasons. The angle of the block: morning sun, afternoon sun, evening light. Ventilation was important. And then there was colour: paint or wallpaper or a combination. A sunroom was a must, as was a built-in bar in the lounge, as they called the living room these days. An open-plan kitchen–dining room would add a modern touch. A study for Malcolm. 'What am I going to study?' he'd asked her. She'd brushed him off. Care had to be taken with the southern side to ensure that mould was kept at bay.

The plan had gone to the builder for costing. Malcolm had thought it too extravagant but had allowed her to hand it to him anyway. She'd have to learn the hard way. Insurance would cover some of the cost but on his salary they couldn't afford half the extras she'd planned. But he wasn't going to say. Let the builder break the bad news to her. He couldn't be bothered arguing. But in the end, the government had given a sizable grant enabling most of Marion's desires to be fulfilled.

———

As the bus pulled out into the flow of traffic going south, Marion saw the schoolchildren of the town straggle out across the footpath, getting in the way of pedestrians, turning this way and that, jeering at one another, tossing their school bags over their shoulders. She spotted Robert at once, darting across the road, his quick eyes taking in the surroundings. Louise was taking her time, dawdling up the street with a group of girls. They were huddled together, their heads inclined to one girl in particular. Shirleena. That dreadful girl from the fish and chip shop. Marion stiffened. She'd have to remind Louise to discriminate between who was possibly a good friend and who was an acquaintance. Vicky Bumford was there as well, apparently hanging on Shirleena's every word, nodding and looking round at the other girls. Louise was at the back of the crowd, straining her head forward. Her blazer was down around her shoulders as if it were an evening stole, and her hair was in a high pigtail fountaining out from the top of her head. *How ridiculous!* Marion thought. *How old does she think she is? One year into high school and she thinks she's seventeen!* Tiny curls had escaped Louise's rubber band and one long sensuous lock curled its way down over the nape of her neck to her shoulder. That hair had to go. A sensible bob was what the girl needed! Who did she think she was, parading along the street like that?

Robert burst through the door into the kitchen. 'Hi Mum.'

'Hello dear,' Marion replied in her 'I want some information' voice. Robert picked it up straight away. 'How was school?'

'Alright.'

'Would you like cup of Milo and a biscuit?'

'Yes, thanks.' Robert slid into his place at the kitchen table.

'Anything happen at school today?'

'No.'

'Nothing at all?'

'Nup.'

'You did go?' Handing him the Milo.

'Yep.'

'What's the name of that girl that works at the fish and chip shop? You know, the one that hangs around with Vicky?'

'I dunno.'

If Robert wasn't going to cooperate, she was at a dead end.

'I'm going down to the slab,' he said, referring to the concrete slab at the back of the police lockup. It was a great place to practise bowling. He'd drawn at set of wickets on the high brick wall at the side of the flat. Above the wickets he'd drawn a very life-like portrait of the cricket coach. He'd enlarged the eyeballs and added glistening red veins, snarling, canine teeth and dribble.

Louise sauntered into the kitchen and dropped her bag in the middle of the room. Marion smiled and kissed her. Now was not the time for a confrontation about dropping bags in the middle of the room. She put on her bright voice: the carefree happy voice. 'I've made an appointment for you,' she said, knowing that Louise rarely knew if she was telling the truth or not. In any case, she'd make the appointment tomorrow. (And convince Malcolm to give her the money.)

'What for?' asked Louise.

'For your hair! In the salon,' said Marion. 'Shampoo and blow wave. The works! And a trim.'

'Oh, Mum! That's great!'

Marion smiled and pulled at the loose strand of hair hanging down from the rubber band. Louise could be placid and dreamy, or she could be steely and stubborn. Marion had caught her at the right time. 'A shaped bob. Or even shorter. Sort of like Mia Farrow? What do you think?'

'Oh, Mum, that would be great! Thanks.'

A neat haircut, thought Marion. And none of this dishevelled kitten look.

'And perhaps we can buy you some nail polish. Only clear, mind you!'

'And some eyeliner to go with the Mia Farrow?'

'Absolutely not!'

On the Bus

Scotty picks up his school bag and holds it against his crotch. He moves up the aisle. His face is pale, with a concentrated, preoccupied look. His eyes staring at nothing in particular. The bus jerks and he shifts his weight, grabbing the handle of the seat at his side. Louise and Sally are sitting there, laughing hysterically as the bus bumps along a rough patch. Sally takes the opportunity to grab Louise just above the knee and squeezes hard until she yelps in agony. It's an old game, but always good for a laugh. Louise throws her head back in exaggerated pain and crashes into Scotty's hand. He feels the knock of her head against his fingers.

'Sorry!' she says. 'It's not my fault!' Laughing and groaning as Sally's grip continues to hold her. Scotty smiles: a lightning flash of white teeth. He re-positions his bag. His groin stirs. Sally lets go and flops back against the seat. Louise sighs and holds her legs in a prone position, the red marks of Sally's fingers imprinted on her thigh. 'Look what she's done to me!' she says, lifting her eyes to Scotty.

Oh! And look what you've done to me, he thinks. *Keep the bag steady . . . keep it in front of me . . . look careless . . . like I'm not interested . . . oh my God . . . .my dick's on fire . . . oh my God . . .*

I've got to get off the bus . . . Everyone can see . . . I've got to get off!

The cold air revives him and brings his erection under control. He lets the bag hang over his shoulder. His elder brothers had told him what would happen: the sweating, the rubbing, the excruciating, delightful agony. They didn't tell him that it was the most amazing experience in his entire life. He doubts he will be able to think of any ordinary thing ever again.

His mother becomes a blur as he moves quickly to his shared bedroom and positions a chair in front of the door.

Chapter 20

MELANIE TURNED AROUND AND GAZED at the great wide expanse of the school oval. 'Here he comes,' she said. Julie turned around as Ronny Cracknel raced up behind her and grabbed her round the waist. She lifted her face to him and kissed him on the lips. Melanie took the bag of lollies from Julie and held them out to Ronny. 'Want a freckle?'

'Yeah, thanks.' He took it and held it between his teeth, proffering it to Julie. She covered it with her mouth and their tongues swirled around the sweet chocolate.

'Youse are disgusting!' said Melanie.

'You bet!' replied Ronny. He flicked Julie's bra strap and raced away to the middle of the oval where a football was hurtling through the air. He was a ruckman, and a good one. No-one was talking VFL, but if he played well and consistently he would end up in the local first division. That would be a good start.

Julie gave a little skip, just to prove she could. Melanie imitated it. Then Julie did another. Melanie did the same. And around the oval they went like a pair of crazy Morris dancers, skipping and dancing and jumping. The strong green grass coating their shoes with moisture. The pines at the end of the oval holding the wind up high. Julie smiled and turned to Melanie.

'I'm going to marry him.'

'I know that!'

'We'll have to wait forever. Four more years!'

'I know! You'll be old by then.'

'I've seen his thing,' said Julie. Melanie stopped dead and faced Julie.

'You haven't! Have you?'

'Yep. It's only little.'

'When did you see it?'

'It fell out of his shorts when we went rowing on the river. Now that I've seen it, I know it will be alright. I know it'll fit. I'm normal down there.' She pointed to her crotch.

With complacent certainty about Julie and Ronny's future, the girls finished the sweets and popped the paper bag.

———

The only time Scotty moved with any purpose in his step was towards the music department. He'd put his head down and stride deliberately through the yard. In all other subjects he was woefully behind, but in music, he was a star. Ron Jolliffe was quick to diagnose Scotty's reading problem and devised a method of colouring in the notes to identify their various pitches. It worked like a dream. In no time he was reading the manuscript fluently, even helping others who were struggling. Every lunch hour he'd be in the practice room working on scales and arpeggios. Although Ron encouraged Scotty to take home an instrument, the boy refused to do so. Ron didn't press him. The lad would have his reasons, and remembering Scotty's elder brothers, he imagined that they wouldn't take kindly to the sound of a musical instrument. His brothers were loud, belligerent clowns who spent their school years jeering at teachers, eating exam papers, throwing books and pens around the rooms, and clambering over furniture.

Scotty was different. He was small and slight. Quiet and self-conscious. His father joked that he must have been sired by the milkman. His mother joked that there wasn't a milkman within cooee of the place. Of course they called him the runt of the pack: the little poofter. The one that should have been a girl. His father didn't bother with him much. His three other sons were strong and capable: they could work in the bush, had plenty of endurance. He didn't need Scotty.

One day Scotty would buy his own trumpet. He'd have a place of his own, a flat or a house. He'd need plenty of space so that the sound wouldn't annoy any neighbours. And he'd stand at the open window or out on the front porch and he'd blow the trumpet as loud as he wanted to. He'd let the sound ring out to the sky and the hills. He'd feel his heart and soul move in the liquid gold notes and he wouldn't stop till he was utterly exhausted. In the meantime, he'd keep his talent a secret. He wasn't going to give any of his family an opportunity to pour shit on him.

On the Bus

Teenage love is a strange and powerful thing.

It's as if the others on the bus conspire to leave the seat next to Louise empty. The only empty seat. And Scotty the only one looking for a seat. It's as if the air has parted and drawn him through a vacuum that ends with her: as if his feet have only enough strength to get to where she sits. He drops his school bag nonchalantly on the floor and swings round and sits next to her. He notices his breathing and controls it with a brass player's concentration.

She remains completely paralysed.

Their guardian angels, resting on their shoulders. Playing poker. Occasionally lifting their eyes to each other. Crossing legs at the knees and rearranging a diaphanous swathe of ectoplasm around their bodies. Sighing briefly and throwing down the cards. Eventually touching each other: reaching out a hand to stroke a face, the heat of the exchange causing an explosion of molten angel dust.

Louise knows no more than the warm spicy smell that he brings. For one brief moment she looks at his hands: the veins like powerful rivers underneath his beautiful olive skin.

She rises to go as the bus approaches her stop and realises in panic that she has to negotiate his knees. He pulls back in anticipation, trying not to distress her. When she's free he looks up at her.

'See you tomorrow,' he says, and gives her his smile.

It fills her body.

'Yes,' she says, completely hypnotised.

Chapter 21

THE STOVE IN THE NEW house took a bit of getting used to. It ran hot. It was fast and efficient. Marion had to be on her toes. Roasts could burn, white sauce would catch if she wasn't constantly stirring, and vegetables could boil dry in an instant. Malcolm had wanted a slow-combustion stove. 'It'll warm the whole house! And heat the hot water. Free hot water, Marion! They're back in fashion, you know. Even Flo and Barry have one. Firewood doesn't cost much, and Robbie and I will keep the wood up to it. Cost virtually nothing.'

Marion remembered the old stove that had been removed from the Cunninghams' house when they first came to the valley. It was a giant of a thing and although Vonnie had sworn by it, she wasn't taken in. Wood stoves were smoky and dirty and demanded constant attention. For Flo and Barry, the slow-combustion stove was a source of endless irritation. Barry was tardy in supplying chopped wood and Flo felt like a slave to the thing: forever having to monitor the wood supply, juggle the various flues and empty the ash. She'd christened the stove 'YOU BASTARD!'

But Malcolm imagined a slow-combustion stove as efficient and efficacious. He saw himself as the head engineer, stoking the fire, keeping the heart of the house going. He would be responsible for the warmth and comfort it would provide: Marion, for the wonderful aromas of home cooking. He would be with her, at the core of domesticity. Each reliant on the other. Each with their own contribution to the home.

In the end the expense had put them off. Marion was relieved, but Malcolm merely put it on hold. Five years down the track, he said. He was itching to prove to Flo and Barry how a stove should be run. Whenever he was at their house, he'd fiddle around with it, opening and shutting the flue, repositioning wood, emptying the ash. 'I'll put it in your compost,' he'd say as he lifted the heavy bucket and headed for the back door. Flo would raise her cigarette with a resigned wave of her hand.

'Whatever, Malcolm.'

———

Since moving into the new house, Marion had made a few decisions about her life. Firstly, she'd use the car to do the shopping herself. Having lived in town for eighteen months, she'd grown used to having all the facilities at hand. She'd become a familiar face on the street. The butcher was friendly (even a bit flirtatious). He always gave her good cuts of meat. The grocer always drew her attention to the freshest vegetables, telling her their origins, giving advice on cooking and storage. All the shopkeepers were friendly towards her, laughing and joking. Previously, Malcolm had done all the shopping. She simply prepared a list for him and he'd do it in his lunch hour or do a quick run around after work on Fridays. It was never very satisfactory. Sometimes he bought cheaper brands and sometimes left items off altogether, considering them unnecessary. He always bought plenty of the things he liked: lots of bacon and cans of baked beans. He loved to see them lined up in the cupboards. Robert did point out that sixteen cans of baked beans was probably enough, but it never stopped him buying that extra can or two.

Living in the flat had been a delight for Marion. She joined the Country Women's Association and went to regular meetings. She also helped out at the school tuckshop. New friends came around for coffee in the afternoons. Now, back in Happy's Road, she didn't want her social life to dry up. Having the car occasionally was the first thing to see to.

'I'm rostered on for the tuckshop on Friday,' she said.

'So?' Malcolm knew what was coming.

'Well. If I could have the car, I could do the tuckshop, then the grocery shopping as well.'

Malcolm leant back on his chair and spread his legs. 'Marion, does it ever occur to you that my car is just that. MY CAR? I need the car at work. What if I need to visit someone outside the office? Have you thought of that?'

'Has that ever happened?'

Malcolm felt a burst of fury. 'Don't you ever question me like that, Marion. I provide a good living for this family. Your job is here.' He banged on the arm of the chair. 'In this house! Looking after our children. Have you got that?' Self-righteous anger took hold. 'And the next thing you'll want the car for is drinks with the "girls". Oh yes, Marion. I've heard about women like that. And I'm not having it. Have you got that? I'm not having you racing round the valley with your stupid friends.'

Marion was close to tears. He tried to soften. 'You know you're not a good driver, Marion. You know that. What if you had an accident? Where would that leave me?'

'How am I to become a better driver if I never have the car?' She heard her own voice, a snivelling whine.

'We can do a little drive on Sunday. Up on Willows Marsh. There's no traffic up there. Would that satisfy you?'

'Yes. That would be good.' She left the living room and went outside, fighting tears. Face crumpling, she rammed her fists into the pocket of her apron.

She stood on the edge of the concrete block by the clothes-line and tried to look busy in case the children saw her. Quickly she wiped her eyes with her apron. All the possible retorts came to her: did he have to borrow the toaster if he wanted to use it? There were plenty of women drivers in the valley who were just as good as men. Some even drove trucks! Flo had the car all day anytime she needed it. Barry didn't mind. He just took the bus to Hobart. Why hadn't Malcolm told her about moving the seat forward? That had made all the difference. Why had he kept that from her? He never used the car at work. She knew that for a fact.

'Right!' she said to herself. 'Sunday it is. I'll make sure he moves the seat forward. If it's more practice I need, I'll make sure I get it. One thing at a time.'

Marion decided to look on the bright side. He just needed softening up. She had gone about it the wrong way. If she'd been more patient, the right moment would have presented itself. She had to fight the urge to get to the point. It was simply a matter of time before he saw reason. If he appeared to be stubborn and reactionary, she would see it as being steadfast and traditional. If he was demeaning and critical, he was only trying to protect her from the cruelties of the outside world. If he was tight with money, he was simply being economical. If he seemed to be controlling, he was really being protective. It all depended on your point of view.

———

Doing the shopping would mean asking for money, and that would be difficult, too. Malcolm had short arms and long pockets. He behaved as if the money was his and his alone: decisions about groceries and household items were made by him and he'd vet every single item on a list. Marion found it tedious and demeaning. Even with sanitary napkins, he'd challenge her to find a cheaper brand. Simply having the car, and access to money, would make her life a lot easier. She'd have to give it a little more time. He'd come round eventually, she hoped.

The other great change that she'd set her heart on was a part-time job. She'd looked on the community noticeboard outside the newsagency. Apple sorters were needed in the main shed off Cooper's Road. Pickers were needed at the Bouldgers' orchard (no Catholics need apply). A typist was need two hours a week at the lawyers. Forty words per minute, minimum. Nothing for her.

She fantasised about seeing an ad that would make her dream come true: an advertisement meant for her and her alone. She would be the only applicant, the only qualifier. It would read: *The council is seeking an experienced dance teacher for the new Dance School. Must have experience in all dance forms. Adult and children's classes.* If it had council endorsement, she thought, Malcolm was bound to agree.

She knew she'd be good at it. Since she was a child, she'd helped Bo-Bo and Mum in the dancing school. Teaching came naturally to her and she was familiar with how the accounts were drawn up. By the time she was fourteen she was taking the under-sevens class, helping the men in the adult ballroom and keeping up with her own tap and Latin. But it was a daring thing to do. Flo had thought it a great idea. She'd promised to help with advertising. There was nothing like it in the valley. Would the community want a dancing school? And where could she have it? There was a small hall attached to the primary school, and the music teacher might be amenable to being an accompanist? The dream seemed too grand. Perhaps it was not for the likes of her to start a dance studio. But the fantasy persisted. It played on her mind in the dull afternoons. As she waited for the children to come home from school, she'd kick off her shoes and go through a few routines.

One Friday night after tea, she mentioned it to Malcolm. He'd had a pre-dinner sherry and was in a mellow mood. In her bright conversational voice, slightly offhand and by-the-way, she mentioned a friend from the primary school who was starting a women's fashion store in the town. 'She's doing it all from scratch. Her husband's a farmer, but there's no money in the apples these days so she thought she'd have a go at retail.'

Malcolm laughed. 'That'll come to no good,' he said. 'No-one shops here for fancy stuff. They can go to Hobart.'

'But they don't,' she replied. 'There are people that live down here that have never been out of the valley. Look at the council members: at least two of them have only been to Hobart once in their entire lives!' Malcolm snorted. Dismissing the conversation.

But Marion had prepared for this all afternoon. She wasn't going to be put off. She'd waited long enough. The children sat at each end of the kitchen table; the door to the lounge was slightly ajar. They could hear every word.

She knew as soon as she started that it was a lost cause. But she'd promised herself she'd mention the dance school. The prepared speech in her head had its own momentum. Her throat became dry, her voice high and scratchy. 'We could use a little extra money. When the children finish high school, they'll need to go to Hobart for Matriculation. They will have to board and that will be expensive. A small dance studio can make quite a lot of money if it's run properly. Flo thinks it's a great idea.' She tried to keep her tone light and up-beat. Marion remembered her mother and Bo-Bo and the woeful mess of accounts lying on the benches and the last-minute clean-up as they heard the children clatter up the stairs in their tap shoes.

'Don't make me laugh, Marion!' Malcolm guffawed. 'You couldn't run a chook raffle! Oh, and if "Flo thinks it's a great idea" then it's definitely not. Have you got that? There's no way my wife is going to be running round town in a pair of dancing shoes. I'd be a laughing-stock. You've got to think about my position as a council employee. What do you think they'd think if my wife up and started a business? No. You're only thinking of yourself, as usual. Your place is here, making this our home. And another thing! If anyone's going onto Matriculation College, it's Robbie. I'm not wasting good money on the girl. She can leave school after Grade 10, if she gets that far. There's no point in her going any further.'

Marion's voice became very low and tremulous. Louise and Robert had to strain to hear her. 'Louise has never achieved less than a B-plus for any of her grades.' Her voice was shaking and the words came hissing out of her mouth. 'She deserves an education as much as Robert!'

Malcolm threw his arms up in an exaggerated gesture as if he was having to explain something to a petulant child.

'Marion, don't be stupid! You just have to take one look at her! There's no point in wasting money on her. If we had any extra money, which we don't, the best thing we could do would be to buy a couple of cows and put them in the back paddock.'

Robert sprang up from the table with a loud 'moo'. He grabbed the back of the chair and started performing a plié, mooing with every bend of the knees. Louise smiled and flicked a rubber band at him. Malcolm came thundering into the kitchen and whacked Robert across the head.

'Ow! That hurt!' Robert cried. Louise closed her books and prepared for a quick getaway.

———

Malcolm felt the rising panic of his world tumbling out of control.

Robert no longer spent time with him playing cricket. He'd made the high school cricket team, and he wasn't going to spend his weekends learning cricket from his dad. He had friends of his own. They congregated in his room and played loud rock music on the portable stereo. It was dreadful music. Malcolm couldn't understand why they listened to it. There was no melody to it. No beautiful voices. Only ugly nasal twang. Well, they could keep their Creedence Clearwater Revival. It was a load of codswallop as far as he was concerned. When he'd had enough he'd go into Robert's room and tell them all to clear off. They'd hop on their bikes as quick as a flash and disappear down Happy's Road. Robert would be sullen for a while.

And that dreadful Flo! Trying to influence Marion: trying to make her into some sort of Women's Libber. He wouldn't have it. His wife was not that sort of woman. It went against nature. Whenever he thought of Flo, he had that vision of her on that day. The day of the fires. Her dress plastered to her legs and the Saltmarsh babies clinging to her. She'd put her hand on his shoulder when she'd seen the ruins of his house. What did she think he was going to do? Cry or something? He wasn't soft.

———

Marion sifted a cup of self-raising flour and added a tablespoon of caster sugar and let the mixture sit for fifteen minutes. She was anxious to get this right the first time. There was a lot hanging on this batch of pikelets. At the CWA, Marion's pikelets were much admired. They were light and never doughy. She took care to make sure all the ingredients were at room temperature before starting, and she always made sure they were cold before placing them in cellophane packets. Every member of the CWA had a number. This was to maintain anonymity for the purchaser and to prevent obvious enmity between members. Nevertheless, Marion – number 24 – proved to be very popular, and any cakes, biscuits, jams or pickles she made always sold quickly. When the Hobart branch rang with a specific request for pikelets, lamingtons and scones, Marion was the obvious choice for the pikelets. The order was for ten dozen pikelets in half-dozen packets. They were for a function at Government House. The excitement was palpable. Marion would be carrying the reputation of Golden Valley to the capital city. She could hardly believe it herself. She couldn't wait to write and tell Mum and Bo-Bo.

Opportunity had smiled at her. Breathlessly she told Malcolm about it. He chuckled indulgently. 'The others must be upset about you being chosen. You're not the only pikelet maker, surely?' Well, if it would keep her quiet for a while, all the better. Better she was making pikelets than dreaming about a dance school. And it'd give her a bit a pocket money.

But when Marion asked for the car to make the delivery at the CWA headquarters in Hobart, all hell broke loose. She explained to Malcolm that it would be impossible to travel by bus. The pikelets had to remain flat and cool. Not only that, but Molly Driscoll was cooking the lamingtons and Vonnie was cooking the scones. Two big trays of each. A car was required so they could place the cakes in the boot, where it was cool. Molly didn't drive, and Vonnie couldn't leave the shop, so it was up to Marion. The delivery had to be made on Friday.

Malcolm was beside himself with rage. How dare she make an arrangement without consulting him! Marion said she had already mentioned it the week before, and he hadn't had any objection then. Malcolm asked how he was supposed to get to work. Marion said she would come with him to work, drive home, collect the pikelets, drive to Vonnie's, then Molly's place, drive into Hobart, drop off the cakes, come back to Golden Valley at the end of the day, take Molly home, take Vonnie home, then come and collect him from work. Malcolm countered: that was far too much driving for an inexperienced driver.

'And Hobart? On a Friday? Have you thought of that? You'll have to do a reverse park in the main street. Have you thought of that?'

Marion responded in an even tone. 'There's a car park at the back of the shop.'

Malcolm leapt into the details. 'Have you seen it?'

'No,' she said, 'but Molly's been there before. Molly said there's room to turn the car around in the car park.'

'Is the entrance one way or two ways? These are important details, Marion.' She said she didn't know. 'How are you going to get back onto the main street? Do you turn right or left? If you don't know now, how are you going to find out? And getting back? It's a long, tiring drive, Marion.'

'I'll take a thermos. We'll stop at the lookout.'

'And what about the children?' he said. 'Will you be back in time for the children when they came home from school?'

'They're old enough to spend a couple of hours by themselves.'

Marion had a brief flashback to her own school days, coming home to a bare kitchen while the piano thumped overhead. She was in charge of her siblings: filling them up with bread and jam and waiting for Mum or Bo-Bo to come downstairs in the bleak cold afternoons.

'Flo's home if they need anything,' she countered, 'or if they want company.' The mention of Flo made Malcolm's blood boil all the more.

'That stupid woman! I don't know if I want my children hanging around that house! Does she think she's still going to Africa to live with the ning-nongs?'

'Yes,' replied Marion. 'They're off at the end of the month. And good luck to them.' She flicked out a tea towel and folded it over the oven handle. She was determined to win this battle. It wasn't much to ask. Just having the car for one afternoon. Flo said that if the worst came to the worst, she would drive Marion and Molly into Hobart. Barry could catch the bus to the university and they could collect him after work.

She was just about to mention Flo's offer when the doorbell rang. Robert, never far from the action, opened it. Darryl burst into the kitchen.

'Marion! I've heard the news! Government House! Whack-oh! Waddya reckon Malcolm!' He gave Malcolm a punch on the arm. 'Just think! Those bludgers from Government House are going to eat your pikelets, Marion. You're famous now. Everyone in the valley is talking about it. Molly's beside herself about the lamingtons. Apparently her blood pressure's gone through the roof. Vonnie's not so fussed. She says she's too old to get excited about a batch of scones.' Darryl pulled a couple of longnecks from a brown paper bag. 'I thought we could have a little celebration. How about it Mal? Just happen to have these with me.'

Malcolm pulled open the drawer of the kitchen dresser and rummaged noisily till he found the bottle opener. He took two glasses off the top of the dresser.

'Did you want one?' he said to Marion. She shook her head.

Malcolm sighed as he poured the sparkling amber fluid into the glasses. It would take the edge off his anger. Once he had had a couple of glasses in him, things would look better. He had no idea why he felt so angry. But he did know that it was the right way to feel about this situation. Marion was scheming behind his back. She was trying to do things without telling him. He was being kept in the dark. His greatest fear was that somehow she would make a fool of him. Maybe the pikelets wouldn't be cooked properly and someone at Government House would be taken ill. And it would be all her fault. Did she really know what she was doing? She wasn't a trained cook. Surely Government House ought to be supplied by properly trained chefs. What did they think they were doing, interfering with ordinary people's lives? He'd have to point all this out to her. But not at the moment. Not with Darryl here with a couple of bottles of beer.

Malcolm took a long draught. 'It's great, Darryl. But there's one problem. How are they going to get these cakes to Hobart? They don't think these things through. You can't ask a housewife to down tools and just rush off to Hobart at the drop of a hat. Marion's got things to do. There's the kids to consider. And Vonnie – Vonnie's always busy. The shop's too much for her as it is. Look at how she has to take care of Merv. No, it's inconsiderate.' Malcolm warmed to his topic. 'These blokes up at Government House don't know what they're doing when they ask for something like this. Oh, they think it's very nice... very quaint... to ask a simple housewife to supply them with scones and pikelets, and the like, but they don't consider the impact this is going to have on the families concerned. For instance: how are the girls going to get their cakes to Hobart? Have they considered that? No. So it's an imposition on us, their husbands and their families.' Malcolm took another long, justified swig of beer.

'Oh, no Mal,' said Darryl. 'You've got it all wrong! There's no problem with transport. I can take them up in one of the council trucks if need be. There's no problem there.

The girls don't even have to come. I spoke to Cliff Bumford before I came. He's very keen. Reflects well on the valley, he said. Mighty proud of our housewives, he said.'

Malcolm shifted gear. 'Oh, there's no need for that. So Cliff's heard about this?'

'Yes, he reckons it's a great idea!'

'Well... I can take them up myself. Might even be able to take the afternoon off. Even if I can't, Marion can take the car.'

'Are you sure, Mal?'

'Yes, of course. She can have the car whenever she likes.'

Marion took a quick step away from the sink and busied herself in the overhead cupboard. She would have the car for the Friday trip to Hobart! There would be no backlash! She was overwhelmed with gratitude to Darryl.

Darryl breathed a sigh of relief. He refilled Malcolm's glass and settled himself on the kitchen stool. Conversation settled into its familiar patterns: what the children were up to, council business, Marcia's new hairdo (a blow wave), cars (the Valiant was in decline), footy (the Saints were in good form), finance (inflation was rising).

Robert made an entrance and Darryl gave him a sip of his beer.

'Come and see my drawings before you go?'

'I certainly will, matey.'

When the beer was gone, Darryl marched up the hall to Robert's room. On the way he rapped his knuckles on Louise's door. 'How ya doin' Princess?' Louise sprung open the door.

'All the better for seeing you, Dazza!' She gave him a big hug and just as quickly shut the door.

Darryl looked at Robert's paintings and sketches. He was serious and earnest and gave each piece a long, considered appraisal. 'What do you call this, Robbie?' he asked, pointing to an oversized eye.

'It's an Egyptian eye. It's the Eye of the god Horus,' said Robert.

'Egyptian, eh,' said Darryl. 'Ya gunna do another one to match?'

Robert smiled. 'No. There's only one.'

'Gawd! Struth! Bloody Egyptian gods wandering around with only one eye! It's not gunna lay a curse on me or anything is it?'

Robert laughed. 'No, it's for good luck.'

Malcolm came in as Darryl picked up a sketch of the river with the road running beside it. The telegraph poles diminishing in perfect perspective. 'And will you look at this Mal? He's got the perspective right down to a tee. You've got to hand it to him.' He turned to Robert. 'Young Robert!' he said. 'I don't know much about art and that, but even I can tell you're very talented, my boy.' Malcolm looked over Darryl's shoulder. He hadn't been in Robert's room for some time. 'My goodness, Mal. Your young man's got a lot of talent. Just look what he's done here.'

Malcolm gave an indulgent glance to the array of sketches and paintings. 'He's costing me a fortune in paper and pencils,' he said. Robert's face stiffened.

'I pinch most of it from school.'

Malcolm felt a mighty desire to pull attention away from Robert. It was infantile, he knew. Why couldn't he let the boy bask in a few compliments every now and then? It wasn't as if Darryl was an expert. He didn't know what he was talking about most of the time, let alone on the subject of art. Why did he feel this incredibly strong urge to belittle the boy? His first instinct on hearing Darryl's comments was to point out that art wouldn't get the boy a job. Art wasn't a job. Darryl's praise would give the boy a swollen head. He should be keeping his feet on the ground. It seemed such a waste to be fiddling away with pencils and paints.

Robert was small and fine-boned like Marion. He had a delicacy in the movement of his hands that Malcolm didn't like. Even the way he'd pick up a piece of toast seemed overly precious. Underneath Robert's playful personality, however, was a steeliness. Malcolm could sense it. It was beginning to show itself more and more.

Malcolm waved Darryl's ute out of the driveway with mixed feelings. It seemed this Government House business was something to be proud of, and he wouldn't be made to look a fool.

———

Malcolm turned the television on and plonked down in his chair. 'Stone the flaming crows! I can't hear a bloody thing!' He got out of his chair and turned the volume up. The clarion call of the ABC news bulletin filled the house.

'Dinner's ready.' Marion called from the kitchen.

'And about time. Why is it so bloody late?'

'Robert was late getting home from practice.'

'Oh, Robert's fault is it? Not you gas-bagging on the phone.'

'I haven't talked to anyone all day. Malcolm, do we have to have the TV up so loud?'

'What do you mean? This is important news, Marion.' The Vietnam War spilled out into the living room. 'You need to know about this Marion. What if Robbie gets conscripted? What'll happen to Mummy's little boy then? Eh?'

Robert sauntered into the living room. 'I think I'd object. But I do like the uniforms.'

He was goading. Malcolm knew it but couldn't control his anger. 'No son of mine is going to be a conscientious objector!'

'For heaven's sake, Malcolm. Turn the television off and come and sit at the table. Robert's twelve years old. He doesn't know a thing.'

'Oh! And now I'm being told what I can and can't do in my own house?'

Malcolm moved his chair right in front of the television. He grabbed his dinner and sat down with it. Marion sat down at the table with the children.

'Did you have a good day, darling?' Marion said to Louise. Louise lifted her head in a questioning gesture. 'A good day. Did you have a good day?' A little louder this time.

'Yes,' Louise mumbled. 'Yes!' She tried again at the top of her voice.

Robert started laughing. Then he moved his lips in a silent parody of conversation.

'Robert, eat up and go,' said Marion.

'What?'

'You heard me.'

'What's that? Once again?'

Marion gave up and silently ate her dinner. Louise felt sick. She swirled her mashed potatoes together with the peas and carrots. 'You can have my chop, Mum.' She forked her lamb chop onto Marion's plate.

———

Whether it was Marion and her schemes, or Robert's seeming

indolence, or Louise's secrecy, Malcolm found that since the fire there was always part of him wanting to rage against something. He wanted to re-experience that moment again. Anger seemed the way he could touch that intensity in an explosion of passion. And it felt right. It always felt right. The actual moment was pure, beyond dreaming. It transported him. Took him to a world outside of himself. But it always left a trail of devastation.

He knew it was affecting him at work. The morning had started badly. The report on bridge reconstruction was due at the end of the week. He had a preliminary version on his desk. Scanning it through, he started muttering to himself. 'This'll all have to be done again.' He marked the page with a red slash. He used such force that it ripped the paper. Picking it up, he marched to the typing pool. 'Who's responsible for this?' He held up the torn sheet.

'I am, sir,' said a young woman.

'Don't you know how to indent a paragraph? Didn't they teach you that at typing school? What do you think you're doing?'

'I'm sorry, Mr Johnstone. We were taught to—'

'I don't care what you were taught, girly! In this office it's my way or the highway! Have you got that?'

The young woman hung her head and started crying. The senior typist stood and approached Malcolm.

'That's enough, Malcolm,' she said. 'She's new. She's doing a very good job. I think an apology is in order.'

'Do you now?'

'Yes, I do.' She held her ground.

'Well, what I want is a bit more attention to detail. Have you got that?' He marched out of the room.

On Thursday night they had an early dinner. The children helped with the washing up and left Marion to make the pikelets. The ingredients were lined up in regimental fashion on the kitchen bench. The eggs were fresh from Vonnie's chooks. They were still warm when she'd picked them up in the afternoon. She had the caster sugar and flour at room temperature. The butter had been out of the fridge all day to make sure it was soft and easy to melt. Even the salt she'd considered, making sure it was dry with no lumps. She'd taken four fresh bottles of milk out of the fridge to rest on the bench, their necks filled with a rich plug of risen cream. She'd shake them well before pouring them into the saucepan and warming it just slightly. It was one of her tricks for a perfect mixture. She'd scrubbed the milk saucepan till it shone.

Robert and Louise quietly left the kitchen, as if they were leaving a sacred temple where a grand ritual was about to take place. Malcolm settled in the living room watching the television. Marion cracked the first egg into the large mixing bowl, feeling the clear white of the egg drip from her fingers. She added the warmed milk, cleaned the whisk with a fresh tea towel and entered a trance.

She had borrowed every cooling rack she could lay her hands on. Some of them coming from Alice Saltmarsh, via Flo. By the time the children were getting ready for bed, the sweet smell of sugar mixed with flour was wafting through the house.

The evening dragged on until the very last batch. Her legs were aching and her eyes were sore. She'd started out in breathless excitement but now she just wanted it to be over. Carefully she spooned the batter onto the barely greased pan. Six little pikelets all in a circle. As if in slow motion, the mixture heated and gradually a fine line of bubbles formed on the surface of each. Deftly, she flipped them over. Some were fine grained yellowy-brown in texture, others motley with large dark brown freckles on a golden background. But each acceptable. She gazed as they lifted and stretched, as the flour and egg and milk coalesced to a light delicate cake. Their circumference formed a dark brown rim and the interior opened out as the pikelet rose, giving a pale cream to the sides, springy and soft.

Now she could begin putting them in their cellophane packets, making sure they were cold but dry. If she left it till morning, they'd absorb the damp night air and become soggy. As she lifted the last pikelet out of the pan and flipped it onto a rack, Malcolm came into the kitchen.

'Time for bed, darl,' he said. 'You won't be long will you?' He leant his elbow on a vacant part of the bench. Winking at her, he picked up a pikelet and shoved it in his mouth.

'What?' he said, looking at her horrified face. 'They won't miss one.'

'How dare you? Malcolm! Why did you do that?' Marion was so outraged she could hardly speak.

'Do what? Oh, Marion, come on! It's only a pikelet.'

'I need to have the right number. I need ten dozen.'

'They won't notice one less.'

'Yes, they will.'

'Don't be stupid! One little pikelet! You're making a mountain out of a molehill. Come on. Pack it in and come to bed.

You've done enough. That's enough pikelet-making for one night.'

'Get out!'

'What did you say?'

'I said get out of my kitchen!'

'Marion, I think you're getting this out of proportion.'

'I'll need to make another batch now. Don't you see that?'

'You're being stupid. Just stick them in their packets and come to bed.'

'I'm not coming to bed till this job is finished.'

'For God's sake, Marion. Get things in perspective. They won't miss one.'

Marion rinsed the mixing bowl and turned the hot plate back on.

'Oh well if that's your attitude,' said Malcolm as he helped himself to another pikelet. 'When I ask my wife to come to bed, I expect her to come to bed!' Marion was silent. 'Fine. I get the message. Well, get this one!' He turned around and swooped the trays of pikelets onto the floor.

———

Louise heard the ruckus and came running up the hall. Malcolm strode past her to the bedroom and slammed the door. Marion stood with her lower lip trembling, tears running down her face. Louise could see nothing of her mother, her vitality, her exuberance, all her spark. She was a void, emptied out. Suddenly grown old and decrepit. Louise put her arms around the shaking figure.

It was an end point for Louise. A completion. The final shift into the women's world. On her knees in her pyjamas, she helped Marion pick up the scattered pikelets, brushing any dirt from them and carefully placing them in the cellophane packets. They laughed about getting out the iron and flattening out the buckled ones. Marion stopped crying. She sticky-taped the packets with trembling hands. They placed them with the good side up for the best presentation possible. Louise made sure every packet was uniform. She made an extra batch and they waited hand in hand while they cooled.

Marion explained to Louise everything she'd done wrong. She shouldn't have challenged Malcolm. She should have dropped everything and gone to bed. She could have got up early in the morning and finished the last batch. She shouldn't have put herself above his needs. But she'd been obsessed. Wanting them to be perfect. She needed so much to get this right. To do something for herself. Something that reflected in the outer world. Something that showed her competence and individuality. A challenge that she'd met. A chance to show off what she could do. And of course, some extra money that she could keep for herself and the children. But she'd got above herself. Letting her pride dominate. And she'd paid the price. It was not his fault, Marion said. Men didn't understand.

Louise wondered what it was that men didn't understand. She knew Marion was wrong to blame herself. She knew that Malcolm's behaviour was unjustified. She decided she would no longer come at his bidding. She would not kiss him goodnight. Nor would she sit in the front seat of the car. Whenever she could, she'd catch the bus. She'd communicate through Robert. If there was something that needed saying, or a request, she'd ask Robert to do it for her. She would not look him in the eye. She'd let her eyes glaze over and slide away from his face.

They lay together. Two frozen stick figures. Marion's body felt weightless, as if she were hardly touching the mattress or the pillow. The very cells in her body felt different. As if her flesh has been replaced by air. Like an insect that hovers above a flower, she felt an intense vibration in her body that seemed to hold her outside of time. With crystal clarity, without artifice or fantasy, without false hope and expectation, she saw the trajectory of her life. She saw the banality of her existence: its rawness, its baseness; monotony edged with nervous alertness. The seemingly endless mine-field of trivia and minutiae. The constant giving and giving and giving. The managing of Malcolm's vulnerable ego. She felt the nameless longing inside her darken. She took air into her lungs, then released it, feeling a blankness in her mind expand like a cancer, killing all the joy in the world, all delight and ambition, all her little plans and projects.

Eventually Malcolm leant in towards her. He felt sick with shame. He wanted to show that he loved her. He didn't know why he'd acted so badly. If she hadn't been so uptight. If she hadn't put all her attention away from him. 'I'm no good with words,' he said. She knew it was an apology. She reached out and took his hand.

On the Bus

In righteous anger, Louise sits bolt upright on the bus and tells Sally and Vicky of the great injustices of the domestic world. But Vicky tells of greater atrocities against the female sex: a few pikelets was nothing compared to a black eye and broken teeth. 'At least Dad paid for her falsies,' Vicky adds.

Sally ponders on the sadness of the world. She watches as Louise changes in front of her eyes when Scotty sits down beside her. She sees how Louise changes instantly, leaving her conversation with Sally and Vicky, giving her undivided attention to Scotty, her body softening, her anger gone and a warmth coming into her smile. *She's gone*, thinks Sally. Shrouded in a new and foreign world.

Chapter 22

MALCOLM FELT FINE THE NEXT day. He'd been provoked. He'd reacted badly, but he hadn't hit her. In retrospect, he was proud of that. No-one would have blamed him if he had lashed out. No. He'd shown restraint. Marion had a good life and should learn to be more grateful. No right-thinking man would condemn him for his behaviour.

And if Louise had a problem, he'd sort that out too. She wasn't too old for a whack across the bum. Surly little minx that she was turning into. But she was a looker, just like Marion. It wouldn't be too many years before she found a nice bloke and settled down. A few grandchildren. The more the merrier. Some little blokes to go fishing with. Play a game of cricket.

He could sense the alliance that the females had formed. Well. Two could play at that. He and Robbie were mates together. And he'd work at keeping Robbie in his corner. He'd show more interest in his drawings and paintings. He'd make sure he concentrated and listened when Robbie talked about his music. But it was difficult. Always the thoughts and the judgements intruded. Why did he feel this wild anger? Robbie must be made to understand that art and music weren't real subjects. Why was he wasting his time on things that weren't going to help him get a job? Couldn't he see that he should be focusing on maths and science? Subjects that would lead somewhere. He'd need to join the

Cadets next year. That'd knock some sense into him. Bit of army discipline would be the making of the boy. At least Robbie was good at sport. At least he was getting that right.

And indeed, Robbie was excelling in the cricket team. He was a good spin bowler and had the best batting average in the team. His record clearly made him captain material, but the coach was unwilling to allow such a quixotic character to ascend to the captaincy. He was the centre of attention for all the wrong reasons. As the self-appointed clown of the cricket team he'd present at the crease wearing a purple tutu or fishnet stockings beneath his boxer shorts. His team mates enjoyed the fun. Visiting teams were appalled. Parents complained. It often earned him a reprimand, sometimes the cane. But it was always worth it. The moment of hilarity was like the top of the wave to a surfer. There was no holding it back.

Malcolm monitored Robbie's academic progress. At teatime, as he cut up his lamb chops and spread them with relish, he'd lean one elbow on the table. 'How'd you go in the maths test today, Rob?'

'Yeah… alright I think. We don't get the results till Friday.' Robert could keep him at bay until then. He would give Malcolm a man-to-man look and cut his chops in the same way that his father did, same concentrated look on his face, same angle of the knife, the same lifted shoulders and furrowed brow. Then he'd pile relish on top. The parody complete.

Marion looked at Louise smirking beneath a curtain of hair. Her father never asked about her subjects. They were irrelevant. He seemed to think that as long as she could cook and clean, she'd be fine.

And Louise appeared to be dreamy and preoccupied. She could twirl a lock of hair, or roll her eyes, or swing her skinny hips and no-one would ever guess that she was top of her class in all subjects. She'd fold up her English essays and stash them in her bag before anyone had a chance to see them. If any of her friends asked about her marks, she'd fob them off. She instinctively knew to keep part of herself sheltered. That part of her belonged to her teachers: to books, learning and writing. Marion was aware of it but stood back. A silent witness, approving but not participating, proud and a little frightened.

The next week passed with its unfaltering rhythm of meals, washing, ironing, cleaning. Marion's life blending in with the smooth sway of grass on the hills outside the kitchen window.

On the Bus

But on the bus, a world beyond words envelops Louise and Scotty. Eons pass. They sit side by side. Gradually, his gentle, warm hand folds over hers. They keep their eyes straight ahead.

Chapter 23

W HO DOES YOUR TIME BELONG to? Marion wondered. My time is my own when neither he nor the children are in the house. If they saw me outside of their time, what would they see? Would they see their mother, their wife doing this or that, or would they see me: a person apart and separate from them? Do they simply see me on hold until they enter the house, as if I'm only activated when they pass through the door? Have they any idea of the thoughts that race through my head. To see someone apart from what they can give you, would be a gift. Certainly they'd see someone who loved and cherished them. But would they see any separation from their own demands and desires? Am I only alive in another's gaze?

Only when she sat down to write a letter home did she deliberately pull the shutters down on her present life and drift to the past. As the cat flopped down on the hearth and the warmth of the room settled around her, Marion would open her writing pad.

> *Dear Mum and Bo-Bo,*
>
> *Hope all is well with you. I can't believe that spring is here already! I've nearly finished the cardigan for Lucy. I can't believe she's the only one at home these days!*
>
> *As she's going to be sixteen, I thought to make it in a dark blue. It's all the rage here. The teenagers are all going for the dark colours. Thank you for*

sending the photo of her. It made me cry. Malcolm is doing well at work and has been given a pay rise. He's very popular in the office these days, ever since the fires. Robert is doing alright at school but he could do better. He only tries with the subjects he's good at like Art and Music. English he's pretty good at but with Maths and Science he's not even trying. I feel like shaking him sometimes! It's very frustrating. But there's not much I can do. It's up to him. His father's not impressed with his grades and is always on at him. It does no good.

Louise is doing very well. She seems to enjoy studying and every night she does at least 2 to 3 hours. Sometimes we have to stop her so we can have a game of Monopoly or cards. All her grades are good but you'd never know. She's very modest. I think she has a secret boyfriend. He's a nice quiet lad from up the valley. Very polite. He plays the trumpet beautifully. He played at the school concert. It was the best item on the programme. Louise was asked if she'd sing, but she's too shy for that sort of performance.

I'll be thinking of you as the winter comes. Would Bo-Bo like some house socks? I have a lovely pattern with fake leather soles. Enclosed is a photo of Robert and Louise in the backyard next to the Daphne bush. Who do you think Louise looks like?

Lots of Love from everyone here,
Marion

Marion found the knife-edged balance between out-and-out confrontation and completely giving over to the demands of her husband. She found the art of compromise: to talk from his point of view and allow him the chance to see hers. Discussing the details of every procedure gave Malcolm the chance to give directions as captain of the ship, while Marion would act as chief bosun and point out the perils. Whether it was painting a fence or planting broad beans, getting the children off to school or planning Marion's all-important CWA trips to Hobart, it worked for Malcolm and gave him a feeling of control and a clear picture of what was to happen in any given event. Marion learnt to duck and weave, ask all the necessary questions, point out what it was like from her perspective: 'But from my point of view, Malcolm . . .' And Malcolm learnt to listen. 'Yes, I concede that that could be the case, Marion . . . but on the other hand . . .' And the broad beans would eventually be planted outside the north wall, in full sun, rather than inside the flower garden next to the Daphne bush.

Robert enjoyed the arguments they'd throw at each other, the to-ing and fro-ing of their conversation, the whittling away of Malcolm's seeming advantage, or Marion's deference. He'd see her argue like a lawyer and Malcolm become bewildered and angry. He'd hear her say, 'Very well, Malcolm.' Malcolm feeling slightly guilty about the win, Marion feeling put upon. But Robert knew she was saving something in reserve. For Marion, straight answers had to be carefully examined for the advantages further down the track: for the pitfalls that might not be apparent at face value; for the possible advantage for her at a later date or as a point to debate and apparently lose, giving her an upper hand when she needed it.

He loved to inject his own conversations with wit and pedantry, especially when talking to teachers.

'Robert Johnstone! Why are you loitering around the gym when you should be in class?' Headmaster Norman Dillon roared at him.

'Well sir, strictly speaking the gym is a classroom. If a classroom is where we learn, then the gym is definitely a classroom! Only the other day I learnt how to fall off a balancing bar without breaking my neck, sir. Very useful, sir! The law of gravity, sir! I've definitely learnt about the law of gravity!'

'Enough of your rubbish!'

'Yes, sir! On my way, sir! As you can see, my legs are moving in a northerly direction: off to B block, sir. My anticipated time of arrival will be one forty-seven p.m. precisely. Good afternoon, sir!'

'Just go, Robert.' An exasperated Mr Dillon straightened his tie and threw his shoulders back, while Robert quickened his pace, taking short steps and flipping his feet outwards like a cartoon duck trying not to bend his knees, and crashed into maths class seven minutes late, playing air guitar and singing Pink Floyd's 'Gnome'. As the song said, the sky, the river – they were indeed good.

On the Bus

The Road and the River by Louise Johnstone

You cannot imitate the road,
River.
You can bend and sway:
Pull beside the rushes,
Cleave to the high bank.
Beyond the splash: the sparkled light.
Ravines of light halt in smothered darkness.
The cold hums below the surface,
River.
What twisted caverns yawn
Far below the fishes home
Where the softest clay
Powders into no colour
And time folds:
Endless falling
Like the whirling stars.

You cannot imitate the river,
Road.
Cling to the earth
Like a vast claw.
Those that ride you push the air
Never looking down to your
Nobbled spikey skin
Gripping rubber
Time and time again.

Time and time.
Again.
Time.

9/10

Well done Louise! Another exceptional poem. Even though you're writing free verse, you have introduced pattern into the form that reflects the content and concept of this fine piece of writing.

Sally hands the piece of paper back to Louise as the bus veers into the verge at Stop 17.

'More of your usual crap!' She laughs. Louise snorts and pulls Sally's plait.

'Here comes lover-boy.' She peers at Louise, batting her eye lashes. 'Should I move? Make way for… "poetry in motion"?'

'Nah, you stay put. He can stand for once.'

Sally and Louise continue laughing and giggling, heads together, leaning in towards each other. They're quiet for a while, then explode into laughter as one or the other presents a funny face, a sneer or a gormless blank stare to those around them.

Scotty looks to Louise as he moves up the aisle.

'She's mine today, lover-boy!' Sally yells out to him. He smiles.

'No worries, Sal.'

There are empty seats further down. Shirleena is sitting all alone on the back seat, her simian eyes scanning the scene. Scotty halts two seats back from Louise, drops his bag and holds onto the rail as the bus pulls out.

Louise is like a magnet. He can't move beyond a certain

radius. The longing for her is so visceral it pulls from inside his guts. The Sunsilk smell of her hair and its endless swirl of curls and colour and texture fascinate him. Even the shape of her bony knees, sticking out from the check school skirt, seems perfect. When she looks at him, he's filled with calm alertness, drenched in feelings beyond the mundane world. There's a kernel of life that starts to exist outside of his current reality: outside of the here and now and the boisterous rush of mates and brothers and parents and teachers, footy and band and everyone he's ever met or is likely to meet and certainly beyond the banter in the locker room after footy practice. It's outside of all the opinions in the entire world that say to him, '*She's too good for you, mate.*'

Only in music does he find some equivalent feeling: some resonance that speaks to the yearning in his soul. When he plays the trumpet the sound balloons out of the instrument, coming from his mind and his heart and his body all at once, and the quickening nerves on his skin feel washed with electricity. When he plays the solo in *Trumpet Voluntary*, he feels the inevitable steps of the crotchet beat, marching forward certain, unhurried, righteous and true. Simple, straightforward and bold, coming to the final cadence as certain as the rising sun. The certainty of the tune gives him confidence and a feeling of rightness.

Yes, he will do it. He'll ask her if she wants to go fishing! No-one could object to fishing. Even her nervous little mother couldn't object to that. She might even like a fresh blackfish from the river, or a delicious whipsnake eel. Nah… she'd probably draw the line at the eel. Ugly looking things.

But he knows. Everyone says so . . . *She's too good for you, mate. Only thing you can do is play the trumpet. You're in the bottom stream, mate. Below the tradies. You'll probably end up on the coun-cil with a pick and shovel. Mate! She'll be on the council! She'll be running the bloody show! She's the smartest cookie in the jar. You've just crawled out of the swamp. Just look at your brothers. What a bunch of Neanderthals! The logs of wood. Thick as two planks the lot of them. You're no different. You skinny little runt.*

But that doesn't stop the feeling. And Louise, two years younger, has no concern beyond his good looks. She can feel his eyes on her as she sits chatting to Sally. Part of her becomes removed from the conversation, alert to the feeling at the back of her neck. Knows that he's there, just behind her, looking in her direction. She flicks her hair. He's enraptured and hurt beyond measure. He shuffles his feet. Looks out the window... *Better make a move soon, mate. Before she finds someone a lot better than you. She won't be young and stupid for ever. You've only got one chance. Go for it, log-head!*

Scotty sighs and looks to the back of the bus. Shirleena's dull eyes are looking straight at him. He quickly looks away. He's paralysed with his own inaction and lack of knowing what to do. Oh, he knows what to do in the mechanical sense. His brothers have explained every aspect of the mating game from snapping a bra strap, to full-on sexual intercourse. In plain terms. In terms of a quick fuck behind the sports centre. But he couldn't do that. Louise deserves a lot better than that. But what, he doesn't know.

The bus pulls into the school yard and disgorges the rabble onto the tarmac. Shirleena descends like one of the glamorous chorus girls on *The Dean Martin Show*. She hesitates on the last step. Ray Brown comes up to her and puts his arm around her neck and inserts his tongue into her mouth. When he releases her, he says, 'I've had a shave!'

'I can tell,' she replies. Oblivious to the smears of red lipstick across both their faces, arm in arm, they make their way towards A block.

Chapter 24

'I'M NOT CARRYING THE SPUDS!' Carl picked one out of the bag and hurled it at his brother Max.

'Yes, you are!' said Sally. 'If you two are coming, then you carry the spuds and Max carries the snags.'

'We won't need the snags if we catch some fish,' said Max.

'No, but that's unlikely,' replied Sally.

'I don't want to carry the spuds!' yelled Carl.

'Then go back home!' Sally yelled back at him.

Louise bent down and picked up the bag of potatoes. 'There's a lot in here.'

'Yes, well,' said Sally, 'there's quite a crowd coming on your quiet, intimate luncheon date.'

Ronny Cracknel and Julie Butler, hand in hand, came slowly down the track, Julie hardly limping at all. Melanie Squires followed close behind. Robert was already larking about at the camp site and Scotty was knee-deep in the river. Bending over the water, he looked up and gave Louise a quick smile then cast his eyes down with a look of intense concentration. His arm moved ever so slowly through the water. Fingers soft, turning gently this way and that, feeling under the surface of the bank, letting his hand drift without disturbing the brackish residue that stuck to the fallen branches and the boulders. His feet were freezing, and his thighs were one step away from shaking. But he held himself still. Then his face lit up. With deft, swift movements he pulled a fish straight out of the water and wrapped it in his tee-shirt, holding it fast against his stomach. Keeping his movements slow and steady, he made his way to the bank.

'Cor!' he said. 'Hasn't anyone lit the fire yet?'

He was pleased with his opening remark. He'd been filled with anxiety thinking of what he might say to Louise: how he might be able to impress her in some way. Now he'd done it! He'd caught a blackfish! Straight out of the river. Right before her eyes! The icy cold water had been a test: a test for a hunter, a hero. He'd already set the fire. All it needed was a match. Ronny, with a cigarette between his teeth, winked at him and held out his hand, pulling him up onto the bank. 'I'll set some lines,' he said. Scotty pointed out a spot further upstream where the bank folded in, and the roots of a large blue gum curved into the water.

Louise and Julie, Melanie, and even Sally slipped into the prescribed roles; without thought or question or hesitation, without even knowing, they wrapped themselves in the cloak of domesticity and organised the camp site. Courting was in the air and things had to be organised. Primal roles established – ancient archetypes descending on the supple young bodies. Sally (who knew how to catch blackfish, gut it and mount it on a stick or cook it in a frying pan) gave way to the mood of hunters and gatherers. She only gave it a passing thought before unpacking Louise's knapsack and laying out the food. This was Louise's day. Not hers. She would do the expected in the background, play the home-maker: the kitchen here on one corner of the tarpaulin; cushions piled high in the middle; raincoats and jumpers in the far corner; an umbrella to huddle under in case it rained.

The grass was tall and lush. Close to the ground it was still wet from recent rain. The track, which always dried out in the summer and gave a satisfying thump to running children, was still muddy and slippery. It was September. The sun had some strength in it, but the days were still short. The silver wattles were in full bloom, the Ovens wattles close behind and the crimson gums already in their full glory. But there was still snow on Sleeping Beauty's hair.

The fire pit had been there ever since anyone could remember. Sally pulled a box of matches out of the back pocket of her jeans, crouched down and put the flame to it. The crackle and spit and hiss drew everyone's attention. They gathered round, watching the flames take hold, mesmerised by the growing tongues of fire. The smoke drifted up in leisurely, slow-motion curls. When the moment of reverie had passed, they continued with their allotted tasks.

Carl, Max and Robert started washing the potatoes. Ronny told them to move downstream so as not to disturb any nearby fish. 'How far down?' asked Robert. Ronny picked up a spud, weighed it in his hand and then hurled it downriver.

'That far,' he said.

'Ah, great!' whined Carl. 'Are we gunna have to walk all the way down there to clean the spuds?'

'No worries, mate,' said Robert. 'I'll give them a full toss from here and they should be clean by the time the fire's ready.'

Max was onto it. He pick up a couple of potatoes and started tossing them in the water.

'Max! Robert!' Louise said. 'You'll lose half of them!'

'Nah,' said Max. 'I know where they're going. Just wait and see.'

Louise, Julie and Melanie pursed their collective lips.

Melanie put her hands on her hips for good measure.

'Leave 'em alone,' said Ronny. 'It'll keep them out of the way.'

The river was wide and shallow. There was an island of boulders midway, with a stunted myrtle growing almost horizontally. On either side the water ran fast, turning and churning, the surface bubbling, the current rolling this way and that, sometimes lifting, sometimes turning back on itself. The slower eddies near the bank flowing upstream in a reaction to the force of the water. A pair of wattle birds in tall peppermint gums spread their wings and let go like high divers on the ten-metre board, falling slowly till the first slow-motion flap of their wings took them gliding across the river. They were soon replaced by a flock of ravens, calling loud *wac-wac-ahh*s to each other as they strutted along the branches, their sleek black wings and tail feathers glinting through the trees.

The sun was stronger now. Julie shielded her eyes. 'I know I'm supposed to wear a bloody hat. I don't need any more freckles.'

'Don't worry,' said Louise. 'I'll make you one.'

She grabbed a sheet of the newspaper that Scotty had used to light the fire and proceeded to fold it.

Ronny and Scotty waded upriver. Barefoot in the freezing water they moved slowly, unsure of their footing. 'Jesus Christ, Ronny!' said Scotty.

'I know! Don't think about it. Just look as if you know what you're doing.'

'I'm bloody freezing!'

'Me too. Don't look back! Do you want them to think we can't handle this?'

'I don't think I can.' And he started giggling.

They held off for as long as they could before heading for the bank. Ronny set a couple of lines while Scotty ran on the spot to get his blood flowing.

Back at the camp, Louise, Sally, Julie and Melanie unpacked the knapsack – Marion's carefully packed wicker picnic basket having again been transferred by Louise. The basket was prissy and ostentatious, and she didn't want the others to see that her mum had packed the picnic. Besides, the old canvas knapsack would be easier to carry. For Louise, it was the difference between playing at picnicking and actually having a picnic/date. She didn't want the occasion gentrified by Marion, appropriated in any way. It was enough that Marion had cut the sandwiches and baked a cake. Louise said that she was meeting Melanie and Julie… maybe Ronny would come along. She didn't mention Sally and certainly didn't mention Scotty. When Louise said that Robert, Carl and Max might tag along, as they usually did (a slender bit of truth to disguise the omission), Marion chopped some celery sticks. 'Those boys' teeth are always dirty,' she said.

To Louise, it seemed only a slight deception not to mention Scotty, to hide the picnic basket – to lay a trail of crumbs leading in the opposite direction as her soul shifted, and pledged allegiance to a new deity.

———

In any case, Marion was preoccupied. Word was out (via Vonnie) that Elizabeth Petch would be running for president of the local chapter of the CWA. Elizabeth Petch! Good Lord! She'd only been in the valley five minutes and already was trying to take over and make her mark. She'd already offended poor Mrs Smith (said Vonnie) by criticising her lemon icing. Well! Mrs Smith had been using the same method to make the icing for the past twenty-five years! *And here comes this dreadful woman, straight off the boat from England, trying to lord it over everyone. Well! As if her icing's any better. Just because she's English! Thinks she's dealing with natives. We'll see about that.* Marion's loyalty lay firmly with the local crew. Elizabeth Petch could get off her high horse and serve some time in the rank and file. President! Ah! Not if Marion had anything to do with it. Elizabeth Petch might be able to turn her hand to a sponge, but her pikelets were dreadful!

———

In no time at all, Scotty had lifted another slumbering blackfish out of the river. This one was bigger. He was wet through from its thrashing. Its fin had caught in the fabric of his tee-shirt and scratched his belly. Wounds from the hunt. Ronny caught two rainbow trout in quick succession.

They returned to the camp site, conquering heroes with their catch gutted and cleaned. Much discussion ensued concerning the cooking. Sally was keen to use the aluminium frying pan that was hooked on a nail on the trunk of a gum tree: there for communal use. Ronny wanted to use sticks. 'Nah,' said Carl. 'They always end up falling in the fire when you do that.' In the end they had a vote. Louise sided with Ronny and Scotty, while Melanie, Julie and Sally opted for the sensible frying pan. (It even had a Bakelite handle!) Robert and Max disqualified themselves by being downstream having a fight with the potatoes.

It was a grand day. The air was fresh but the sun was strong. After the bitter cold of winter, the day gave promise of a fine spring and summer to come. A feeling of freedom imbued them with raucous energy. The mood was high as they cooked the fish and sausages, roasted the spuds in their jackets straight onto the hot coals and waited impatiently for them to form a hard ash shell. When they were cooked, Sally deftly cut them open, and placed a dollop of butter on each one. She placed them on strands of bark and handed them around as if they were canapés on fine bone china.

Julie and Ronny sat on the cushions sharing a cigarette, gazing at the river. Melanie and Sally collected the enamel plates. Max and Carl and Robert drifted away, taken by the afternoon torpor. They wandered through the long grass, their voices rising and falling, thrown high among the tall heady grasses, laughing and scattering, gradually diminishing until silence seemed to fill the void they left.

Without a sound, Julie and Ronny stood up and stretched. Gathering a couple of cushions, they moved into the long grass, away from the river. Soon they were obscured by the gums. Louise and Scotty watched.

'Reckon they're up to no good.' Scotty smiled.

'Probably,' said Louise.

'Hope he remembered to bring something.'

'Do you think they would? Do it I mean?' Louise was incredulous.

'They've already done it.'

'Really?'

'Oh, yeah! But she's a lot older than you.' Scotty set to reassure her.

'Only two years.'

'Yeah, but that's a lot. You're only fourteen.' He chewed on a grass stem. 'I'll be seventeen in a few months. Dad says I can leave school after next term.'

'What are you going to do?'

'Dunno... Dad says I should join the army. Become a *man*!' Scotty laughed.

Louise looked at the fine brown skin of his arms, soft and with a dark shadow of hair. The sinews of his hands were taut as he clutched his knees, thinking hard. She waited. Eventually he stretched out on the tarp, yawning and enjoying the sun. His bare, skinny chest rising and falling with the delicious air.

'That's a nasty cut you've got,' she said, hating herself for sounding like her mother. 'Do you want a Band-Aid?'

'Nah, best thing for it is spit. You can give it a lick if you want.' He cradled his head behind his hands and smiled at her. His eyes held more sparkle than the river. Louise laughed and hugged her knees. 'Do you know what's gunna happen next?'

'Yes,' she said. 'It's going to rain.'

The wattle can be in its finest glory and the bees can be a corona of movement, a symphony of hums around the crimson gums. The giant tree-ferns can unfurl their croziers as the parrots descend to snip the underside of the old fronds, and the endless daffodils can stretch graceful heads to greet the returning sun. But nothing will spoil a fine spring day like the rain. Slow at first. Large drops on warm skin. Then the clouds. And winter returns.

The wind picked up, and the river became opaque, choppy. The fire was just about out. Melanie and Sally abandoned the campsite at once, quickly packing up the picnic and grabbing the tarp and umbrella. They ran up the path towards the road.

'Youse'll get wet!' Sally yelled. Louise and Scotty looked at each other and laughed.

'Do you think it'll blow over?' Louise asked.

'Nah... we're gunna get soaked.' He smiled at her. Daring her to stay put. She smiled back, feeling rain pit against her forearms. She held tight, not moving her eyes: questioning. 'Come with me,' he said and held out his hand. 'This way.' A track led them up a slope and into a clearing. A large blue gum stood on the far side. 'Over here.' The trunk had been hollowed out by fire. There was enough room inside for two people to huddle together. They sat down on the dry, ashy ground.

From where they were, high above the river, they could see the storm closing in. They could see the river, now alien and remote, churning and twisting, roaring and leaping. Around them the vegetation drooped towards the ground. The blackwoods deepening in colour as the grey clouds rushed across the sky.

They sat side by side, knees to chin, huddled in the small enclosure. The rain grew stronger. Even the guttural sound of the frogs seemed muffled and far away, the rain thrumming all around them.

There was only one thing on their minds. As Scotty slowly stroked Louise's hand, she leant in towards him and brushed her lips against his cheek. He turned and they kissed.

The raindrops swelled on the blackwood leaves, holding the kiss in a thousand reflections. Splash! went the kisses, into the runnels of water creating a miniature landscape of fiords and tarns, flat plains long thin gorges.

They kissed and cuddled, laughed and joked. The day had turned. The rain threatened to turn to hail and the westerly wind flew horizontally across the river. Inside the tree, they were dry, enclosed, cocooned, huddled against the wind. Curtains of cobwebs hung above them. The only two people left on Earth. Outside of time: sheltered from the storm. They created their own world, their own quirky way of laughing at the world, of seeing their friends, their family, their teachers. All to be examined and analysed. Their own language of gesture and caress. Reading each other's minds, feeling the right time to touch, to kiss, to pull back, to talk, to be silent. Feeling the weight of the soul's isolation lift. Feeling the relief of knowing one another.

On the Bus

THE KISS. A SOFT, SLOW-MOTION kiss. Or a tight, puckered kiss. A quick kiss: on the cheek, on the ear. A fun kiss with a peppermint between the teeth. A languid kiss, soft and breathy. A pash! A snog! An osculation! A noisy kiss with sucks and smacks and pops.

Falling into each other's orbit. Eyes locking. Foreheads resting gently against the other. Noses sliding together. Each mouth searching for the other. The outer world fades away. They're bold and carefree.

On a crowded bus, a stolen kiss is hardly noticed. There is the normal ruckus of bags being thrown on overhead racks or under seats. Pencil cases being handballed from one end of the bus to the other. Cigarettes being passed around. Love letters conveyed by trusty courier across the sea of uniformed adolescents. Shoes dangling out of windows. Pencil shavings surreptitiously placed in women's hats. Ties knotted to the stop bell. A constant roar of sound: voices vying to be heard above the straining engine.

On the bus, a stolen kiss is hardly noticed, except when sitting directly in front of Gert. 'Outrageous behaviour!' she declares, whacking them both with her handbag. 'The audacity of this young Jake-o-Napes! And you!' she says, pointing at Louise. 'You shameless hussy!'

Or Mavis Curtis, respectable matron, circumspect and cautious, clucking her tongue and crossing her legs. Her son, John Curtis, sits quietly next to the girl with the high forehead. He blushes from the top of his head to the tip of his toes. The girl with the high forehead blushes as well, then blushes again, seeing him blush.

Jennifer and Annie: eyes agog. 'Oh, get over it,' says Susan, rolling her eyes.

Wilf and Marco, workers from the Electrolytic Zinc Company, eye off the kiss from across the aisle. 'It's all goin' to the dogs, Marco,' declares Wilf. 'They've got no respect for the older generation. We were never allowed to behave like that! Aye! My dad would give me a good walloping if he caught me at it like that! Didn't mean I didn't have me fun with Betty behind the factory wall!' And he laughs a wheezy laugh. Marco doesn't respond. He directs his gaze out the window onto the golden, green landscape. His eyes are watery and sad.

The Schiller children look away: pretending not to see. They're from the Catholic school. Sister Ignacia has told them that the state school children will be paraded naked before the devil in the afterlife. Ingrid Schiller wonders what that might feel like.

Harry the Drunk leers at Scotty and Louise, thrusting his

right forefinger through the circle of his left thumb and forefinger: the age-old symbol.

Alice Saltmarsh: anxious. Hoping the child doesn't make the same mistake that she did. She doesn't want the lovely Johnstone girl to be tied to family life at such a young age. She doesn't want Scotty to be burdened at the beginning of his adult life. They should feel that they have the world at their feet. She thinks of Sally. Both Louise and Sally should feel they have opportunities in the future. Life for them shouldn't be confined to the valley. They are both bright. They deserve an education, even though it's a remote possibility.

Flo, making a mental note to give Louise some sex education: maybe even some condoms. She'll buy some *Dolly* magazines, and the new *Cosmopolitan*. Yes! The *Cosmopolitan* is much more explicit. Is Louise too young to read *The Female Eunuch*? She'll make sure she's aware of her own sexual response. God only knows what her mother has taught her! Marion makes Flo laugh and despair at the same time.

Sean O'Hara sits aloof, seeing the trajectory: this could go either way, he thinks. He hardly has to look at them to see what's going on. He can practically feel the kiss himself: the first kisses of youth, fresh as spring. Envy is beneath him but he does feel regret and melancholy at the passing of time. His sees his own adolescence on display. The land of youth, full of energy and sparkle, vitality, raucous and spontaneous, careering through time, carefree and careless, sovereign and blessed. It brushes his heart and he smiles.

Shirleena, guarding the treasured back seat: stony-eyed.

Chapter 25

NORMAN DILLON FIDDLED WITH THE cord of the venetian blinds, peering through the slats, looking down on the school yard.

'I don't think there's anything to worry about, Norm,' said Ron Jolliffe. 'It's just puppy love. Bit of kissing ... no harm in that.'

'Yes, Ron. No harm in that. It's when they stop kissing you've got to start worrying. That's when you know they're at it. There are five pregnant girls at this school at the moment. It reflects very badly on us. Very badly. Head office is sending down a sex education officer next year. But it's only for girls in Grade 10. Nothing for the younger ones. The times have got away from us, Ron. We're way behind on all fronts.'

And he thought of the new social studies teacher, with his hair bouncing off his collar, his paisley tie and double-breasted check suit, playing folk guitar to a bevy of girls during the lunch hour. Or the new chemistry teacher – a woman! Wearing a bright orange baby-doll dress that hardly covered her thighs and revealed her cleavage ... Not that she had anything to show ... poor thing was as flat-chested as a man. Norman wondered if the study of chemistry had anything to do with it.

'Oh, it's highly unlikely, sir. He's a good lad and I can't see her letting him go too far.'

'He's a good lad ... unlike his siblings ...'

'Oh, no sir! He's not like his brothers at all. Really, he is very conscientious in the music department. Yes, he's wonderful. Any little thing that goes wrong with a trumpet, he's onto it. He can fix it. It's no trouble to him. Off he'll go to the metal-work rooms and come back with a new valve or whatever. He did it the other day. We had young Silvia Brodvich, caught her hair in the slide of a trombone. First time we've had a girl play trombone. But she's a big lass and she's doing well. Hair should have been pinned back, not all over her face like she has to hide behind a curtain. Anyway, Scotty fixed it in no time. She lost a bit of hair. He's got a very good mechanical mind has our Scotty. I know he's no good academically but in practical matters he has a lot of skill. And memory work! I've never known anything like it! Once he's learnt a piece of music, you can throw away the manuscript. It's in his memory forever! Aye, I wish I had that talent.'

Norman Dillon let the blind go with a clack. 'He can leave school anytime he wants now. He's over sixteen.'

'Aye. I for one will miss him. I hope he finds some trade. That would set him up. As I said, he's a practical lad.'

'Even for trade work he'll need some basics in maths and English. Best he can do is find some family friend that'll take him on. Someone who understands how his mind works.'

The fog of cigarette smoke in the staffroom began to clear as teachers stubbed out their cigarettes. They gathered up their books and folders and hit the corridors with grim determination, as if going to war.

Norman Dillon sighed deeply. He felt left behind. The curriculum had changed. History and geography were no longer history and geography. They had morphed into 'social studies'. He felt a creeping uncertainty. What was being lost here? What new ways of thinking were being introduced to students? Would they be able to fill in the countries of Europe on a blank map? Or tell the difference between an alluvial plain and a glacial valley? They were being asked to think about things before they had any facts in their heads. At least he could have some impact with English. He was a stickler for good grammar. Next year he'd take the top English class. *Less poetry and more grammar. Give them a good foundation and move them away from self-indulgence. Poetry's all very well, but this free-form stuff doesn't do anyone any good. Rigour. That's what they need. Rigour!*

On the Bus

'I'm leaving soon.' Scotty hangs his head, not looking at her.

'Leaving school?' asks Louise.

'Yes,' he says. 'Dunno what I'm going to do though... Dad says it's time to leave.'

'You could finish the year out.'

'Nah... won't make any difference. Dad reckons I should join the army. He can make that happen, he says. With this war... It's a lot worse than people say. Dad reckons the Chinese will come down here to Australia and take over. He says it's the Domino Effect. Once they take over Vietnam, they'll take over the next country then the next, and then the next, till they get to Australia. They'll turn us all into communists and we'll lose our freedom.'

'They'd never get as far as Tassie.' Louise laces her hand through Scotty's, as if she could keep him home by holding on. But Scotty's sounding like the Channel Six news commentary.

'Dad says we've got to nip it in the bud. He'd enlist himself if he could... Says his best days were in the army, fighting the Japs. He said he wanted at least one of his sons to be in the army... I guess that's me. They have brass bands in the army. I could play with one of them! I know the Last Post already ... it's a piece of piss. Although you should have heard Jolly when I was learning it. He came into the practice room and took the trumpet out of me hands. "Never play it on a trumpet, boy," he said. "The trumpet's too harsh. It's not to be played harsh." And he got out a bugle. His own bugle! It's silver and so beautiful and the notes are all soft and round not like the trumpet. He was right of course. It's a lot harder but worth it. He stood there looking at the floor, just lifting his hand every now and then, when I got a bit sharp, or wasn't breathing in the right spot. And he said I was never to play that tune without me heart in every single note. And he looked so stern. I'd never seen him look like that. I tell you what, playing without valves is so hard. It took over an hour! I missed double maths. But that's ok. He said he'd fix it for me. He's good like that.'

Louise listens. She can't argue with anything he's said. She's just his girlfriend. His real life belongs elsewhere: with his quiet little mother and his great bellowing father and his raucous drunken brothers. She's just a small piece of his life: a cuddle and a kiss and a squeeze. She's seen his concentration veer away from her in a flicker when the school bell rings. He races away to the music room, his thoughts no longer on her, his turn sudden as he leaves her stranded, still dreamy and not knowing what she wants, what she might ask of him or what she might give. She knows she's a part of him – but only a small part. If his love is a fierce, strong, concentrated beam of light, hers is a gentle corona, encasing her like a protective fog: wrapping her in a feeling of security, lightness, warmth, as if her bones are filled with air. She feels lifted, buoyed by an opening out to the world, but at the same time shielded and protected.

He keeps talking. He hasn't touched her once during this trip. Little eye contact. Part of him is already there: already in the army fighting a strange foe.

'The Viet Cong are very small, but they can fight! Like those feral cats out the back of our place... Fierce! And they all wear black pyjamas. Even the women. Dad says that you can't tell whether it's a woman or a man you're fighting. And they live in these tunnels under the jungle. Hundreds of them! And they're cannibals! They eat the liver of anyone they kill! Dad says it'll all be over soon. He says to enlist now, so I can see a bit of action. He says it'll make a man of me. But he's always saying that! "Chop some wood, son! It'll make a man of you! Eat your meat, son! It'll make a man of you. Come and stand in the pouring rain and help me fix the guttering. It'll make a man of you!"... I'll be glad to get away from the old bugger.'

Louise thinks of Scotty's life as a series of tumultuous events. His father, loud, belligerent and often drunk, lording it over his sweet little mother. His raucous brothers, like a litter of boisterous pups, venturing into a life full of accidents: machinery, trees, fishing boats, cars – everything a potential disaster. The unexpected happening at every turn. Scars and broken bones: emblems of a warrior cult. The enemy is the natural world. They feel an urgent need to hurl themselves at the bush, armed with axes, picks, chainsaws, and trucks of all description. They can load a truck in five minutes flat with cigarettes dangling out the sides of their mouths, laughing and exchanging banter. Nothing is ever serious. Every life situation is an opportunity for danger and amusement.

Whereas her own life seems so muted and measured. The regularity of Malcolm's job dominates the household. Sporting events for Robert are the next most important thing. If her netball match is not in the near vicinity of Robert's football match, she'll have to miss out and make the dreaded call to Miss Bedford, the coach. Malcolm can't be in two places at once. Sunday's priority is Marion's baking. Monday morning, the trip to the CWA shop. Even the neatness of her room, the regular study times, the regular meal times, fall into prescribed patterns. It's all planned and laid out. There are no accidents or broken bones. Only Robert's chaotic and subversive behaviour brings some semblance of spontaneity. She'll laugh and smile at his antics at the dinner table until either one of her parents admonishes them both. Always the personal touch is aimed at Louise: 'Never laugh with your mouth wide open, Louise,' her mother will say. 'Do you realise how ugly you sound when you laugh like that? Use the serviette! Put your knife and fork down when you're talking.' But Robert seems above the rules. He has some immunity to the strictures governing the household, whereas she is tightly bound by the potential for ugliness and shame.

Chapter 26

THE GIGANTIC *EUCALYPTUS REGNANS* TOWER straight above the forest, oblivious to the raging southerly gales and the steep gradient of the land. Patriarchs of the bush, always reaching up, up, up; trunks stretching white with death and only a few tufts of leaves on the outer ends of the branches. When they fall they make a mighty roar, bellyflopping into the understorey, scattering their brittle branches; their inhabitants – possums and birds – fleeing. But before the fall, there is an eerie silence. A vacuum like an in-breath. A shaft of nothing in the ether, only discernible to animals and madmen: a warning in the negative. And then like all vacuums, filled by the bolt of life and death in one confusing dance.

The loose-leafed bedfordia bedraggled the path. Native cherries stood aloof and contained, their dark folds of branches hiding the minute berries, their roots clinging to the mush of dead tree-ferns. Louise felt cutting grass whip her bare legs. It broke her stride and slowed her gait, but she said nothing.

'You're not used to roughing it?' Scotty smiled back at her.

'I've been on two girl guide camps,' Louise responded, anxious to show that she knew a thing or two. Scotty let out a hoot and swung his body round a small blue gum.

'I suppose you all sat round singing "Kum Ba Yah".'

'Yes we did, actually.' There was no use denying it. It had

been one of the most magical moments of her life. Sitting round the camp fire with Brown Owl softly strumming the guitar and their young, clear voices rising up with the smoke, entwining the branches and then rising further, as if heaven itself was drawing up the smoke and their voices and their souls. And so, in a simple act of self-betrayal, she leant against the blue gum. 'It was god-awful,' she said. How could she accommodate the magnitude of a child's soul with what she felt now? With the pull of the earth and her strange body and the fascination with this boy-man? He leant in and kissed her. The smell of eucalyptus mixing with the comforting smell of his sweat.

The weight of the backpack pulled against Scotty's shoulders. Large and bulky. Filled with Nan's eiderdown. She wouldn't miss it. She was in hospital having her veins done. He'd have it back before she even knew it was missing. The track rose steeply. Stepping-stones for giants formed its foundation. Tiny bells at the waist of Louise's skirt rang an impatient ting-ting as she stretched her legs up and over the boulders. Scotty looked back, smiling, stretching out his hand.

'Nearly there,' he said. 'Do you need a rest?'

'No, I'm fine.' She wished she'd worn jeans, but the skirt was so pretty. Fine Indian cheesecloth, multi-coloured, full and luxurious. She'd take it off slowly, letting it fall to the ground. Her heart was pounding from the climb. 'Well, maybe just for a minute?' Scotty found a dry boulder just off the track, big enough for both of them to sit. They shared a cup of tea. He was pleased he'd remembered to pack a thermos.

'Just over that scree slope.' Scotty pointed to a tumble of

football-sized rocks: giants emptying their playthings down the hill. 'That's the worst bit. Once we're over that, it's easy.' He screwed the top back on the thermos. 'If it's too much, we can go back. Not a problem.'

'No, no! I'm fine. I can manage.' She took his hand. 'I wore my sensible shoes for a reason!' She jumped to her feet and danced a soft-shoe shuffle, stretching her arms to the racing clouds above. Scotty marvelled at her perfect beauty and gently put his hand on her calf. He let it drift up her leg until the dance was done and he could feel the elastic band of her pants. The rush she felt was greater than the wind in the ghost gums, or the clouds pulling themselves up from the west, or the torrent of the waterfall far below. They kissed slowly and seriously, conscious of a rite of passage anointed by the elements. Their souls conjuring their own magic, their own language, ancient and as sure as rising sap.

Louise knew now for certain. She was doing the right thing. This was the time to give her body, give her love to Scotty. He was going away. He'd become part of the Anzac legend. To give yourself to a young man who was off to fight a war, off to help liberate an oppressed people and stop Australia from invasion, was a noble thing. It was the least she could do.

As they scrambled across the scree slope, the cave opened before them. It was larger than she expected. A wide sandstone lip opening out to the valley. The back of the cave was dark and damp. An old mattress stood upright against the inside wall. Scotty laid it on the floor and spread the eiderdown. A large plastic witch's hat, pinched from a council work site, lay in the corner. He quickly repositioned it at the entrance.

'Just in case there's anyone around.'

———

The eiderdown. Nan's love: cosy and warm, slightly musty. Scent of lavender. The gentle hands of an old person conjuring a cocoon in which the babies sleep. Gravity diminished. The cool air a potion. The rustling bush, a lullaby. The sky dimmed by cloud. The cave a small pocket of stone perched high above the valley, swinging in the clouds. A window to the world. A dull, unblinking eye. Scotty heard the *thunk* of a wallaby's tail through the skein of his dream. He opened his eyes, looking out. About four o'clock he guessed. He lifted Louise's arm off his chest. Time to get moving. Emptying the remaining tea into the cup, he gently woke her. 'Here,' he said, as if offering something to a sick child. She sipped it as if it were communion wine.

The descent was much more precarious: managing the scree slope on their hands and knees, crawling like crabs, laughing into the wind. Once they were under the shelter of tall eucalypts, it eased off. When they came to the understorey at the base of the valley it was calm and humid. Louise looked up and saw the top of Scotty's head bending to avoid a branch. Then he swung round like she knew he would, smiling, and held the branch back for her to pass beneath. As they made their way down the final stretch, Louise felt the semen slip out of her body. The crotch of her pants dampened. She smiled to herself. Now she was a woman. And because the semen had gently eased out of her body, she reasoned that there was no fear of pregnancy. Shirleena had told her with confidence that no-one gets pregnant the first time they have sex.

Louise followed Scotty down the track. Looking at the back of his head, she already felt him moving away from her. He was off to the world. Off to Vietnam. She would be alone. The magic of the trip to the cave, of the natural world, the young man and her own desires coalescing into an overwhelming experience, was already losing its intensity. But she'd done something. She'd acted independently. She knew what she'd done was against the moral code of her parents, but the world was changing. No longer would she let Marion make every decision, from her socks to her hair; choose her friends, decide when and where she was allowed to go. She hugged the secret to her and walked back down to the valley with a clear heart and a shining, noble spirit.

But the blind sperm that dances on the wide surface of the ovum knows nothing of human intentions. It knows only to wriggle and burrow, to move and swim.

On the Bus

Shirleena looks around. 'Youse don't know nothing.' She slowly scans their faces.

'What is it that we don't know, Shirl?' asks Sally.

'For starters, babies don't come out your bum.'

Sally laughs. 'We all know that.'

'They come out of your vir-gin-a,' Shirleena continues. 'And it really hurts. Sex hurts too, although not as much.'

'No it doesn't,' Sally says. 'No-one would do it if it hurt.'

'I know,' insists Shirleena.

'Have you done it?' Louise asks.

'Yes. Lots of times.'

'What's it like?' Louise wants to know.

'It's different each time. Sometimes it's real nice. Other times it's not so good.'

'Well. That's helpful,' says Sally.

'Youse'd better be careful when you start. Make sure he wears a franger.'

'What's a franger?' asks Louise. She's willing to be seen as a complete drop-kick in order to attain some information.

'I'll show ya,' says Shirleena. She reaches into her inside blazer pocket and takes out a small packet. She rips it open and takes out the condom. 'You've got to put this over his dick.' She shakes it out to its full length.

'Oh! How disgusting!' says Sally.

'It looks sort of... wet,' says Louise.

'Have a feel,' says Shirleena.

'No way! There's no way a slimy thing like that is going inside my body!' says Sally.

Louise touches the limpid object. 'It's all swishy.'

'Get used to it,' says Shirleena. 'You'll be needing them. But you won't need it the first time. The first time it always hurts, but you can't get pregnant.'

Louise and Sally watch in horror and amusement as Shirleena rolls the condom over her thumb. She laughs, rips it off and flicks it towards the back of the bus.

Chapter 27

A THOUSAND FLIES DANCED ON the screen door at the back of the Donohue house. The sweet smell of roasting forequarter filled the air. Out in the yard, Mert threw an empty longneck into a forty-four-gallon drum: the satisfying sound of breaking glass. He contemplated whether the lamb would be ready soon or whether he had time to start on another beer. Bugger it, he thought and went to the outdoor fridge. Grabbing another Cascade Blue he held the top to the edge of the workbench. With one swift blow of his fist the top came off and skittered onto the concrete floor.

He wandered round the yard with beer in hand. Picking up the axe, he let it fall onto the chopping block just to hear the satisfying *klok*. The innards of a Bedford engine littered the yard. Already the weeds were growing through the gearbox and a pardalote was nesting in one of the brake cylinders. At least he'd had the forethought to put the electricals in the shed. He looked at the tyres and gave them a kick. He'd have to tell her sometime. Taking another swig of the beer he pulled the screen door open, and dozens of flies flew into the kitchen.

'Shut the bloody door!' Doris yelled. Mert swung round, still with beer in hand and held the door open. Flies swarmed in. He slammed the door as hard as he could. It bounced back on its hinges and remained open. Doris threw a tea towel on the kitchen table.

'Look what you've done!' She knew there was no point in aggravating him, letting his belligerence explode. 'I'm gunna find Scotty.'

'Well you won't find him!' Mert looked at her. 'He's gone, Doris. He's gone up to the barracks. You won't be seeing Scotty for a while.'

'You bastard, Mert! What have you done?' Doris put her fists in the pockets of her apron. 'Mert!'

'What have I done?' He raised his voice, putting his huge ugly face right up to hers. 'The boy's a man, now. If he wants to go to war you can't stop him. And if my son wants to go to war, I'll let him! If my son wants to leave home and stop hanging round the kitchen like a girl, I'll let him! If my son wants to make himself into a man, I'll let him!' His voice was one long crescendo. Mert took another mouthful of beer, then placed the bottle carefully on the table and lowered his voice to a hissing whisper. ''Cause he is my son. Isn't he, Doris!'

Doris held herself in check. She picked up the tea towel and wiped the bench. 'You should have told me,' she said, her voice catching. 'Why didn't you tell me?'

Mert belched and picked up the beer. His face was puffy and red.

'No point.'

Doris turned to the swinging screen door and walked out into the yard. From there she ran to the pine tree that sheltered the chassis of a '58 Dodge. She climbed through the barbed wire fence beyond it and kept running. When she came to the escarpment she stopped. Here, a hundred yards from the house, the land fell away. She stood at the edge. Every cell in her body felt as if it had turned to stone.

Only her heart kept pulling at her chest. She leant against a pine tree lifted her head and hit it hard against the trunk.

'No!' she cried. 'No! No! No! Not my Scotty!'

Doris had always tried not to make Scotty special. But it was useless. It was like being in love. She couldn't help but light up when he came into a room. He was different from his brothers: shy, soft and kind. Intelligent in his own way. Not like her other boys. What if he did spend more time with her? What did that matter? He was more of a friend than a son – and friends were few and far between, stuck up there at the end of the valley. Unable to drive, Doris had to rely on Mert or one of the older boys to take her into town. It was a remote, lonely life. And them – Mert and the boys – always putting her down. Treating her like a servant. A slave.

She hit her head again. Hard, until it really it hurt. And then she yelled. It was like a banshee's curse, screaming high and loud across the escarpment. She sucked breath into her lungs and let the cry out. Then she did it again and again and again. The air around her felt brittle. A flock of green rosellas took off down the valley.

Chapter 28

L IGHT FROM THE WINDOW LAY across the bed. Late afternoon, and the sun was getting low. Louise stretched her feet into the patch of sun, feeling the instant warmth. Stretching her legs out and arching her back, her jeans didn't feel too tight. It was only when she leant forward that she felt some constriction around the lower back. There was some discomfort there. *Yes*, she thought, *definitely some pain*. Her period was definitely on the way. She rolled onto her right side. She could hear Marion coming down the hall.

'Darling?' she called out.

'I'm in my room.'

Marion popped her smiling face around the door. 'You'll be needing these,' she said and placed a packet of Modess pads on the dressing table. 'I've bought you some mini pads as well. Just for the last day or so.'

'Thanks, Mum.'

'Are you feeling alright?'

'Yes...just an aching back.'

'Take a Disprin if you need to.'

'Thanks.'

Marion had been preoccupied. The run to the Hobart CWA was now a regular event. And one of the cafés in Huonville had asked her to supply them with scones, pikelets and two sponge cakes every week. She could choose the type of sponge and the icing. There was a spring in her step.

Robert was doing reasonably well at school and hadn't been in trouble for some time. Malcolm's veggie garden was bursting with produce. If she could only get him to wash the potatoes and carrots in the laundry instead of loudly plonking them on the kitchen sink, clods of dirt falling on the floor. Everything was on an even keel. She felt happy and exuberant.

She looked at Louise and simply registered that she was lying on the bed. As she was moving back down the hall, Marion felt a blank spot in the flow of time. The clouds robbed the house of the last of the direct sunlight. A nail on the roof constricted and scraped against the iron. The sun seemed to take the oxygen with it. Her feet came to a halt.

In her mind she re-ran the conversation she'd just had with Louise. She thought about the last two – or was it three? – periods that Louise had had. She'd been pleased that she'd taken responsibility for washing her pants separately and making sure she took the pads out to the incinerator and burnt them herself, so that Malcolm and Robert didn't have to see them. Louise had taken on all the responsibilities of becoming a woman. But Marion hadn't actually seen the pads, or the trips to the incinerator. She remembered the look in Louise's eyes: the sun warming her feet, her face pale and her eyes dark and anxious.

Marion put her hand on the telephone table to steady herself. Slowly she turned around and walked back into Louise's room. Silently she looked at her daughter. Louise turned red and her eyes swelled.

'Mum?' Her face crumpled. 'Mum!'

Tears came flooding down.

'What have you done?' Marion's voice was low and trembling.

She looked at her daughter and felt her entire life hollowing out. Everything that was joyous and good, everything that she had ever wanted in life: their happy home, the good husband, the beautiful country life. All of it evaporating, vanishing. Her rage was intense.

'What have you done?' She yelled this time and struck Louise hard across the face. 'How could you do this to me? To us? You've ruined yourself and your family!'

Louise sat on the bed hyperventilating, holding a pillow against her body. 'I didn't know, Mum! I didn't know!'

'What didn't you know, you stupid girl? What precisely didn't you know?' Marion hissed the words at her. 'Who did this to you? It was that Scotty boy wasn't it.' Louise didn't answer. Still holding the pillow, she looked up at her mother.

'They said it wouldn't happen. They said it couldn't happen the first time.'

'You stupid, stupid girl! Well you've proved them wrong haven't you! How could you believe such a thing?' Marion felt her world tumbling down, her past coming up to meet her.

Louise heard the change in Marion's voice. She sounded old and weary. The anger was over. It was swift and stinging but now she was in recovery. 'Just as well your father's not home.' Then Marion did something that completely took Louise by surprise. She sat down next to her and folded her in her arms. 'We'll get through this,' she said. 'God knows how, but we will.'

How could she not have noticed! How could she have let her daughter fall into this trap? Surely Louise should have been able to see through all that stupid girl-talk: other girls telling her lies and fables. She'd made sure Louise knew the basic facts.

But not the facts of love. First love, like an electric current searing through the body. The physical need for touch, like a return to infancy, filling the mind with a sense of grandness, a greatness eclipsing any common sense that might have stayed her actions. The mind-blowing feeling of being close to someone: feeling that there was one person who understood implicitly, that they were the one person on earth who could make you feel whole and complete. That they alone could take you to other worlds: worlds of feeling and sensation that were beyond dreaming, worlds that eclipsed the everyday, the mundane. Yes, Marion knew that feeling. And she knew the consequences. How could the trajectory of her life rebound in this way?

Marion thought quickly: Louise would go to school for the rest of the term. Then she'd stay home till the baby was due. Then into Hobart for the final few weeks. She'd be able to find some excuse for her absence at school: a trip to the mainland, or visiting grandparents. The child could be adopted out, and that would be the end of it.

Deep down Marion didn't care what others thought of her. She always appeared to be particular about other peoples' impressions of her, but she wanted to impress in a detached way, to feel that good impressions were made: that Malcolm and Marion were of a type. They had their place in the world and could be seen as good people, good citizens.

All that changed in an instant. She would protect her daughter. Fierce mother-love welled up in her. She'd protect her from the gossiping neighbours, although she knew there would be little she could do about that! She'd draw her in close. Wrap her in warmth and trust. Keep her close. Keep her in the house and protected from her so-called friends.

Marion hugged Louise to her and looked out at the sun's last rays slanting over the paddock. The immediate threat was not from the outside.

———

As Malcolm swung the car into the garage, the headlights swept through the darkening kitchen like a search light. Marion braced herself. Louise was in her room. Robert was in the living room watching TV. She could hear his laughter. Already, she had made some calculations. She knew from quizzing Louise that it was too late for a curette. Louise was at least two months pregnant. How could she not have noticed? How could she be so blind? She knew Malcolm would blame her. She might as well accept that.

Her mind was racing. The most important thing was to protect Louise. She knew she couldn't put off the confrontation, so it might as well happen straight away.

Malcolm came through the back door with a weary look on his face. A perfunctory kiss and he sat down on the kitchen stool.

'You won't believe this, but we had five people at that meeting that swore that daylight saving was going to ruin their pasture. They insisted that an extra hour of daylight would dry their paddocks out. Can you believe that, Marion! Did these people ever go to school? They sit there and fold their arms and just look at you. There's nothing I or anyone else can say that will convince them that they're wrong. Even the mayor can't convince them! They think it's a conspiracy by New Zealand farmers to steal their market! As if anyone here is going to buy New Zealand mutton! I tell you what Marion, there's a big problem with education in this valley, or else there's a big problem with people being really stupid.'

Marion poured him a beer and gave herself half a glass. She stood in front of him with her legs crossed and her arms folded. There was no way to ease into this conversation. No way to soften the blow. Their life was about to be plunged into dark waters. Robert had always been Malcolm's chief worry. But he seemed on an even keel these days.

'Well, you won't believe this,' said Marion, putting down her glass. 'Someone told Louise that you can't get pregnant the first time you have sex.'

Malcolm went still. He looked at her. 'What are you saying, Marion?' He put down his beer. 'What exactly are you saying?'

Marion turned white. 'I don't know how this could have happened. To our daughter! To our lovely daughter!' She was crying now and couldn't control the pitch of her voice. The words came out loud and shaking. 'Malcolm, it's not her fault. She didn't know!'

Malcolm stood up so fast that the stool toppled over. 'I don't believe this! Where is the little slut?' Malcolm stomped down the hallway hitting the wall with his fist as he went. 'Louise!' he yelled. 'Louise!' He kicked the door to her room open, expecting to find her cowering on the bed. But the room was empty. 'Marion! Where is she? Marion! Do you hear me! I said WHERE IS SHE?'

Marion had come up behind him. He swung round and his fist hit the wall next to Marion's face. The plaster cracked.

'I don't know! Malcolm, I don't know!' Marion was trembling now. He stood in the hall, blocking the way. She couldn't move. 'She only told me this afternoon. Malcolm, I'd no idea!' She tried to duck under his arm, then sank to the floor. If he was going to hit her, at least she could roll into a ball, protect herself. Malcolm paced in front of her like a wild animal.

'This doesn't happen in my family, Marion. This sort of thing doesn't happen here! Is this a joke? Are you joking with me Marion?' Marion looked up and saw his huge red face.

'I'm sorry, Malcolm. I'm sorry!' It was all she could manage.

'Find her, Marion. Find her! If you'd been keeping an eye on her . . . If you had your wits about you instead of carrying on with your stupid friends and your stupid cooking! You should know what's going on with her. That's your job Marion! That's your job! I'll find her myself. And when I do she'll wish she'd never been born!'

'Louise isn't here.' Robert stood at the far end of the hall. 'She left ages ago.'

'Where did she go?' Malcolm yelled at him.

'I don't know and if I did I wouldn't tell you!' Robert turned and ran.

———

Robert was out the back door and across the back paddock before Malcolm could catch him.

He ran and ran and ran. He climbed a fence and followed a small creek up to the tree line. Once he was in the bush, he had a good vantage point and could see down onto the house. The lights were all on now. Doors were banging. Malcolm was yelling. Robert sat down, out of breath. Hugging his knees, he watched and waited. His instinct had been to flee, to get out of there as soon as possible. But he also had a growing feeling of being a player in the world, a person who had opinions and a voice to express them. His other instinct was to stay and protect Marion. But this was not possible. He was just a boy, physically no match for his father. He felt ashamed. He wanted with all his will and might, to defend his mother. He wanted to stand up to the bully: to be filled with righteous indignation and defend his mother and his sister. But his legs had just about given way when he'd answered Malcolm. He'd heard the row but he'd no idea what it was about: the banging on the wall, the crunch of the plaster. All he knew was that he was against his father; that his father was standing over his mother threatening her. She was small, cowering beneath him, her hands on her face, sinking to her knees. But he'd find a way to get back at him. He'd find a way to protect Marion.

He watched and waited. The front door opened. Marion raced out. She headed up the road towards Flo and Barry's place. She stumbled, still in her apron. She was limping and sobbing, going as fast as she could. Then he heard Malcolm. He was outside the back door, his hands cupped around his mouth and yelling, 'Louise! Louise!' The sound was so alarming Robert trembled. Malcolm was directly below him, the cry seemed to be funnelling up between the trees. 'Louise! Louise! Louise!' Malcolm paced up and down the back yard, yelling at the top of his voice. His whole body concentrating the sound of her name. 'Louise! Louise!' Robert was transfixed, witnessing his father without being seen. He waited and waited, trying to decide whether to stay where he was and sleep under a tree, or if he might cross the paddock and find sanctuary at Flo and Barry's.

'Louise! Louise!' Malcolm was unrelenting, roaring and pacing. Then Robert heard a change. Malcolm stood still. 'Lou!' It was no longer a scream or a yell. 'Lou! My darling! What have you done? Oh, Lou! You're my darling! You're my darling little girl!' Malcolm put his hands over his face and cried.

Robert sat motionless. Stunned at the sight of Malcolm sobbing on his knees on the wet grass. His mind was racing. Had Louise run away from home? Had she died? What had happened to her? Was she lost? Had she killed herself? He'd seen her leave the house in a hurry. Robert's rage and distrust of his father evaporated. Part of himself wanted to despise Malcolm, to look down on his father and loathe the beast kneeling on the ground, his shoulders heaving with pain. He wanted to belittle the passions of his life. Robert wished to see himself as a grand soul with unfortunate parentage: to be greater, more spirited, more alive than Malcolm. He wanted his life to have a great trajectory, to rise above the small-mindedness of the valley, to hurl himself at the outer world, to be a part of a grand vision, great ambition, exert great talent. He wanted to be taken out of the twilight of his current existence, out of pettiness and simplicity.

He felt his spirit kindred to Marion's: quick and light, effervescent and quirky but not veiled by caution, not inhibited and circumspect, muted and dulled by routine. He sensed a great buoyancy behind Marion's personality, and her determination to check herself at every turn. But he also felt his father's earnestness, his dogged determination, the stolid, practical truths of his life and his simple quest for uncomplicated love.

All these thoughts ran through his mind. Standing up, he realised he'd already made that move out of his current existence. He'd already left the valley with its narrow, limited culture. Whether that decision came first, or whether later, as he put his arms around his father, he couldn't say. He made his arms as large and as wide as he could.

'Oh, Robbie!' Malcolm cried. 'Robbie! Robbie!' He turned and held his son. Robert could hear Malcolm's heart, thumping with grief. They went inside the house, Malcolm taking great gulps of air, his diaphragm shuddering with each out-breath.

'What's happened, Dad? Has she run away?'

'I don't know, Robbie. I don't know. But she might as well. The stupid bitch. She's pregnant, Robbie. She's pregnant.' Malcolm said it as if he were practising to say the word.

The phone rang. Malcolm lunged at it. The low, steady voice of Merv came down the line.

'Malcolm, listen to me. Malcolm you're a good man. You're a good man and this could have happened to anyone. You're not the first and you won't be the last. She's with us. Vonnie's putting her to bed now. She fine. She's safe. You need to keep your distance for a few days, Mal. We'll look after her. No harm will come to her under this roof. Are ya there, Mal? Can you hear me?' Merv lifted his gravel voice up a register, just to make sure.

'Yes, I'm here.' Malcolm's voice was croaking.

'We don't need any stupidity from the grownups. There's enough of that going round. It's this damn war that's the cause of it all. Now, Malcolm. She's staying here until she's ready to go home. Ya listening?'

'Yes, Merv.'

'As I said, you're not the first. Same thing happened with my second daughter. All worked out in the end. And a lovely kid she had too. Took her a while to get hitched but she did in the end. Now, I know Louise is different. But she'll find her way. Have a glass of whisky, Mal, and go to bed. Things will look better in the morning. Are ya there?'

'Yes, Merv. Thank you, Merv. I'll do that.'

Malcolm put the phone down. He was exhausted. 'One daughter found. One wife missing.' He put his arm around Robert. He righted the kitchen stool. Robert felt a welling of sympathy and had a fleeting glimpse of Malcolm's loneliness. 'There's some whisky here somewhere.' Malcolm started looking through all the cupboards. Eventually he found it behind what Marion affectionately called the dry goods larder. Johnny Walker Black Label. The good stuff. He filled two Vegemite glasses to the brim.

'Here, Robbie.' He handed Robert a glass. 'Let's put ourselves to sleep.' Malcolm downed it in one gulp. Robert put the whisky to his lips and immediately felt the burning. He took a sip and his mouth was on fire.

'You finish it, Dad.' He handed his drink to Malcolm. Malcolm took it and threw his head back, emptying the glass. 'I think I'll have a ham sandwich,' he said.

'I'll make it, Dad. You stay there.' Robert was keen to help. He busied himself with the preparations. 'Toasted?' He looked at Malcolm.

'Yes, toasted would be nice.'

'Mustard?'

'Yes, thanks.'

'No worries. Toasted ham and mustard sandwiches coming up.'

It was almost like a normal conversation. Malcolm was on his third whisky when Robert put the plate in front of him. He looked up through tears. 'I love you, Robbie. I hope you know that. I love Louise too. I love my children. You're good kids and I love you both.'

'I know, Dad,' Robert replied. 'I love you too.'

———

Merv put down the phone and swung his chair around. There was no point in taking risks. Malcolm was a good bloke, but in this situation things could get out of hand.

'I'll sleep out front darling,' he said to Vonnie.

'That's very wise. I'll make up the outdoor bed.'

'No. You don't have to do that. I'll sleep in me chair. Just a couple of pillows and I'll be fine. You go and look after the girl.'

———

Louise had been breathless when she got to Vonnie's shop. It was closed so she knocked on the side door. Vonnie steeled herself. She knew who it was and what it was about.

She'd been watching the young girls for years now. Knew all their little habits. Who liked Aero bars and who preferred a Kit Kat. There was often a lot of discussion as they made up their minds. Sally, of course, was the most forward of them. 'Vonnie, Darling!' she'd call her. And 'Mr Vonnie' for Merv. Cheeky little thing! Behaved as if she were a relative. Well, she might be at that.

Louise was more reserved, as you'd expect. She was dreamy most of the time, but Louise was very quick on the brain work. Before you knew it, she'd add up the change while Vonnie was still taking the pencil from behind her ear. Then she'd give Vonnie a big grin.

Vonnie hadn't seen that smile for some time. Louise had become quiet. She seemed indifferent and distracted. Normal teenage stuff, thought Vonnie. Then one day as Louise was leaving the shop with a packet of seed potatoes for Malcolm, Vonnie glanced at her back. Louise was wearing her normal jeans and a pink tee-shirt with a lovely scalloped neckline, the sort of tee-shirt you could only get in Hobart. Marion must have got it when she went up for the CWA. Yes, she definitely saw a difference. Louise had broadened out across the back. Usually, she was as thin as a pin with the tiniest waist, but now her back, below the ribs, had filled out like a sturdy tree trunk. *Trouble ahead*, thought Vonnie. *That wretched Donohoe boy!* She thrust her hands into the pockets of her apron. *Can't leave them alone! They find something beautiful, something precious and all they want to do is destroy it! They pull the wings off butterflies! They feed gravel to chooks! Just to see what happens. Brutes! The lot of them!*

The next time Louise was in the shop, Robert was with her. He wouldn't understand, so she said it anyway. She took Louise's hand and held it tight.

'If you need anything, darl,' – she looked into Louise's eyes – 'If you ever need anything or any help in any way, I'm here for you. So's Merv.' Vonnie let her hand go. That's all she had to say.

———

So when the urgent knock came she knew what to expect. Louise was numb and mute. She couldn't say a word. She just looked at Vonnie with terror in her eyes.

'No harm will come to you here, darling.' She sat her down at the kitchen table and fed her a plate of silverside and boiled potatoes. 'Does ya mum use the stock from the silverside?' she asked in an offhand way.

Louise found her voice. Slowly and deliberately, she answered. 'She sometimes uses it but only if she's boiled the meat in two lots of water. She says you've got to get the salt out. But by the second or third lot of water, it's mostly gone. Then she makes a vegetable soup.'

'Yes, it can make a lovely soup. But I think this lot will be too salty. I didn't even wash it. I was about to, when the bell rang and that Flo woman came in asking for some brown rice. "Brown rice!" I said. "Never heard of it!" Well, she wasn't impressed. Bought some rice anyway. Keeps well, rice.'

Vonnie nattered on. Keeping things light, telling her little tales about the shop, and the customers. Nothing to upset the girl; tried to put her at her ease.

'Now tonight, you and me are going to sleep in the big bed. There's plenty of room. Merv's going to stay on the verandah. He loves being outside of a night. It's no trouble to him. Not that anything's going to happen. If your dad comes looking for you, Merv'll talk him down. Men can get over-excited in these situations and we don't want anything nasty to happen. Your dad's a good man but it's best to be on the safe side.'

Vonnie took Louise into the bedroom. A large mattress sat on a bed base that was four inches high. Just low enough for Merv to be able to swing his body up onto the bed, if he was on the floor, and just high enough that he could propel his body out of the chair and have a soft landing. If he'd forgotten to put the brake on, the chair went shooting across the room. Vonnie would fix it and line it up with the ramp at the foot of the bed. Merv didn't like to use the ramp to get into bed and he liked being at floor level. It meant he had some control. He could get in and out of bed as he wished and use his hands to propel himself along the floor. He'd become real fast at it. When the kids were little, he'd been able to give them a run for their money. Larking and screaming as he chased them round the house. But those days were over now. He was old and stiff. The grandchildren could climb up to him. He wasn't going to scurry across the floor anymore.

Vonnie found a brushed-cotton nightie in the shop, and a toothbrush. *Normal things: settle her down.* She gave her one of Merv's Mogadons and a glass of milk. *That should do the trick*, she thought.

'Things'll look different in the morning,' she said. 'One thing at a time, Lou. You just get as much sleep as you can.'

She came to bed herself, propped up with pillows and the *Women's Weekly*, and tried to do the crossword. She looked over to see if Louise was still awake, but she was out like a light.

Merv grabbed a couple of blankets and the big cushion off the couch. He wrapped himself in the thinnest one and folded the thick one over his lap. Vonnie would come out in any case and fuss about. He put the big cushion behind his head and crossed his arms. The porch light was on. This was what he wanted. He wanted the light to shine on his face. If Malcolm came down the road hell-bent on destruction, the first thing he'd see was Merv's eyes. A man with no legs learns to use his eyes. First thing he'd do was assess Malcolm's state of mind. That was the easy part. All he had to do was look at him: sort of stand behind him. Feel what it was like to be Malcolm at this particular point in time.

That wasn't hard! He'd been there himself. Daughter number two. Jennifer. By God she was a handful. Daughter number one, Helen. Textbook case of what to do. Everything in the right order. No problems with any of life's transitions. But Jennifer? Nothing but trouble from the word go! Alright in the end, but a lot of effort to get there. Malcolm needed to know that it wasn't his fault. Or Marion's fault. They were doing their best to raise their kiddies. This would change things. Yes. But it wasn't the end of the world.

Merv sighed and looked out to the road. Blue gums were silhouetted against the fading sky. It had been a warm day, then a blazing sunset. *Good for the sailors*, he said to himself. Pulling the thick blanket up to his chin he felt the warmth envelop him. A mopoke called from the blue gums. A sad, lonely call, then the sudden silence. Merv gave himself a task. He'd watch the sky till the last of the light had disappeared. He'd keep his eyes on that colour until the moon came up and made everything soft and lovely. He'd watch till the last little patch of light behind the gum trees merged with the dark of the trees. Then he'd turn his concentration to something else. Maybe the sounds of the river. You didn't notice it by day. Too busy. But at night it was a constant gurgle. Just in the background almost in the back of your mind. At night you had time enough to really listen to it. Hear its undulations. The tinkle at the top of the sound and the lower sound, the swish and glumph as the water poured over the rocks. Funny how sound separated out when you really listened to it.

Now that he was warm and settled, his mind clear and calm, he could stay in this state for hours. Even if he did doze off for a minute or two, he'd be woken by the sound of feet on the gravel road. He'd be ready for Malcolm. And he'd go through the code in his head before he finished listening to the river.

All the lights were on at Flo and Barry's house. The garage door was open, and Barry was heaving cardboard boxes up against the back wall. Marion came up behind him. He didn't see her.

'Flo! I can't fit any more boxes at the back!' he yelled at the top of his voice. 'It's either make a second row, or throw some stuff out!'

'Barry . . .' Marion limped into the garage. Her leg was bleeding. 'Barry . . . I . . .'

'Marion! Good Lord! What's happened?' He moved towards her and put his arm around her, taking her hand. 'Come inside. Come inside. Flo! Come here. Come here, now!' Flo came rushing out. She was ready for a fight if Barry thought she was going to throw out any of her possessions. She rounded the corner of the garage like a boxer ready for action. Then she saw Marion.

'Oh my God! Marion! What happened?'

They took her inside and moved several boxes off the couch, using one to prop up Marion's leg. 'Put the kettle on, Barry.'

'I don't know where the bloody kettle is! Shouldn't we call an ambulance?'

'No!' said Marion. 'I'm alright. Really!' I tripped over Robert's bike. The pedal caught me on the shin. It'll be fine. I just need to put it up for a while. Louise is pregnant.'

'What?' said Flo.

'Louise is pregnant.'

'Oh Marion! I'd no idea. We've been so busy with the packing … We're expected in Chad by the end of the month. I haven't seen Louise for ages.'

'Well, she's pregnant. And not a little pregnant! She's at least two months, possibly three. Oh! I'm such a fool! I'm such a fool, Flo! Why didn't I see this coming?'

'It's not your fault,' said Flo. 'Are you sure it's too late for a termination? I know someone who has contacts in Melbourne.'

'No, she's too far gone. Anyway, Malcolm wouldn't allow it.'

Barry found the kettle and made the tea. 'Would you like Earl Grey, or just ordinary?'

Marion just looked at him.

'Just ordinary, then.'

'No. I can't stay. I have to find her. I thought she'd be here with you.'

'Marion, you can't walk on that leg. Barry, go and see how Malcolm is. Louise is probably at the Saltmarshes'. I'll stay here and bandage that leg.'

Barry was thankful for the instructions. He raced out the door and jumped in the VW. When he got to the Johnstones', Malcolm and Robert were eating the ham sandwiches.

'Want one?' Robert proffered a large plate to Barry. Barry took one.

'Louise is at Merv and Vonnie's,' said Malcolm.

'Oh,' said Barry. 'Marion's at our place. She's damaged her leg somehow. Something about a bike?' It's rather nasty. Flo's putting her to rights. Well. All accounted for.' He bit down on the sandwich without tasting it.

———

The worst was over. Louise stayed for two more days with Merv and Vonnie. She helped in the shop. It was such a relief to be away from her own family. 'When you're ready, love, you go home,' Vonnie said to her.

When she was ready, Vonnie and Louise made a batch of Anzacs and a beef casserole. Vonnie put them in a wicker basket. 'Before you go, say goodbye to Merv. He's gunna miss you. He wanted to have a word before you go.'

Merv turned off the races and swung his chair around. He looked at Louise quietly, with a steady gaze, just letting his eyes settle, just letting his love wash over her. Before he'd said anything, she'd started to weep. 'You're a good girl, Lou. You're good. And you'll go a long way. You're bright and quick. Vonnie says you're the best assistant she's had. But that aside, you've done the wrong thing, Lou. And you know that. I know, I know, it takes two to tango. But that boy's gone now. We don't know what's going happen to him. He may not even come back. War's a terrible thing, Louise, and I know you thought you were doing him a favour. It was like that in my day too. Girls would just give themselves to you if you asked! Don't tell Vonnie about that. Now things are gunna be different. I know you feel ashamed and that's normal. But you've got to look forward, Lou. Life goes forward. You're a sacred vessel, Lou. You're holding life inside ya! And you have to look after yourself. Now, I don't know what's going to happen with your baby, but for now, you're in charge of that little life. So don't do anything stupid, that's what I'm trying to say. Vonnie and me'll always be your friends, so just remember that. And your dad's a good bloke. So you give him that casserole and see if that doesn't put a smile on his face.'

Louise bent down and hugged his great bull neck. He patted her on the arm.

'Off you go, now. And good luck!'

———

She opened the back gate. Malcolm was in the veggie garden planting peas. 'Over here, Lou,' he said. 'Grab the end of that bit of string and hold it tight. I know it's a bit late getting them in, but we could get lucky. What do you think?'

'It's worth a try,' she said, putting the basket down. She held the string against the ground. The earth smelt fresh and clean.

'Come on,' said Malcolm. 'You can help me put them in. They only have to go half an inch deep. I'll make a drain and you do the seeds. A couple of inches apart. Zigzag them a bit. Give them a bit of room.' Louise picked a handful of pea seeds out of the paper bag slumped against the spade.

Malcolm came up the row towards her. 'Do you think we can get three rows in here?' He put his hands on his hips. Louise could smell his sweaty armpits. She thrust her arms around him, pushing her head into his chest.

'I'm sorry, Dad. I'm so sorry!' Her muffled voice choked.

He held her close, rubbed her back. 'We'll get through this, Lou.'

Chapter 29

Norman Dillon shut his office door, straightened his tie and pulled his waistcoat over his paunch. He set out for B block. This had to be done quickly. His feet tapped out a military stride on the polished linoleum. The sound gave him confidence. Without hesitation he opened the main door to the Home Economics room. Louise Johnstone stood in the middle of the room in her underwear.

'Mr Dillon!' exclaimed Mrs Bradshaw, the home economics teacher.

'Sorry, Mrs Bradshaw. My apologies, Louise.' He half closed the door so as to be out of sight. 'Get dressed immediately, Louise. This can't wait.'

'Well… yes, headmaster,' replied Mrs Bradshaw. She quickly handed Louise her school dress.

'We'll do it later, when Mr Dillon's finished with you.' *Poor little thing*, thought Dulcie Bradshaw. She only wished to adjust her dress by taking the darts out of the back: make it seem less obvious. This was the third one she'd had this year.

'Come with me.' Norman Dillon was tight-lipped. He strode along the corridor with an urgency; Louise had to almost run to keep up. He opened the door to the gym. Rows and rows of Grade 10 students sat behind desks with exam papers in front of them. There was a spare desk by the door. The exam paper on the desk had 'Louise Johnstone' written in pencil in the top left-hand corner.

Louise looked up at Norman Dillon. 'I'm not in Grade 10, Mr Dillon. I'm only Grade 9.'

'Today you're in Grade 10,' he replied. 'Sit here. Do your best. There's another exam this afternoon and two more tomorrow. Louise... just do your best.'

'Yes, sir.'

'If you need anything: a glass of water, or to go to the toilet, just raise your hand.' He turned to go, but then swung round. 'You'll need this.' He took his fountain pen out of his breast pocket and placed it on the paper.

Norman Dillon had never done anything so rash. But times were changing. Everything was in flux. Women were pushing themselves forward. And quite rightly, in his opinion! The female staff members were progressive, some would say strident, harsh, selfish and arrogant. But the traditional view of women as home-makers was giving way. And very quickly. Until now, women who wanted a career had had a choice: teaching or nursing. If they didn't like the sight of blood, they became teachers. But now, there were women entering science, and law. The students at his school were at the opposite end of the scale. The prevailing view was that students were privileged way beyond what was necessary for an education. Their parents had experienced war and depression: their education had ended at age fourteen. To them, to remain in school till the age of sixteen was giving them far more than they deserved. The stunted, pinched, narrowing, hard-bitten parochial attitudes of many parents sent shivers down his spine. The 'what was good enough for me' way of thinking prevailed with most of the parent body.

Norman Dillon was changing as well. He was changing with the times. He'd seen the devolution of girls who had left school too early: seen the light go out of their eyes as they trudged behind strollers and shopping trolleys; drinking a shandy while they waited in the car park as their no-hoper husbands emptied their pay packet in the pub. *Divine rights of men*, he thought: *the divine right to get as pissed as a billy goat three times a week. Drop-kicks, the lot of them!* Well, he'd have none of it. If this country was going to pull itself into the twentieth century, the education of women was going to be the key. Things were moving fast. There was talk of computers and how useful they'd be in the science lab! Imagine what that was going to do for education. Not many of the staff could see it now, but there was going to be a revolution. Even if some old fuddy-duddy from the woodwork department carried on about the devil and electricity and changing vulnerable brains, God's will and god knows what else. It was coming fast and everyone ought to be ready.

'Morning, Mister Dillon.' Malcolm strode into the head-master's office. Norman Dillon rose and shook his hand. 'Thanks for seeing me. I know you're a busy man.'

'Not at all, Mr Johnstone. Can I call you Malcolm?'

'Yes, of course.'

'And I'm Norman. No need for formalities these days.'

'Norman. Well, the fact is ... Louise would like to take some time off school. I know she's a good student, but she needs to help a bit at home.' Malcolm was floundering. Norman coughed and leant back in his chair.

'We've got a bit of a business going at home.' Malcolm brushed imaginary lint from his trousers. 'You see, Marion's a very good cook. She's getting quite a reputation around the neighbourhood. Louise needs to give her a bit of a hand. Just for a term or so.'

Norman nodded and resisted the temptation to rest his elbows on his chair and steeple his fingers. 'I quite understand, Malcolm. The baking industry is a noble profession. I wish your wife and Louise the best of luck.'

Malcolm's face relaxed. 'Oh, we're all putting on weight in our house, I can tell you! On the other hand, you'll still have to put up with Robbie.'

Norman smiled. 'Oh, we all need a bit of levity in our lives, Malcolm.' He rose from his chair and shook Malcolm's hand.

If Norman Dillon could give Louise Johnstone a chance of getting to Matriculation College, he would. She had a good brain. Under normal circumstances, she might or might not have had the chance to get that far. He'd always argue with parents to go that extra two years. It made all the difference, not only to job prospects but also to widening their social sphere. And he'd heard all the arguments: 'They'll just go off and get married anyway… It'll turn their heads! They won't want to stay in their proper place… It's a waste of money. It costs a cow to send a child to Matriculation College: only for the boy.' Even if he's the stupid one.

A scholarship was worth two hundred dollars a year, plus fees and textbook allowances. Some of those textbooks would be the first books inside some of those homes. Ten thousand scholarships across the country. If he could get half a dozen in his school he'd be a proud man. If one or two of them were girls, even better.

Chapter 30

'FOR GOD'S SAKE MARION! WHAT were you thinking?' The sound of her mother-in-law's voice down the line sent Marion into shock. She stepped backwards, knocking over the telephone table.

'I found her in the newsagency buying cigarettes with some dreadful girl. Both of them looked appalling! Well you don't have to say anything. It's all bleedingly obvious! I've taken her out of that place. It's filthy and depressing. My granddaughter does not belong in an institution for unwed mothers. How could you let this happen to her? Oh, I suspected something was wrong when I didn't see you for Graeme's seventieth. I was so embarrassed. Surely a family can make some effort. But no. You said you had something else on. Well! I see now! She's had the baby and God knows where it will end up. She's with us. She hasn't said a word. She's lost her voice completely! She's completely traumatised. I don't know if she'll ever get over this. Ever! Graeme's very upset. Very upset! You know she's always been his favourite. Some grandmothers would give her the cold shoulder. Cut her out completely. Well, I am not going to do that! But we're particularly hurt that this could happen in our family. I know there's a war. People are going mad. Girls give themselves thinking that it's their patriotic duty or some such nonsense. But girls need protecting! Louise needs protecting. She's so young. She's only fifteen, for God's sake! I don't want to hear the details. But I do want you to know that whatever lapses in care, you and Malcolm, yes I include him in this, whatever lapses in care and diligence you have shown as parents, will be made up for in this household. Is that clear? Until further notice, she remains under this roof!'

Marion heard the loud clang of the phone being forced into its cradle.

———

Elizabeth Johnstone had not been fooled by Marion. The first time Malcolm brought her home… flaunting her legs as she strode across the Axminster. Obviously a hoofer, with the strength in those calves – and, of course, ankles to die for! Graeme couldn't keep his eyes off her. Nothing sturdy about the woman… a gold digger… a cheap little hoofer from the East End of London. What was Malcolm thinking? Did he think that all English people were the same?

She should have known! Oh, yes, that first meeting: Marion offered to help with the tea – well she'd already done her worst by marrying her stupid son – and then she put the milk in first! Extraordinary…! Well! Graeme noticed but didn't say anything. Always the gentleman… He kept look-ing at her legs.

'Quite a good match,' he'd said when they (thankfully) left. Quite a good match! Well! Malcolm never listened to her… never any time for his mother… He was all sport and adrenaline. Stupid boy! The navy was supposed to knock some sense into him. But if anything he was worse when he was discharged… And Graeme was no help. Off to the club whenever he could sense trouble. Or to his infernal study. How long did it take to read the *Times*? Golf, club and gardening and that was it with him. Never any attempt to inculcate some common sense or culture into the boys. No sense of discrimination or taste . . .

At least Simon had done well. A degree in engineering. More than Malcolm could ever do! And a lovely wife. Lovely! No need for her to flaunt her charms. A pure and delightful girl. Not quite up to him in the intellect department, but nevertheless a good, solid type – she'd never put a foot wrong. Sensible. Unlike that Marion!

Just as well they were down in the country. She couldn't abide them being close by . . . And Robert! How could a boy become so eccentric and precocious at such a young age? Unnerving. Very artistic. Well, he'd have to be very artistic to make a career out of it . . . Hah! Malcolm deserved him.

———

Elizabeth flung the tea towel on the kitchen bench. The room was cold. The grandfather clock in the hall struck the quarter hour, its pendulum heaving itself from one direction to the other: the infernal effort of marking time. *Needs must*, she said to herself. But then the thought of company softened her.

It would be nice to have Louise in the house . . . Some company for a change. And it would be a chance to try to make things right for Louise, fill in the gaps in her appalling education. They could do things together . . . galleries, the theatre, the cinema . . . First things first. Feed her. Nutrition. The girl needed decent food and regular meals. No more cigarettes and Mars bars. She was as skinny as a rake. Regularity. Rest. Breakfast at seven thirty. Dinner at one o'clock. Supper at seven. Bed at ten thirty.

Graeme was more like a piece of furniture these days . . .

keep him fed and watered, neatly clothed and he'd go about his business without so much as a by-your-leave… Having Louise to talk to would be a welcome change, as soon as the girl found her voice. Dear, dear girl! So beautiful… so young. *'Damaged goods' as they say … She'll never be the same … Never be that carefree spirit. Stupid! Stupid Malcolm! Stupid! Stupid Marion! They've no idea what a treasure they had … And now it's a matter of putting back the pieces. But she'll never be the same. That darling little girl has gone – and she's gone for ever.*

———

Louise heard the grandfather clock strike the quarter hour. Sitting on the bed she looked at the wallpaper, its patterns of lilacs and primroses in vertical rows. Every fifteenth row, the pattern repeated. On the thirteenth row, the yellow of the primrose on the outer most edge was missing, the ink having run out. Every lilac seemed to be exactly the same. Every lilac seemed to be exactly the same. *Every lilac is exactly the same. Exactly the same. Exactly the same.* Louise repeated the phrase over and over in her head.

The clock struck the half hour. Elizabeth knocked gently on the door.

'I have some towels for you, dear.' She put the towels on the straight-backed chair by the window. They smelt of mothballs. 'When you're ready … a nice hot bath. That'll do you good!'

Louise went on staring at the wallpaper, the rhythm still running through her head. Her eyes flickered for a moment.

'I'll come and check in half an hour, shall I?'

Louise rallied enough to give the slightest nod.

Suddenly Elizabeth sat down heavily on the bed. The

mattress squeaked. She wrapped her big, heavy arms around the girl. 'Buck up! Louise. Buck up, girl! It's not the end of the world. Now listen to me. We're having roast beef for supper. And baked apples for pudding. How does that sound? You need feeding! Dear girl!' She held her tight. 'We love you!' she said. 'We love you, Louise.'

Louise felt the crushing arms around her. It was suffocating. Granny smelt of lard and Velvet soap. She would have liked to be left alone with the wallpaper. To be left to listen to the circles of her mind repeating aimless patterns and feel the increasing numbness take her away. It would be nice to notice nothing. To feel nothing. To remain within the perfect rhythm of the paper. To become two dimensional. Spread her thin body out so that it became nothing but skin against the brick wall. Squeeze her insides out: like a rolling pin pressing all the viscera out of her body. To become a flat object. To only hear the tiny voices of insects, the rustle of leaves, the hollow wind. To mark the time with the boom of the clock. To be nothing but a film of light. A thin quivering thing without nerve or moisture.

Elizabeth could see only blankness in Louise's eyes. Dullness. Sometimes a frightened, nervous flicker. Louise wouldn't meet her eyes but gazed at the floor. Her breathing seemed deliberate, as if she was making a special effort to breathe. In. Out. In. Out. In and out again. A conscious effort to stay alive, as if, if she didn't keep her breath going, she'd simply fold onto the carpet and disappear.

But Elizabeth was a talker. She began to hold Louise afloat with a constant stream of chatter.

'Don't mind me, dear. Just hold this can of bulbs for me. Will you listen to that traffic? I think the council should put some bumps in the road. That'd do the trick. People think they can come up here as a short cut to town. Or for free parking. Well! I'm one step away from writing to the council. Or better still I'll get Granddad to do it for me. His name carries more weight.'

The minutiae of every thought were given oxygen. Elizabeth would talk to the running water in the bathtub. She'd berate flies for slipping through the screen door. She'd curse the heavens for a shower of rain on washing day. She'd savagely pull the door of the oven open and yell at the crackling roast. 'Are you ready yet?' The *dong* of the grandfather clock and the quick punctuation of Elizabeth's voice wove a net over Louise's trauma.

In her mind, Louise would follow the voice. Hearing it through a long dark tunnel, way in the distance, mumbling sounds without meaning. She repeated the words. Holding the sound and texture in her mind. Trying to make sense of the ups and downs of it. Trying them out in her mind like a child learning to talk. She'd pull on each strand of Elizabeth's voice. She knew she had to try to lift her mind out of the quagmire and pull the fragments together.

—

'Go and tell Granddad that lunch is ready.' Elizabeth held her breath as the girl went up the stairs.

'Lunch is ready,' she heard Louise say.

'What-ho! Jolly good! What's the old girl got on the table?' Graeme's voice boomed cheerfully.

'It's a pie she's made from scraps.'

'Oh! I love a good Scrap Pie!'

And the spell seemed to be broken. Louise's voice was back.

Elizabeth had a bit of a cry and made light of it, wiping her eyes on a tea towel. 'The onions,' she said.

Every night, when Elizabeth and Graeme had gone to bed, the grandfather clock seemed to become alive and erratic. It struck at strange intervals of time, sometimes the hour, then straight away the half hour: as if time and space had twisted and doubled up on itself. Order was left aside. The relentless pendulum pushing the dusty air this way and that, striking the quarter hour again and again, as if it were spreading a layer of dust over the fusty furniture. Louise's body buckled and her hands gripped the pillow. She cried. Sometimes soundlessly. Sometimes out loud.

Elizabeth put down her book on the bedside table. She could hear the sobs from down the hallway. Graeme lay beside her snoring like an elephant. He was no use to her. *It'll take time*, she said to herself. *It'll take time*.

The sobbing eased. Elizabeth picked up her book, relieved. Then she heard voices. She could distinctly hear Louise's voice in conversation with someone. She put the book down again. Yes, it was Louise's voice. Then a silence. Then Louise again. Was there someone in her room? The conversation seemed to go on and on. With dread in her heart, she slipped out of bed and along the passage.

Louise's bedroom door was shut. Elizabeth bent over and looked through the keyhole, cursing that she'd left her glasses on the bedside table. She held her breath as she tried to make out what was happening. All she could see was a fuzzy outline of the bed. Louise was sitting up. She wished she'd left her glasses on! Elizabeth stood up and stretched out her back. The talking had stopped. She opened the door and put her head into the room. Louise lay on her side facing the wall. She appeared to be asleep. There was no-one else in the room. Relieved, Elizabeth gently shut the door and went back to bed. She finished the chapter in her book and dozed off to the sound of Graeme's snoring.

The next night was the same. Elizabeth heard Louise talking. It was an animated conversation. She seemed to be saying 'I' a lot. 'I' this and 'I' that. Laying down the law to someone, being aggressive, being commanding. Bold, as if she were lording it over someone. There were long periods of silence and then Louise's voice again. This time calm. Relaxed, almost mesmeric. Droning on and on in a commanding tone.

Again, Elizabeth crept out of bed and along the passage. This time she took her glasses. The voice was bold and loud. 'You think you know me,' she heard. 'I know more than you will ever know. You have no idea what I know! What I see. I see your ambition. Your stupid ambition! I see your ignorance. Your judgement. I know everything about you. Do you hear? Have you got that? I know everything! Have you got that? Have you got that!' There was an iron ring in the voice, edged with hysteria.

Elizabeth clenched her fist to her heart. She went straight to the kitchen and made a cup of Horlicks. Carefully she held it in both hands and took it in to Louise. She was sitting bolt upright in bed, her eyes wide, her mouth tight and hard. Elizabeth offered the mug, but Louise didn't take it. She didn't see it.

'I'll leave it here dear. It's just here on the table. Drink it all up, there's a good girl. You'll sleep better.' Elizabeth put her hands on her shoulders and kissed her forehead. There was no response, only her rigid body slightly rocking.

Louise turned her head to the wallpaper and looked for the changing pattern. Looked for the thirteenth row.

———

'Althorp,' said Graeme.

'Althorp?' Elizabeth looked up from her knitting.

'Yes, you know ... Althorp from the club.'

'That Althorp! Dreadful man! He tried to touch me up at a dance once. I pity Alison having to put up with him.'

'Anyway, Althorp says it's an epidemic. Teenage pregnancy. He says it's everywhere. Right through society. It's the war. And it's the pill. Makes them think about sex. But they don't go on the pill. Their mothers wouldn't let them. Then they do it without a thought. Louise isn't the only one. Althorp says he's had three this week!

'What I'm saying, Elizabeth, is that it isn't anyone's fault. Malcolm and Marion are doing their best. Times are changing. Look at fashion! Dresses right up to the thighs! It's unheard of. In our day you'd be put in jail for indecent exposure. And their hair! Lord! Even the boys. Have you seen what boys are doing to their hair? Down to their shoulders, covering their faces.'

Graeme hadn't said so much for twenty years.

'Do you mean to tell me you've been talking to Althorp about Louise?' Elizabeth glared at her husband. 'Is that what you talk about at the club?'

'Well, that and other things. Sometimes we just sit quietly. Do you know what that feels like?'

Elizabeth huffed and put her knitting on her lap. 'I'm worried, Graeme. I'm terribly worried. She's losing her mind. If I'm not talking to her, she'll drift off and end up chasing fairies. I – we have to stop it. You could help, you know. Talk to her more. Take her out?'

'Take her out?' he said. 'Where would I take her?'

'Well... I don't know.'

'We could walk down to the yacht club. That would be a nice stroll.'

'No! Don't go anywhere near water. Don't take her down there. Why not the museum? There's always something interesting going on there. Or the library. They have lunch-hour concerts in the library these days. That would be lovely.'

———

Graeme thought the concert might be the go. They sat on plastic chairs and ate ham and salad rolls. A strand of red onion stuck to Graeme's chin. The orchestra shuffled in. Students from the conservatorium. Among them was the girl with the high forehead who used to love sitting next to Robert on the bus. Louise lowered her eyes, hoping not to be seen. The lead violinist was barefoot. *Lord!* thought Graeme.

Albinoni's *Adagio* for strings filled the small auditorium.

Louise sat. Her hands were sweating. She could still taste the onion from the roll. Its smell was overpowering. Graeme belched. As soon as the music started, she felt tears in her eyes. Any outer defence to the world was peeled back. She had no defence against the truth of music. The lead violinist pulled his bow slowly and inexorably across the strings. Every note pulling at her soul. Her blood seemed to fill with the sound as her heart pounded in a visceral reaction.

She was drenched in perspiration. The back of her legs so sticky with sweat that she wondered if she'd wet her pants. Every nerve of her skin was on edge. The sounds caressed and inflamed her skin. She concentrated on breathing. She hoped no-one would look at her. The sound rolled over her like the breakers on South Arm beach. She dived in and out. With each wave came a new way of feeling that filled her with sorrow, anguish, surprise and knowing, pulling deep inside her body.

And all the time, as she heard the sounds, the slow-motion change of the harmonies, the quivering rasp of the low cellos, the plaintive cry of the violins, she thought to herself: *I know. I know every note. Every feeling that comes from this sound belongs to me. I'm the one whose soul they are playing. I know every nuance, every change, every quietening and expanding in the sound. I know all this. It is me they are playing. It is my soul on exhibition for the whole world to see. It's my life they are talking about. I am that music. I am that sound.*

It was beyond her imagining to think that she could ever play music. Never in her wildest dreams could she see herself playing an instrument. Yet she knew every note and cadence. Every haltering, straining bow, every shimmering vibrato and slow gliding crescendo. She knew it all. It all made perfect sense. There was knowledge beyond her that folded over her and pulled her jagged nerves in one direction, then another. It coiled around her like a thick light. She had no defence against it. Her throat seemed to open up and pull back towards her spine. She felt like singing or simply making a noise, a high thin lonely note: a keening. It was like a hand reaching into her throat pulling out the sound like a thick ball of wool. It was echoing through her body as if she were a hollow chamber. It was crawling up the back of her neck. She tried to focus on the orchestra. Her bowels felt tight, stretched and watery all at once.

The barefoot boy leading the orchestra seemed to be a wise old sage in the guise of youth. Someone that knew the depths of human emotion. His hair was dirty and lank. He wore a kaftan shirt over a pair of jeans. She was certain he knew everything. He was some kind of god put there to heal her, to entrance and enthral her. He was a magician conjuring thought and feeling. She couldn't look at him. He knew the sorrow of the world. She was sure of it. He knew the sorrow of the world and its inevitable weary resolution.

The velvet cellos, holding their notes like a hand holding her head under water. Holding it there till she learnt to breathe. Breathe with the water. Cool and clear. Each long sound, each note, holding her there in that new world.

There was no escape. She didn't have the strength to avoid the experience. She was frozen and static. She tried to focus on the sandals of a cellist. She said it in her mind. *The sandals are leather. The sandals are leather. The sandals, leather. The straps criss-cross the feet. Criss-cross the feet. Criss-cross, criss-cross. No-one will see me. Keep my head down. No-one will see me. Don't look up. Everybody knows. Everybody knows. The sandals are leather. The sandals are leather. Criss-cross. Criss-cross. My hands are shaking. Keep them still. Keep them still. Tight! Tight! Keep one hand in the other. Don't move. Breathe quietly. Look at the floor. The carpet is grey. The carpet is grey.*

The players moved like swaying grass. They were one being. And the conductor was a god, pulling them this way and that. Pulling with his hands and arms making them breathe together, drawing sound out with his fingers. The cellist with the sandals played a passage by herself, the orchestra a bed of sound: uncertain and disquieting. The colours changed. Mournful and dark when the cello sang, then piercing and bronze when the solo violin played, birdlike and throaty. And it was all a part of her. Part of her heart, part of her broken body, her shredded soul. Part of the great sorrow. The inevitable great sorrow. A laying down of life's darkest corners: a bed of impenetrable sadness. A soft film of disquiet underlying all of the joy of the world. And yet there was resolve and knowing. Inevitability. Ineffable grace and knowledge. Wisdom and clarity.

One thing she knew when the music eventually, mercifully died away. She knew she was not alone.

Graeme belched, and wiped the red onion off his chin.

———

Her eyes were closed. Her spine was straight. *All's well,* thought Elizabeth. *All's well. She's saying a prayer . . . quietly meditating.* She felt such relief. Perhaps things were looking up. Louise's face was calm and she was breathing deeply. She looked young. Her old self again. She looked balanced, composed. Her head was tilted to one side, angling towards the head of the bed. Elizabeth glanced at the head of the bed. There was Louise lying down, facing into the room. Her hair a tangled mess on the pillow. She was fast asleep, facing in towards the room, one arm above the blankets. Elizabeth pulled back in shock. She rubbed her eyes and positioned the other eye to the keyhole. Yes, that looked better. There she was, fast asleep.

Chapter 31

'Mal?' Darryl stuck his head round the door to Malcolm's office. 'There's drinks in the lobby. You wanna come down? Amanda's leaving. She's getting married on the weekend. She'll be wanting to say goodbye to you.'

'Down in a minute, thanks.' If he put it off as long as possible, the party would be winding up by the time he got there.

'Don't leave it too long, matey. They're all getting sloshed.'

Malcolm busied himself for another fifteen minutes. When he got to the lobby the jokes were running thick and fast. He assumed a compliant smile and stood by the door. Amanda sidled up to him.

'Next time you see me, Mr Johnstone, I'll be a married woman!' She giggled and sipped from a champagne glass.

'Best of luck, Amanda. I hope everything goes well for you.'

Amanda looked up into his face, but he didn't meet her eyes. She turned around to see who he was looking at. There was no-one there. 'Anyway,' she said. 'Thanks for all you've done for me.' Malcolm quickly glanced at her then looked away.

As soon as he could, he left.

———

At home, Marion was preparing dinner. He sat on the kitchen stool, sipping a beer. 'Would you like a drink? A shandy?'

'Yes, I would, thank you.' Malcolm poured out half a glass and topped it up with lemonade. Marion took a sip, then another, feeling the alcohol and sugar rush through her body. 'Whoa! I think I've turned to mush!' She put the glass down. Malcolm looked at her with a steady gaze. He held his arms out to her. She rushed to his side and cradled his head against her breast. Malcolm let out a long sigh. She kiss the top of his head. 'I'd better cut the carrots.'

'Bugger the carrots.' He pulled her tighter into his body. Tears ran down his face. He brushed them away on her chest. She stroked his face and neck.

Robert sauntered into the kitchen, his nose in a Marvel comic. 'What's for tea?'

'Picked eel's feet,' replied Marion. He looked up.

'You beauty!' He rolled up the comic and playfully tapped her on the head. Before she could react he pulled her apron strings undone.

'Robert!'

Malcolm stood up. 'It'll be a little while yet, mate.' He positioned himself in front of the chopping board. 'Come over here and I'll show you how to chop carrots.'

'No way!' Robert looked at him in mock horror. He skittered out of the kitchen and down the hallway.

———

For Robert, it was a great calamity that he didn't understand.

'Will she ever come back?' Robert asked as he dried the dishes.

'I don't know,' Marion said.

'I hope she comes back and brings the baby with her.'

'That won't happen.'

Robert looked at the suds in the sink. They were popping as tears fell on them.

'Go and do your homework, Robert. I'll finish here.' Marion didn't look up.

Robert left the kitchen. He remembered the day Lou had left. Marion had packed a bag and Malcolm was warming up the car, impatient to get going. Lou was like an elephant. A huge stomach protruding outwards. She got in the front seat of the car.

'No you don't!' Malcolm yelled at her. 'You get in the back. And lie down. I don't want anyone seeing you. Have you got that?'

Louise got into the back seat and obediently lay down. Robert ran to the car. 'Bye, Lou, bye!'

'Bye, Robbie,' she whispered, looking up at him.

———

Dear Mum and Bo-Bo,

Hope all you lot are well. We've had a wonderful summer here. It hasn't been too hot, which is a blessing. The garden is beginning to look good. I planted a rose by the front gate and it's been flowering all summer. It's a David Austin. They're all the rage down here. Malcolm's garden is doing very well, although he has had white moth in the cabbages. One cabbage lasts a long time! We seem to be living on cabbage. If you put a slice of bread over it when it's cooking, the smell won't go through the whole house.

There's still a lot to do around the house but we're

gradually getting there. I'll send you some photos soon.

Robert's doing very well at school. He actually managed to win a prize at the end of the year. It was in Art, of course. Everyone says he has a talent.

I have very sad news, Mum. Louise has slipped up. Must run in the family. I don't know how it could have happened. I kept such an eye on her. She's with Malcolm's parents at the moment. We've no idea when she'll come home. Malcolm's been beside himself. He's been angry a lot. And drinking too much. I can't go and see her by myself. I don't know what's going to happen to her. I wish you were here. I miss you all so much.

I love you both more than I can say.
Marion

A reply came by return mail.

Dear Marion,

My dear girl, don't be disheartened. It's not the end of the world. As Bo-Bo says, 'Children are born every day. They bring their own charm and love with them.' Look at Lucy. She's the light of our lives! We wouldn't be without her. She has brought so much love into our lives. She's such a blessing. And I'm sure Louise's baby will be the same. You're not too old to pass it off as your own. No-one will care anyway. Take heart dear girl. It may seem like a long haul at the moment, but the sun will come out again.

All our love, Mum

———

Alice and Sally made a special trip up to Hobart. It took two buses to get to Battery Point. Sally gazed out the window. Alice sat quietly. Each had a present for Louise. Sally had some sandalwood incense. Alice had bought her a loose-fitting tee-shirt, red and white stripes. 'She can wear it anywhere,' she said. 'Nice for her to have something new.'

When they arrived on the doorstep, Elizabeth was in the garden.

'Hello! Hello! Alice! Well, it has been a long time. And this is your daughter. Sally, isn't it? What a lovely name! And you're pretty, just like your mother. Louise has told me all about you. Well! Come in, dears. I'll make some tea. Louise has been busy making an orange sponge.'

Sally helped Louise in the kitchen. They were awkward with each other. Solemn. Reserved. When the cake wouldn't come out of the tin, Louise started crying. Sally leapt into action, finding a spatula and scraping the burnt crust from the base of the tin. She laughed as she lay the ruined cake out on a plate. 'Well, this was worth the trip!' she said. The old connection was re-made. They fussed about decorating the cake with icing and thin strips of orange.

'We present you with a *convollipop d'orange!*' Sally placed the plate on the coffee table, laughing and dancing and flinging an apron around.

Elizabeth and Alice talked of weather and gardening. The girls went upstairs to Louise's room. They lit the incense and talked of school.

After a silence Sally asked, 'Has your mum been to visit yet?'

'No. She doesn't get on with Gran. I think she's coming up next week. I'm not sure. I don't know if she wants to see me. I know Dad doesn't. He hates me.'

Sally looked at the floor. 'At least you're in Hobart. Are you allowed out?'

'I suppose so. But I don't know anyone.'

'Are you coming back to school?'

'I don't know. Gran's enrolled me at Tech for a typing course. She's got an electric typewriter I can use.'

'That's great! You'll be able to get a job!'

There was another long silence.

'Was it really awful?' asked Sally. Louise just nodded. 'Everyone misses you at school.'

The visit dragged on. Neither girl knew what to say. When they left, Alice and Sally took a walk around the neighbourhood looking at all the gardens, the lovely picket fences, the wrought iron verandahs.

'You see that house over there?' Alice pointed to a two-storey Georgian cottage. 'I grew up in that house.' Sally stopped dead. She looked at her mother.

'You're joking. You grew up... there?' She pointed across the road. 'In that place there?'

'Yes.'

'Mum, your family must have been really rich! Is that why you know Louise's granny?'

'Yes. Elizabeth has always been good to me. She's not as conventional as she looks.'

'Does your mother still live there?'

'I'm not sure. They cut me out when I got together with Salty.'

'How could they do that? To their own daughter? Do you

think that's going to happen with Louise? Are her parents just going to ignore her? Just pretend that she doesn't exist? Everyone makes mistakes. And they were strict with her. Much stricter than you and Salty are with me and the boys. They wouldn't let her out at night or even go shopping by herself! I don't think I ever want to meet your parents. They must be horrible. You're better off without them!'

'Yes,' said Alice. 'I'm much better off without them.' She looked at the cottage, wanting to stand there, tall and proud. She wanted to say to her mother: *'Look! Look at this lovely child! She's a free spirit. She's clever and lively and beautiful. She loves life. She loves me. She loves her father. She lives in a shack. And we all love her. And your cold stone house is filled with nothing but ambition and misery. A curse on your sterile existence! A curse on your stupid society friends and your shallow life!'*

———

When they had gone, Louise opened an exercise book and started writing.

> *Blue angel at my window*
> *Against a pale sky.*
> *Late afternoon time slips*
> *Slow and thick.*
> *The wind outside*
> *Wild amongst the trees,*
> *The cool whisper on my arm.*
>
> *I miss the purring wind in the long grass.*

Chapter 32

'GRAEME,' ELIZABETH CALLED FROM THE bottom of the stairs. 'Gra-eme! I'm off to Cassandra's. Can you hear me? She needs a model for a few hours.'

'Yes, dear.' Graeme came out of his study onto the landing. 'Don't catch cold. Give her my love. Louise and I are going to listen to Sibelius.'

'Oh... the violin concerto? Tossy Spivakovsky?'

'Yes, of course.'

'Well I hope you both enjoy it. I'll get some fish on the way home.'

———

Elizabeth opened the heavy stained-glass door. 'I'm here,' she yelled, dropping her bag on the mahogany hall table. Taking off her shoes, she unzipped her skirt and let it fall to the polished floor. Pulling her blouse over her head she made her way to the back of the house. In the kitchen, with its wide flagstones, she peeled off her underpants and left them on the back of a chair. She undid her bra and hooked it over a cast iron pot hanging on the dresser.

A maze of small corridors led to the studio. The large room was filled with plants. Aspidistra sat in pots on either side of large, glass doors. Rubber plants stretched up to the ceiling. Monstera and calathea sat in large tubs. The garden beyond was alive with the wind rustling through a gigantic elm.

An easel stood on one side of the double doors. A large table with turned legs held the accoutrements of the painter. Behind rows of sword grass and orchids was a large carved bed. Cassandra lay there, smoking a cigarette. She stubbed it out and pulled back the sheets. Slowly and leisurely they made love without conversation.

Cassandra leant over Elizabeth and lifted a strand of hair off her forehead. She kissed her gently.

'How are things going? Are you being a good granny?'

'Doing the best I can. She's an awful mess, Cassie. She's been split asunder.' Cassandra ran a finger across her brow. 'At least Graeme's trying to do his bit. He's introducing her to music. They're listening to Sibelius as we speak. Violin concerto. Tossy Spivakovsky. Did you ever meet him? A girl in fourth form went out with his brother... We were just preppies... Wonderful player! She likes it. She likes music. And she humours Graeme. She's very polite. One never knows what she's thinking. But at night she goes quite mad, Cassie. Quite mad. She talks to herself. Fighting and arguing. Raging arguments. And crying. Lots of crying, of course.'

Cassandra sighed and sat up rearranging the pillows. 'You'll have to be kind, darling.'

'What do you mean? Of course I'm kind!'

'Not to Louise, Lizzie. I know you are kind to Louise. Marion. You'll have to be kind to Marion.'

Elizabeth said nothing for a while. 'Stupid woman! Why should I bother with Marion? She's a lost cause.'

Cassandra laughed. 'I do need you to sit,' she said. 'There's something new I want to capture. She traced her finger round Elizabeth's face.

'What is it? Another wrinkle?'

'Possibly,' she smiled. 'Your eyes are different. There's uncertainty... fear... hope. Compassion.'

'Compassion? Ha!' Elizabeth snorted. 'You're making that up just to make me more compassionate.'

Cassandra laughed. 'Darling! Please take the throne.'

Elizabeth sat herself heavily into the model's chair. Her flesh settled around her bones, succumbing to gravity, sagging into little mounds and valleys. Her belly relaxed and creased into her thighs. It was warm in the studio. She sighed and laid her arms along the chair. The elm seemed to lift and dance outside the window.

Cassandra turned her mind to painting, no longer seeing her lover, only the flesh, the angle of the sloping shoulders, the shadow of pendulous breasts, the corona of grey hair.

'You're ruthless,' Elizabeth said.

'What do you mean?' Cassandra looked up from the easel.

'Once you pick up that brush, the shutter comes down. That's it. I no longer exist for you. I'm just a heap of flesh.'

'Nonsense! I have to concentrate.'

'Yes. That's it. It's concentration. Takes you away from me.' She brightened. 'It's alright. I understand. Artists are ruthless. They have to be.'

'How's Graeme?'

'Totally besotted, of course. He fumbles his way through. Well he's always done that... Totally accepting. I'll give him that! He deals with things if and when they cross his path. His haemorrhoids are playing up. Apart from that he's fine.'

⸻

Gradually a healing of sorts took place. There were times when Louise wasn't thinking of the birth, or the baby.

Mostly she moved forward into each day with a jerkiness, a stumbling determination, as if each small action was being learnt for the first time. Her mind told her body to move, then she moved. The pain still reverberated. It would be there, first thing in the morning. A cloud of shame, panic and nausea enveloped her each day before she was fully awake. The effort of getting out of bed seemed monumental.

The typewriter helped. Learning a new skill drew her mind into focus. The rhythm and coordination locked all her thoughts in the front of her brain. There was no room for phantoms or introspection.

Elizabeth's endless chatter was a thread to grab hold of. She'd hear the words and repeat them in her head: sifting and sorting, slowly finding the meaning behind them, giving the appropriate response, going through the motions of communication, knowing that this was required of her. She'd feel the dark phantoms hovering when she shut her eyes and tell herself that the voice, Elizabeth's voice, was the lifeline to sanity. She'd hold the words, their texture, their meaning and lilt in her mind, savouring them, trying to imbue herself with the sounds and meaning. Elizabeth was patient. Often repeating herself.

Graeme's music was powerful medicine, drawing out the poison, stitching up her broken heart. She had such a visceral reaction to it: becoming sweaty and teary, her heart racing. The music moving inside the cells of her body. It was like a wild, sorrowful beast telling her the truths of life. She no longer felt alone. The sounds were knowing. The sounds came from deep within her and yet were known to anyone who heard them. The intimacy of music seemed appalling, shocking, yet universal.

And the monotony of the typewriter numbed the nervous edges of her psyche. Concentration and coordination pulled her mind and body together. Monotonous repetition soothed her. *The quick brown fox jumps over the lazy dog.* Again and again and again.

———

Eventually she had her first certificate in typing. 'Look!' She waved it at Elizabeth and Graeme.

'Goodness me!' said Graeme. 'I never thought we'd have a typist in the family.'

'Well done, dear. How many words a minute did you manage?'

'Forty-two. With two typos. I got "perhaps" wrong. It came out as "prehaps". And I misspelt "enliven". I started it with an "a". I know how to spell it! It was silly mistake, but when you're under pressure you haven't got time to think.'

'Never mind. You've done well,' said Elizabeth. 'I've got some good news for you. Your mother's coming to visit tomorrow. She's coming for the whole day. She's catching the early bus. I think she said she'd be here about nine o'clock. We'll have to make something special for lunch. What about a quiche? I'm sure she'd like that.'

'Yes,' said Louise. 'That sounds good.'

'Then she thought she'd take you out shopping, and to a film perhaps?'

'Yes, that sounds good.'

Louise was quiet for the rest of the afternoon. The grandfather clock boomed out the hours.

———

'She's here, Elizabeth.' Graeme opened the front door. 'Marion!' He took her in his arms.

Elizabeth came up the hall. 'My dear! Come in. Come in!' She gave Marion an awkward kiss. They moved into the kitchen.

'Hi, Mum.'

'Darling.' Marion rushed towards her, held her tightly. She sobbed and sobbed, her heart pounding. She didn't care what Elizabeth and Graeme thought. At long last she had her daughter in her arms. Louise held onto her. Quietly crying.

Elizabeth and Graeme shuffled out of the room. 'Tell me when the kettle's boiled,' said Elizabeth.

For both Marion and Louise, it was an enormous relief. Just to be together was enough. They didn't talk about the birth.

They laughed and cried through *Butch Cassidy and the Sundance Kid*. Marion thought Paul Newman was the most handsome. Louise preferred Robert Redford. Under the cover of the dark cinema, Marion looked at Louise, trying to read her. Louise seemed her old self again. Marion reached out and took her hand.

At the bus station, Marion reached into her purse. 'Dad wrote you a letter. He misses you so much.'

Louise took the letter and put it in her pocket.

Marion waved and waved till the bus turned a corner and was out of sight. Louise opened the letter.

> *Dear Lou,*
>
> *The weather here is not as warm as you would expect for this time of year. I don't think any of the*

tomatoes are going to ripen on the vine. What we need is more rain and a bit of heat in the sun. I can't believe Australia lost the cricket to the bloody poms! Here's a word from Robert.

Hi Lou, I miss you.

Love, Robert

Anyway, that's all for now. And well done about the typing. That will be very useful.

Love, Dad

Chapter 33

Iᴛ ᴡᴀs Lᴏᴜɪsᴇ's ᴅᴇᴄɪsɪᴏɴ ᴛᴏ return home. It was late autumn and the country dry and melancholy. Graeme drove. Elizabeth and Louise sat in the back seat. When they arrived, Darryl and Marcia were in the driveway, a spontaneous visit that sent Marion into a spin.

'Malcolm, mate! I had no idea Princess Lou was coming home today! We were just passing and thought you might like some cockie salmon. They're running at the moment. Been down to Dover. Left when the sea breeze come in. We'll just say a quick hello, then we'll be off.' Darryl put a bucket of fish in the laundry tub and made his way to the front of the house, leaving Malcolm trailing behind.

'Mr and Mrs Johnstone! I don't think we've had the pleasure! This is my wife, Marcia, and I'm Darryl.' He took Graeme's hand enthusiastically and then Elizabeth's. 'And here's our lovely Princess! Oh my goodness! More beautiful than ever!' Darryl gave Louise a bear hug. In the moment of silence and recovery, Marcia chimed in.

'Oh yes! You're looking lovely, Louise, with your hair all straightened out like that. No-one would recognise you. And it was a nice holiday you had in Hobart was it?'

Darryl glared at her.

'Come into the living room, everyone,' said Marion, wondering how she'd survive this nightmare.

'Oh, no, we'd better be off... or just one beer if there's

one in the fridge, Mal? Youse'll have a lot of catching up to do I'm sure.'

Marcia sat down on the couch and took out her knitting. 'Just a cuppa for me, Marion.'

Robert came sauntering into the room. He gave Louise a satirical smile.

'Oh, here he is,' said Darryl. 'The Van Gogh of the valley!'

'Hi, Dazza. Marcia. Hi Gran. Hi Granddad.'

Louise sat down on the pouffe. She felt like laughing. Not a mean laugh, not a loud hysterical laugh, but just a laugh of recognition. A simple laugh that acknowledged that this was home: this weird space, this conglomeration of disparate people. She'd straightened her hair and pinned it up in a topknot. It made her feel different, a new person. She wore the tee-shirt that Alice had given her and a new pair of jeans, high waisted and baggy legged. She sat differently. Emulating Marion's straight back and her focused expression: the art of seeing one thing at a time when faced with multiple stimuli, producing a veneered stare, directed singly, as if the outside world were filtered through a precise and accurate camera.

Malcolm didn't know what to do. Here was his daughter, home again. She'd come back of her own volition. And he wanted her to know he was somehow worthy, of what he wasn't sure. That she had made a choice to come back was a sort of honour for him. He just wanted some quiet time. Maybe they'd have a game of Monopoly latter in the day, then he'd show her round the garden. He'd like it to be just him and Robbie and Marion. He wanted to just sit and be with her. She didn't have to say anything. Just be.

But there was all this loud chatter and bluster. Marcia

was carrying on about her infernal knitting . . . clackety-clack-clack. Darryl was talking loudly about what a bloody great artist Robbie was . . . Marion was fussing around like a blowfly – there was an air of ruthlessness in the way she placed cups and saucers, sugar bowl, milk jug, Anzac biscuits.

'Show me your garden, Malcolm.' Graeme threw him a lifeline. Heads lowered in serious pursuit of coddling moth and aphids, they made their escape. Graeme had always known Malcolm had not the intellect that his other son possessed. Yet he loved him more. He doubted that Elizabeth loved him at all. For her, Malcolm was a dumb animal blundering through life. For Graeme, he was a refreshing change. There was no irony in Malcolm: no pretence or wiles. He was straightforward, honest in his emotions. Indeed, he had emotions. Graeme suspected his other son had no emotions at all. No, it was refreshing to be with Malcolm: in the garden, looking at the cabbages, tasting the parsley.

'I think she'll be alright, Malcolm,' he said. 'She's very delicate at the moment. Very delicate.'

'Oh, I can see that,' Malcolm replied, looking up to the sun.

When they went back inside, Marcia was holding forth on the virtues of plastic knitting needles as opposed to steel. Clackety-clack, clack, clack. Marion placed a cup of tea, milk no sugar, beside her on the small coffee table. Marion questioned whether cable needles were absolutely necessary when working a small cable stitch – say, three stitches. Marcia was adamant that it was a sin against the purity of Knittery and in any case, cables were always even-numbered. Louise hugged her knees and smiled. Robert slurped his tea loudly. Elizabeth thought she might turn into a ball of suet and roll across the floor.

'Would you like to see my artwork, Gran?' asked Robert.

'Why, yes! Lead on, D'Artagnan!' She plonked her teacup in the saucer and followed Robert to his room.

She stood in silence and looked about. Immediately she had the feeling of substance, of depth and quality. She didn't look closely at any individual sketch or painting. She let her eyes roam, feeling the whole rather than the individuality of the work. She deliberately wanted to gain an impression of Robert's life: not just the display before her, but his room, his bed, the clothes strewn across the floor. She wanted to feel the youth of him: his adventurous spirit.

'This is what I'm working on at the moment,' he said. 'I'm experimenting with perspective. It's called "Eye's the Fly".' In the eye of an enormous fly was the reflection of a classroom. Looking carefully at the detail, Elizabeth saw an orderly row of students, some heads down, some looking up to an unseen teacher. In the back row was a gallows with swinging corpses.

'Robert,' she said, 'there's someone I think you should meet.' They stayed in Robert's room for another half hour, talking about painting and perspective, the prospect of art school and what the future might hold. Elizabeth thought it might not be a wasted journey down to the valley after all. Robert was elated. *My gran knows stuff*, he said to himself.

Everyone was back in the living room when they returned. Marion asked Robert to get the milk out of the fridge. Marcia was on her third cup of tea and showing no sign of leaving. *Glued to the couch*, thought Marion. Robert pulled himself up to his full height and assumed a hero's stance.

'To the fridge I shall go!' he proclaimed. 'Never let it be said that Marcia was denied milk in her tea in this household!' Everyone laughed.

As he swung open the fridge door, an unopened envelope fell to the floor. It had been sitting on top of the fridge for weeks. He picked it up. It had a double window and was addressed to Louise. Without a thought he held it in his teeth as he poured milk into the milk jug and returned to the living room.

'This came for you,' he said, handing it to Louise. Marion and Malcolm had both forgotten about the envelope. They were immediately alarmed. They thought it might be in relation to Louise's pregnancy or her school attendance.

Louise grabbed it. 'You've slobbered all over it!' she said in fun, and went into the kitchen.

Malcolm hoped against hope that she'd leave it and deal with it later and called upon everyone to voice their opinion on the state of the nation.

'So what do we think of that galah Gough Whitlam?'

Everyone started talking at once.

Louise slowly entered the room and leant against the door. 'I've got a scholarship,' she said. 'I've won a scholarship to Matric!'

'Let me see that!' Malcolm reached for the notice.

'You haven't done Grade 10!' Marion said. 'There must be some mistake.' Robert leant over Malcolm's shoulder. He was grinning from ear to ear.

'Aw ... You beauty, Lou! Listen to this. *Louise Mary Johnstone, the Commonwealth Government of Australia is pleased to inform you that you have won a Scholarship to study Years Eleven and Twelve. This includes, $50 book allowance, $250*

living allowance and $500 boarding allowance, if required.
Lou, you've hit the jackpot!'

'There's obviously some mistake.' Marion shook her head.

Malcolm felt cold. 'What's this all about, Louise?' he asked.

'Mr Dillon made me do the Grade 10 Commonwealth Scholarship exams. He said it was an opportunity not to be wasted... that I could... if I tried... I don't know! He just sat me down with the Grade 10s and made me do them. He even lent me his pen.'

'You never mentioned anything about this!' Malcolm felt betrayed. 'Why wasn't I told?'

'Oh, Mal! Isn't this wonderful!' Darryl piped in. 'We all know how bright you are Lou, but this is just unbelievable! Oh, Mal! To think that you and Marion have a scholarship girl here! It's just amazing! I've never known anyone who's won more than a chook raffle, let alone a scholarship! Cor blimey! You must be so proud!'

Malcolm didn't know what he felt. He looked around the room. Marion had tears in her eyes. She sobbed and hiccupped at the same time.

'You can stay with us, darling,' said Elizabeth. This was manna from heaven. The girl could be given a life after all. Stuck down here in the country with the sheep and the cows. It was no place for a young person. 'You agree, of course, don't you Graeme?'

'Of course! Of course! No question about it!' replied Graeme. 'What would you like to do when you leave school, Louise?'

'I'd like to be a primary school teacher.'

'Just hold your horses!' said Malcolm. 'We don't know anything about this. This could be a hoax of some sort.'

Robert sniggered. 'Dad, it's got the Commonwealth

Government logo all over it.'

'Well, we need to talk it over. We can't make decisions on the run.'

But he knew it was an open and shut case. Louise would go to Hobart Matriculation College. She'd board with Graeme and Elizabeth and come home on the weekends.

Malcolm stood back as they crowded round her. *Ooh-ing and ah-ing like she's a film star or something. Not like she's coming home with her tail between her legs . . . not like she wants to make up for what she's done.*

She'd only just come home, and Malcolm was losing her again. He wanted to keep her close: keep a good eye on her. Start the growing-up all over again. He wanted a clean slate for her and for himself. Quiet time together, just her and him. He didn't have a clue what he'd say to her or what he would talk about, all he knew was this dreadful feeling of her being wrenched away. She already looked different. But there was no use fighting them. He didn't want to look a fool. He put his hands in his pockets, brushing his fingers over small change.

'I'll just go and check on the wood situation,' he said to no-one in particular. 'Might be nice to have a fire tonight.'

At the wood pile he picked up the axe, then let it fall to the chopping block. The *clonk* seemed to echo all around the valley. He looked up at Sleeping Beauty. There she lay, her impassive face always looking at the sky, her curves and folds spreading out to the foothills and creeks, rivers and mudflats. Nothing was as he imagined it would be. He had no idea about the future. No idea in what way he was responsible for what happened. All he knew was how to put one foot in front of the other. *Best get on with it.* He would keep his sadness to himself and be happy for her.

He heard footsteps behind. He turned around and Lou was right in front of him.

'Thanks for the letter, Dad.'

How big is your hand?
Reaching up to take a hand,
Looking up: wondrous eyes.
Is your uniform too long? Too wide across the shoulders?
Will you give your teacher a toothless grin?
Would I recognise my own genes
If you lifted your head amongst a sea of faces?
And if you looked directly and smiled blindly
Or kicked off a sock and displayed a purple blotch?
Your only imperfection: perfect child.
Of my mind.

When the high winds raged
And the valley's updraught lifted the limbs of
clattering gums
And the pale lichen pulled its strength against
the boulders
And the soft mosses dipped their roots in trickling creeks
And the creek's gentle song murmured to the world
And the clouds, the heavy breath of gods, shimmied
earthwards
And our skin was the sun's wild heat
I held your hand as a cluster of hot cells

Swam through my body
Blindly seeking home.

One day one day one day
Perhaps the sounds that made your bones
Will sing to your unknown soul
And I will look to the sky,
The infinite sky,
And feel the cells of my body
Brushed by unknown winds.

www.ingramcontent.com/pod-product-compliance
Lightning Source LLC
Chambersburg PA
CBHW030508120726
47904CB00005B/1394